DREAMS of the CENTAUR

ALSO BY MONTSERRAT FONTES

First Confession

DREAMS of the CENTAUR

A NOVEL

Montserrat Fontes

W. W. NORTON & COMPANY
NEW YORK

The text of this book is composed in Granjon
with the display set in Albertus
Composition and Manufacturing by the Haddon Craftsmen, Inc.
Book design by Chris Welch

Library of Congress Cataloging-in-Publication Data
Fontes, Montserrat.
Dreams of the centaur : a novel / Montserrat Fontes.
p. cm.
I. Title.
PS3556.o55D73 1996
813'.54—dc20 95-5822

ISBN 0-393-03847-5
W. W. Norton & Company, Inc., 500 Fifth Avenue, New York, N.Y. 10110
W. W. Norton & Company Ltd., 10 Coptic Street, London WC1A 1PU
1 2 3 4 5 6 7 8 9 0

Con admiración y respeto
para el pueblo Yaqui de Pótam

Para mis munitos de sangre y alma:
Lorenzo y María Cristina

Acknowledgments

Authors depend on the work of others. I am forever indebted to the finely honed scholarship and guidance provided by Dr. Evelyn Hu-DeHart's *Yaqui Resistance and Survival;* Edward H. Spicer's *The Yaquis: A Cultural History;* John Kenneth Turner's *Barbarous Mexico;* and Jane Holden Kelley's *Yaqui Women: Contemporary Life Histories.*

En el Pueblo Yaqui de Pótam, Sonora: Profesor Hilario Molina, Lucía y Hermenegildo Buitimea y María Jesús Olívar de Quiróz, gracias por su ayuda y atenciones. En Ciudad Obregón, Sonora: Ramón Iñiguez Fránco. En El Museo del Yaqui: Alberto Sánchez Ramírez, Lillian Rivera Valle.

My thanks to the National Endowment for the Humanities for a grant to study the Mexican Revolution under the caring tutelage of Professor John Tutino, Ph.D., at Boston College.

In Tucson, Arizona: Mi amigo y guía Tito Carrillo, Advocate for Yoeme Autonomy; mi cuate Jim Mahoney; mi amigo el distinguido Raúl Ramírez; mi fina y generosa amiga Becky Tapia of Old Pascua.

In Oxford, Mississippi: Ernie Lowe, M.D., for sharing his skill and expertise; University of Mississippi Chief of Police Mike Stewart, for his ideas and straight talk; and my friend and guide Cathy Stewart, who led me to the right people.

For twenty-one years of nurturing support, thank you faculty and students of University High.

Closer to home, my thanks to Jan Steward, for sharing her love and knowledge of horses; Judy Serlin, for taking that scary first journey with me; Norine Dresser for remaining my oldest friend; Gordon Culp y su ratoncito; the pebble-moving team: Howard Lager, Jeffrey N. McMahon, Michael Meyer; the survivors of El Carmen's Third Street Writers: Gerald Citrin for his support and inspiration, especially with the final assault; Janet Gregory for her unstinting energy and those questions—so painful, so needed; Lisa Teasley for the present tense. And a special bow to Katherine V. Forrest, fine novelist, loyal friend, razor-sharp reader, whose wisdom led me out of many a boxed canyon.

Y los de la casa: Lorenzo González Fontes, gracias por tu kinán, tu lealdád y tu inspiración; Cristina Fontes de González y Lorenzo González Martínez, mis manitos fieles, mis guías; Aída Fontes tu energía vive siempre en mi, Tía Marta D'Emilio por tus memorias de Santa Cruz; mi amor Laurence Taylor; mi hermano Paulino Fontes y hermana Angela Fontes—todos mil gracias. My continuing love and gratitude to you, Gillis. As always, with this, as with all that is good in my life, the source is you.

My thanks to my editor Amy Cherry, for her level sight and steady hands.

"Centaurs—whose name etymologically signifies 'those who round up bulls'—were a primitive population of cowmen, living in Thessaly, who, like American cowboys, rounded up their cattle on horseback. Their behaviour was rude and barbarous, whence the savagery which was always attributed to Centaurs— gross creatures, cruel, and given to lechery and drunkenness."

Larousse Encyclopedia of Mythology

El Corrido de los Durcal

Ésta es la historia señores
de dos compadres rivales
que la amistad terminaron
por un caballo de males.

José Durcal lo montaba
de buena ley lo ganó
con sus tres reinas en mano
a Esteban se lo quitó.

Al Moro negro deseaba
Esteban gran hacendado,
y en una noche sin luna
dejó a José balaceado.

El día del juicio señores
al rico no ajustició;
y el hijo Alejo Durcal
a la venganza se dió.

En la cantina "El Estribo"
un solo tiro le dió;
rabiando al padre lloraba
y a su padrino mató.

Alejo va detenido
porque a su padre vengó;
su madre llora en silencio
y el pueblo lo defendió.

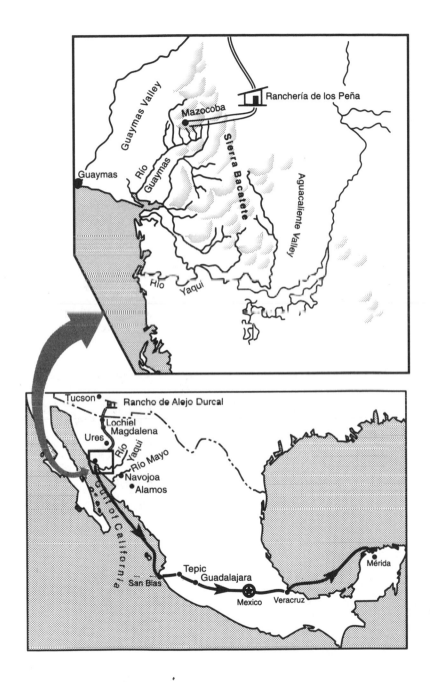

PART

ONE

1

*1885—the Durcal Ranch,
Alamos, Sonora, Mexico*

MARRIED AT SEVENTEEN, FELIPA WAS TWENTY WHEN SHE knew that she would never bury an old husband. His death would be early, sudden, violent.

The face of the dead José came to her one afternoon when she saw Rosario, a Yaqui Indian girl—no more than fifteen—running through a row of orange trees. The laughing Rosario ran, Yaqui sandals in one hand, while the other lowered her long calico skirt.

From where she stood, Felipa could see the girl more clearly than who was chasing her. The girl and her pursuer zigzagged through the trees toward the back of the house. Soon the pair were out of Felipa's sight.

Stunned, angry, Felipa steadied herself by leaning against a post of the net-screened porch. Her suspicions were temporarily allayed when José reappeared moments later from the opposite side of the house.

He was combing his wavy black hair with his fingers as he entered the wide front porch where Felipa, eight months pregnant with her second child, stood waiting. Felipa pressed the head of Alejo, their two-year old son, into the loose folds of her black skirt.

Felipa's suspicions returned when she saw that José was obviously surprised to find her there. He smiled. His powerful calloused hands straightened her shawl; he leaned over and tenderly kissed her swollen belly.

Felipa stepped back. "I saw you with the girl."

"You should be resting," he replied, still smiling.

"José, I saw you with the Yaqui girl."

"Felipa, you saw nothing."

He walked past her into the spacious house that no one but himself had built. As usual, he paused in the doorway. Felipa watched him gaze into the long, rectangular room that served as parlor, kitchen, and eating area. She knew what he was thinking. That the long table, the four chairs, the eight-by-eight hand-hewn beams had come from his hands. That unlike most ranch-home families who endured hard, tamped dirt floors, his family enjoyed a level, wooden floor—splinterless—safe for bare feet. And soon he would travel to the port of Guaymas to bring his wife furniture worthy of the house.

He had hammered every nail, mitered every joint. The thick adobe walls kept his family cool in the burning summer months. Unlike the big houses in Alamos that used firepots, his house held a rock fireplace that burned mesquite and sweet fruitwood during winter.

Starting when he was nineteen, José Durcal had toiled for a decade to prepare a ranch where he would proudly place his family. Long ago, wealthy hacendados had claimed the best land. José had taken what was left, labored eight years burning the tenacious chaparral, breaking the sunbaked land, digging wells and irrigation ditches, planting oranges, wheat, alfalfa, and hay. Determined to make his land yield, at first he had worked alone; when he had money, he hired Yaquis. Felipa had heard ranchers gossip of José

Durcal and his Yaquis. "It's one thing to hire them, but to live with them? Never."

He also multiplied his cattle, and often spoke to Felipa of his dream to breed stock sturdy enough to withstand the hot Sonora climate.

Every skill he acquired working the land he had transferred into building his home. Countless times Felipa had heard of how he savored the long, two-year ordeal. How he refused help, refused to sleep in the house until he could share its sheltering roof with Felipa.

José turned, opened his arms, and motioned Felipa to enter. She raised her hand, gestured "wait."

"Come, Alejo," José called.

The boy hid deeper into his mother's skirt.

"Alejo."

Felipa pried Alejo's fingers loose and gently nudged her reluctant son toward his father. Alejo looked up at her once more before darting off into his father's arms.

He hoisted his son onto his shoulders. "I'll cut wood for you, Felipa," he offered.

Holding on to his father's hair, Alejo watched his father's hands move with a hatchet. Small logs became kindling, which José tossed into the stove. The flames lapped up and the hands slid the griddle over.

Felipa remained outside, rested her hands on her belly, and waited for Rosario to finish feeding the chickens. Her back rigid, the girl refused to face her. Felipa's wrath returned. She wanted to order the girl off the ranch, to send her walking into the fierce desert until she dropped dead. But Felipa said nothing as Rosario lowered the bucket and hurried toward her family's home.

Rosario's parents, a Yaqui couple with five children, lived a field away in a mud-and-cane house on the other side of the well. They had their own goat and made cheese, which they sold in the Alamos market. The father worked the range with José; the mother and young children hauled water to the Durcal orange trees and vegetable garden.

As Felipa came closer to term with her second child, José had insisted that the strong, quiet Rosario take over the washing, ironing, cooking. When had he noticed the girl's smooth skin? The firm limber body?

Felipa fumed. Reluctantly, she entered the house, closed the front door, then, remembering her premonition, lowered the heavy crossbeam.

"What are you doing?" asked José. His blue eyes narrowed in anger as he lit the kerosene lamp. "You know I never bolt my door—never need to."

He put his son down, strode past her, and lifted the crossbeam.

"José, the Yaquis," she stammered. "What if . . ."

"*I* have no reason to fear Yoemem!" he shouted.

Felipa shuddered at the word "Yoemem." Why did he insist on calling Yaquis by the name they used for themselves?

She locked eyes with him until his glare forced hers down. Defeated, she went to the kitchen to prepare the evening meal.

The incident with Rosario enraged her, shamed her, frightened her. No matter what he said, Felipa felt sure that today, José had irrevocably endangered their lives.

Yes, she knew Indian women were subject to the whims of their patrones. But these weren't any Indians. Was José mad? These weren't Opatas or Mayos. These were Yaquis! A band of marauding Yaquis had killed her mother. Felipa's hands violently kneaded the dough for flour tortillas.

No matter what José said, he and his family were what Yaquis detested most: Yoris, the Yaqui word for whites or any other outsiders.

She tried to convince herself that they were safe. Hadn't José always been fair to his laborers—Indian or Mexican? Didn't he always praise them? Say his dream could not exist without Yaqui loyalty? But what if Rosario told her father?

Unlike other Indians, Yaquis had always refused allegiance to Mexico. Everyone knew they were untamable. Her grandparents had described in awestruck tones the successful attack on Alamos led in 1826 by Yaqui captain general Juan Banderas. "A Yaqui with a stick can kill ten Mexicans," her grandfather had marveled.

It irked Felipa to hear that on his banner the rebel Banderas had carried an image of the Virgin of Guadalupe, the same Virgin who was Felipa's only confidante.

Holy Virgin, give me the strength to forgive my husband. Spare him justice.

Because now a new Yaqui rebel threatened Sonora.

Cajeme.

Her husband and his fellow ranchers uttered this name with respect, almost reverence. José described Cajeme as "the greatest man in Sonora." To Felipa, the name brought only dread.

She wondered how much of what she heard about Cajeme was true. The elusive Yaqui rebel never slept, they said, nor did he touch liquor. He supposedly could read and write. That she doubted. Cajeme spoke Spanish and, before his rebellion, had risen to captain in Sonora's militia. Then foolish Mexicans had made him mayor of the Yaqui River area, trusting him to placate Yaqui rebels. But he suddenly changed his name from José María Leyva to Cajeme, announcing, "God placed men in every region, and us Yaquis he placed in the valley," and he started fighting Mexicans. This, thought Felipa, *proved* Yaquis can't be trusted.

Her pulse quickened. What if Cajeme succeeded in uniting Yaquis against Mexicans? Just this year his followers had attacked the railroad stations, haciendas, and ranches around Guaymas and Alamos. Rumors were that even the powerful hacendados, men who had their own armies, had sent their families to Europe.

And yet her own husband would have her share a well with a Yaqui family, and today he might have placed their lives in peril.

The squeal of her son's laughter filled the house. José had lifted Alejo onto the table to play the game she detested. Alejo would let himself fall off the edge of the table and just before he crashed onto the floor, José would catch him. Hands trembling, she placed scrambled eggs and onions in front of José and Alejo.

A TALLOW CANDLE burning by her bed, Felipa lay on her back, a sleeping José on one side of her and a quiet Alejo on the other. She thought again of her husband and the girl. Again she saw the face of a dead José. She shook her head.

Alejo played with the tip of her braid. She looked at the long, slender fingers and narrow wrists of her son, at his immense brown eyes, his thick brown hair, his accentuated widow's peak. Alejo had her face.

The only sign of José in Alejo was a scythe-shaped birthmark at the base of the spine. José had boasted, "This is the sign of conquerors."

No, her son would not be a conqueror. He would be like her, she hoped. She studied Alejo's hands. José too had once had tiny soft hands. What turned men's hands into heartless tools? Not these hands, she vowed. Not ever. She pressed Alejo's hands to her lips.

The boy looked up and playfully blew into her face. He was trying to cheer her up. A shaft of pain crossed her heart. When she felt lonely here at the ranch, Alejo would stroke her forehead with his tiny hand as if to smooth away her sadness. The gesture only made Felipa sadder. He should not know about feelings like this.

But two-year-old Alejo always seemed to know when she was upset. Tonight after dinner, he had followed her every movement as she cleaned up the kitchen. She took to her bed earlier than usual just to be rid of what she called her "little shadow."

She remembered the pronouncement of her outspoken Tía Mercedes on the day of Alejo's baptism: "Now that you're a mother, you will never know peace."

The same aunt had warned her, "When you marry a man, you marry their dreams and their dirty habits." Then Tía Mercedes had ranted about men's sacks and the huevos they carried between their legs and how when the huevos filled up men went crazy until they emptied them into a hole.

Felipa felt she had to believe her aunt. The youngest of her grandmother's brood, Mercedes was nevertheless the family matriarch, a role she had earned by being big, strong, blunt, smart, and impatient.

Tía Mercedes had married and buried three husbands. She had had a son by each husband, but one by one her sons had left her, gone south, into the interior of Mexico to seek their fortune.

Mercedes expressed no resentment toward her sons. "My prayer is that I never live to bury them. Men are easy to raise. They don't get pregnant. If they succeed, they will forget their mother, especially if she doesn't need them. If they fail, and return, I'll put them to work."

To Felipa and anyone who would listen, Mercedes loudly insisted that her sons were wrong about leaving. "No place in Mexico is as magnificent as Alamos. After Guadalajara, we are the richest and greatest province. All the gold and silver men could want lies beneath our feet."

Standing at her mill, both hands on her hips, Tía Mercedes entertained her clients while Felipa lifted sacks of grain off wagons. Felipa loved to hear her aunt's stories of the days when Spaniards ruled Mexico. "Every January and July, eight hundred mules, each carrying two solid bars of silver, were needed to carry the treasure of Alamos to Spain. Those gachupines were greedy. But," she would add smiling, "even they couldn't take all of it."

Lying in bed, her husband's back to her, Felipa remembered how Tía Mercedes had encouraged her marriage to José Durcal. "He has land, a strong back, blue eyes, and most important, he's not from Sonora, so chances are you're not cousins."

José always slept on his side with an arm thrown back over her leg. The weight of his arm bothered her; she moved slightly to cast it off.

He jerked awake. "What's wrong?"

"Nothing."

"Is Alejo asleep?"

"Almost," she replied.

Alejo was afraid of the dark, and she kept a candle burning until he fell asleep. José took a deep breath and lowered his head to the pillow. He swung an arm back and dropped it on her leg. She felt trapped, wedged between husband and son. And inside her, a baby, restless from the beginning, threatened to kick her belly to pieces. How different this second child is from Alejo, she thought.

Holy Virgin, give me a daughter. I know nothing about the world of men.

She barely remembered her father, though she looked very much like photos of the handsome Spanish-born Octavio Robles who had abandoned wife and three daughters to search for gold in Las Californias. Although the famed Silver City of Alamos prospered from its gold, silver, and copper mines, it belonged to the hacendados. Octavio refused to believe that the gold up north was gone. He left, sent money at first, then only letters; eventually they too stopped.

Ugly rumors reached Alamos that a man resembling Octavio was living with a woman in Guaymas. Deaf to family protests, Felipa's jealous mother was on her way to find him when Yaquis raided the coach, killing all passengers and the driver.

A returning coach brought back the bodies of three men and two women, one of them Felipa's mother. At the well-attended public funeral, Felipa heard indignant curses against Yaquis and etched those curses into her mind.

Felipa was eleven, her sisters, Teresa and Catalina, ten and nine, when they started working at Tía Mercedes's mill. Only Felipa liked the work. Her aunt taught her to hire and fire day laborers, and to ignore farmers' pleas for lower prices to grind their grain.

Alamos was shocked when her father, half dead, returned three years later, tied to a skeletal burro with a note scrawled in charcoal, *I am Octavio Robles from Alamos,* sewn onto his frayed shirt. The burro stumbled into the Plaza de Armas, and a townsman hauled Octavio, delirious with mine-camp fever, by cart to the mill.

Felipa didn't recognize her father. She hurried her frightened sisters to a neighbor's and returned in time to see Tía Mercedes single-handedly lift her father off the cart and carry him into the house. Felipa helped her aunt strip away the rotting clothes, wash and dress Octavio in clean cotton garments left over from one of her husbands.

Later, Tía Mercedes explained to Felipa, Teresa, and Catalina, "One of my husbands died from this fever. It will rise until he bursts."

The doctor confirmed that nothing could be done about the fungus that grew in the lungs.

Surrounded by neighbors, all with rosaries in hand, Felipa, sisters, and aunt sat up all night watching the fever ravage Octavio's lips and eyes. They buried him next to his wife in the family plot, and the women returned to the mill.

Lying in bed with her husband and son, Felipa recalled the morning José Durcal and his rich friend Esteban Escobar came to the mill to have wheat ground.

A laughing Esteban paid Tía Mercedes for his grain and announced, "I'm off to drink mezcal and taste the women."

José waved Esteban off and stayed at the mill. Dressed in a clean white cotton shirt, new denim pants, and shiny boots, he spent the day leaning against an adobe wall that faced the mill and stared at Felipa as if she were a long-sought treasure, a special ornament to be placed in a guarded alcove.

He tilted his hat low on his forehead, but Felipa could feel the gaze of his narrow blue eyes taking in her hair, her mouth, her chin. Then the gaze moved lazily across her shoulders, lingered at her breasts, took in her waist, passed across her hips, and dropped to her feet. His blue eyes followed her every motion. Desperately she wished that her face, arms, and hair weren't covered with stubborn mill dust.

"What does he want?" she whispered to Tía Mercedes.

"Perhaps a wife," her aunt replied. "We'll see when the day ends."

José did not offer to help Felipa and her sisters as they loaded the heavy sacks of flour onto his wagon.

Felipa blushed hot when Tía Mercedes announced loud and clear, "It seems that some men like to see if a woman is as strong as a mule before they make an offer on her."

At the end of the day, José brought Tía Mercedes slices of pineapple, which she accepted with a nod and shared with her nieces. When a smiling, shoeless and shirtless, mezcal-soaked Esteban returned, José bid Felipa a silent farewell by raising his hat.

For days Felipa could not stop thinking about him, nor could she quiet her sisters' excitement. But except for his blue eyes, she had no memory of what he looked like. No man had ever paid attention to her.

Early one morning ten days later while Felipa was alone sweeping the mill, José reappeared with a sack of oranges. She was barefoot and had not combed her hair.

"These are from my land," he told her shyly. "I also have wheat, alfalfa, hay, and beans. When I finish the house, and if your family gives us permission, I will return for you—if you like. Soy blanco y decente."

At first Felipa was overwhelmed. He was twenty-nine and she was sixteen. She could barely speak. She covered her feet with the broom and tried to dust off her dress, a useless gesture, she knew. Then she ordered herself: pay attention; notice this man. She stepped back to see him more clearly.

The narrow blue eyes that had studied her so closely seemed bluer, and were framed in long black lashes. She followed a line down his face, from the inquisitive furrow between dark brows, to a long narrow nose, to the cleft in his chin that ended the line. His wide mouth was set in a determined jaw. His muscular arms contrasted with the sharp angles of his face. She thought she smelled rose water on him.

Felipa managed to sputter, "I have only my aunt."

She didn't see him for two months. He reappeared one Sunday afternoon and in front of her sisters and Tía Mercedes said, "My house is ready for Felipa."

Although to the entire town Tía Mercedes had already voiced hearty approval of José, she challenged him anyway. "We know nothing about you or the mule that bore you."

José flushed, then politely explained, "My mother was a decent woman who raised me well. I never knew my father."

Tía Mercedes rose and ushered everyone out of the room, including herself. "Then I will let Felipa decide."

Alone with Felipa, he asked her if she had any requests or conditions prior to the wedding.

Felipa knew that marriage to José meant leaving Alamos and Tía Mercedes, so she gave his question serious thought. She decided not to tell José of the teary farmer who came to the mill with his friend and begged him, "Get drunk with me. Today I must hang or shoot my old dog." Crying, the friend had said yes. Later, she had told her aunt about the incident. Tía Mercedes had scolded, "What else can one do with an old dog?"

"I never want a dog," Felipa blurted to José. How simple I sound, she thought. Impulsively she added, "I like birds."

"Birds? All right. Dogs are important on a ranch," he explained, "but if you don't want any, we won't have them."

She agreed to marry him, and after he left, Felipa asked her aunt, why would someone like José choose her, one of "the Robles mill girls," to be his wife? Alamos was a wealthy city. José had many girls to choose from, rich girls with dowries, sheets, shoes, girls whose fathers had not abandoned them, girls who bought their dresses in stores instead of from the traveling Lebanese vendors.

Tía Mercedes had suggested that since José himself had no history that they knew of, perhaps he wanted to start his family with someone as new as the land he had claimed.

"A man without a shadow has less weight to carry," said Tía Mercedes.

So Felipa stopped questioning and came to trust that it was her he wanted. With the pride this brought to her, she had blossomed into beauty.

On their wedding day the following year, he barely spoke when he took her to his ranch. Upon arrival, he whispered, "The mattress has been stuffed with fresh hay—unused by anyone."

That first night she had cried for her family, especially for her aunt, whose only advice had been, "There's nothing a woman can do but wait until the man is finished."

Finished with what? she asked herself. José did not touch her the first week. She slept on the bed alone every night, he on a pallet by her side. "Call me when you want me as your husband," he said.

Every sundown she wondered what needed to start that required finishing. She dared not pray to the Virgin for assistance. Wise as the Virgin was, she was a Virgin.

Felipa cried, and as soon as José saw the tears begin, he demanded she walk around the house. He would point to the thickness of the walls, hit them with a stick, insist that she too hit the walls until she agreed that he had built her the strongest house in the valley.

Finally one early morning she called him—not out of need or love—but because she wanted the matter settled. "José," she said. "Now."

She closed her eyes and lay perfectly still. He took her gently, reverently, silently. When he was finished, he thanked her and kissed the palms of her hands. Then he heated water and left her alone to wash herself.

The act had given Felipa no pleasure.

Life on the ranch was quiet; the air was dry, clean. She noticed that she could sleep entire nights without coughing and wondered if the mill had caused her coughing.

Other more obvious changes took place in her. She started to grow. When she first met José, she had to look up to his eyes; a few months after their marriage, she could look directly into them. After Alejo was born and she had regained her strength, she could see the top of her husband's head.

The morning they went to register Alejo's birth at the church, Tía Mercedes asked, "José, what do you grow on your land that makes your wife grow so tall?"

He laughed good-naturedly. "It's the nectar of the Durcals, Doña Mercedes. We make everything grow."

The two had laughed at their joke. Felipa knew he had noticed her height, but this was the first time he had mentioned it. She was thankful that humor, not rancor, was his response. Life with him will be good, she had thought.

Her secret wish remained that she could enjoy her husband's physical love. She suspected herself of doing something wrong. Yet had she not given birth to a son? Surely that proved she was all right. But why did the marriage act hurt her so much?

She was too embarrassed to ask Tía Mercedes or her sisters. Both Teresa and Catalina had married as soon as they had turned seventeen; both had moved away—one to Guanajuato, the other to Guadalajara.

On days when José worked the range and left her alone from sunrise to sundown, loneliness weighed heavily. Ranch work was harder than mill work. Only sundown ended the day's labor. She felt herself grow stronger. Her endurance increased, and that made her proud.

But she missed the noise of the mill, the millstone grinding the precious grains raised in the dry Sonora. Life at the ranch had taught her how precious indeed were those grains, how much farmers had to work to make the dry land yield. She missed bantering with farmers, missed visiting with their wives and daughters.

The mill was the hub of Alamos, and Tía Mercedes could charm secrets out of a rock—so everyone said. Customers stood in line to gossip with her. At the end of a busy day, Felipa loved counting the money with Tía Mercedes.

At the ranch she seldom saw money—only after the harvest, or when José sold a few head of cattle. José was strange with money, Felipa thought. He liked to convert paper money into pesos fuertes, gold coins that came in denominations of two and a half, five, ten, and twenty pesos. He hid the gold coins in little niches inside the house and even made a tiny safe under the wagon's seat. "You can go anywhere with gold," he told her.

But who would want to leave Alamos? she thought. She missed the grandeur of Alamos—two hours away from the ranch by wagon—the winding, shiny cobbled streets, the elevated sidewalks beneath white colonnaded arcades. She missed the evening promenades around the Plaza de Armas in front of the Purisima Concepción, which, Tía Mercedes said, was the model for churches in the Americas. True, the Spanish had never completed the second tower, but to Felipa that only doubled the beauty of its single steeple.

Without question she accepted the lore that Alamos was founded in a sacred valley where the jungle and the desert met the orchid and the cactus, where the deer of the mountain met the boa constrictor.

She knew that Alamos, like the state of Sonora, was far from Mexico City. However, she liked to think that Alamos was not so much isolated as it was protected. To the north was the vast Sonoran Desert, to the south was dense jungle. The ocean was west and the mountains were east. That, she told herself, was all she needed to know.

For all its sturdiness, the Durcal ranch house lacked the internal beauty of the Alamos homes, whose whitewashed fronts stood flush to the sidewalk, presenting a fortlike front. On hot days residents of those homes opened the doors to share their beautiful patio gardens with passersby.

A memory she had of her father was strolling by those homes to admire the tile-and-mosaic interior patios with potted plants and tree-shaded gardens open to the sky. The bedrooms were arranged around the garden.

"The Moors left us this custom, Lipa," her father had explained. "They believed that in a house, as in a person, true beauty should remain hidden in the center."

At the ranch all was outside. The barn in front of the house. To the right the vegetable garden, to the left the orange trees. A corral was in back of the house.

Unable to discern beauty in her surroundings, Felipa sought comfort in ranch sounds—the rooster scolding his chickens, a coyote's lonely night howl, the grunt of José's horse when he threw the saddle on, the squeak of wagonwheels. The best sound came at the end of the day when José returned from the range, tired, sweaty, and proud—his voice recounting his day's achievements and listing the next day's plans.

Lying in bed, Felipa recalled the timbre of José's voice as he detailed his future dreams. Its resonance always excited her. Again, she thought of Rosario.

Useless to fight doubts, thought Felipa. Something did happen between the girl and José.

Grudgingly, Felipa remembered a piece of advice from Tía Mercedes: "Never ask your husband to admit to infidelity, because if he says 'So what?' what will you do?"

She saw Alejo's eyes were closed and put out the candle.

2

Seven years later, 1892

FOR NEARLY TEN YEARS, FELIPA HAD HEARD OF JOSÉ'S PLANS TO travel to Guaymas to purchase animals, tools, and furniture that would raise the status of his ranch.

José complained that everything cost more in Alamos, because wealthy hacendados set the price. "Nothing's impossible for them," he screamed. "They bought Europe and brought it to Mexico."

To Felipa's embarrassment, José often stood at the mill and openly criticized President Porfirio Díaz for encouraging American investors. "He's ready to let the gringos into the Yaquis' carbon fields, salt pits, and oyster beds," José railed.

"José is right," said Tía Mercedes, and she had explained to Felipa how a partnership between Americans and hacendados would crowd out Yaquis and men like José.

Felipa was secretly pleased when José's biggest obstacle in getting to Guaymas proved to be a Yaqui: Cajeme. The charismatic Yaqui leader had united the Indian tribes against Mexicans, Americans, and other foreigners.

Infuriating Felipa and neighbors, José had applauded the routing of Mexican troops by Cajeme, a man he described as having "more nobility in his little finger than all the Mexicans put together."

If José spoke of Cajeme as the man who could save Sonora from outsiders, José also knew it was foolish to leave his wife and three sons unguarded when Yaquis were rampaging throughout Sonora raiding railroad stations, haciendas, train stations, and coach travelers.

José reminded his wife and neighbors that Yaquis were the only warriors who, after defeating the conquistadores, had asked for peace from those they had *defeated.* "Name me another people who did that," José challenged.

Finally after twelve years of battling Yoris, Cajeme had been apprehended. Accounts of what happened in the last days of Cajeme found their way to Alamos and to the grieving José.

Caravans of citizens and officials had traveled from various parts of Sonora to see and question the mythic warrior who had successfully outwitted soldiers and ranchers. They saw an articulate, thin, soft-spoken man of medium height with a ready smile.

How many Yaquis did he really have in his fort, El Añil, when he repelled General Topete's six hundred men?

Cajeme smiled mischievously and answered, "Under three hundred."

"Impossible!" exclaimed his interrogators.

Keeping his smile, Cajeme added, "That's because little Indians multiply when they have weapons."

Asked to explain why he had lost so much weight, Cajeme said, "It's not the same for a man to eat and sleep well every day as it is to live in hiding, cross mountains without food, and almost never sleep."

Cajeme was kept under custody until the eve of April 21, 1887, when he was escorted aboard the steamship *Democrata*. The day he was taken out of prison he surrendered his belongings to the chief of police and asked that they be returned to his family. The chief told Cajeme that he need not worry.

Cajeme answered, "This is not the time to waste jokes on a man who is about to die."

Arms and legs bound, Cajeme was marched by government soldiers along the Yaqui coast and through the Yaqui villages until four days later he was executed by a firing squad.

Hearing of Cajeme's last moments, José wept openly. And Felipa refused her husband any words of comfort. And José didn't seem to care. Alone or in public he sang corridos about Cajeme—not the songs that described his death, but those that heralded his hero's bravery.

> *Dicen que ya viene "El Once"*
> *a apaciguar el Estado*
> *y Cajeme les responde:*
> *—Madrugando, no hay cuidado;*
> *yo no les entriego el rio,*
> *aunque muera fusilado.*

> *They say "The Eleventh Battalion"*
> *on its way to appease the State*
> *And to them Cajeme answers:*
> *"No need to worry as long as I rise early;*

I'll never surrender the river to them,
though my death come from a firing squad."

During José's extreme despondency over Cajeme's execution, Felipa lost her fourth child, a girl, at birth.

For days afterward, she suffered a high fever. Tía Mercedes remained by Felipa's side, funneling liquids down her, and cooling her body with alcohol rubs.

Alejo ate and slept on the floor next to Felipa; though semiconscious, she could hear him pleading with her not to leave him. She could feel his hand—tiny yet heavy—on her shoulder. At the height of the fever, José and the two younger boys, Hector and Andrés, stood at the foot of her bed.

Angry, she tried to tell them to leave her alone, to let her rest *over there.* Her words remained unsaid. In her thoughts she begged them to please let her rest. Faces swirled through her—among them, the face of the dead José as she had seen it years ago. She ordered herself: return.

And so Felipa resigned herself to life. Her fever broke, and she worked to regain her strength. She was by now twenty-seven.

After her convalescence, she noticed that her sons looked to José, not her, for guidance. Had she been that sick? she wondered. Why, they had even learned songs about Cajeme!

No, she thought. She must take back her sons, and the quickest way was to send him off to Guaymas.

"You're still too weak," he argued. "You almost died."

"Your Cajeme died, not me. Go!"

He wanted to take the boys. "I want my sons to know their country."

"They stay with me until they're men," she answered.

He left with his friend Esteban Escobar.

As Felipa reclaimed her sons, she silently mourned over the loss of her daughter.

*   *   *

IN THE PORT of Guaymas, José bought furniture, a sealed trunk full of books, a plow, a prize bull, parrots, and stuffed animals. From the Yucatán Peninsula he ordered logs of precious hardwood and rope made of the finest henequen.

On a hot September morning, José and Esteban's caravan returned to Alamos. A crowd gathered around the plaza while the two travel-weary men showed off their goods. The center of attention, however, was not José's bull and birds, but Esteban's two-year-old black stallion, a wild-eyed, unbroken steed barely contained with three hemp ropes.

Proudly, Esteban proclaimed the horse's name was El Moro.

People came as close as they dared to the beast and agreed that he was well named.

"Tell them I found him!" José shouted, for all to hear.

Esteban laughed at José. "It's true. My friend is angry because I outbid him for the horse. I'll tell you what, José, you can be the godfather of El Moro. On the Fiesta de San Francisco I'll have this demon tamed and blessed on the same day. Don't be angry with me."

Esteban smiled, and his teeth were white, straight, and very small. His fair complexion had bronzed under the Guaymas sun; his light brown hair contained strands of gold.

NINE-YEAR-OLD ALEJO saw his father's caravan while it was still a mile away. He called out the news to his mother, saddled the mule, and rushed to meet his father.

José had been gone six months and had left Alejo in charge. With the help of his brother, seven-year-old Hector, Alejo had rotated the cattle in the fields. Although the animals were thin, not one had been slaughtered to sell for hide. His father's arrival meant fresh meat for the family.

His father would be pleased to hear how his sons had worked together. Even five-year-old Andrés had helped by gathering eggs and milking cows. July and August brought little rain, but with careful watering the family had kept up the fruit trees and the vegetable garden.

Alejo's excitement waned as soon as he saw his father. José's face looked drawn, the curve of his mouth down. The trip did not go well, Alejo thought. Yet all three wagons were loaded. And he had the Zebu, the bull that would make their cattle the best in the valley. Alejo marveled at the fleshy hump that crowned the light gray shoulders of the bull. Perhaps Father was tired.

Alejo told Hector and Andrés, "Make sure no one has to ask for anything." The boys filled the trough and every gourd and cántaro with water so the laborers could drink their fill and splash the dust off their faces.

In the kitchen, Felipa cooked stacks of big paper-thin flour tortillas, beans, scrambled eggs mixed with shredded beef jerky, peppers, tomatoes, and onions. She hurried. José had directed the workers to transfer crates and cages into the house, feed the mules and horses, and when they finished, "Go wait in the porch. My wife will feed you."

Hats lowered to their eyes, the men sat on their haunches. In silence they waited to be fed. Hector helped her carry the steaming plates to the workmen. Young Andrés brought out a bowl of salt, which the men sprinkled liberally over the food.

Alejo followed José and studied how reverently his father untethered the bull and led him to the stall he had built before he left for Guaymas.

"There!" José said. "Another of my dreams has come true. Alejo, name him."

Alejo fed the bull some hay. "I can choose the name?"

"Who else?" José hugged his son.

Alejo thought. He looked at the muscular beast with its downcast ears. He bent down and pointed to the big, low-hanging testicles. "There's our new cattle."

José laughed. His blue eyes sparkled for the first time since his return. "Yes, that's where the bullets are. His rifle is this big." He measured out three feet.

Alejo laughed with his father. "Call him Sueño."

"Sueño? A soft name for a powerful animal."

"Dreams are powerful," said Alejo seriously.

José knelt before his son and kissed him. "Next to your mother, you are my happiest dream." José lifted his shirt and grabbed both of Alejo's hands. "Here is my heart," said José, his voice low, harsh. "Do you feel it?"

Frightened, Alejo nodded.

José opened Alejo's hands. "Swear to me that if I fall, you will complete my dream."

Confused, Alejo asked, "Fall?"

"If I die," snapped José, "or if something happens to me, swear to keep the Durcal name alive. Make the Durcal ranch a wheel that turns by itself." He squeezed Alejo's hands until they hurt. "Swear!"

"I swear," said Alejo, now truly frightened.

José wrung the boy's hands. "Louder! Now, upon your father's heart and by your mother's love and by all the gods in all the heavens, swear!"

"I swear!" shouted Alejo. He dared not breathe.

José embraced then released him.

Legs shaking, Alejo followed his father out of the barn. Perhaps tomorrow he would tell about Guaymas. Perhaps he would tell what dream did not come true.

SITTING ON SARAPES, the five men rested against the side of the barn. Alejo walked through the black night and gave them two bottles of mezcal. "From my father. He said tomorrow we will have fresh meat. He said he would be pleased to have you stay."

The men mumbled among themselves. A voice said, "We will stay as long as Don José has work for us."

"As long as there's enough mezcal," slurred another.

"Too many Yoris pay us with mezcal," said a serious voice.

Alejo tried to see who had said those last words. Too dark. *"Dios emchanía,"* said Alejo in Yaqui. God help you.

"Dios emchiokue." God forgive you. The response came from the man sitting farthest from the group.

Pleased with the exchange, Alejo returned to the house. Tía Mercedes had taught him those phrases last Sunday.

Alejo liked talking to Yaquis whenever they came to look for day work. He had tried to learn their language. His father spoke Yaqui and had taught him many words.

But Felipa put a stop to it. "He should pray that God protects him from those murdering thieves."

Mother mustn't know that Father had hired a Yaqui. Would she make him leave?

IN UNSPOKEN ACCORD, Felipa and José delayed their private reunion until everyone else was asleep. José took Felipa into his arms. He kissed her eyes, her hands, her mouth. She tasted mezcal. She took his worn boots and put them in a corner. José tore off his clothes and threw them over the boots.

"Burn it all tomorrow," he said.

He stood before her, naked in the flickering flame of the kerosene lamp. His hands were coffee-brown; so was his face, up to his forehead where his hat had rested. The rest—arms, legs, torso, and forehead—was sallow, sickly. Although absolute nakedness was rare between them, Felipa's eyes were drawn to his protruding ribs, flat stomach, and narrowed hips.

He's not as handsome as when he left—but he seems sweeter, she thought, more like a boy, a ragamuffin. "José, have you been ill?"

"No. I've been without you, without my life." He sat on the bed. "Come to my side."

Something about his nudity bothered her. She found a fresh nightshirt and tossed it to him. Smiling, he shook his head and put it on.

She calculated. He had been gone six months, and prior to that, he hadn't touched her for at least five months. She had been too sick with her last pregnancy. She couldn't help wanting to know: "Were you with other women?"

José frowned. "Esteban and I drank too much, slept little, ate nothing. We gambled, waited for ships and trains to arrive. Tomorrow you will see what I have. I brought you gifts."

"I want to know about the women." I am sick with jealousy, she realized.

"Women follow Esteban because he's rich. He buys them gifts. I don't. Every gold coin I spent is in those crates and in the barn."

Half in jest, she pulled his thick hair with both hands. "So, Esteban paid for your women."

He grabbed hold of both her hands and held them. "Felipa, why do you worry? You have three sons, a ranch, and a husband who lives only for you."

Laughing, he took her in his arms and crushed her to him.

Felipa pulled away. "Don't, José."

His eyes narrowed. "I won't be punished, Felipa."

He wasn't.

He loved her twice that night and, despite herself, the second time she allowed herself to return his embraces, to take pleasure in his touch, and, for the first time, to enjoy stroking his fragile frame.

Forgiveness flowed generously from her. His thin frame made her feel powerful. She obeyed the willful, pointed hunger that trembled within her. Her body made demands, and her strong arms guided his body to reach deeper, to slide closer, and grant her a rare new joy.

She heard herself wildly demand more. José was still laughing when he fell asleep. Left with the burden of her satiety, she thought, thank God no one can hear through these walls.

THE FOLLOWING MORNING she was grateful that José's single preoccupation was uncrating his purchases.

He unpacked, hammered, and decorated all morning. "You need to know Sonora's animals," he said to his sons.

The deer's antlers had eight points and a thirty-inch spread. José hung him over the main fireplace. The majestic buck's black eyes stared unflinchingly at the opposite wall.

Next José draped two ocelot pelts—heads left attached—on each end of the new couch. Amused, Felipa watched her youngest sons run their fingers through the soft fur. Hector looked into the pink mouths. He tested the teeth's sharpness with his fingers. The gentler Andrés traced a finger over the ocelot's intricate rosettes and rubbed his cheek against the coat.

Felipa looked for Alejo, and found him hiding by the stove in the kitchen. She tried to coax him to join his brothers, but the boy shook his head and pressed his face into her hip. He was shaking.

"Come here, Felipa," called José.

Alejo pushed her away. Afraid to ruin her husband's morning, she returned to the living room to find that on one side of the main door José had placed a peccary with a prickly pear in its mouth, and on the other, a bighorn sheep, head in butting pose.

José laughed. "They can greet company." He put the coyote with a chicken in its mouth on the front porch.

"Here are your birds you said you wanted," he said to Felipa as he uncovered a pair of yellow-headed parrots. "The heat killed the canaries." He moved the parrots to a larger cage. "These parrots are from the Enchanted Forest near Guaymas. They will live a long time and have babies."

"Will they talk?" asked Hector. He moved to inspect the birds.

"Not if they're together," Felipa said. "Only one can be trained to talk. They're beautiful. Alejo, come see the birds."

Alejo moved slowly into the living room. He stood next to Felipa. "The house is full of eyes," he said.

"All these animals are from Sonora," José said. "Someday I will take you to the Sierra and you can hunt your own trophies."

"We don't have rifles," said Hector, looking around.

"Now you do," said José, pointing to a long narrow box. "But first I will teach you to shoot."

"Show me the rifles," pressed Hector.

"They're packed," said José firmly.

Felipa remarked at José and Hector's similarity, especially now that both were angry. José might well have been arguing with himself, except that Hector's eyes were dark brown like hers.

José moved to another crate and took out a stuffed quetzal. "This bird comes from Guatemala—near Yucatán—where our wood is from. They say Guatemalan forests are so thick it always looks like night."

Alejo looked at the long, curved emerald plumes of the bird, its burnt-orange breast pressed against a dry lacquered branch. Its tiny, yellowed beak was half open; the gold eyes with black rims gave it an angry look.

"I don't see where they killed it," said Alejo. "Where's the hole?"

"They plugged it up," said Hector impatiently. "What else did you buy?"

"Is that true, Father?" asked Alejo. "Have all the holes been covered up?"

José shrugged. He searched through more of the boxes. "Ah!" He peeled layers of paper off an oblong cedar box, which he gave to Felipa. "For my wife. Sit down and open it. Boys, sit with your mother."

Felipa rested the box on her lap. Alejo held down the base as she lifted the top. She gasped.

A hand-carved statue of the Virgin of Guadalupe lay inside the red-velvet-lined box. Alejo helped his mother hold up the two-foot carving. Speechless, she looked at her husband.

"Now you have your own Virgin," he said. "I will build an altar so you can pray to her whenever you want."

Felipa took her gift into the bedroom and shut herself in. She sat on the bed and pressed her head to the Virgin. Then she remembered her ardor of the night before.

What had happened last night that hadn't happened before? What hadn't she been doing? Was it *right,* that reventón that almost made her faint? Her loins grew weak. Quickly she stuffed the statue of the Virgin back in the box.

Alejo's screams pierced through the adobe walls. Running, she found José at a loss to steady his trembling, hysterical son. She looked for the cause of the commotion. Hector and Andrés were holding a tiny stuffed black bear cub. It stood on its hind legs, its mouth shaped to an eternal smile, its front paws extended in greeting.

Later that night, Alejo lay on his bed on top of the covers, his face flushed, his dark eyes ablaze. He clasped Felipa's hand over his heart. She could feel his despair.

"I know what they did. They *had* to kill the mother first," Alejo argued with her. *"Then* they killed the baby. They *killed* the baby, didn't they?"

Felipa had no answer.

José and her other two sons were long asleep. Alejo had refused to let her leave his side.

The day had soured after José unpacked the cub. He had not found time to kill a steer. The promise of fresh meat gone, the men had asked for their wages and left to look for work at the nearby mines. Just as well, thought Felipa; one of them was a Yaqui.

In tears, Alejo had run off on José's horse. When he didn't return after an hour, José and Felipa hitched the wagon and went looking for him.

They found him throwing rocks in a ditch. The sun was high; heat waves shimmered from the silent baked earth. José scolded him for leaving the horse in the sun without water or shade. Alejo offered no defense. He came back willingly but stayed outside to tend the horse.

When Felipa and José returned to the house, another shock awaited them. In front of the fireplace, they found two black onyx marbles lying next to a limp scrap of black fur. Piles of cotton, wire, plaster, and burlap lay in a heap. Hector had sliced open the cub.

Enraged, José shouted at the seven-year-old.

Hector stood his ground. "It's a toy. I wanted to show Alejo that it's a toy."

Andrés picked up the pelt. "I'll keep it." He petted it and was unwilling to part with it for the rest of the day.

Refusing dinner lest José take the pelt away, Andrés had taken it to bed with him.

FEELING THE EFFECTS of the day, Felipa pried her hand free from Alejo's grip. He sat up in bed and pushed back his hair.

"How big was his mother?" he asked.

"Black bears get big."

"Bigger than you?"

"They're much stronger, stronger than either your father or me. They're dangerous."

Alejo started to speak but paused. He closed his eyes; Felipa knew by the expression on his face that he was reaching a painful conclusion.

"If someone kills your mother, everything terrible can happen to you. That is the truth, isn't it?"

"Follow me with the candle," whispered Felipa.

They returned with the cedar box. Felipa took out the statue, placed it on the stand next to Alejo's bed. She poured melted wax from the half-burned candle onto the top of the stand and fitted a new candle into the hot softness.

"With the Virgin, nothing can happen to you."

Felipa pulled back the sheet; Alejo crawled into bed. She followed the dark gaze of her son as he watched the flame send pulsing rays of light up the pink gown of the Virgin. The green mantle fell gracefully from the golden crown. The feet rested on a bed of delicately carved roses.

Felipa watched her son look at the holy oval, his breath steadying.

3

ASHAMED BECAUSE HE COULD NOT STOMACH THE DEAD ANI-mals his father had brought home, nine-year-old Alejo sought José's respect by working long hours clearing the fields of brush. The boy made sure the trough and cántaros in the house stayed filled with fresh water; horses and mules were fed before José rose. Hector, seven, and Andrés, five, worked beside Alejo.

Alejo was embarrassed that his younger brothers worked so hard to cheer him up. The serious-minded Hector played games to see who could haul more water on shoulder yokes to the fruit trees so their father would not have to seek help. The mines and railroads paid higher wages than the Durcals.

Alejo studied how José pampered the new bull in the corral in back of the house. "Sueño needs to fatten on oats and clover. He lost weight during his long train trip."

"From where?" asked Alejo.

"Tejas. His calves will be here by spring and summer."

Alejo was also embarrassed with his mother. He had not allowed her to remove the statue of the Virgin from his room. He had tried to sleep without the Virgin, but when he imagined the cub's horror as it saw its mother killed, then his own horrors surfaced, and with that came an involuntary shaking in his legs that no yerba buena tea could quiet. Only the presence of the statue granted him sleep.

José had scolded him for keeping his mother's gift. "It is the only thing in this house that I bought for her alone," José said.

"It's just a borrow, Father." He understood his father's resentment.

One day while watching José plane the new wood for the altar,

Alejo saw the solution. He would carve a statue for himself. He would make his own Virgin of Guadalupe.

She needn't be as fine as Mother's, he thought. He did want it as tall. She wouldn't be as beautiful. But She would be his. Practicing on his father's scraps of wood, Alejo spent every free moment carving. Finally, after many late nights, he learned how to order his hands to shape the wood into images he visualized. The power lies in the blade, he realized. Hearing his parents fight over the Virgin made him work harder.

José argued, "It's yours. Take it back."

She retorted, "José, if it's mine, let me do with it as I please. The Virgin hears my prayers in Alejo's room. Our boy is frightened. You don't understand his fear. But I feel it *here*." She pointed to her heart.

"When I finish this altar, that statue will go in it. He can pray and sleep there if he wants. You too!" Blue eyes narrowed, jaw clenched, he added, "But in there, I won't give you what you want."

She flushed. He was shaming her for desiring him. After this, she vowed to stay away from him at night. And if the scorching heat of day lingered into evening, her desire remained in check. But if dawn brought moments of dry coolness, and if his hand rested upon her thigh, she relented and hated herself afterward.

Sometimes she controlled herself for three, four days, then desire came and, full of self-loathing, she would feign sleep and roll into him. She never fooled him. Nor did he ever deny her. José always responded, always rejoiced at her need for him.

This is madness, not love, she chided herself. She yearned to ask another woman if her body craved this, this *thing*, this insanity. When she drove the wagon into Alamos for Sunday mass, she looked at the women in church and wondered if any desired their husbands as she did José. She saw nothing. But she needed to know.

Tía Mercedes.

"As husband and wife—we're not as before," Felipa stammered one Sunday. It was almost time to return to the ranch. She had waited all day to be alone with Mercedes. As usual, her aunt had had many visitors.

Smiling coyly, Mercedes nodded as if she understood. She sat down. Her dark eyes glowed as she ironed her skirt with her hands. "Oh yes, I saw it in your eyes. You ripened after he returned from Guaymas. Some women are damned for it. Their husbands are afraid of it. They deny their wives and give it all to whores. My second husband was that way. My third one didn't last long enough. With the first, I didn't care. I didn't know anything—neither did he." She threw her head back and laughed.

Felipa could feel herself color.

Mercedes sighed, and reached for Felipa's hands. "You make me envious, Felipa. The body has no principles—so the church warns us. But you have a husband. You have no reason for shame." Mercedes grew sad. "Old bodies are in danger of a rezbalón—losing reputation and years of virtue for one moment of friction. Felipa, it's the old bodies with desire that should be ashamed—and pitied."

Felipa thought she heard self-reproach in her aunt's voice. But Mercedes rose, moved quickly to the kitchen, and returned with a small sharp knife and a rucksack full of wood. "Give this to Alejo. The knife is from Toledo."

"Why does he need a knife? We have plenty at home. We have wood too."

"He should have his own for his carvings. Besides, I'm his godmother."

Felipa laughed. "You've baptized half the children in this town."

"That doesn't keep me warm. And it's bad for business. Godchildren expect to be charged less at this mill." Tía Mercedes gathered her skirts and waved goodbye.

Wishing she could stay longer, Felipa boarded her wagon, took the reins, and clicked the mule team home.

A few miles outside the town's borders, Felipa heard the report of rifles. From the road she recognized the light-colored hats of rurales, federal government troops that had been coming into Sonora in greater numbers.

She halted her team. "What is it?" she called. No answer. She could hear the officer yelling at the rurales.

"What is it?" she repeated, hands cupped to her mouth.

The officer, a young thin man, rode to meet her. He tipped his cap. "Sorry to alarm you, señora. We caught the Yaquis that have been stealing cattle."

"They're dead?"

"Executed. The colonel sentenced them this morning."

Felipa stayed in the wagon and waited until the detachment passed her. Four soldiers, rifles between their legs, sat in the bed of the wagon, driven by a civilian. Dragging behind were the bodies of three men, bare feet bound, their heads covered with grain sacks.

Felipa was relieved she wouldn't have to come to town for another week. She knew the rurales often let the bodies rot on the outskirts of town.

The incident with the soldiers enraged José. "Díaz is giving Sonora to the gringos! The train, the telegraph, the mines—it's all theirs. Yoemem are starving in their own lands, and if they steal food, we shoot them."

"The Yaquis," she corrected, "will kill us quicker than the gringos." Felipa wondered if José would ever see that his beloved "Yoemem" had no love for him whatsoever.

"They defend their lands! Are you blind? Sonora is full of Americans, Spaniards, Germans, Arabs, Chinese—all of them here to steal from Mexicans and Mexico's primera gente, the Indians, and especially the Yoemem."

"Yaquis can't be trusted. They murder, burn, steal . . ."

José wasn't listening. An ugly darkness had come upon him, and when these moods beset him, she remembered the face of the dead José she saw seven years ago.

She saw he was still angry. ". . . now even Esteban makes deals with gringos. Mining has no soul. It's avarice. Esteban, my good friend, ha! Stole my Moro. *I* found that horse." His eyes sought her out. "On the Fiesta de San Francisco, that horse will be mine!"

THE STARS WERE still visible on the morning when José, Hector, and Alejo rode out to introduce Sueño to the herd. José had rounded the readied cows into a dale protected by cottonwoods that grew near a season-dry riverbed.

José placed his sons far enough from the herd to avoid distraction, yet close enough to keep the two-year-old Sueño from wandering away. The first two cows refused Sueño's mount. The bull grazed, wandered in the dawn, then grazed again. José led a third cow to him.

Alejo was half asleep on his mule when he heard his father bellow, *"Toro!"*

"Did it happen?" asked Alejo.

"Of course it did!" shouted José, elated.

José dismounted and cautiously approached the newly mounted cow. That morning, Felipa had given him a red braided ribbon to mark the cow that first received Sueño.

In honor of San Francisco, that cow and its offspring were to be spared. His sons clapped when he slipped the red noose around her neck.

Sueño returned to the same cow two more times.

Before José left, he ordered his sons to watch Sueño. "Keep count! I'm going to town."

Alejo saw the next mating. A strange tingling ran through his legs. Sueño goes fast, he thought. Faster than donkeys. He joined Hector at his end of the range.

"Watch Sueño." Alejo dismounted and handed Hector the reins to the mule.

He took out the knife Tía Mercedes had sent him and cut into a rectangle of pine the size of his hand. Again, he would try to make a rounded edge. The previous night he had traced the head of the

Virgin onto the block with a piece of charcoal.

Alejo jumped when Hector bellowed, *"Toro!"*

"Fool! You made me cut myself!"

"No, *you* cut yourself," Hector scoffed. "Watch Sueño."

Alejo lowered his mouth to the cut and swallowed his blood. He looked at the sky. Clear and hot. He didn't want to be here. He should be in town for the Fiesta de San Francisco.

But last night his father had announced that today Sueño would go to pasture, "And you two will take care of him." That meant they would miss the fiesta. That meant his mother would stay home too. The whole family had always gone to town on fiesta days. Why did Father want to go alone?

FOR YEARS AFTER this Fiesta de San Francisco, Alamos spoke of the poker game at Madame Carmelo's. Narrators added or deleted details, but people agreed on key points.

José Durcal arrived in Alamos early that morning. He was alone. He visited Felipa's family. At the plaza he chatted with friends, patted heads of children, bought candy, ate churros, and drank hot chocolate. He attended church services and walked in the procession behind the priest and sacristan during the blessing of calves, goats, dogs, roosters, and mares.

The sun was already high when Esteban arrived leading El Moro; the horse scattered people in all directions. Esteban laughed at the sight. With him was an American, who also enjoyed Moro's wildness.

From a respectful distance, the priest blessed the horse. Then Esteban and the American wended their way through the crowds, cutting a visible swath toward the back streets and Madame Carmelo's. The next detail people recalled was that José had loaded his wagon to capacity with feed and followed Esteban.

*   *   *

MADAME CARMELO WAS a heavy-bosomed woman with short crimpy red hair, large hips, small blue eyes, and pasty skin. Men trusted her. Her girls were clean and kept their mouths shut. When Madame went to market she spoke to no one unless spoken to first. And in public, she called no man by name. She said she was French, though her accent was German.

In the parlor of her brothel, no one but Madame herself sat between the players and dealt American cards onto a black silk flowered Spanish mantilla. José, Esteban, the American businessman named Billy Cameron, and a Chinese called only El Chino sat down to play early in the afternoon. Billy Cameron, ruddy-faced and broad-shouldered, carried a look of happy anticipation. He smiled frequently. Onlookers wandered in and out of the whorehouse, waiting for the real game to start.

Esteban and Billy drank mezcal. José drank only water and lime juice. El Chino took occasional sips of water and smoked constantly. All four bought a thousand pesos' worth of chips from Madame Carmelo. Such amounts were rare.

Esteban laughed. "My compadre José came to win Moro from me," he said to Cameron.

To José, Cameron said in a low voice, "Friendship should never hinge on a horse."

José smiled at Esteban. "I've come to take Moro where he belongs. *We* know how it was."

"Esteban says you have a big ranch, Don José," said Cameron. "Says you worked on it ten years. I'd like to see it."

"I'm still working on it. But he's right, my land has been good to me. Why are you here, American? Land?"

Cameron hesitated before answering. "I don't know—Yaquis worry me."

José looked at Cameron and waited for what seemed a long time before answering. "Yoemem are no problem if Yoris stay out of their land. Gringos want their carbon fields, their salt mines, and their oyster beds."

"Perhaps," said Cameron. "But the fact is, Yaquis are not developing what they have. Their lands are rich in silver too. Why don't they work them? Or let others work them? They'd be well paid."

José's blue eyes narrowed. "Are you a miner? Are you here to survey Yaqui land?"

Esteban cut in, "Billy's here as my guest. And we want to play cards."

JOSÉ AND ESTEBAN seemed to be playing without heart. They bet lightly, folded quickly. Billy Cameron was ahead for a while, then left the table when he lost to El Chino. Cameron pulled up a chair and watched the game. El Chino quit when he was five hundred pesos ahead. He sat next to Cameron. The game was down to José and Esteban. Summoned by an unvoiced signal, the room filled with spectators.

Esteban downed his last mezcal. He left the table and washed his hands and face. José did the same. When they sat back down, José pulled a leather pouch from inside his shirt and counted twenty gold coins.

Murmurs of surprise vibrated the room. Responding to the crowd, José winked, reached back into the leather pouch, took out two rattlesnake rattles, clasped them between index and middle fingers, and kissed them. Gentle laughter rippled throughout.

Esteban left the table to confer with Billy Cameron in a corner. Cameron accepted a signed note from Esteban.

"My friend has agreed to cover my note for the game," Esteban said to José.

José shrugged. "No need. Get your note back. My gold against Moro."

Pointing to the gold coins, Esteban said, "That's more than I paid for the horse."

José shrugged again. "I'm playing for the horse, Esteban, only for the horse."

Luck sat with Esteban for the afternoon. José never bluffed—so it seemed. If the cards didn't come, he folded. Near sundown, he was down to two coins.

Madame dealt a new hand. Esteban opened; José asked for two cards; Esteban raised a finger to show that he was still in the game. José threw in his last two coins. Esteban raised his finger again.

José announced, "Let all witness, that I bet Sueño, my Zebu."

Esteban burst out laughing. "By the skirts of the Blessed Virgin, what in hell would I do with your bull? Use it to haul my silver?"

No one laughed.

José dropped his hand over the snake rattles. "Let all witness that I bet my entire ranch."

Esteban paled. "José, what are you doing? Think of your sons. Felipa. Your fields. No, José. I cannot let you do this."

"Accept the bet," said Cameron, dead serious.

A voice called out, "No, Don José!" Other voices echoed the plea.

"My entire ranch. You owe me this."

With visible regret, Esteban accepted. He put down a full house—two tens, three jacks.

José lowered his cards—two nines, three queens.

THEN PEOPLE RECOUNTED how neighbors helped José tie Moro to the wagon. On the outskirts of town, José picked up Tacho, an old Yaqui, sitting by the side of the road. He seemed to be waiting for José. Tacho, a veteran from the Cajeme wars, now made his living as a day laborer.

Those who followed José home heard him thank the Indian as he returned the rattlesnake rattles. Witnesses claimed that Tacho seemed to know José would leave Alamos with El Moro.

THAT NIGHT, ALEJO saw four horsemen silhouetted against the darknesss riding alongside a wagon. As they neared, Alejo saw a horse, the mouth and neck covered in foam, the animal's head controlled by a bitless bridle that pressed into his nose and jaw. Two short ropes fastened to the back axle of the wagon kept the horse from rearing and hurting himself.

Moro. That must be Moro, thought Alejo.

Slowly, José drove the loaded wagon into the back corral. The men watched but kept their distance. José unhitched the mule team but kept Moro tethered to the wagon. The stallion's angry shrieks filled the balmy night.

From behind a juniper post, Alejo, Hector, and Andrés watched their father water down the horse with a gunny sack. He started at the withers, down the shoulders, to the chest, back to the ribs, the belly, and the flank. Moro's shrieks grew louder with each stroke.

"Tell Andrés he's not hurting him," whispered Alejo to Hector.

"We know," said Hector.

Then Alejo saw a small narrow man slowly enter the corral. He placed a bucket of water before the horse. The horse shied. Moving like a shadow, the man boarded the wagon—the wheels remained silent under his weight—and handed a wooden manger to José, who lowered it without making a sound. José opened the lid of the manger and the shadow tossed down hay, alfalfa, and clover into it. Next the shadow tossed sacks of oats. José motioned Alejo to carry the sacks to the barn.

Alejo raced lest he miss anything. Hearing a new shriek from the corral, he looked back and saw the silhouettes of two lariats in the air—they followed each other like mating birds as they fell over the horse's head. More shrieks.

Alejo feared the stallion would strangle himself. "Noooooo!" he hollered.

A strong hand shut his mouth. Felipa.

"He must drink water before he can eat," she whispered gently to Alejo. "Watch. That's Moro." She kept her hands firmly on Alejo's shoulders. "They'd never hurt him."

José and the narrow man tied the lariats' ends to opposing posts. In a flash, the man removed the horse's harness. Free of the wagon, the stallion reared high on his back legs, his front hooves pelting the night. José and the small narrow man dragged the wagon out of the corral, then José swung the gate shut.

"My Moro is home!" he shouted to the sky.

Again, Felipa saw the face of her dead husband.

Let me be wrong, Holy Virgin. Let José's victory bring joy, not blood, to this house.

4

ALEJO WAS TO MARK MORO'S ARRIVAL AT THE RANCH AS THE turning point in his family's life. The horse threw an ominous light over his brothers and him. They were known as sons-of-the-man-who-owns-Moro.

It didn't seem fitting that the oldest son of Moro's owner feared sleeping alone, so Alejo returned his mother's statue. And he abandoned the idea of carving the Virgin's image. He began crafting his own designs onto pieces of wood, focusing on a statue of Sueño.

Once he mastered the rounded edge, the head and hump came easily; but the tranquil look of Sueño's eyes eluded him. His father encouraged his progress and gave him larger pieces of Yucatán hardwood. Ecstatic over José's attention, Alejo doubled his efforts to master tools.

He learned how to work every tool on the ranch, and for a reward, his father bought him his own hand plane, chisel, straight gouge, saws. José taught him how to use strips of wet hide as clamps, how to whet his blades. "Alejo, with these tools a man can build a life."

Alejo discovered that he could figure how machines work. José bought a gold pocket watch and taught the boys how to tell time. He opened it up and showed them the intricate mechanism. Fascinated, Alejo traced the connection between the center wheel and the smaller wheels that moved the minute and hour hands.

The word "school" entered the house. "Someday my sons will be important men in Alamos. They can't marry well if they can't read. They can't sign contracts, read newspapers or bulletins."

Aware of her limited education, Felipa agreed. Three times a week she drove her sons to La Escuela de Doña Severita, run by a Swiss couple brought to Alamos by an eminent family. The change excited Hector and Andrés. They made friends, learned quickly, and clearly preferred the town to the ranch. "The town has ice," Andrés explained sheepishly to his mother.

But after a month, Alejo quit school, insisting that he could teach himself to read from the still-unopened trunk of books his father had brought home from Guaymas. "I'm too tall to be there," he said. "Besides," he added, "I love the ranch."

And he missed his mother. If the ranch was his center, the center of the ranch was Felipa. Whether out on the range moving cattle or working quietly on his wood, he knew where she was and he directed his pulse toward her. If she is safe, he thought, remembering the stuffed bear cub, we are all safe.

Felipa interceded for Alejo; his absence made her days unbearable. She could do without the younger boys but not without Alejo. The headmaster told Felipa that Hector deserved more schooling. "He has a rare gift for learning," the headmaster told her. José agreed to let Alejo stay home on condition that he learn to read— and if the younger boys attended school full-time.

The matter was settled. Five days a week, Hector and Andrés went to school and lived in town with Mercedes. When they came home, Hector happily taught Alejo what he had learned that week.

It was Hector who broke open the trunk of books. In it were old French novels illustrated with copperplate reproductions of narrow-footed heroes and heroines in the throes of dueling or despair. Hector insisted that he could read the stories, until José convinced him that they weren't written in Spanish.

For Alejo, the drawings opened a trove of ideas to copy and expand. He transferred sections of the drawings onto wood pieces and whittled them. From town his brothers eagerly brought him charcoal, soft lead, and paper. Soon Alejo was teaching Hector and Andrés how to draw.

Another change. The small, narrow-framed Tacho stayed. He didn't sleep at the ranch; but he appeared daily when the family rose. In the evenings he ambled off and disappeared into the horizon. Alejo had recognized him as the quick shadow that had worked with José in the corral the night Moro arrived.

Alejo saw that sometimes Felipa gave beef jerky to Tacho. This too was a change. Alejo suspected his mother's kindness to a Yaqui had to do with the breaking in of Moro.

Felipa had begged José not to tame the horse himself. Nevertheless, José left one morning with Moro tied to the wagon, plus food, water, straw mats, a saddle, and Tacho.

Before leaving, Tacho said to Felipa, "Nothing will happen to Don José or the horse while he is with me. You have my word."

They were gone three days and José returned riding Moro.

MORO BROUGHT JOSÉ power. José came to represent an ascendancy of ranchers over miners. "Alamos will die if we only rely on mining," he claimed to one and all. "Yes, the mines bring money and miners buy what we grow. But when a mine is dead, miners take their silver and leave behind them men without work—peasants without land. Our crops will rot." After his victory over Esteban, farmers and cattlemen listened to him.

José shared his good fortune with his neighbors. Ranchers brought their mares to Moro at the back corral and spoke of the poker game. Those who could paid José with money; the poorer ones signed notes promising grain or other crops. He never pushed for payment, nor was he ever too busy to listen to questions or give advice when consulted.

At night when he saw Felipa at her new altar, praying to the Virgin, he always said, "Thank her for the three queens."

THE FOLLOWING YEAR during the Fiesta de San Francisco, José rode to town with his family. Alejo was surprised how many people knew his brothers, especially Hector.

Alejo noticed that rich, well-dressed men tipped their hats to his father and mother. Men took his father aside and in low voices priced the use of Sueño or Moro for their stock.

Eventually, the municipal president of Alamos asked José for Moro to sire a foal from his prize mare. José refused. Word of the refusal spread. José proclaimed, "His mare will know Moro when he admits that land—not mining—is the life of Alamos."

José warned against foreign investors from the United States coming into Sonora to colonize Yaqui lands. He pushed for a Mexican-owned railroad to link Alamos to Guaymas and Hermosillo.

He demanded that the ranchers' tax money not be used to pay soldiers' salaries in the ongoing wars against Yaquis. "Send the rurales home. Why do they chase the Yoemem in their own lands? This state will die without these workers. Leave the Yoemem and their lands alone."

His stand for Yaqui autonomy drew angry criticism from friends. Felipa never argued with his long tirades, but it was clear she could never be convinced of Yaquis coexisting peacefully with Mexicans.

José refused to cooperate with government orders that miners, ranchers, and farmers count and report the number of Yaquis they had working for them. He urged fellow ranchers not to obey the authorities. "Why do they want to know?" he asked, not caring whether he was in the plaza, in a cantina, or at Madame Carmelo's house playing cards. "Why should Yaquis be counted like cattle? To round them up? To *sell* them to Tejas, again? Lock them up in Hermosillo jails?"

On the subject of Yaquis, Alejo was torn between his adoration of Felipa and respect for José. He simply avoided his parents when they spoke of Sonora or Yaquis or gringos.

What Alejo knew was that he loved Tacho. In secret, Tacho had taught him how to make and use a bow and arrow, how to shoot the old gun his father had tossed out when he bought the new Colt. And although Alejo was already an excellent horseman, Tacho showed him how to care for horses and cattle, how to anticipate illness, drain boils, deliver breached births.

Tacho also simplified time. "Everything starts with Ash Wednesday," he explained. "The year has two parts. The first is winter and spring. The second is summer and autumn."

That makes sense, thought Alejo. Sonora is either green or brown. What didn't make sense was that according to Tacho, the sufferings of Jesus Christ had taken place in Yaqui country. Or that flowers grew from the blood that fell from Jesus while he hung on the cross. Alejo knew that under Cajeme, Tacho had been a temastian, a religious teacher, and when the old man's religious teachings confused him, Alejo begged to hear about warriors or battles.

The old man's loving description of the ritual of becoming a Yaqui warrior never bored Alejo. It seemed grander than any hacendado wedding.

Only the bravest and strongest could aspire to be a Yaqui soldier. Surrounded by a group of older warriors, a captain would enumerate the aspirant's strengths. After that would come the solemn pronouncement: "For you there is no more sun. For you there is no more night. For you there is no more death. For you there is no more pain. For you there is no more heat, nor thirst, nor hunger, nor rain, nor air, nor illnesses, nor family. Nothing can intimidate you. All is finished for you, except one thing: to do your duty. Where you are assigned, so shall you stay. There you will remain in defense of your nation, your town, your race, your customs, your religion. Do you swear to obey the divine mandate?"

To that, the warrior would simply answer, *"Ehue."* Yes.

* * *

As the frequency of José's trips to town increased, Tacho was ordered to hire peons to work the ranch. He hired Yaquis—but Felipa ordered that they be Yaquis without wives or children.

A government edict had classified Yaquis into two categories: pacíficos, tame, or broncos, wild. The wild ones had a subclassification: bandits or rebels. Bandits raided the haciendas' cattle. Rebels fought for Yaqui Nation autonomy.

"How can we tell the tamed ones from the wild ones?" Alejo asked his mother on one of many days when they were alone.

"No one can, not even your father. All Yaquis are wild. The ones in the fields help support the rebels. They buy them arms and supplies. Your father prefers them to other workers. Someday, he'll learn otherwise."

"I think Tacho is tame, don't you?" asked Alejo. "He taught me how to mend harnesses, and without him La Cocinera would have died. I can't imagine the ranch without her."

La Cocinera—The Cook—was the name of Sueño's firstborn. The calf was orphaned when lightning struck the mother while standing under a tree, the cow still wearing Felipa's red braided noose around her neck. Crying, the horrified boys had insisted on collecting what was left of the cow and burying it behind the house.

Tacho had worked day and night to save the calf. Afterward, La Cocinera was raised in the kitchen by the boys and Felipa. All took turns cutting wood to keep the kitchen warm. They force-fed her through a makeshift udder Tacho fashioned from cheesecloth. La Cocinera was a pet who answered to her name.

"Mother," Alejo repeated, "isn't Tacho tame?"

"Only because he's old, and . . ." She closed her eyes as she did when she prayed. ". . . and because he takes care of your father."

Of late, that old foreboding that she would never bury an old husband had returned with renewed persistence. Every time José mounted his wild horse, and left her alone with Alejo, she steeled herself: *Will it happen today, Holy Mother?*

Guilt lashed her when she thought of José's death. Since his return from Guaymas, José had doubled the size of the ranch. He had more money to spend, but she saw him less. Breeding Sueño and Moro took him out of the house, leaving her and Alejo in the care of Tacho and his workmen.

JOSÉ BOUGHT HER colorful silks, Spanish shawls, and a plumed hat. The gifts embarrassed her. Did he buy them because she was less pretty? What woman had he admired in that hat? He made her wear her new finery to church and she was miserable.

"I feel ugly," she explained to Tía Mercedes. "People will think I'm putting on airs."

Tía Mercedes scolded her. "You're not the mill girl he married. You're the wife of an important man. What I wouldn't give to shed these mourning rags and dress like you! It's time a woman in our family married money and kept the husband."

"I know I was happier before." Tears came to Felipa's eyes. "Why doesn't the Virgin give me more children?"

Mercedes shrugged. "She herself only had one. Some women would gladly give you theirs." She lowered her voice. "Does José come to you as before?"

Felipa nodded. José did come to her—though at times she feared he was no longer flattered by her newfound desire of him.

"And you still receive him with the joy of a ripened woman?"

"Oh yes. But," Felipa whispered, "am I still comely, Tía Mercedes?"

"More than ever," said her aunt, emphatically. "More than ever! Your skin is fairer, now that you don't work in the fields. You're the envy of all who know you. Your job is to keep your husband wanting you."

Felipa saw her husband walking toward her. He had never been handsomer, more robust, more full of vigor. Nor had he ever played cards as much. Gambling filled him with plans to expand his holdings.

"I've figured out if I sit and gamble with men who drink, gamble, *and* own land, I'll eventually own some of that land," he had boasted one night in front of Alejo. She had seen awe in Alejo's face.

José had held one winning streak for four hours and come home with a full pouch of pesos fuertes. He hid the gold coins behind her altar.

She found herself hoping that José's good fortune would end.

NEIGHBORS SOUGHT OUT Alejo's skilled hands. His reputation as a quick clean worker spread. He still worked on the ranch, but he also reroofed barns, mended saddles, reshod mules. Felipa beamed with pride. Alejo deserved praise, especially since so much was made of Hector's achievements.

One day while she and Alejo transferred the parrots into a new cage he had built, she noticed how much he had grown. Watching him play with the parrots, which had multiplied into a noisy colorful aviary, she saw a resemblance to José—not in the face, but in his stance. Manly. Alejo had always looked like her. She looked again, but the resemblance was gone.

Sadly Felipa recalled the thin pale José who had returned with treasures from Guaymas. How she longed to have him back.

Alejo turned and said to her, "I'm glad he's not as skinny as he was. I like him strong."

"How did you know what I was thinking?" she asked, afraid that she had spoken her wishes out loud. "Did I say something?"

Alejo stood still. "I don't know. Didn't you say something?"

"I don't think so. Try to remember."

"I can't remember," said Alejo. "Sometimes I don't know if I hear you inside or outside. Don't you hear me, like that?"

"I can feel when you're afraid."

"I can feel when you're sad." Alejo took his mother's chin and directed her gaze toward a parrot nesting in a corner. "That mother doesn't know that the eggs she's sitting on won't hatch."

5

Five years later, 1899

FELIPA HAD GROWN ACCUSTOMED TO JOSÉ'S STAYING OUT LATE, but he had never stayed out entire nights. Eyes closed, she lay in the dark, her palm caressing the empty pillow, the emptiness weighing heavily upon her. She heard the rooster crow, and knew the day she feared had come.

She rose, lit the stove, opened the front door, and found Moro—haggard, riderless. She took the hanging reins and led the horse to the barn, unsaddled him, watered and fed him.

In the barn, La Cocinera rose to greet her. Automatically, Felipa reached into a sack of oats and gave some to her. While the animal ate, Felipa rested her forehead on the cow's soft neck and wept.

"It's happened, Cocinera." She hugged the cow tightly to her. The beast could not warm the coldness in her center.

Outside, the sky lightened. She left the barn and saw the small figure of Tacho ambling toward the house.

"Moro returned without him," she said.

Tacho hitched the wagon and headed toward town.

Felipa entered the house and woke Alejo. "Your father didn't come home."

He sat up. "I don't believe he's dead," he said. He dressed, not caring that his mother was present.

In the candlelit room she could see José's legacy—the scythe-shaped birthmark at the base of Alejo's spine. All three sons bore the mark. None had his blue eyes.

"Stay here, Mother. I'll ride to town."

"Tacho's already on his way."

"They'll tell me more than they will him. Hector will help me."

Felipa followed the tall wiry figure of her son to the barn. He saddled Coqueta, the roan mare, fathered by Moro. She had been José's present to Alejo on his fifteenth birthday. That was over a year ago.

Since then, Alejo had sprouted, was taller than José, and would undoubtedly keep growing. And, Felipa lamented, as she watched her Alejo hoist himself onto the mare without using the stirrup, her dearest son seemed to have started a secret life that didn't include her. Every day, he raced through his ranch chores, mounted Coqueta, and left.

Tacho returned to the ranch hours later. "Nothing on either side of the road to town. Don José was playing cards with Esteban at La Carmelo's last night. Her house is still closed Alejo is at Doña Mercedes's."

"Come into the house," said Felipa.

Tacho removed his hat and set it on the bighorn sheep near the door. "He may be hurt somewhere," he said, reaching for the clay cup of coffee Felipa held out to him. "Perhaps he went home with Don Esteban."

Felipa locked eyes with him. "Tacho," she said forcefully, "that's not what happened. Now search the road to Esteban's. You and your Yaquis find José before the buzzards. Take the wagon."

He put down the cup and left.

ALEJO AND HECTOR went to Madame Carmelo's and hammered at the front door. A woman's angry voice told them to return in the afternoon.

"I know what to do," said Hector. He mounted Alejo's Coqueta and returned with Tía Mercedes riding on the mare's haunches. A frightened Andrés, barefoot, clad in trousers and nightshirt, trotted behind them.

Hair still in its night braid, Tía Mercedes stood in the middle of the street and called to Madame Carmelo and her girls. "Sonya! Sonya! Angela! Cristina! Bettina!"

The front door had barely opened when Tía Mercedes slammed it back on its hinges. Alejo held back his brothers to allow their aunt to enter first. Surrounded by Alejo, sixteen, Hector, fourteen, and Andrés, twelve, Mercedes demanded "the whole story" from Sonya Carmelo.

The dark, airless brothel smelled of stale cigar and liquor. In a grave voice Madame Carmelo recounted the events of the previous night. "They played and bet as they have since José won that horse, years ago. Last night José bet his entire spring herd against Esteban's five hundred acres with the river running through it."

Hector stepped forward. "Who won?"

"Your father. I saw that. They were still arguing when we went to sleep." With an air of helplessness, she said to Mercedes, "They leave when they're ready, you know."

"River land for an entire spring herd is more than playing! Friends don't bet that way. Think, Sonya," ordered Mercedes. "What else did José do or say? Ask someone else—one of the younger girls."

Madame returned with a message. "Bettina says Don José insisted on seeing the land last night—even though it was past midnight and cold. Don José was happy—said he wanted to bathe in *his* river." Madame's face brightened. "Maybe the two fell asleep there!"

The family left the brothel. Alejo and his brothers woke up Sheriff Antonio Alcázar. The burly, dark Alcázar immediately sent riders in all directions.

"They could both be hurt somewhere," Alcázar suggested. "We'll find them, don't worry." He patted Alejo's shoulder.

Alejo shrugged off the sheriff's hand and mounted his horse. "I'm going to Esteban's," he announced. He spurred Coqueta to a gallop toward Esteban's hacienda on the opposite side of Alamos from the Durcal ranch.

The sheriff chased after Alejo, bringing him to a halt by firing his pistol in the air. "Take hold of yourself, Alejo. José is a friend of mine. I care about him—care about both of them. Follow, but wait outside."

Alejo watched Alcázar trot toward Esteban's house, saw the sheriff dismount, remove his hat, and run a hand through a thick mane of hair. Alejo wondered if Alcázar would remove his hat if he were going to question anyone else. Not likely. Alcázar climbed the wooden steps and knocked on the vertical etched glass of the wide front door.

Alejo dismounted and remained on the foot of the steps. His fingernails digging crescents into the saddle, he appraised Esteban's big white house. This house was made for him, he thought with disdain. Father made his own.

Esteban opened his own front door. Alejo strained to hear Alcázar's murmurings. He saw a bleary-eyed Esteban make wild-gestured explanations. The sheriff kept both hands on the brim of his hat, nodding respectfully as if he understood.

Alejo raised his face to the noon sun. He feared breathing lest he explode. His hair, a sweaty black mass, clung to his scalp. He looked at the two men talking on the porch, saw Esteban's mouth move erratically—first one way, then another. Little control. Alejo narrowed his gaze. Concentrate on the mouth, he told himself. Each time he starts to say something, he changes his mind. Esteban's lying. That's why he can't control his lips. The feeling came clear to Alejo: *Esteban killed Father.*

"Son of a bitch!" Alejo sprinted up the steps.

Eyes wide with fear, Esteban slammed the front door. The sheriff intercepted Alejo at the top step. He wrapped his thick arms around the youth's waist and carried him down. "Alejo, there's been an accident. He told me where to look."

TACHO FOUND THE dead José, body face down, stuffed beneath a narrow ledge of rock. José had a bullet hole in the center of his chest and another in the neck. The body had been wedged deep enough to protect it from buzzards, but not from a coyote that had gnawed off a foot.

Felipa was standing in front of the house when Tacho arrived. She waved away the field hands. "Tacho and I can carry him in," she said, tossing a sheet over the body. She slid her hands beneath José's head and shoulder blades and lifted him off the wagonbed. Tacho took the knees.

They laid José on the wooden table. Felipa removed the sheet and looked at her husband. His arms were outstretched in a rigid arc above his head. Red ants scurried out of both wounds.

Felipa said, "I'll heat water to wash him. Cut off his clothes."

"The bullet is still in the heart," said Tacho. "The one in the neck went straight through." He stared at José's stump. "Maybe the coyote didn't like the acid on his new boots. He should be buried with both boots on."

Felipa leaned against the stove to steady herself.

"Señora," Tacho said, "I'll do this alone. He had pride."

ALEJO AND ALCÁZAR rode toward Esteban's river land. Looking at the tracks on the trail, Alejo thought he recognized the Durcal wagon wheels. He dismounted and looked closer.

"My mother or Tacho has been here," said Alejo. "Look at these wheels. They're especially wide." His father had said wide wheels were best to carry loads of hay and salt up to the hills. "Whatever happened, happened here."

"Don't make too many conclusions," advised Alcázar.

Looking closer, Alejo saw splotches of rust leading from the trail to beneath the low rock ledge. He followed two sets of grooves that carved a path to a ledge beneath which blood had clotted to a brown pool.

He lowered his palm into the solid pool and tore a hole into its center. He released a low "Aaahhhh." He raised the claylike earth and blood to his face, breathed it, kissed it. Mouth smeared, shaking with rage, he faced Sheriff Alcázar. "I swear this death will be paid for."

"Alejo, control yourself. Esteban admitted he didn't know if José was hurt. They were drunk. We know what that means."

"Someone dragged Father's body there!" yelled Alejo. "Look, boot heels—" He traced the line from the trail to beneath the ledge. "You're a coward—afraid of Esteban's money."

"Don't say things you'll regret, Alejo. These men have been friends for years—before you were born—before José met Felipa. Friends don't kill each other one night over a poker game—no matter how drunk. That's not the world of men."

"Father won Moro. That ended everything between them. Esteban has never come to our house since then. You're a fool to believe a murderer."

Alcázar bristled, "You have no right to insult me. If it was murder, we have laws, judges, and juries."

"José Durcal has three sons."

A stern-faced Alcázar looked at Alejo. "His three sons should first take care of their mother. Only you can work the ranch if José is dead."

HEAD COVERED, AND dressed in black, Felipa met her sons as they arrived at the ranch. Behind them, several wagons filled with neighbors dotted the road leading from Alamos.

"I rang the church bell. Hector told everyone to come—the priest—everyone is coming," announced Alejo. His horse's mouth and neck foamed white. "Father should be buried on the ranch."

Felipa looked at her son, saw an angry stranger. "The sheriff must come before we bury him. Your father's been shot. This is not a public matter, Alejo."

"Alejo's right, Mother," said Hector, urgency in his voice. "Do what he says, please. We have a plan."

"Plan? Your father's been murdered. We've sent for Sheriff Alcázar. We will demand an investigation." Felipa's voice softened. "Your father's in here."

Respectfully, Alejo dismounted; Hector and Andrés followed him. He signaled his younger brothers to wait and entered the house alone. Still as a statue, his mother stood by the table. The parrots chattered.

A sheet covered all of José except his arms. They were fully stretched out above his head as if he were reaching for something beyond his grasp. His hands were cupped.

Numb and cold, Alejo tiptoed toward the body. The wooden boards creaked beneath his boots. He motioned to his mother to pull back the sheet.

The face was swollen, the mouth slightly open, showing only the tips of his front teeth beneath the thick mustache. Though his eyes were not entirely closed, the blue didn't show. A thick bandage was wrapped around the neck.

Alejo pointed to the bandage, his face asking for explanation.

"One of the bullet wounds," whispered Felipa. "The other is in the chest."

Alejo lowered the sheet, saw that a folded cloth had been placed beneath the shirt. He gritted his teeth. "Hector! Andrés!"

Barely looking at the table holding the body, Andrés ran to his mother, buried his head in her chest, and sobbed. Hector took Alejo's arm and stared at his father's face, then slowly, he wrapped himself into Alejo and wept quietly.

Felipa looked at Alejo. "First, the investigation."

"There won't be one. Esteban killed Father—claims it was an accident—told Alcázar he was shooting at something that scared the horses. Alcázar believes him."

Felipa shook her head in disbelief. "Esteban would never murder your father. Perhaps it was an accident. But first Alcázar must see the bullet wounds. Tacho said José's body was hidden. Maybe someone else was involved."

Hector stomped his foot. "See?" he shouted. "You're fooled too! Madame Carmelo told us that last night Father won river land from Esteban. River land! If people see Father's wounds, we'll have witnesses. Alcázar won't come."

"We'll wait and see," Felipa said. She saw José on the table, saw her sons, their faces ugly with pain. She let Andrés lead her to a chair.

Alejo pointed outside to where their neighbors stood waiting. "Bring them in. Show them the wounds," he said coldly. "Make sure you tell them where Tacho found Father."

Hector opened the door. "Come in, friends."

Alejo stood aside and watched farmers, ranchers, wives enter in silent single file—the women had their heads covered with black rebozos, the men wore black armbands. Alejo did not recognize the pudgy priest who walked directly to Felipa and extended his hand. She kissed it. The black-robed clergyman whispered words that allowed Felipa to cover her face and weep aloud. In chorus, the women keened with her.

Annoyed by the noise, Alejo led his brothers outside and away from the house. In the distance he saw a wagon. "Tía Mercedes," he said, relieved. "Come on," he urged gently. "Mother will listen to her."

The wagon pulled in. "Alcázar is not to be found," Tía Mercedes said angrily. She leaped off the wagon and hurried into the house. The keening stopped.

A different flurry of activity started. The boys unloaded food and candles for the vigil. Inside, neighbor women cut enough stovewood to cook dozens of paper-thin flour tortillas to feed everyone. Felipa took out every dish and eating utensil she owned.

The men went outside, unloaded picks and shovels, and looked to Alejo for direction. Alejo said, "Tacho, take Moro. Lead him up the hill where Father will be buried. Slaughter a steer. Cook it in the back corral."

Half the men crowded into a single wagon and followed the old Yaqui leading José's horse to the gravesite. The other half joined their wives in the house.

Alejo had decided that José would be buried on the highest part of the hill, an area that looked down on the small valley where Sueño had first been led to the herd. The hill was visible from the house; beyond the hill were other fields José had set his heart on owning.

To four men who counted themselves as special friends of his father, Alejo said, "We have sent a rider to look for Sheriff Alcázar. I suspect he's hiding. You saw Father's wounds. Alcázar knows we must bury my father before the body turns. We need time to search every part of town for Alcázar. He must not be able to say that he was somewhere we did not look."

Alejo lowered his voice so that only the four could hear. "We need to preserve the body. While I build the coffin, will you wrap Father's body in cheesecloth and canvas and lower it into the well?"

The men exchanged glances. "What about the vigil?" asked one, warily.

"The rosary will start soon," added another.

"I'll put Father's hat on the table. They can pray around that," said Alejo. "My father's body must not rot. The coolness of the well will give me the time I need."

The men hesitated. Hector by his side, Alejo gazed at each man singly. Finally, the first one nodded; the rest followed.

"Andrés!" shouted Alejo. "Fill every cántaro and gourd with water. We can't use the well until tomorrow." To the four, he said, "Draw enough water for you and the others."

The men filled barrels, canteens, troughs, then went into the house. Alejo expected a protest from his mother. None came.

The wrapped body roped tightly, they lowered it into the rock-lined well until it rested just above water level.

ALEJO ON ONE end, the younger brothers on the other, they hauled a Yucatán log from the barn and set it on X-shaped sawhorses held together by barbed wire.

"To mill the wood, we have to work together," Alejo explained to Hector. He handed him a two-handled saw. "The saw will quiver and want to go its own way. Don't let it. Follow my lead. When I push, you pull at the same time, and Father's planks will be straight."

Hector nodded.

"What do I do?" asked Andrés.

"Watch Hector so you can replace him."

"The town has coffins, Alejo, or we can help with the sawing," offered a neighbor. "José was our friend."

Quietly, firmly, Alejo said, "I thank you, but we will make his coffin."

The neighbor raised his eyebrows in disbelief. "That log is two hands in diameter."

"I know," said Alejo. "We have more." He nodded to Hector. "Ready?"

"Ready."

Alejo extended his arms and pushed his end of the saw. The saw lunged forward and the long blade made its first cut. Hector's hands slipped off and the saw handle struck his chest.

"Trade places with me," said Alejo quietly. "We'll start again. Dig your feet into the ground. When the saw comes, pull it toward you, then push it back to me. Stretch out your arms."

As Alejo pushed his end, Hector pulled at the same time, and shoved it back with all his weight. The blade curved wildly into the log.

Alejo shook his head. "Hector, you moved your feet. Use your arms and back." He looked down at the log. "This side is ruined. We have to pull out the saw and turn the log over. We'll start again."

Hector reddened.

The neighbor sat down and leaned against the side of the barn. He rolled himself a cigarette.

Andrés sat cross-legged on the ground and watched nervously while his brothers turned the log over.

Alejo pantomimed what he wanted Hector to do, then made Hector repeat the motion several times. He pushed Hector hard, testing his stance; Hector's feet held.

"Rhythm is more important than speed," Alejo told Hector. José had taught him that.

In unison, Alejo pushed; Hector pulled. Andrés clapped. The neighbor smiled. A slow, steady whoosh, whoosh sound continued until the first log was finished. They started a second log and worked until Alejo saw that Hector's legs were shaking.

Alejo stopped and trained Andrés as he had Hector. The twelve-year-old held out through two planks.

The wagon returned with the men. "The grave is finished. It's level and deep," Tacho said. "I'll go choose a steer."

A woman brought out fried beans with hot tortillas for the men. Alejo and his brothers ate. Hector paused before taking up the saw. Alejo checked his hands. Blisters. He took off his shirt and tore it in half. "Wrap them."

Whoosh, whoosh, whoosh.

The sound combined with the murmur of prayers and chattering of parrots as the sun descended. In back of the house, mesquite burned into coals and a steer hung upside down and drained clean.

Four hours later enough wood had been milled for Alejo to hand-plane the planks. Without needing to be asked, the neighbors made faggots and dipped them in oil. They gave enough light for Alejo to continue working. Fighting sleep, Hector and Andrés watched Alejo. Inside the house the prayers continued. On a spit, the steer cooked above a pit of the coals. The air was thick with smells of burning oil, fresh tortillas, and readied meat.

Alejo stopped suddenly. "Tacho!" he called. "The glue! Start the glue!"

Tacho hurried to the barn and returned with an old, sooty black pot. Into it he threw a solid mass of animal fat. He dug a hole, filled it with red-hot mesquite coals, and placed the pot over it.

"We need milk," Tacho said to Andrés. The boy jumped. To

Alejo, Tacho explained, "It makes a better binding."

Alejo nodded approval. "Hector, stir the glue. She's a slow cooker. And she's going to stink to the heavens."

"Remember," Alejo said, turning to the group, "it was the glue, not José Durcal, that smelled here tonight." He laughed when the group laughed.

Alejo planed the boards, then cut them to width. But the length puzzled him. He dropped the saw and sat down. Will Father still be rigid? he asked himself.

The thought of having to break his father's arms was unbearable. The coffin would have to be long—very long. He nearly collapsed in despair when he saw that he would not have enough wood.

A soft voice entered his head. "Don José will be ready, Alejo. We will fold the arms across his chest. I give you my word." Alejo looked up into the small black eyes of Tacho.

With renewed confidence, Alejo rose and cut the length. Fresh energy filled him. He joined the boards by placing one-by-two-inch cleats across. He put them on the inside for the top, and on the outside for the bottom. There! he praised himself. That way we can lower Father easier.

The rotten smell of the glue mixing was stronger than that of the cooking steer, the bread baking, and oil-burning faggots. Amused by the disgust on Hector's face, Alejo whittled the pegs for the butt joints. Only a half-dozen neighbors remained awake to hold the torches while Alejo carefully matched the holes to the pegs. He called for the glue and set end grain to face grain. Wet strips of hide from the slaughtered calf served as clamps. Near midnight, he finished the bottom of the casket.

Alejo looked up at the clear night sky; his neck cracked in pain. He emptied a cántaro of water over his face, splashed his body with the cool water, the drops hitting the hardened earth with a thud.

He entered the house. Four candles burned on each corner of the dining-room table—José's hat lay in the center. Rosaries in hand, the women mourners sat around the table—some asleep, others awake. The men had sat themselves against the wall; still in work clothes, Alejo noted. They had left work to be with Father. He smiled at the sleeping ones who had tipped over into each other.

The front of his cassock full of breadcrumbs, the priest recited the litany to the Virgin and the group answered, *"Ora pro nobis."* Sitting tall, Felipa sat next to Tía Mercedes. They're fortunate to have each other, thought Alejo.

No, he can't ask her to come see the coffin. Saddened that his place was outside with the men, Alejo returned to the yard.

Dead asleep, Andrés was slumped over, hands buried between bent knees. Hector sat erect, but his eyes were closed. *We* will sleep next to Father, he decided. He spread straw mats around the well and placed the sleeping Andrés on one of them. He thanked the neighbors who were still awake with an embrace, then led Hector to a mat. Stretched out beside his brothers, Alejo slept till dawn.

"WE MUST RAISE the body," said Tacho, shaking Alejo awake.

Alejo tried to sit up. Every joint in his body was locked. "Help me."

Tacho rubbed Alejo's shoulders and back. Slowly, Alejo unwound himself upright.

Tacho had brought two other Yaquis with him. Together they hoisted up the body. Alejo felt the canvas. It was cold and hard as a rock.

Alarmed, Alejo asked, "The body, will it be like this?" He pointed to the immovable canvas.

"Only for a while," said Tacho. "That's why we brought up Don José now. Finish your work. I promise his arms will be folded across his chest."

Alejo didn't argue. He watched the Yaquis carry the long, rigid body into the house. A foul stench filled his nostrils. He lowered his head deep into the well and inhaled. It wasn't the body. The smell came from the glue.

His brothers were as he had left them. Alejo blew into his hands and rubbed them together. He opened and closed his hands, certain their bones would snap. Legs aching, he hobbled to the coffin and tested the joints. Solid.

From the barn he retrieved a can of axle grease and a sack of tapered nails made by the town blacksmith. The grease would seal the wood. He would close the coffin with the finishing nails José had ordered for a special occasion.

No time to carve the word "Centauro" on the top. The initals "J.D." were all he had time for. He looked at his torn hands and wondered how he would manage that.

A WHITE SURPLICE covered the priest's black cassock as he led the procession up the hill. Behind him was José, inside the newly built casket carried by his three sons and Tacho. Alejo had asked Tacho to be the fourth pallbearer.

José's arms were crossed over his chest as Tacho had promised they would be. Dressed completely in black, Felipa walked alone behind the casket. Mercedes followed Felipa. Then came families who had known José Durcal—farmers, ranchers, wives, children.

Alejo didn't notice if anyone cried. He knew he couldn't. Perhaps he was too tired. He couldn't see his mother's face; it was covered by a black veil that someone had lent her. But he was certain she wasn't crying either.

The priest blessed the earth and casket. Then Alejo and Hector stood at opposite ends of the coffin and, with ropes, gently lowered the coffin into the neatly dug grave. A sigh escaped from Hector.

The brothers took turns shoveling the earth into the grave. With each shovelful, Alejo buried his father deeper into his head. By the time the grave was filled, José was locked away.

AFTER THE BURIAL, after the neighbors had eaten the steer and left, Felipa lowered the bar across the door and faced her sons. "Now," she said, simply.

They rushed into her strong arms. She held them tight, and let them sob freely, loudly, as they had when they were children. Their tears were for José, for each other, for themselves.

No one of her sons uttered his fears; no one dared.

Hector and Andrés were to leave school and return to the ranch to work with Alejo. Before leaving, the priest had warned the young men: "Ignore the code of vengeance. The memory of your father must not be soiled with more blood."

Those words did not sit well with Alejo. Later that night he tried to remember where or when he had seen the pudgy priest. The man was a total stranger.

6

A WOMAN'S FACE ENTERED ALEJO'S SLEEP. HE SAT UP, SHOOK himself awake. No, he thought, she must not haunt his dreams. Perhaps if he visualized the three months with Ana María, took it from beginning to end, he could bury it deeper than the body of his father. Perhaps he would be finished and free of her.

Alejo had known the lawyer Rafael Castillo all his life—though only recently with a wife. The thin, delicate-framed lawyer had married late. His wife, an American-born Mexican woman from Arizona, was much younger. Nineteen. Castillo had first introduced Ana María to the Durcals right after José had won Moro. His father had needed the lawyer to draw up contracts with people. His mother had tried to befriend the young bride but had given up because "she won't talk." Alejo thought it cruel that people had dubbed Ana María "La Muda." Why should she have to talk? He himself could go days without speaking to a single soul—other than his mother.

Six years after their wedding, the Castillos bought a house in an area of new homes on the outskirts of town. As a present, his father volunteered Alejo to build cupboards for their kitchen. "He can make anything Ana María wants," his father had boasted. Alejo didn't look forward to working with the young woman—pretty, to be sure, but melancholy. He only recalled her thick brown hair that tended to curl itself around a serious oval face.

The first day Alejo went to the Castillo home he measured the space for the cupboards. His plan was to make them at home and install them upon completion. He arrived at eight in the morning, and briefly saw Rafael Castillo as he hurried off to his office. Alejo was ready to leave, but Ana María offered him yerba buena tea and served him bizcochos. They sat at the kitchen table and talked. She spoke of Tucson, saguaros, red verbena, fields of golden poppies and primrose, and sunsets, "much redder than anything in Sonora." He spoke of Moro, Coqueta, Sueño, Tacho, La Cocinera. No, he thought to himself, he had never seen *this* Ana María before. He had never noticed the clear brown of her eyes, nor the tilt of her nose, nor her small firm breasts and small waist. She was of a piece, all compact. His stories amused her; she laughed aloud. Never had he felt so successful. He heard himself combine words as only Hector could. At six in the evening, the lawyer came home and Ana María stopped talking. Embarrassed, Alejo rushed off. Never had he known such a day, he thought on the ride home. *He* had made Ana María's pouty mouth laugh with genuine delight. Yes, her paleness vanished when she laughed. All night he relived the day; all night he rushed time so he could sit before her again, and from there regard how she cradled a cup with both hands, parted her lips barely enough to slip in a bite of bizcocho. Loins aching, he returned the following day, and the next, for three months. After the cupboards, he had learned to make a bathhouse, and to refloor a bedroom.

It's just to talk, he told himself at first. Other than his mother and brothers, he had no real friends. Ana María would be his friend. He would learn about *her*. She was twenty-five, he fifteen.

Her father had insisted on a professional man for his daughter. One day, after the cupboards and before the bathhouse, Ana María was in midsentence explaining, "Father chose a lawyer for me—" when Alejo reached across the kitchen table to take her hands. He needed to stroke the fine wrists, but the act swelled to include a kiss of the soft narrow palms, and then a warm moist mouth pressed into the dip of his neck. He held his head still to prolong the stay of her lips against his flesh. To reach his neck, she was standing on tiptoes. Her heels shook from the strain. He thought his heart would break. He rose to full height and lifted her off her feet, and, as he raised her to him, he knew how it would end. He slid her into him, and felt her legs wrap themselves around his waist. Entering her was right. Sweet. They never spoke of their act. But each time he went to her, he found her trembling with anticipation, eager to receive him. Always, the sweetest moment was her shudder of completion. Afterward he advanced the work he came to do, and they coupled again before he left. The second time was always rushed.

He was in the process of expanding the front porch when Castillo left Alamos unannounced. Ana María too was gone. That was a year ago. He had heard people speculate that the couple had returned to Arizona. Some said they were in Tejas, others said California.

As he lay in bed, Alejo visualized the three months as a narrow tube which he made narrower and narrower, then smaller. He locked it deep in his head until, *Pas!* it vanished.

THE SOUND OF a rider racing toward the ranch snapped Alejo out of his reverie. He lay still, let the rap-rap-rap, rap-rap-rap of the canter speak to him. One horse. The rider was light of weight, possibly young. Alejo rose; as head of the house, he must meet the rider.

José had been dead ten days.

The rider reached the ranch courtyard and from his horse called out, "Señora Durcal! Letter from the sheriff."

Alejo ran out of the house and saw a young man his age. The horse's neck was lathered; foam framed the muzzle. Alejo took hold of the bit, steadied the head of the panting animal, and checked its mouth. The rider had worked the bit into the vulnerable flesh.

"This isn't your horse, is it?" Alejo asked.

The rider answered by waving the envelope in front of Alejo's face. "I have a letter for Señora Durcal. She must go to the courthouse tomorrow morning for the inquest."

Alejo reached up. With one hand he yanked the rider off the horse, with the other he grabbed the envelope before the messenger crashed onto the dust.

Alejo placed his boot squarely on the fallen man's chest and pressed down. "My mother's name is not yelled out by you or anyone else. You'll return to town when I say that horse is ready to ride again."

Alejo stuffed the envelope inside his shirt. *Hector can read this to all of us later,* he thought. He unsaddled the horse and led him to the water trough. The stunned messenger remained where Alejo left him.

THE FOUR DURCALS arrived at the courthouse half an hour earlier than the summons requested, Felipa shrouded in black. Hector and Andrés wore black pants and white shirts with black mourning bands tied around their upper arms. Alejo wore José's black linen coat.

After the sheriff's notice arrived, Felipa had washed then boiled her sons' white shirts in lye and ironed them. Her sons had taken turns scouring the cuffs and collars to cold white.

Alarmed at the size of the throng waiting for them, Alejo searched and found Tía Mercedes. He relaxed slightly when he picked out his father's friends standing a respectful distance away from the family. He was counting on their support against the Escobars. Rafael Castillo had not returned from Arizona. Just as well, he thought.

Alejo braked the wagon. Almost simultaneously, and seemingly out of nowhere, a darkly clad Esteban Escobar appeared, accompanied by Billy Cameron, the smiling American who had come several times to admire his father's ranch. Esteban's fair hair was oiled. The bloat of his face was less than when Alejo had seen him the morning of José's death.

Before Alejo could say or do anything, Esteban was helping Felipa down and was escorting her into the courthouse. Alejo fought his impulse to chase after them. He wanted to pick up the coiled whip beneath the seat and snap his mother back to his side. Hands shaking with rage, he tied the reins, forced himself to breathe slowly, deeply. *Not now, not here.*

Hector and Andrés jumped off the carriage and rushed to Alejo's side. "What's Esteban doing?" asked Hector. He shook the wagon. "Do something, Alejo."

"Look," said Andrés, eyes wide. "He's touching Mother." He pointed to Esteban's hand that held Felipa's elbow.

Alejo drew his brothers to him. Controlling them brought him self-control. "People are watching," he said, voice level. "Go with Tía Mercedes." He gave them a gentle push and entered the courthouse after Esteban and his mother. Over his shoulder, Alejo saw Billy Cameron gaping open-mouthed at the horde crowding into the courthouse.

Esteban was shorter than Felipa. He angled his head up toward her ear and whispered hurriedly. Alejo could see Esteban's tiny, even white teeth. All he could make out was the word "sorry." He was unable to discern whether his mother acknowledged anything Esteban was saying. A black rebozo over her head, she seemed to be staring straight ahead, oblivious to Esteban's words or to any other part of the proceeding.

Alejo approached; Esteban smiled uncertainly. Barely nodding,

Alejo placed his arm around Felipa and hugged her. Her shoulders and torso were stiff. Good, he thought, she hasn't been listening to him.

Esteban left them and joined Billy Cameron. Together they walked toward an elegantly tailored white-haired man. The man's pointed chin and the long thin nose with a slight bump made it clear: he was Esteban's father. Alejo remembered that the Escobars were from Hermosillo, the state capital. He's come for his son's trial, thought Alejo.

The courtroom was filled to capacity. Sheriff Alcázar came out of a side door and announced to all, "Because this is not a trial, the judge will hear the testimony in his chambers. Only the two families will be present." He pointed toward the doors he had just come through.

The courtroom buzzed with displeasure. Esteban's father motioned the sheriff over to him. After a brief murmured conversation, the sheriff announced to the crowd, "The windows in the judge's office will remain open so that all may hear the proceedings. We want no secrets here." A scrambling toward the exit followed.

The judge's office had two French windows protected by grid ironworks on each side. The windows opened to the street, allowing ample room for people to see and hear the testimony. The townspeople pressed their faces to the window grates. Sheriff Alcázar led the four Durcals into the office and pointed to a bench. Alejo and Felipa sat down and placed Hector and Andrés between them. Esteban and his father followed and sat across from them.

When the judge signaled, Esteban rose, told his story. He spoke as if to a child. They had played cards and drunk mezcal until past midnight. José insisted on seeing the Escobar river land. They rode out there—still drinking. Something spooked the horses. It was dark. Esteban shot. He did not think he had hit José. He thought José had fallen down. Confused and unable to remember what happened next, Esteban claimed he had come home. His plan was to

82   MONTSERRAT   FONTES

retrace his steps the following morning to find José. It was not the first time he and his friend had lost track of each other during a long night of drinking and playing cards.

Esteban was the only one present at the shooting; no one could contradict him.

The judge said that unless there was testimony to the contrary, he would have to rule José Durcal's death as accidental manslaughter.

Complete silence followed—indoors and outside among the spectators.

Hector's voice broke the pall. "How can you say that?" The boy stood. "Who's higher than you?" Felipa swiftly pulled him down. She turned to Alejo; her mouth framed the sound of his name. Seeing his name leave her lips made him feel as if he might be freed from the eyes that held him captive in that room.

Alejo walked to the center of the room. His throat felt like a narrow, frail reed; his hands were heavy, useless. He tried sheathing them in the pockets of his father's coat but his fingers were too long. He chose to let them hang by his side. He looked to the windows and was heartened by the familiar faces—but not enough.

Again he turned to Felipa. He gazed at her until he could envision the planes of her face encompassing the entire room. His words were then set free.

"Esteban Escobar claims the shooting was accidental. He claims both bullets were fired to hit a snake or whatever frightened the horses. Isn't it strange that either bullet could have killed my father? Both bullets were well placed—aimed."

Esteban rose, pain across his face. "I did not *aim* at my friend," he said. "I could never do that to José." He looked at Felipa. Her black eyes returned the glance.

Slowly, casually, Alejo positioned himself so Esteban and Felipa could no longer see each other. "You made no mention of the land my father won from you that night," said Alejo. "According to Madame Carmelo and other witnesses at her house, you bet and lost the river land called Valle de los Espejos."

Esteban shook his head. "That's impossible. True, José wanted to buy that land from me. We went there because he insisted on seeing it. He has been after me to sell it to him for years." He stopped to look at the crowd. "Many of you have heard us argue about it. It's an old story that always comes up after long nights. But that property is not mine to bet or sell. That land belongs to my father, who is here to testify to that effect. If Madame Carmelo has a statement to make about this, where is she?"

Esteban turned expectantly to Alcázar. "Señora Carmelo has refused to come," said Alcázar to the judge. "She says she has nothing to say other than they were there past midnight. But I will go for her myself." He left the room.

Outside, the crowd buzzed with displeasure.

The two families waited in silence for the sheriff to return. The crowd grew louder; fragments of pro-Durcal statements flowed into the room. This pleased Alejo, who frowned at Hector for waving at José's friends.

"Perhaps now Don Escobar could testify about the ownership of Valle de los Espejos," Alejo suggested to the judge. "Lost bets must still be paid, no?"

Suddenly Esteban rose and, in a voice that everyone outside could hear, spoke to Felipa. "I was José's first friend when he came to Alamos. Silver was good. He could have made money in that. But no, he wanted land, even though he was almost penniless. So I lent him what he needed for his land. Several of you farmers and ranchers out there"—he pointed to sunbaked faces at the windows—"joked about our friendship. How could a lazy man like Esteban be friends with a hardworking man like José, you asked. Well, we were. Often you heard me say that I slept like an innocent after watching José work so hard. That too is true." Some members of the crowd smiled. "But I admired José Durcal." Esteban turned toward his father. "And I know that my father wishes I would be as hardworking as my friend." The older Escobar's nod was slight, but definite.

Esteban continued. "I was at his wedding and I baptized his oldest son, the young man who now accuses me of murder. How could I murder José Durcal?" he pleaded. "I am innocent. I know some of you remember the break in our friendship after our trip to Guaymas, years ago. Well, the true and shameful cause of that break I will now confess."

Esteban lowered his head and paused. All eyes were fixed on him. "I acted dishonorably on that trip. José found Moro first and had sealed the bargain. I was jealous of his good fortune and doubled the price. I admit I took the horse that rightfully belonged to José."

Esteban paused again and laughed. He scratched his head and smiled. "I don't know what I thought I could do with that horse. Moro nearly killed me. I never could ride him. Who could?" he asked, shrugging. "José. Only José Durcal, El Centauro Durcal, could ride El Moro. And we all remember how he took his revenge with his three queens. Believe me," Esteban chuckled, "more than once I have thanked God for José's three queens."

The crowd at the windows laughed with Esteban.

Alejo sought to lock glances with Esteban, but Esteban kept his head turned and looked only to the outside crowd.

He has fooled them, thought Alejo.

No one seemed surprised that Sheriff Alcázar returned without Madame Carmelo.

The judge's ruling remained unchanged.

With one arm Alejo hugged his mother and Andrés; with the other, he drew a scowling Hector to him and whispered hurriedly into his ear.

THE BROTHEL WAS closed, the shutters pulled down.

Inside, an angry Hector paced the floor; Tía Mercedes towered over Madame Carmelo. "Why apologize to me?" Mercedes shouted. "Your silence robbed José's family of justice and land—both!" She leaned forward and asked, "Sonya, how many years was

José your friend? You knew him as a young man." She stressed the word "knew."

Madame Carmelo sat slumped over the Spanish mantilla that covered the table where she had dealt the most important poker games in Alamos. Her usually crimped red hair lay flat on her head. She kept her face hidden and let out another loud sob.

Tía Mercedes snatched the mantilla with both hands and shoved it into Madame Carmelo's face. "Why didn't you tell the court what you told us? Why? You, you pile of filth!"

Eyes blackened by tear-run mascara, the weeping woman cringed. "Have pity, Mercedes," she whimpered. "You would have done the same." Her sobs grew louder.

"*Puta!*" Mercedes threw the mantilla to the floor. "If I believed that, I say, God, kill me where I stand."

"You can still tell the judge about the poker game, señora," argued Hector. "Tell him what you told us—nothing more. No one would blame you for changing your mind."

As if in great pain, Madame Carmelo slowly raised her head. "Look at me, Mercedes," she implored, pointing dramatically to herself. "This pile of filth, as you call me, has no young men to defend her. I have nowhere to go. Who cares about women like us? Who asks how or where we will die?"

Her quavering voice broke. "But that very question is what all putas ask themselves. How? Where will I die?" She paused; her small blue eyes darted back and forth between Hector and Tía Mercedes. "This house is all I have. This is where I planned to take my last breath. Esteban's family could take it all away." She narrowed her eyes and snapped her fingers twice. "Like that!"

"No!" cried Hector. "They can do nothing if you and everyone swears to the truth! Just the truth! Señora Carmelo, here in this house you saw Esteban Escobar bet river land and lose it to my father. If he bet dishonorably, he still must pay. Don't be afraid of the Escobars. Trust us. My brother said to tell you that we'd protect you."

Madame Carmelo lowered her head again.

He turned to his aunt. "What happened to our friends? Our neighbors who came and saw the bullet holes in Father? Alejo is right. Those bullets were aimed. He killed Father. Why is there no trial, no more questions, nothing?"

He shut his eyes and violently shook his head as if driving out forbidden images. "No. No! Truth must mean something!" His voice thundered throughout the brothel. "Someone must hear us!"

Startled, both women stared at the young man, whose dark eyes burned in his pale face. Hector stared back and drew himself to full height. "You think that because I'm fourteen I don't know truth can win, even against the powerful Escobars. You look at me and see only a boy." His mouth curled bitterly. "You too, Tía, no?"

"You're wrong," answered his aunt. "I fear I see the death of a boy." Her voice was hard. "In you I see what Esteban and your father's games will finally cost this family. Before my eyes I see the birth of a vengeful man. Don't let it happen, Hector. As Felipa's son, you are also mine. For five years you have gone to school and lived with me. I know you. Your father too, I loved like a son."

Hector pointed a finger at Mercedes. "And would you allow your son's death to go unavenged? No trial, nothing?"

"I'm doing what I would for my son. Maybe Sonya's right. Maybe the judge from Hermosillo has no ears for women like her." Mercedes turned to Madame Carmelo and reached for the weeping woman's hand and moved it up and down. It rose and fell— weightless. "She's as powerless as we are."

Nodding, Madame Carmelo bowed her head and grasped Mercedes's hand.

Hector continued. "If she who saw the poker game and the neighbors who saw the bullet wounds will not speak out against Esteban, it's clear what José Durcal's sons must do. Are we to live in the same town with our father's murderer?"

"The code of vengeance is not for children, young Hector,"

warned Madame Carmelo. "The Escobars are among the most powerful families in Sonora. Felipa Durcal is blessed. She has land and three sons to help her."

"Don't speak my mother's name in this house," said Hector. He walked to the door. "Tía, I'll walk you home before I ride to the ranch."

The sun was low when Tía Mercedes and Hector left the brothel. They hurried down the winding cobbled streets that led toward the square. Hector held his aunt's elbow as she stepped onto the high stone steps beneath the arches in front of the plaza. A group of men speaking quietly stood aside to let them pass.

A tall rancher tipped his hat and respectfully said, "Doña Mercedes, young Hector, we share your grief."

"Gracias, señores," said Tía Mercedes. She nodded and nudged Hector. He stared straight ahead. "Bad manners will get you nothing," she muttered under her breath.

Loudly Hector proclaimed, "I have no manners for cowards, cowards who saw the bullets in my father's body and said nothing today in front of the judge."

Tía Mercedes seized Hector by the collar and drew him to her. "As you act, so shall you be treated," she scolded harshly. "If you're so eager to be a man, shoulder your pain like one." She turned his body around to face the group of men. "Apologize to your father's friends."

Hector tried to wrest himself free but was unable to break her hold on him. He pressed his lips shut and defiantly thrust his chin out for all to see.

"No hay cuidado, señora," said the tall man.

The men tipped their hats again and resumed their conversation.

"YOU WON'T LEAVE until you eat," Mercedes said to Hector. She demanded that he finish the entire plate of beef stew, tomatoes, onions, garbanzo beans, and flour tortillas. She watched him gulp down his food.

"Thank you for coming with me to Madame Carmelo's," he said. "I'm sorry you were ashamed of me."

"You say foolish words because you don't understand the way things are, the way things are in true life, Hector." Mercedes picked up a fork and started eating with him. "Your father never accepted the way things are. He always wanted more."

"He always worked for more, Tía," Hector corrected. "Father always said 'worked.' That's why we're rich."

Mercedes laughed. "Rich, are you? Time we had a talk."

Hector heard that although his father owned Sueño and Moro, and although he owned land, and townfolk came to him for advice, the Durcals were not a wealthy family. According to his aunt, Sonora had families far richer, far more powerful.

"José's dream was to make the Durcal name as famous as the Almadas and Maytorenas," she explained. "And who says that can't be? Who knows what God has planned for you, eh?" She reached over and playfully chucked him under the chin. "Hector, you're the most handsome of Felipa's boys." She stroked his dark hair. "You have José's best features."

Hector frowned and pulled away. "What do the other families have that we don't?"

She scraped her garbanzo beans onto his plate. "Maytorena has land—lots more than José had. Your father liked Maytorena. Together they've fought to keep their Yaqui workers from being sent to the Yucatán henequen plantations. But it looks like the Díaz government isn't going to let Yaquis stay in Sonora. I heard they're taking the women and children now."

"We still have our workers," said Hector.

"Pray the government lets you keep them." She shook her head. "This is a terrible time for Yaquis."

"Tía, tell me more about the rich families. What do you have when you're really rich? More horses? Cattle?"

"Well, there are the Almadas. They have mines—like Esteban's family."

"Why didn't Father like mines?"

Mercedes shrugged. "Well, as Esteban said today, José liked land. He liked his ranch, his horses, his crops. He liked to see what he owned." She laughed softly, her fingers gently rearranging loose strands of hair at the base of her neck. "He was always telling me what his next plan was. He loved making lists. He loved land. A person is blessed when he loves what God gave him."

"That's like Alejo." Hector sighed. "He loves the ranch. It's too quiet for me. Sometimes nobody talks for a long time. One day I was out on the range with Alejo. I had already made up my mind not to talk first. It was a contest I was playing with him, but I didn't tell him about it. Well, he never noticed my silence. He rode his horse and he carved his animals. That's why I told Father I shouldn't have to come to the ranch when school is closed. They didn't need me." He lowered his voice. "Now, I'll have to stay there all the time and, and . . ." He struggled for control. "I hate ranch work, Tía Mercedes. I've tried to like it. I can't. It's just one big circle—always the same—day in day out."

She took his hands and turned his palms over. Scabs had formed over his blisters from working on José's coffin. "I know. You're restless. That's how my sons were," she said, sadly. "They couldn't wait to go away."

"I don't hate Alamos," he added quickly. "Did they?"

She laughed. "They were afraid I'd use them in the mill. And I might have. So they left. God bless them."

She made the sign of the cross. "But I had my Felipa to help me. You should have seen your mother then, Hector. What a brave strong girl! She was younger than you when she came to the mill. By the time José came to take her, the mill was working. I tell you, Hector, a mill is like an endless vein of gold. No matter what happens, people will always need to have their harvest ground."

Hector wrinkled his nose in disgust. "I don't want to work in a mill either. I want to see Guaymas and Madrid. I want to be rich and cross the ocean." He curled his hand into a fist. "But first, Esteban has to pay."

"Hector, don't let hatred poison your heart," Tía Mercedes scolded. "We will never know what happened that night. José is gone, but his sons are strong. José taught Alejo everything. You know how to read and you understand numbers. Andrés will do anything you tell him to. You boys could become rich, if that's what you want. But nothing will happen unless you take that dagger out of your hearts. Sonya Carmelo was right. Felipa is blessed."

Hector leaned into his chair and locked his hands behind his head. "Well, everyone is blessed today," he said sarcastically. "Tía, the whole town knows what happened. They expect us to take revenge."

"People like excitement," Mercedes said. She looked directly into Hector's eyes. "Their talk goads fools to do crazy things. All you and Alejo will get out of meddling with Esteban is jail, hanging, or both."

Hector scoffed. "No one in town would hang us. They know us." He pushed his plate away from him.

Brusquely she cleared the entire table. "Now you're talking like a boy of fourteen—a tired, stupid boy. You think the rurales won't hang you and your brother if you raise an arm against the Escobars? That family is connected all the way to the Capitol. Look at what they do to the Indians! Their families can't bury them until the bodies have rotted."

"Tía, we're not Indians!" Hector shouted.

"You're not Escobars!" she shouted back. "You're fatherless ranch boys with only a mother to protect you."

Mercedes stood, threw the table out of her way, and grabbed hold of Hector's shirt. "No more burials in this family! Understand?" She shook him until he had vomited his entire dinner onto the floor and onto her.

*   *   *

ALTHOUGH THE SUN still had no heat, Alejo was already exhausted. All week Tacho had tried to teach him to ride Moro. Daily he had pressed his will against the horse and lost. He was angry at himself for failing with Moro, angrier at his mother and brothers for witnessing his falls. The previous night Alejo had taken a swipe at Hector for boasting, "I can ride him."

He asked his mother to keep away the stream of neighbors who came to give her their condolences. "Go stay with Tía Mercedes," Alejo begged his mother. "It will save them a trip out here. I don't want anybody to see me with Moro." Felipa refused to leave the ranch.

Lips cut, back and shoulders bruised and limping, Alejo entered the corral where Tacho waited with the blindfolded Moro. Grabbing reins and mane, he carefully mounted. "Maybe today he won't throw me too far," he said to Tacho. He tried to smile but it hurt too much.

Tacho grunted, "Hmmm. When you talk like that, you already gave Moro permission." Barely moving his lips, Tacho repeated his instructions: "Moro knows only Don José's weight. Use your knees. Make him feel your strength." He held a crop out to Alejo.

Alejo refused the crop. He pressed his knees and trotted the horse inside the corral several times. Moro tried to shake off the blinders wrapped around his eyes. He jerked his ears forward, then back; his nostrils flared, every pore desperately reaching out as if asking air and dust, where am I?

Alejo smiled. Through his loins he compared Moro to his own mare, Coqueta. Father and daughter. How generous she was with him. Why did Moro hold back?

The horse had only known kindness from him. He had helped care for him since that dark wonderful night when his father had brought him home. And Alejo had kept a respectful distance from Moro, never assumed a familiarity that was not his. So why, Alejo wondered, does he refuse me so cruelly?

Alejo saw Tacho raise an arm. At the signal, Alejo pressed knees and heels into the stallion until the horse broke into a canter. Alejo glided. He was sure that should Moro want to, he could tear himself free of all dust that powdered his hooves.

Tacho swung the gate open. Moro's ears moved. Alejo pressed harder and the horse maintained his stride. Keeping him at a canter, he left the corral. Obediently, the blindfolded Moro circled the house and barn, then returned to the corral. The gate swung shut behind them.

Tacho signaled again, and Alejo reined the horse to a halt. Willfully Moro yanked his head forward. "Pull and hold!" shouted the Yaqui. "Never ask a horse permission!"

"I don't want to hurt him," said Alejo, embarrassed at his own words.

Expressionless, Tacho asked, "Why? He'd kill you." He unwrapped Moro's eyes. "Trot. Let's see how long he'll let you stay on."

All morning they worked the horse without blinders. At noon, bored with the trot-canter routine, Alejo decided to press for a gallop. Moro responded immediately. Elated, Alejo felt the horse gather his hind legs beneath his powerful body, then extend his forelegs far ahead of him, and then came that magic instant when all four feet left the ground at the same time. Rider and steed fused. Boy became suzerain. The sour taste in Alejo's mouth turned to nectar. Heady with delight, he looped around the trail again and extended the route, prolonging the ecstasy.

Out of the corner of his eye he saw Tacho frantically waving him back. Alejo drew back the reins, slowed Moro to a canter, then down to a crisp trot. Grateful, Alejo leaned over and stroked Moro's sweaty neck as he had seen his father do, then headed him toward the corral.

At the entrance, Moro suddenly swung into the post. Alejo raised his leg to protect his thigh from being crushed. Effortlessly, Moro flung him high into the air.

From the air, Alejo saw the distance grow between him and the ground. He saw Tacho's dark eyes follow his ascent. He saw Moro, neck arched, snap at the air with his back hooves and with a stroke of his tail, brush the day farewell, and stride toward his stall.

Felipa seemed to be waiting for Alejo to touch ground. Tacho stood behind her. Crashing, Alejo felt his body touch the earth in segments—shoulders, head, buttocks, heels. Air rushed out of him and a benign blackness embraced him.

Coming to, Alejo saw two heads. Felipa's pale, frightened face, and Tacho's smiling brown countenance.

"A broken man can't work this ranch," she said. She unbuttoned his shirt and checked his ribs and shoulders.

Alejo shook his head and pulled himself away from Felipa's searching hands. "Almost! Almost!" he said to Tacho. "True? I almost had him."

Tacho extended a hand to Alejo. "Almost," he chuckled. "Moro *almost* let you be in charge."

Nursing his right leg, Alejo stood up, letting Tacho's small figure slowly lead him toward the house. They left Felipa behind.

"No blinders tomorrow," said Alejo. "I'm sure Moro will let me ride him."

Tacho pursed his lips in disapproval. "No, Alejo. Moro's still a one-man horse. He must learn to see only you. That can only happen in the hills."

Pointing to the barn, Felipa threatened, "I'll shoot that demon before Alejo leaves this ranch with him."

Looking directly at her, Tacho asked in a cutting monotone, "How can Moro accept Alejo with you around? The horse knows you're in charge."

Felipa ran at them, her tall frame a shaking tower of rage. Too angry for words, she ripped off her apron and slapped it wildly at their heads. They accepted her blows in silence, without resistance.

When she had finished, Alejo asked with tears streaming down his dirt-stained face, "Do you want Esteban's words to come true? Will José Durcal be the only one to ride Moro?"

Undaunted she replied, "The devil take Esteban! I want you

whole. That horse has brought me only pain." She disappeared into the house.

Alejo whispered to Tacho, "Gather what we need. We leave tomorrow."

"What time?" asked Tacho.

Alejo answered in Yaqui, *"Tua machiapo."*

7

ALEJO AND TACHO LEFT FOR THE HILLS DURING THE BLACKEST part of night. The moon had set; the sun had yet to rise. They hitched the wagon and tied Moro to the back.

Alejo wasn't ready to leave yet. He had never moved directly against his mother's will. Never had he disobeyed a request of hers. He had hoped to see a light in his mother's room—perhaps hear her footsteps in the barn as they loaded the wagon with food, water, machetes, two rifles, straw mats, hay, oats, ropes, blankets.

Tacho had not allowed him to feed Moro or to load José's saddle onto the wagon. Alejo, too preoccupied over his mother, had not questioned the orders.

Something gnawed at his center. He ordered her, *Don't fight me when I need you.* Alejo reproached himself for needing her consent.

He and Tacho left, and as they made the final turn—as they took that last twist in the road from which the house was visible—something forced Alejo to look back for what had to be the last time. A tall silhouette filled the door. The profile waved the lantern toward the wagon. Through the light the connection with his mother returned. The emptiness in his center disappeared.

*   *   *

DAWN CAME. IN silence Alejo and Tacho rode toward hills where Durcal cattle had never grazed. Tacho drove while a content Alejo whittled on a small rectangular piece of wood. Since his father's death he had not tasted the sweet stillness that came when his fingers guided blade over wood to release the picture inside his head.

His plan was to carve a soaring eagle, wings spread wide. He had seen an eagle in one of Hector's books. But before he tackled the full piece—his largest to date—he needed to practice shaping the back and wings on smaller blocks. The parrots he had carved had come too easily to him. No, he thought, the eagle has strength and grace. He admired the grace that warned *stay away*. Could he make power and beauty flow from the same form at the same time?

As they neared the first set of hills, Alejo noticed that Tacho bypassed the visible trail that led to the top. Instead he circled the hills, then headed toward a second set that from a distance looked almost identical to the first. Alejo wanted to ask where they were going but was afraid to appear childish. The sun told him that they were riding north and west. I know where home is, he assured himself.

When they reached the second set of hills, Alejo was disappointed to see that they were smaller than the first—no more than high broad mounds. Tacho drove into the cleavage and steered toward a narrow but dense wall of dry, dead chaparral. He tossed Alejo the reins and hopped off the wagon. "Drive through," he said.

Tacho ambled to the wall of chaparral and searched beneath the brush until he unearthed a frayed piece of rope. He pulled back the rope and the entire chaparral wall moved with him.

Out of the corner of his eye Alejo saw that the old man was waiting for a response. Alejo pressed his lips together and drove the mule through the narrow passage. Moro snuffled.

Tacho pulled the chaparral wall closed behind them and climbed back onto the wagon. With his chin he pointed to narrow ruts on the dirt. "Follow those all the way to the river."

"What river?" Alejo murmured, expecting no answer. He felt the sun's full rays on his shoulders; ahead of him he saw chuck-holes, chaparral, and mesquite.

Tightening his hold on the reins, he clicked the mule forward. The road coiled around the base of the small hills; the wagon wheels rose and fell unevenly. The jolts awakened Alejo's empty stomach. A satin dust filled the air, forcing the animals to snort their nostrils clean. Turning his head, Tacho also cleared his nostrils before signaling Alejo to stop.

The wagon creaked to stillness. Alejo shut his eyes, cupped his nose, waited for the dust to settle. Tacho nudged his chest with an open canteen. Grateful, Alejo splashed his face, rinsed his mouth, and drank. He assessed the road ahead: impassable.

"Get Moro," said Tacho. He jumped off and began unhitching the mule. "Only you touch him."

Tacho led the mule single-file through the pass. Alejo and Moro followed. They went down a steep incline that fanned out to a wide clearing where tight rows of cottonwoods bordered the edges of a wide flowing stream. The air here was cool, sweet.

Tacho watered and fed the mule and hobbled it away from Moro. "Let Moro hear and see only you," he said. "Give him water—no food. We want him hungry."

Wagon unloaded, they sat down to eat in the cool shade by the water. Fine ripples traveled over the dark stream, and Alejo controlled the impulse to test the current. He was ravenous.

"Keep your stomach light," said Tacho, tossing Alejo an orange. Tacho filled a flour tortilla with tomato and beef jerky, sprinkled it with salt, and folded it in half. "You have to ride him today."

Alejo looked around the clearing. "Where?"

Again Tacho jutted his chin toward the stream. "In there."

Too hungry to ask how he was to ride Moro, Alejo tore the orange open and finished it. "I still need a taco or at least some tortillas—without meat."

Frowning, Tacho tossed him two. Out of his full rucksack he pulled out a small tin can. In it were matches, corn husks, and finely chopped tobacco. From the corn husks, he rolled himself a cigarette, licked it tight, pinched the ends, lit it. He took a long drag and sucked the smoke in deep. He took another drag; the cigarette burned down almost to his mouth. He pressed out the ember with his fingers.

"Don José always bought me tobacco when he went to town." He leaned back on his elbows, stretched out his legs, and crossed his feet at the ankles. His sandaled feet were ashy from the dust. His dark, beady eyes looked intently at the water.

Alejo chewed the dry tortillas and downed them with water. He studied Tacho. He had never seen the Yaqui move so loosely. He had tossed his body down like an old blanket. His lined face, however, remained on guard. He followed the Yaqui's gaze. He seemed to be searching for something in the stream. Alejo saw nothing out of the ordinary.

This must be a Yaqui hiding place. He's happy out here, Alejo concluded. He felt proud that Tacho had brought him here, but knew to leave questions unasked. "First day I ride Moro to town, I'll bring you tobacco. Did Father come here with Moro?"

"Ayyy!" laughed Tacho, running his fingers through his thick white hair. "No, that was real work. We took Moro to a canyon in the hills. He was too loco for water. Don José was ready to shoot him if he didn't break."

Alejo shook his head in disbelief. His mother had also threatened to shoot Moro.

Tacho sat up and with his finger made a large U on the dirt. "We put Moro in the middle." He made an X in the middle of the U. "That's Moro. Then we ran ropes under the belly and lifted him off the ground—not much." He held up an open hand to signal how high.

He pointed to the two tips of the U. "We wrapped the ropes around these trees and left him hanging there." Tacho put his hands up to his ears and laughed. "That Moro danced and screamed like a witch on fire."

The tortillas lost their taste. "How long?" demanded Alejo.

Tacho shrugged. "Until he stopped screaming."

"He could have broken his back," said Alejo, angry at the image of Moro suspended.

"He didn't," said Tacho. "Your father lowered him, gave him water, rubbed him, touched him, then lifted him again. Moro was like a child. He learned who was patrón."

Alejo disapproved. "Maybe it's better to shoot a horse than do that to him." He felt disloyal to his father.

Tacho turned his cinnamon face toward Alejo and fixed his eyes on him. "Horses and Yaquis get their strength from the earth. Take the earth away and we become obedient children. Your father was good to children, Alejo. He never hurt Moro."

THE SUN MOVED past the hills, leaving their campsite cooler. Alejo stripped down to his long underwear and entered the water. The coldness shocked him. Goose pimples covered his arms and chest. Small pebbles bore into his bare feet. He looked back. On the river-bank stood Tacho with Moro, saddleless but bridled.

"Find the current," ordered Tacho. He pointed to the center of the stream.

Cautiously, Alejo waded farther into the thick sediment that threatened to swallow him. Each step was a struggle. He was in chest-high when he felt the current. It swirled strong between his legs. He trudged beyond the current to the other side of the stream and checked his bearings. The width of the current was about a dozen steps.

He waved to Tacho. The Yaqui threw a lasso out to him. Alejo wrapped the noose around his waist and pulled himself out.

Tacho handed him a small sack with a drawstring which Alejo slipped around his neck. Tacho gave Alejo the reins and said, "Remember all I said." He stepped back, leaving Alejo alone with Moro.

Slowly Alejo led the horse forward. The hooves sank into the soft earth. Moro stopped. Alejo reached into the sack for a handful of oats. Moro sniffed, ate, and dipped his head to drink. With smooth, even strokes, Alejo rubbed neck, shoulders, back, loins. Holding the sack out, he pulled Moro in up to the knees and fed him another handful of oats.

A few more steps—Moro now belly-deep—and again Alejo touched the horse. He whispered, "Moro, Moro," with each stroke. His open hand caressed the powerful chest, moved down to the forearms, traced the curve of the shoulders, then down across the barrel to the ribs, belly, flank, buttocks. More oats, more steps, more caresses.

Moro was chest-high in the water when Alejo ran out of oats. He continued stroking and whispering. The horse tried to turn himself toward shore, but Alejo tugged on the bridle and held him in place. Alejo did not feel victorious. *We've tricked you.* Saddened, he rested his head against the horse's neck and ran his finger down the rigid arc. Moro's eye moved a half circle back and looked at Alejo.

"Moro."

Alejo scanned the riverbank. Tacho was nowhere in sight. The sun's light had weakened; no breeze disturbed the stream's silent flow. Alejo imagined that from a distance he and Moro might appear as strange shapes trapped in a mirror. He closed his eyes and allowed the stillness of the moment, the embrace of the water, to go through him. He tried to see Ana María, José, and Felipa, but their faces were blurred, distant, unreachable.

Moro inhaled deeply. Alejo opened his eyes. *It's time.* He freed his feet from the slush and wrapped his fingers around the horse's mane and let his legs float behind him. "Moro," he said, and smoothly glided his full length onto the horse's back.

Moro stiffened. Again he tried to turn himself around. The water foiled him. Lying over him, Alejo continued stroking, talking. Gradually, he sat up, settled his weight into the dip of the horse's back, and steered him toward the current.

The bucking came—violent—but slow, labored, manageable. Moro snorted; an angry screech stayed lodged deep within. No matter where or how the horse twisted, the water hugged him, penned him. As long as Moro fought, Alejo kept the reins taut, his legs pressed tight to the sides. When Moro gave the slightest sign of slowing, Alejo immediately eased the reins. But Moro ignored the reward and again refused his rider. New resistance met immediate reprisal. The sun disappeared; the fight continued.

He knew that Moro's night sight gave him an advantage. Jaws clenched, Alejo ignored the darkness and pinioned his groin into the horse. In a dervish frenzy, Moro whirled, twisted, spun; Alejo felt as if his waist would snap. He was sure the skin on his knees had peeled away. Then abruptly the horse stopped. Motionless, he snorted loudly into the water. Alejo felt Moro rearrange his lower body, although above the water his head remained perfectly still.

Tense, Alejo was sure he could feel the animal thinking, and he steeled himself. Nothing came. More waiting. Alejo looked around him. Sky and water had become a seamless black sheet. He waited. Still nothing. He used the respite to relax his jaw and to raise his aching legs away from the horse's sides.

Suddenly out of the beast came an ear-piercing war cry. Moro's body crested the water, and in the air, flipped backward into the water. Alejo slid off; he found himself trapped under the animal. The gravel of the river bottom tore into his back. Lungs bursting and terrified of the thrashing hooves, he abandoned the reins, drew knees to chest, pushed himself away from the horse, then sprang to the surface.

Standing in the black water, Alejo could hear Moro's wild throes as he worked himself upright. Finally the outline of the head shot above water. Alejo groped blindly and grabbed the mane. With all his strength, he drew himself back onto the horse, jamming his testicles between his own loin and the animal's spine.

Enraged, Alejo raised his head; he bellowed into the night; his fists pummeled Moro's neck. He wailed, howled angry gibberish until the sounds became feeble whispers; his tired hands clung to the matted mane. He steadied his breath and, pressing his palms against the withers, repositioned himself firmly atop the panting mass of hot muscle.

More twisting followed—but without the prior feral commitment. Alejo knew the fight was now perfunctory. He leaned forward, retrieved the reins, and stroked the pulsing neck. "Moro!" he screamed. The horse swayed to a halt.

Cautious, Alejo softened his hold on the reins, but held the mane. Panting, snorting, the horse remained stationary. Alejo waited in the silent darkness until the horse's throbbing disappeared, then he tried a command: he shifted his weight toward shore, gently increasing the pressure on the reins in the same direction. Moro obeyed.

He dismounted before they reached the bank. When he tried to steady his trembling thighs, he realized he was naked. Only the waist and ankle bands of his long underwear had survived the battle. Under the moon's light he saw the thin loop around his waist; ragged bracelets laced his ankles. He leaned against Moro until he felt blood rush down to his numbed feet.

He led the depleted animal toward unchurned water to drink. Alejo too cupped water to his mouth. On dry land, he ran a slow, deliberate hand over every part of the horse's body. Then, warily, he raised and held each hoof to reassure himself that Moro acknowledged him. In the isolated spot where hay lay waiting, he removed the bridle.

He knew the battle would resume the next day.

THE SMELL OF cooking meat woke Alejo. He found himself where he had collapsed the previous night, naked and wrapped in a blanket. He rose to relieve himself and saw that one of his testicles was bruised. Painful spasms shot across his back and waist when he bent over to study the discolored ridges on his scrotum. Crying out, he discovered that his throat was raw. He remembered his angry screams. Looking down, he saw that the hair on the inside of his legs had been scraped away.

"Leave your huevos," yelled Tacho. The old man walked over to him and handed him a tin cup of pinole.

Hands shaking, Alejo reached for the sweet hot drink made of toasted corn and sipped carefully while Tacho circled him, inspecting his bruises.

"I told your father that horse is bad because he has a bad name. Moros are bad. I know what I'm saying, Alejo." Tacho spoke as if he expected an argument.

Alejo knew of the Yaqui ritual battles between Christians and Moors but thought them reserved for religious fiestas, holidays such as Easter when Christians fought the fariseos—the Pharisees. He was too hungry to listen to such talk.

Tacho motioned him toward the small fire. "Esteban cursed the horse with that name. Today we baptize him," he said solemnly. He held out a pointed stick of mesquite. *"Teku."*

Alejo had never eaten squirrel. He took the stick with crisp meat strips and labored to sit himself down on the dirt. He sprinkled salt crystals over the stringy meat. The salt dissolved quickly. He yanked off a mouthful, chewed fast, inhaling as he ate to keep his tongue from burning.

"Water the animals after you eat. No food for Moro," said Tacho, rummaging through his rucksack. He pulled out two long strips of cotton material, one red, the other blue. "The blue . . ."

". . . is for Christians, I know," nodded Alejo, "and red is for Moors." He unskewered the last of the meat, rolled it, dropped it into his mouth, and licked his fingers clean.

He saw his pants were rolled up by the supplies. Alejo decided not to put them on. Legs and back a solid block of pain, he hobbled barefoot to the water's edge. Standing arms folded across his chest, he looked down at his thin pale frame and compared his torn body to the serene water before him.

He saw his image in the water. Dark matted hair framed his angular face. The few whiskers above his full, sensual mouth failed to hide his likeness to Felipa. He narrowed his large eyes—and clenched his jaw. Still, no resemblance to José. All this, for what? he asked himself. He remembered his fiery assertion at the courthouse. "This son of José Durcal will ride the Moro!" Pendejo.

A weariness crept out of him and deftly enveloped him. He was shocked to hear himself cough deep mournful sobs and he slapped at his mouth, forcing it shut. His brain reeled with the unuttered "Papá, tengo miedo."

"El sueño, Alejo," he chided himself aloud. The dream.

He tore off the piece of underwear that remained around his waist. The dirty bracelets around his ankles he would deal with later, when bending was less painful. The night had chilled the stream, but he forced himself to move, to enter waist high, allowing the cold to numb his bruises. He opened and closed his hands in the water, rubbing them vigorously; he rinsed his mouth, splashed his face, chest, shoulders.

Behind him, he heard Tacho rushing about. Turning, he saw the Yaqui building a long rectangular structure of mud and branches by the edge of the stream. Alejo could see the serious intent on the old man's face and remembered Tacho was a temastian. He knew how to conduct religious rituals.

With the machete Tacho had cut long branches and shaped them into poles that he was now trying to set onto the top of the mound. The task looked too complicated. Alejo shocked himself once more with cold water, then headed for the mule and Moro.

The horse had turned himself around in the narrow makeshift stall. He snorted as Alejo approached, bridle in one hand, bucket of water in the other, and a small pouch of oats around his neck. Moro drew back his ears; Alejo stopped in his tracks and lowered the bucket, waiting for Moro's ears to return to normal before walking farther. If the ears went back, if Moro even breathed resistance, Alejo withheld the water. When Alejo finally placed the bucket

before the horse, Moro turned away and did not drink until Alejo
had stepped back.

From where he stood, Alejo could see how the bit had scraped
the skin of the horse's mouth. He hurts, he thought. Dared he bridle him again? His own groin ached at the thought of mounting.
And what did Moro feel? Would he fight again? Weariness threatened to resurface. Alejo forced it down.

El sueño.

He held up the bridle so the horse could see it. "Moro," he whispered. But now the name bore a different taste. He probed the dark
eyes of the beast and saw its human part. Staring further, he saw the
animal's will to remain whole, and in that, he saw himself.

An unexpected thread of love emerged in him. Afraid to tear the
fragile strand, he closed his eyes and rested his center in its niche.
"Moro," he repeated, and he tasted his own tenderness.

He dropped the bridle and stepped into the horse's realm. His
bare body next to the horse's shoulder, he stroked; the horse stiffened; he rested his palm on the neck and willed his hand to carry
the kinship he felt. He stood by Moro until he visualized their
pulses flowing singly. He gave him all the oats.

Moro gave no resistance when Alejo slipped a noose around his
head and walked him in a wide circle. The gait was stiff; in that too,
Alejo recognized his own exhaustion. This drew him closer to the
horse. Energized, Alejo welcomed the soft morning sun at his back.
A lazy breeze swirled down the hills to the hidden dale; the air caressed his chest and loins. The stream rippled under the same
breeze. The cottonwoods fanned themselves. His weariness lifted.

Looking to the water's edge, he saw where Tacho had finished
his church. It had three arches, a cross over each. The Yaqui had
tied a piece of blue fabric around his head and now sat on his haunches smoking a cigarette.

Alejo sucked in his lower lip and whistled. Tacho waved him
over. Aware that the old man would be angry with him, Alejo
shook his head and pointed toward the supply wagon.

From the wagon Alejo tossed a handful of hay where he wanted Moro to stand. The hungry horse ate. As he chewed, he raised his head, and Alejo slipped on a hackamore bridle. He would work Moro without the bit. Alejo stepped up onto the wagon wheel and, cupping his testicles, lowered himself onto Moro.

The horse's head took a wild swing but he continued chewing. Reins in hand, Alejo waited for Moro to finish eating before putting heels to ribs and riding toward Tacho. Moro's only resistance was toward the water. He shied from the stream.

Tacho scowled. But Alejo was sure he could work the horse on land and without a bit. He was sure Moro was his. "The nose brace will hold him. He's cut," he explained.

"You must work him out there," said Tacho, nodding toward the stream.

"No. He's stiff. Watch his back legs." Alejo turned him around. "See? They're uneven. And he's afraid of the water."

"Alejo, that horse could throw you right now. Why did you feed him?"

"He knows I'm patrón." Alejo heard the foolishness in his voice. He groped for words. "I saw his eyes. He's ready. I feel it."

Tacho lay back on his elbows. He lowered his head and fixed his eyes on Alejo. "Yori, the eagle has no friends."

Alejo was hurt to be called Yori. Tacho had never called him that before. His mother's lifelong distrust of Yaquis shot through his head. He countered his mother's feelings with his father's absolute trust in them.

"Tacho, Moro is not an eagle. He was hungry. He hurts."

"Good. A horse understands hunger and pain."

Tacho stared into Alejo. Diminished, the boy lowered his gaze. "Forgive me," he whispered.

Tacho shook his head. "Mules are smarter than horses—smarter than boys." He went for the mule, slipped on a bridle, tossed a folded blanket on its back, and walked it back to Alejo and Moro.

"Get on the mule," he ordered; he held the reins to both animals while Alejo switched mounts. "Trot Moro with the mule. Give Moro enough rein to run straight. But hold on. Let the mule lead."

"How long?"

"Until I say stop."

All morning Alejo ponied the horse with the mule up and down the clearing. The mule's steadfast gait gave the horse no quarter. If Moro tried to stop, the mule nipped him back into line. Before long, Moro's neck was lathered and Alejo's back was loose again—the pain giving way to the steady pace of the mule. To ease the pressure on his groin, he raised his knees and rode on his buttocks. Alejo craved water; but he dared not stop.

Head wrapped in blue, Tacho also labored nonstop. With a machete he had poked a series of small holes into the earth marking a long narrow aisle that led from the side of the hill to the mud church by the water's edge. In each hole he stuck a green cottonwood stem. The heads of young leaves trembled in the breeze, their lighter, more opaque halves blended with the soft brown earth.

In the center of the pathway Tacho spread out a blanket. He hummed as he shredded cottonwood leaves and tossed them onto the blanket. With each passing, Alejo saw the mound of torn leaves grow wider, higher. Tacho's humming continued. His small strong hands kept pace with the mule.

The animals' chests were white with foam. Alejo's throat burned, his tongue swelled to the roof of his mouth. His loins, thighs, and calves were hot weights. From afar, he saw himself falling off the mule and waking to Felipa's face above his. Her angry caring image eased his pain.

"Alejo!" Tacho's voice broke the reverie.

He waved the boy over. Alejo dismounted; his legs caved. Tacho caught him and led him to the leaf-covered blanket.

"Pick up the corners," said Tacho.

Dazed, Alejo held two ends of the blanket and followed Tacho. They carried the heavy blanket and laid it by the entrance of the pathway outlined by green cottonwood leaves.

"You ride Moro through this path to the water . . ."

"No, he's afraid of it," said Alejo. "He'll throw me."

". . . but when you get to the church, stop and come back. Don't give him his head until the third time—then, make him jump over the church and into the water. There we will baptize this Moor!" He clapped his hands and waved the boy away.

"He won't do it," Alejo insisted.

Tacho pulled out a red cloth from under his shirt and tore it lengthwise.

"Moro's afraid, I tell you." Alejo felt his throat closing and pointed to it. "Water," he managed.

"First the horse." Tacho motioned him toward the entrance of the pathway.

Defeated, the boy obeyed. He brought Moro and held the reins while the old man wrapped the red cloth around the animal's neck. He gave the other strip to Alejo.

"Go for your water. Wrap your head in red. And here. . . ." He reached into his shirt and pulled out a Yaqui rosary. "When you try to attack the church, keep this around your neck and put the cross in your mouth."

Alejo had seen Yaqui rosaries before—simple round hand-carved wooden beads strung together without spaces marking the separate mysteries. His carver's eye was unimpressed. He put it around his neck and put the tiny cross in his mouth.

"The taste, what is it?"

Tacho shrugged. "Animal fat?"

Alejo's impatience grew. He took out the cross and held it away from him. "Why do I need *this?*"

Tacho's dark eyes narrowed. "During the Pascolas, Chapayekas keep the rosary cross in their mouths. The cross keeps evil from entering their hearts."

"Tacho, Easter is far away. Why are we doing this?"

"Today you and Moro will enact the part of Moors attacking the church. I will be the Christians trying to force you into the water to baptize you." He lowered his voice. "If *real* evil spirits try to enter you, the cross will protect you." He whispered angrily, "Inside, you laugh at me, Alejo. Who knows where I will be next Easter, eh? Wrap your head."

Alejo heard the unsaid: every day more Yaquis were arrested and deported to Yucatán. He had always believed their Yaquis were safe, but with his father dead . . .

He hobbled to the stream and drank. Patches in his throat remained dry. He looked down at the rosary. This is useless, he thought. Moro accepts me. What if I demand that we go? What if I load the wagon and go home? Aren't I head of the Durcals? Tacho works for me, no?

Alejo wet the red cloth and wiped the dust off his face. He looked back and saw the Yaqui waiting for him—Moro by his side. Tacho had torn off a piece of blanket and folded it over the horse's back. Touched by this kindness, Alejo wrapped his head in red.

Tacho helped him mount. "Fix your huevos."

Alejo moved his testicles forward and to the side.

"Keep Moro on the path. Remember not to let him jump over the church until the third time."

"What if he throws me?"

"Will he throw you—patrón?" Tacho taunted.

Tense, unsure, Alejo remained silent while Tacho stuffed the shredded cottonwood leaves into his shirt. Then came a sudden sharp slap on the horse's flank.

"Yaaah!"

Moro broke into a canter. Screaming, Tacho chased after them, throwing leaves with all his might.

Moro tried to head toward the wagon, but Alejo held the reins taut and kept him on course. Tacho's leaf shower covered them. Tacho's howls—"Yaahh! Yaaahh!"—confused, frightened Alejo.

When they reached the mud church, Alejo yanked the horse's head to the side. The motion almost toppled him. Tacho continued to pelt them with leaves.

"Two more times!" Tacho ordered, herding them back.

Alejo returned to the starting point; he steadied himself and Moro. Again Tacho filled his shirt with leaves. But this time he walked away and tore a switch off one of the ramadas. He paused to stare at something in the hills. He seemed to be waiting for something. Suddenly, he charged, giving Moro a hard rap with the switch accompanied by the same ear-piercing howls.

The horse reared; Alejo grabbed the mane and steered the galloping animal toward the water amid Tacho's leaf storm. Alejo shook his head to loosen the leaves from his face and to keep the church in clear sight. He brought the horse to a halt. Moro reared again, screeched, demanded himself free of men.

By the water's edge Alejo waited for directions. Leaves clung to his sweaty body and the horse's lathered coat. Elated that the final charge was coming, Alejo hollered, "El bautizo?" Tacho nodded, almost smiled.

Alejo prodded the reluctant horse back to the opening of the leaf-littered pathway. Again Tacho walked away— this time in the opposite direction. Amused, Alejo figured that sudden assaults were part of the ritual.

Moro's ears moved back and forth looking for signs of the attack; his thick, long tail swished at nonexistent flies.

Tacho remained out of sight.

The sweat on Alejo's body had dried and Moro's breathing had steadied when Tacho unleashed his loudest attack. Unseen, unheard, he picked up the four corners of the blanket filled with what was left of the shredded cottonwood leaves and swung the entire sack at boy and mount.

The strength of this blow unseated Alejo. His hands clung to the mane and red kerchief; his legs raced full speed alongside the horse, holding Moro on course by punching the thick neck. His shoulders felt the power of Moro's drive; legs tiring, his naked feet dragged, bending backward at the ankles.

At times Alejo managed to lift his feet off the soft earth as the beast sped toward the water. All he heard was the clamor of pounding hooves and Tacho's howls; all he saw was showers of leaves, mixed with clumps of dirt, as the Yaqui herded Moro and Alejo toward the water.

The horse reared in front of the mud church. Alejo let go completely; the momentum hurled him at the church. His body bent at the waist over one of the arches and his face scraped itself across the dried mud. All air left him. The tiny wooden crucifix flew out of his mouth and disappeared into the water.

He heard the whoosh of a cottonwood switch as Tacho lashed the horse's rear, forcing him to hurdle the church. Above his head, Alejo saw Moro's hooves slice the air as the horse flew over him and into the stream.

Tacho dove in after the horse. Vision blurred, Alejo saw the Yaqui everywhere—with outstretched arms Tacho kept Moro in the water; his quick hands untied the Moorish red kerchief from the horse's neck; he replaced it with his own Christian blue band. All the while Tacho poured water over the beast's head and murmured Latin fragments of the sacrament of baptism.

"In Nomine Patris, et Filii et Spiritus Sancti . . ."

WRAPPED IN HIS blanket, Alejo inhaled the sweet smell of mesquite embers that filled the night air. His belly was full of meat, flour tortillas, beans, and three cups of pinole. He had fed Moro as thoroughly as he had fed himself.

He gazed at the stars that seemed an arm's length away. Lying back, he stretched his aching legs. The gentle heat that warmed his torn feet only set off the painful throbbing again.

He sat up. "This pain won't stop," he said, holding the side where he had crashed into the mud church.

Tacho left his blanket and squatted next to Alejo. His fingers poked the boy's chest and ribs. "Nothing loose." He returned to his blanket and rolled a cigarette in the darkness. He spit into the embers. "Give the pain a face. Sometimes that's the only way."

Alejo was angry. "What are you saying?"

"Close your eyes. Move the pain onto the face. Look at it hard until it goes away."

"What kind of face?"

"Any face. Search your head." Tacho lay on his side and drew the blanket tight around his body.

Alejo closed his eyes and searched. Not Ana María, not his mother, not his father. "Esteban," said Alejo.

"He's too strong for you," said Tacho.

Eyes closed, he held Esteban's face in front of him. Alejo pledged, "I will ride Moro to town as I swore I would. My father's killer will see me—and he will pay."

"Why bring sorrow to your family, Alejo? You are not a killer."

"You know I must do this. Alamos knows it. It's expected."

Tacho raised his head. "You trust a town of Yoris? They will betray you. Never let Yori hands touch you."

"Esteban killed my father."

"Work your land. You're a boy, not a killer. Bullets kill dreams." Tacho grunted and rested his head.

Starting with the torn soles of his feet, Alejo transferred the pain onto Esteban's face, then he moved the soreness of his legs, groin, thighs, ribs, and even his chin where he had scraped it raw on the church's dried mud. He never felt sleep arrive.

It seemed to Alejo that the return to the ranch was coming much too soon. Tacho was traveling fast, using a different route from the one they had taken coming in. The wagon was lighter.

Before leaving, Tacho had surprised him by stashing surplus supplies in a cave on the other side of the stream. The hidden entrance to the cave was small and narrow, but inside, the cave branched out into several small arteries, allowing for little light. Tacho lit a torch and led the way. He lifted a dusty canvas and showed Alejo dozens of singly wrapped American Winchesters and boxes of ammunition.

With pride Tacho had said, "From the times of Cajeme. Yori hands took him."

Exploring further, Alejo saw coiled rope, small traps, oil, flint, bows and arrows, canvas, parts of harnesses, shovels, dried mesquite, and blankets. Tacho packed hay, oats, rope, straw mats, and dried beans.

"Who's this for?" Alejo asked.

"For those who need it," answered the Yaqui. "Only Yoemem and special men know of this cave."

The answer had flattered Alejo; he decided not to protest the Durcals' loss of supplies.

Dressed only in pants and shirt, Alejo rode Moro beside the wagon. He kept his bare feet—still too sore for boots—close to the horse's barrel. The remaining strands of his long underwear had become black rings around his ankles. He would show them to his brothers when he told how he had tamed Moro.

Now, Alejo burned to know more about the cave. But Tacho kept the mule pressed to a brisk trot. Who had used the supplies in the past? Had Cajeme himself hidden in the cave? Why weren't Yaquis using the cave now, when every day brought more arrests and deportations?

"Why are we going so fast, Tacho?"

"The dust—we can be seen from far away. That place is a holy secret."

Alejo checked the horizon and saw no signs of anyone. "Did Father know about this place?"

Frowning, Tacho brought the mule to a halt. He motioned Alejo over. "He knew. But he told no one. You will tell no one. Men go there to do what can't be done elsewhere. When it's done, they don't speak of it again. That keeps the cave safe."

He slapped the mule and Alejo read an end to the conversation.

They rode in silence. Alejo stopped often to reposition the blanket sagging between his bruised groin and Moro's dip. Moro's stride told him that the horse still felt the battle of the stream. A steady pain connected his own body.

Looking back, he saw sameness. The santuario was lost to the brown Sonoran vastness broken by clusters of round hills that bred chaparral, mesquite, and creosote. The santuario with its dark, quiet waters, the arching rows of cottonwoods, the soft earth where he had collapsed, all receded to the realm of memory.

He looked forward under the glaring noon sun; he saw the familiar. Beyond that next set of hills was home. A familiar heaviness overtook him and he tried to lighten the weight by summoning images of his reunion with his mother and brothers. He saw himself riding Moro into town.

He had been gone two nights, but back there, in the santuario, time had had no measure. Yes, he had battled, been hurt, but he had won. Moro was his.

Suddenly, he saw the work that awaited him. Breeding Sueño and Moro, worming calves, branding, planting. And he had plans to kill Esteban! His head whirled.

Beneath this morning's sun, Tacho's words did not sound silly. *You are a boy, not a killer.* So much to do. *I'm sixteen years old,* he explained to no one, to everyone.

Tacho drew in the reins, braked the wagon. "Vienen por mí."

Alejo failed to understand Tacho's words until he heard the clatter of the rurales' horses. A narrow column of four fanned out to encircle them. Alejo recognized the cone-shaped sombreros of government soldiers. A long-bed wagon drawn by four mules lagged behind the riders.

Alarmed, Alejo approached the soldiers' wagon. Inside the wagon lay six bound Yaquis. He recognized two of his day laborers.

"These men are pacíficos, from the Durcal ranch," he explained to the lieutenant in charge. "I am Alejo Durcal."

"Yaquis are Yaquis," answered the young officer. He had light brown eyes and a thin, almost blond mustache that failed to cover the span of his mouth. He opened his canteen and offered to share it. Alejo refused with an angry gesture.

Alejo remembered the two rifles wrapped in his blanket; he saw no way of getting to them. Then he saw Tacho's arm inch back into the wagon. Body tense, Alejo slid off Moro and prepared himself to fight. But no rifles came. In disbelief he saw Tacho pick up his rucksack and jump down from the driver's seat.

"Tacho, no!" Alejo commanded.

The old Yaqui ambled to one of the soldiers and handed him his sack for inspection. The soldier searched, returned it, then followed Tacho toward the government wagon.

Alejo ran toward Tacho. "He's family!"

In a single act, two soldiers drew out their pistols and dismounted. One grabbed Moro's reins; the other pressed a cocked Colt .44 to Alejo's chest. Looking down the well-oiled barrel, he saw that every chamber was loaded. Alejo felt the cold stare of the professional soldier and stepped back. He snatched Moro's reins from the other soldier.

"Our orders are to sweep all ranches in southeast Sonora for Yaquis," said the officer. "We're taking them to Guaymas if you want to get the old man back," he added in an almost genial voice that raised Alejo's hopes.

But then he saw that without prodding, Tacho was climbing onto the soldiers' wagon. Why is he doing this? wondered Alejo. Tacho lay on his stomach, crossed his hands behind his back, and raised his feet. The soldier who had searched his belongings tied Tacho's hands and ran the rope down to and around the sandaled feet.

Never let Yori hands touch you. The soldier's hands had not touched him, Alejo realized.

"Look for me, Tacho!" Alejo called desperately. "I'll find you!" He buried his head into Moro's neck at the sight of Tacho's small frame bound like a calf.

But the old man did not look back. He didn't look at the other

Yaquis, nor did they at him. All stared straight ahead. At what? They could not see over the sides of the wagon.

"When did you receive these orders?" Alejo asked. He tied Moro to the back of his wagon. "We were never told." He spoke loudly so Tacho could understand that he had had no warning of these sweeps.

Perhaps he could reason with the officer, Alejo thought. "My father was killed. My family needs the old man. He goes nowhere. He's harmless. Spare him." He lowered his voice. "We will pay you. I have a good mare at the ranch."

"I prefer Moro," said the officer.

Alejo pretended not to hear, and hurried onto the wagon. He stopped. "All right. The horse for Tacho." Voice trembling uncontrollably, he added, "And a receipt with your signature."

The officer dismounted, untied the horse, and handed the reins to a waiting soldier. "The Yaqui stays with us."

Moro reared once before a soldier's rope caught his neck. The officer climbed onto the Durcal wagon, gathered the two rifles, unloaded them, and tossed them to the wagon driver.

"I'm taking the rifles to save your life," said the officer. He stood with feet wide apart and looked down at Alejo. "Your brother Hector almost got himself killed this morning. We honored Señora Durcal's pleas."

My mother begged them?

Alejo held his breath as he studied the lieutenant's face. He saw no cruelty in the officer's eyes or mouth. Enslaving men and stealing horses is easy for this man, Alejo realized.

He took in every inch of the man. The size of his dusty government-issue boots, the length of his narrow legs, the small nails of his square hands. Alejo would remember all. The thin, light mustache, light eyes, and the even timbre of his voice.

This man turned me into a killer.

Alejo managed, "Is my family all right?"

The officer nodded. "Yes, despite your brother."

Never let Yori hands touch you.

Alejo took up the reins but kept his eyes lowered. "Well, then I thank you, Lieutenant——?"

The officer remounted. Smiling at his men, he pointed to Alejo. "This young rattlesnake wants my name."

Standing, Alejo asked, "Are you ashamed of your name?"

Ignoring him, the rurales returned to double-column formation. In moments they became an indiscernible brown cloud.

Alejo felt as if the land beneath him were slipping away. His head felt weightless. A clear light floated inside. And in that terrible clarity he saw how easily a life is shattered. So this is how it was with Father, he thought. Fast.

"Hijos de puta!" Alejo screamed at the rurales' hoof marks.

But the words held no ardor. The only heat he felt was the narrow stream of sweat that trickled down his neck to his waist.

His center was cold, oblivious to the noon sun.

8

FLANKED BY HECTOR AND ANDRÉS, AN ANGRY FELIPA STOOD on the porch and watched as Alejo drove the wagon toward the house. Her dark hair was pulled back into a thick braid that disappeared into her black mourning garb. Her strong hands cupped the necks of her sons to keep them from running to their older brother.

"Looks bad. No Moro, no Tacho," mumbled Hector. The right side of his face was a mass of bruised flesh.

"Bad, bad," echoed Andrés, sad-eyed.

Felipa decided to postpone her thanks to the Virgin for her son's safe return. Hurt that Alejo had ignored her pleas not to leave the ranch with Tacho and Moro, she was grateful to see Alejo. But now she saw that something terrible had struck down her son, and her rancor was not for the missing horse, nor the Indian. Her ire stemmed from the defeat incised across Alejo's haunted face. His lax hands on the reins surrendered control to the mule.

She extended the pulse of her heart to him, but received no response. He's damaged inside, she thought. Since José's death twelve days ago, she had watched Alejo attempt to uncouple himself from her. She respected his distancing, trusted that eventually he would return.

Alejo leaped off the moving wagon, letting the animals walk themselves to the water trough. Seeing her son's labored walk, Felipa released the boys. Alejo grunted as he gave Andrés a full hug that lifted the twelve-year-old off his feet. He turned Hector's face toward him. The upper lip was torn to the corner; a purple sheen joined cheekbone to eye.

"They hit him with a pistol," Andrés said.

"It doesn't hurt," said Hector, pulling his face away. "They kept Father's gun. They searched the house and took the two Colts." He pointed to the empty wagon. "What happened to you?"

Alejo rested his arms around his brothers but looked at Felipa when he explained, "Rurales. We were almost here when they stopped us—took both rifles, arrested Tacho—took him to Guaymas." He pulled his eyes away from Felipa and said to his brothers, "The lieutenant stole Moro. But I broke Moro—did it in a river."

Felipa assessed the scrapes on Alejo's face, his torn feet and bruised hands. Yes, she reaffirmed, the damage is inside.

"I must find Tacho. And Moro . . ." Alejo stammered, "The lieutenant knew Moro's name. He wouldn't tell me his."

Trying to smile through his hanging lip, Hector sputtered, "I rode to Sonya Carmelo's after they left. He is Lieutenant Raúl Trujillo from Sinaloa. He's twenty-four, stationed in Hermosillo."

Alejo laughed and patted him on the back. "Saddle Coqueta. We'll go see the presidente municipal. Even rurales can't steal horses."

"Inside!" ordered Felipa. She shoved the oldest boys through the door but pulled back Andrés by the shirt collar. "Unhitch the mule," she whispered harshly to him. "Finish the chores. Feed the chickens, horses, mules. Find Cocinera. Lock her in the barn. No one leaves here!"

Alejo and Hector stumbled through the doorway but went no farther. Felipa gave them a second, harder shove, then lowered the crossbeam of the front door. She took José's chair and pointed to the chairs on either side of her.

She joined their hands and placed hers on top. "As men of this house, you will work *here*. Not in Guaymas looking for an old Indian. Not in Hermosillo looking for a crazy horse. Not in town looking for Esteban." She tightened her grip over their hands. *"Here* is the work. If we don't work this ranch, we have nothing. Your chasing around will turn your father's life to nothing."

With equal vehemence Alejo said, "Father brought Tacho and Moro here because he needed them. We need them too. Moro brings us money. Tacho knows crops and animals better than any of us. He finds honest workers."

"We are the only honest workers," countered Felipa. "We love this ranch more than any Yaqui, Mayo, or Opata. Who worked here before Tacho or Moro? Who worked the ranch when your father went to Guaymas? And you were much younger then." She probed their eyes for signs that they too remembered.

Hector tried to wriggle his hand free. Felipa pressed harder. "Swear to the Virgin that you will stay on this ranch."

A tense silence followed. Neither son looked at her. *Holy Mother, am I alone in this?*

Hector turned his face away from her. "Stay for how long?"

His question startled Felipa. She searched herself for the answer. "Until you're no longer needed."

Hector pressed on, "Until we have workers again?"

"She means until the ranch is complete," said Alejo. "Until it's a wheel that turns itself. I swear to work this ranch. Mother, I want

Father's dream as much as he did. I gave him my word when he brought Sueño home." To himself he pledged, *I also swear to see Esteban Escobar dead.*

Hector hesitated, "I'll stay—but not forever."

Felipa saw tears gathering in Hector's eyes. She released her grip. Alejo's fingers locked into hers. Hector wiped a tear from his uninjured eye.

"I don't mean forever," she said gently to Hector. "Just until you're older. I'm afraid for you. This morning when you shot at the rurales—"

"Why, Hector?" asked Alejo, raising his voice.

Cheeks flushed, Hector yelled, "They came at dawn, searched every room, said we were hiding Yaquis. Alejo, they pushed Mother down! What would you have done?"

Alejo clasped Felipa's shoulders. "The lieutenant said you begged them—for what?"

Hector broke in. "Father's gun only had two bullets. I fired. Missed. They tied me, aimed their guns at my hands." He paced the floor. "She threw herself over me." Tears streamed down his face. "It took three of them to drag her off. That Trujillo hit me." He shook his head violently. "Chingado! I was stupid not to check the gun. Mama, I'm sorry!" He knelt and hugged her knees, burying his face in her lap. "I'll stay. I'll stay."

Head bowed, her heart torn, Felipa fervently kissed the crown of Hector's head. She raised her eyes to quiet, watchful Alejo; he too did not believe Hector.

Something struck the door, startling all of them, including the parrots that fluttered and shrieked in the corner. Alejo rose to lift the crossbeam.

Andrés entered, horseshoe in hand. "Why did you lock me out? It's dark in here. Hector, are you praying?" He tossed Alejo the horseshoe and lit one of the kerosene lamps. "I left your bedroll and carving on the porch."

Felipa compared the faces of her sons. Andrés looked worried;

Hector was, for the moment, contrite. Alejo was calm. *Only Alejo understands my demands. The town owns my young ones.*

The four remained still—each looking to the other. *Would that my heart could keep them like this. Would that my womb still held them.*

Hector raised his head. "Alejo, you said the lieutenant knew Moro's name?"

The parrots continued their shrill cries. "One of you, throw the netting over that cage," said Felipa. She rose and walked heavily toward the kitchen. Again their man-talk begins, she thought.

"Yes," answered Alejo, "and how would he know of our horse?"

"Esteban Escobar," said Hector. "I see it! The Escobars are from Hermosillo. Esteban still wants the horse! His talk at the trial about Father's being the only one who could ride Moro was a lie. He wants Moro back."

"Exactly," said Alejo, pleased at Hector's quickness. He felt his mother closing herself off from them; Alejo covered the parrots, then joined her. At a loss for something to do for her, he cut kindling and lit the stove.

Felipa cooked and listened to her sons speak of rurales and the powerful Escobars. Let them do their man-talk, she thought. If I can hear them, I can see them. Nevertheless, anger quickened her pulse as she heard her sons utter the Escobar name—its very sound sent a dark vapor through the house. She too suspected that Esteban was not finished with her family. But she dared not speak her fears to anyone.

If I can keep them here, I can protect them, or die trying.

Through dinner Alejo boasted of his two days with Tacho. The younger boys followed every syllable as Alejo reenacted the battle with Moro. He showed them the dirty remnants of his underwear as if they were medals of valor; his torn feet were battle wounds. Against her will, Felipa found herself wrapped up in the tale.

Moving dinner plates, Alejo re-created the path of cottonwood leaves that Tacho had made and solemnly explained the significance of Moro's baptism.

"Do you believe that?" asked Hector. His fingers shoved his food to his molars. He chewed slowly.

"I didn't then. I do now." Alejo tilted his chair back. Balancing himself with the tips of his index fingers pressed to the table, he gazed at his family.

Yoris can never understand what happened to me at the santuario.

Above the fireplace hung the head of the deer. *Maso.* He felt the religious meaning of that simple Yaqui word.

Maso. Tacho, mi Tacho, his heart cried. He saw the deer and fireplace as a shrine, his own secret shrine where in silence he could mourn the loss of Tacho.

He let his chair drop to four legs. "I believe Tacho knew he would be arrested," he said. "I believe he knew he would be taken. That's why he baptized Moro—to feel like a Yaqui one more time before—"

"They won't deport him," Felipa interrupted. She could feel Alejo's heart swell with pain talking about the old man. "No need to go to Guaymas, Alejo. Tacho's safe. I hear they throw the old ones up north. It wouldn't surprise me to see him back here in a few days."

"I heard they throw the old ones off the boat," said Andrés. "I believe that."

IN HIS ROOM Alejo lay naked in total darkness. He needed to untangle his thoughts.

Ana María, something ugly is eating my life. His mind searched, but the pincers in his head failed to grab that gossamer *some thing.*

He knew one absolute: he had to kill Esteban Escobar. Was that it? Esteban had murdered his father, caused the rurales' raid on the ranch, caused the loss of Tacho and Moro. And, Alejo felt certain, more would come.

Alejo, you're not a killer.

My Tacho, I must become one, he answered. My family, our land—Esteban has poisoned all.

And now he must lie to his mother, pretend that the ranch was his only goal, pretend that he allowed her powerful love to envelop him. Since his father's death, the color of her love frightened him. Her anguish must not enter him. He would lose his nerve. He must close himself to Felipa. He must bury Ana María and Tacho.

I will work alone, Alejo concluded. Alone. I was alone with Moro in the water. He smiled. Wonderful battle! Then the ugly *some thing* surfaced. "No!" he yelled.

He cast his mind outside himself, outside his room, finally outside his house. He visualized himself standing by the well and he peered into the well, into that dark void where the murdered José had hung while his sons made his coffin. How he and his brothers had labored to seal away their beginning. And on the hill, beyond the house, lay his strong, dream-filled father. Yes, all is clear from here, he thought.

Today the Durcals had suffered crucial losses: two rifles, three guns—all their weapons—their workers, Tacho and Moro.

It was obvious. The loss of each had made Esteban safer. Each time Alejo rode Moro into Alamos, people would remember José Durcal and ask, how long before the son avenges his father? Moro was José's specter.

Moro and Sueño had allowed his father to double his holdings in land and cattle. But without Tacho and his Yaqui workers, Alejo and his brothers were tied to the ranch. Sadly, Alejo doubted if he and his brothers could work for the ranch. With the federal government sweeping southern Sonora, soon even Mayos would be forced into hiding. As for arms, Esteban would hear if any Durcal bought a weapon.

Alejo remembered the old Colt .44 his father had stored in the toolbox he kept in the barn. Could he use that to kill Esteban? The black-powder six-shooter had a loud muzzle blast. The gun was exciting to shoot but left a curtain of smoke. In the past Alejo had had to wait until the smoke cleared to see if he had hit the target. Tacho had taught him how to load the cap-and-ball pistol.

Tacho. Tacho, Moro. He felt weaker without them.

His mind reentered his room; he lay still, eyes closed. Again, he saw Tacho go silently with his captors, saw the henequen rope encircle Moro's strong neck.

There was nothing I could do. But he could not convince himself. Hot tears rolled back into his hair.

ALONE IN HER room, Felipa finished braiding her long hair and lay down in the middle of the double bed. Since José's funeral, she had taken to wearing his long underwear beneath her nightgown and had loosened the waist and innerseam to sleep comfortably.

She looked at the carving of the Virgin of Guadalupe on the dresser. A small votive candle burned in a red glass, pulsing rose-colored hues across the Virgin's face. Felipa raised herself on her elbows and spoke to the statue.

They say you were a simple woman like me. Well, how could you let that happen to your son? José is gone. Leave me my sons. For what I am about to do, Holy Mother, guide me.

She would talk to Tía Mercedes about her plan. Under the pretense of seeking advice, she would ask to see Esteban alone. Once there, she would slit his throat. He may be a man, she thought, but the love for my sons makes me stronger.

Yes, a knife. The kitchen taught women how to use knives. He will bleed in spurts, she thought. I must stand behind him—cut left to right—then hold up his chin while he drains.

She thought of her sons and was grateful for Hector's volatile temper. She could not control him, but she always knew what he thought. Andrés's devotion to Hector worried her. Still, Andrés seemed to sense when something was out of balance, and when Hector's rages grew too loud, Andrés came to her.

But Alejo, her major love, now harbored secrets from her. She had long since stopped feeling guilty for loving him more than her other sons—more than José. In Alejo she had nurtured a kindred soul. José's death had hardened the boy. Well, she would kill to keep him whole. He must not be the one to kill Esteban. The Escobar family would make sure the authorities gave her son no mercy.

A comfortable weariness covered Felipa while she thought of her sons. When she bathed them as infants she had spent hours looking at their testicles. Men had so many words for those fragile sacks whose skin spread and shrank with the temperature. As children their sacks were toys they touched, cuddled. Suddenly as men their sacks became their priceless treasure. How could something so delicate be their source of strength? No, she decided, the sacks made men stupid.

WITH PATIENCE AND discipline Alejo retaught his brothers how to work the ranch. The week of his return, he saddled mules and assigned the boys the task of moving Sueño from one pasture to another to keep the younger bulls separate from him. Hector preferred the range, though he tended to hurry the cattle.

"They'll lose weight," Alejo explained.

"I'll feed them double," Hector retorted.

"Feed costs money. The dry season is coming."

Making the rounds, Alejo rode the strong, docile Coqueta and in silence mourned Tacho and Moro. He knew that no matter where they were, they were suffering. He put his back to the work before him and marked the immense vacuum left by the Yaqui and the horse.

ONE LATE AFTERNOON, a fortnight later, Alejo sat on the top rail of the back corral teaching his brothers to wash the heads of "lepes," orphaned calves, subject to lice. To Alejo's amusement, Hector and

Andrés wailed at the task. They used a solution made from boiled tobacco-leaf veins and stems.

"In the ears! Not the eyes!" shouted Alejo.

This was his favorite time of day. And the day had gone well. He had reassembled the .44 Colt—barrel, cylinder, and frame had fit back together perfectly. He had plenty of percussion caps. All he needed was fresh gunpowder. The powder in the flask was at least five years old.

He looked toward the distant blue mountains. A purple haze hovered above them. Closer to him, sweeping brushstrokes of clear blue broke into the white, silver, and violet clouds. I'll carve more on the eagle tonight, he decided. He saw a likeness between the sky and the bird's wings. My strokes are too deep. . . .

A familiar presence invaded his thoughts. Alejo turned.

Awestruck, he saw Moro walking slowly toward the corral, the corral that had confined him the night of the three queens. The horse was dusty and favored his right shank. Alejo dared not speak less the vision disappear.

In silent synchrony, Hector and Andrés brought Moro water and oats while Alejo's trembling hands checked the animal—muzzle to tail, poll to hoof. He found rope burns on the neck, crop marks on the loin, and two deep bullet grazes on the buttocks. Moro stood still while Alejo cleaned the wounds with yerba del manso to prevent infection. He used pork fat so that the tears on the coat would seal slowly.

Felipa's protests were ignored: Alejo slept with Moro in the barn.

The first night Alejo wept prayers of gratitude to his mother's Virgin.

The second and third nights he designed his and Moro's entrance into Alamos.

A Sunday would be perfect. He would wear the silver dress spurs that José had not lived to use. The family would ride the wagon to town to hear mass. He would ride Moro alongside them.

During mass, a well-groomed Moro would be tied to the wagon so that all who attended church would see that he had fulfilled his promise.

Word would spread far and wide—to Esteban. But there, Alejo's plans clouded. The where and how of that fatal meeting were unclear. The violent rage that fueled him daily failed to give him a clear map to follow. He trusted that such a path would open itself to him.

Moro responded to Alejo's care. He allowed the boys to clean and feed him. Recovery was quick; soon Moro was restless to move. He accepted Alejo without challenge, but Alejo kept him confined to Durcal property. Despite his caution to keep himself and Moro out of sight, the priest and a flock of well-meaning women saw him on the horse when they called on Felipa one morning.

Alejo's next move was to send his brothers to Alamos to gather information. He sent cheese, eggs, and meat for Tía Mercedes along with a long list of purchases from various stores.

Hector heard no mention of Moro's return, but he had other news. Esteban had not been seen in Alamos since the judge had ruled José's death an accident. Rumors were that Esteban was in the nearby town of Navojoa. The American Billy Cameron was living at Esteban's ranch. According to Tía Mercedes, Cameron had bought part of Esteban's land to start a small ranch of exclusive registered cattle.

"Maybe he's moved away for good," said Hector.

"No," said Alejo. "Navojoa is close." Esteban can spin his web from there, thought Alejo. *Something else is coming.* "Hector, give me the powder."

Hector tossed him a one-pound can of Remington black powder. "Why do you need it? You have a gun somewhere."

"Did anyone see you buy it?"

"Only the storeowner. Why do you need it?" Hector repeated. "If you don't have a gun, why do you need 3-F powder?"

Alejo wavered—was tempted to tell his brother. He longed to tell someone. He stroked the poised dog on the Remington can and wondered why his mother had never allowed them to have dogs. "Father always kept some on hand," he mumbled.

"You're lying!" screamed Hector.

Alejo laughed at the sight of his brother stretching himself to full height. "You really are a chiltepín."

Alejo had been fourteen—two years ago—the last time he had been to the agricultural town of Navojoa. He remembered little about it other than the old seventeenth-century mission. Navojoa was Mayo Indian country, his father had explained. The Mayos had stopped fighting the federal government back in '85.

"Only Yaquis fight now," his father had added. Thinking back, Alejo thought he had detected some admiration in his father's statement.

Sheriff Antonio Alcázar, two deputies with rifles, and Billy Cameron arrived at the Durcal ranch as the family sat down to breakfast. Arms extended, Felipa barred the door; her tall figure kept the men outside and her sons behind her.

"We have an IOU signed by José Durcal dated a month before his death," explained Alcázar to Felipa. "It is for the bull, the Zebu. Mr Cameron had not come to collect it because he has been in the process of finalizing his own land purchase."

Felipa took the note, looked at the signature. The wild scrawl on the bottom looked like José's signature. She passed the paper back to her sons. "Sueño? My husband would never sell that bull."

"It wasn't a sale, it was a gambling debt," said Alcázar, "signed by witnesses. Mr. Cameron doesn't want trouble. He just wants the bull. He is willing to pay for the purchase of another bull for your ranch. That's very generous."

"Esteban Escobar is one of the witnesses," called out Alejo. "To me that makes the note worthless." He tried to pass by his mother. She held herself rigid against him.

Hector and Andrés pushed their chairs to the doorway and climbed on top of them to see over the heads of Felipa and Alejo.

"Why do you come with rifles?" Hector demanded loudly. "You know we don't have guns. We don't have workers. You know the rurales took everything. Ask Esteban Escobar, he knows. You're thieves! Thieves without a mother, without conscience!"

Felipa reached back and yanked Hector to her. Arms around him, she squeezed his ribs until he groaned; his body grew limp.

"My brother is right," said Alejo. "Why the rifles?"

"I apologize," said Alcázar. "Mr. Cameron feared trouble. The young men . . . you understand, señora . . ."

"He fears my sons?" Felipa smiled. "Just my sons . . . hmmm." Her height enabled her to study the men from the top of their hats to their dusty boots. She took in each one separately, and let her dark gaze linger on Billy Cameron, who stood behind Alcázar and between the two armed deputies. The American smiled as always, but kept his eyes focused above or below the door—away from any Durcals. He's frightened to death, she thought. They all are. She relished the moment. A sweet strength filled her.

Alcázar held out a second piece of paper. "Before coming here, and out of respect for you, Felipa, I took the IOU to Rafael Castillo, José's attorney. He's just returned to Alamos, and has written a personal letter to you that explains why the IOU is valid." Alcázar swallowed. His lips were a dry, chapped white. "I'm sorry, Felipa. This is difficult for me."

She smelled his heavy stale breath. "Difficult for you, Antonio?" She took the paper and put it into Hector's grasping hand. "Four men with documents and rifles come to a woman with three defenseless sons . . ." She laughed at them. "Do what you've come to do. Then I will do what I need to." She stepped back into her house and shut the door.

She felt her sons' expectant stares on her as she moved away from the doorway. Thank God there are no guns in the house, she thought. "Work as if nothing had happened," she ordered her sons.

Hector and Andrés ran to the window by the parrots' cage. "They're going toward the right pasture," said Hector.

"You have a plan to get Sueño back, don't you?" asked Alejo. He spoke low, so only Felipa could hear.

"Your Tía Mercedes and I will speak alone to the American."

"Do you see Esteban's hand behind this?"

"I'm no fool. Cameron will claim the bull is too old for his herd. But first he must keep Sueño long enough for him to make that conclusion. He will return the bull to us."

"When?"

Felipa extended her hand to Alejo. "Before the sun sets, Sueño will be back."

Elated, Alejo kissed her hand and forehead.

NEAR TWILIGHT, FELIPA arrived in Alamos alone. The strength that had quivered through her that morning had grown as the day progressed. Now as she stopped the team before Tía Mercedes's house she trembled with an ardor she had known only with José. She felt light-headed, almost giddy.

Alejo had insisted on staying home, "to guard Moro." The boys stayed with him. She thanked the Virgin.

Tía Mercedes had already heard of Alcázar's visit. "Every beak that came to the mill chirped the same news," she said. "They're all waiting for Alejo to show up on Moro."

"That's why I came. You and I will get Sueño." Felipa fought to control the eagerness in her voice. "Write a note canceling all debts from José Durcal. Say the bull belongs to us. Cameron will sign it."

"Felipa, your eyes dance to a tune unbecoming a widow."

"Tía, help me get Cameron's signature."

"And if he refuses?"

"Tía," Felipa smiled, "I swear to you he won't." She held up José's riding crop and released her laughter. "I will use *this.*"

Mercedes clapped her hands and also exploded in laughter. "Whip a grown man?"

"I saw his face. He's afraid. He expects Alejo—a boy. But he will see us and sign the note. Write it, hurry! We're losing light."

The women rode toward Esteban's hacienda. Once there, they circled the large white house to the outlying fields, where they found Sueño surrounded by fine-looking Zebu cows.

When the Mexican cowhands silently acknowledged them, Felipa was certain they would not warn Cameron. She drove back to the front of the house, aware that from inside, a tall thin shadow watched their every move. That's not Cameron nor Esteban, thought Felipa. She wished she had had a gun to bring with her.

She braked the wagon and got off with slow precision. No movement of hers must disclose fear. Her legs trembled as she walked up the steps. She tightened her grip on José's riding crop, which she hid in the folds on her skirt. But the door opened before they could knock.

A Chinese man stood before them. Felipa noticed that he was taller than she was. His face was smooth, his dark eyes solemn. His braid is as long as mine, thought Felipa.

"Señor Cameron," announced Tía Mercedes.

The man opened the door wider, then disappeared into the back rooms. They stepped in and shut the door behind them. The house looked the same as Felipa remembered.

"Isn't this something?" asked Mercedes, pointing to where the Chinese had stood. Her loud voice seemed even louder inside the house. "I've never seen him in town."

Billy Cameron entered the room. "He's from California. Many are coming to work in Mexico. They're good workers. Now that you're without Yaquis, you might want to hire them."

Cameron speaks Spanish well, thought Felipa. How smart of him to keep that secret. Doubts about the note crossed her mind. Was Cameron really working for Esteban?

"Have you come for the money to purchase another bull?" asked Cameron.

His calm politeness disarmed Felipa even further. "No, I've come for the bull." Felipa could not control the arrogance in her voice. "Give him the paper," she said to Mercedes.

Cameron read the note, then he let it fall. "Impossible," he said, suppressing a chuckle. "We could never allow this."

The word "we" was Felipa's signal. Her arm made a wide arc and lowered the leather crop across his face. Cameron staggered, covered his face with both hands. "Jesus!"

"It is you and Esteban, isn't it?" screamed Felipa. She raised her arm again. Cameron grabbed her wrist.

"Mercedes!" cued Felipa.

Mercedes stepped in. Arms straight, she shoved back the American. Felipa followed, the crop high above her head. "It is the two of you, no?"

She struck repeatedly at the top of his head, his shoulders, his neck. Every blow made her crave another.

"Hong!" yelled Cameron. His eyes darted back and forth, following the swing of the crop. His hands aimed for it, but Mercedes foiled his attempts. Moving behind him, she hugged him around the chest and clamped down his arms.

"Tell me, Cameron," demanded Felipa. "Esteban wrote that IOU."

"Hong!" he screamed, red-faced.

"No chino will help you," said Mercedes. "Not against Mexican women in Mexico. Sign the note before we lower your pants and bloody your talegas!"

Felipa swung her crop across his upper thighs and tugged at his belt buckle.

"Basta!" Cameron held up his hands and nodded. The women stepped aside to let him crawl toward the note.

9

ALEJO HAD KEPT MORO AT A TROT-LOPE PACE FOR OVER TWO hours, since he had left the ranch after he tied up his brothers and left them screaming in the barn. The yellow moon was low as he approached the farming community of Navojoa.

No, not yet!

Throughout the journey he had blocked all thought, had refused to let his mind race ahead to this destination—ahead to killing Esteban. Beyond that deed, all he could visualize was an insurmountable dark barrier, a wall that held no life for him. Yet, on this side of the wall, the only alternative he saw was to kill Esteban. His worth depended on his righting the cruel imbalance that had robbed him of a father, robbed the Durcal ranch of a future.

Tacho's words had burrowed through. *Alejo, you're not a killer.* At times Alejo suspected that the Yaqui was right, and this angered him. No, he did not think of himself as a killer, but the echo of Tacho's warning gave rise to a cold liquid fear that threatened his resolve.

Feeling alone, craving something familial, he stalled before entering the town to savor events of that early evening.

As soon as Felipa had left for Alamos, he had saddled Moro. Carefully, rapidly, he had poured the measured black powder into the Colt .44 cylinder, placed the lead ball on top, and lowered the loading lever to ram the ball into the chamber. He was loading the fourth ball when Hector caught him.

"You lied!" screamed his younger brother.

Alejo nearly dropped the gun. Furious, he slapped at Hector, who deflected the blow. "Leave me alone!"

He had no time to argue with Hector. He must move while he

had enough light to reach Navojoa and find Esteban. Yes, Alejo had reasoned, Esteban was in Navojoa; Cameron's taking of Sueño had followed too fast upon Moro's return.

"Will you shoot Cameron?" asked Hector. "Take me with you," he pleaded, bringing himself under control.

Andrés joined them. "I want to go too."

Alejo found himself surrounded by two eager boys with blood in their eyes. "We'll see," Alejo said, making his voice sound like a weak maybe.

He invited his brothers to load the last two balls into the gun. Patiently, he showed them how to place the gun in the crook of the leg while lowering the loading lever. He taught them exactly as Tacho had taught him.

"One more thing," he added. "Carefully grease the cylinder." He handed them the same tin can that had held the pork fat they had used on Moro's bullet grazes. He looked into his brothers' attentive, fascinated eyes and felt remorseful to be deceiving them. "You don't want a cylinder chain fire." He watched as they reverently rubbed the fat onto the cylinder.

And then, while they worked, Alejo tossed a lasso over them and yanked hard. The gun fell. He doubled the loop and the boys were slapped together. He left them plenty of breathing room as he strapped them to the main post in the barn.

Before leaving, he capped each nipple on the gun. Then he walked to the well, filled a gourd with fresh water, and offered it to his brothers. They refused. Hector tried to kick him; Andrés threatened to burn all his carved animals. Forcefully, he subdued their shaking heads enough for him to plant a kiss on their temples. He had apologized before leaving.

Now, an apparently sleeping Navojoa lay before him. At the far end of town was the Jesuit mission. Around him, the town was dark except for lights that flickered onto the side streets. Find the cantina, he said to himself. There men like Father are drinking and gambling. Esteban.

He reached into the knapsack he had tied around the saddle's pommel. The gun was there. He traced the length of the barrel with his index finger and felt his heart accelerate. The liquid fear rushed through him. He clicked Moro toward the light.

Again, he blocked all thought. Something sour turned his stomach. Anxious, he stroked Moro's sweaty neck and tried to praise the animal, but his speech remained trapped. He tried to work up spit. Nothing.

Moro's hooves clicked over the cobblestones. Too loud. He led the horse toward a dirt street which wound its way to the bright light.

He read the broad red letters outside the cantina. El Estribo. The whitewashed walls looked blue in the moonlight.

Parked in front were wagons, carts, donkeys, and a few horses. Alejo checked the hindquarters of the better breeds. None had the Escobar brand. Of course not.

Alejo, finish it!

Removing his hat, Alejo ran a shaky hand through his hot matted hair. He held the hand out before him, gazed at his long trembling fingers. He shut his eyes, drew the night air of Navojoa deep into his lungs. He smelled dung, bacanora, mezcal.

He put his hat back on, lower, tighter. Dismounting, he peeked over the half-doors of the bar. Playing cards with three other men, Esteban sat against the back wall facing the entrance.

Alejo counted seven men and two women in the cantina. The place was quiet, unevenly lit—the brightest kerosene lamps burned on tables surrounding the cardplayers. One woman rested her head on the counter; the other stared ahead, dumbly waiting while her husband talked to tired farmers.

Tomorrow and for the rest of their lives they will remember this night.

Easing back, he turned, saw the reflection of the moon and himself in Moro's eyes. The vision came: clear, clean.

"You will be what he sees last!" he whispered to Moro.

Remounted, he pulled the gun out of the knapsack and watched a steady hand cock the hammer. Moro had no trouble climbing onto the high step of the sidewalk. Nor did he brake before the half-doors when Alejo's knees urged him forward.

Alejo and Moro entered; the doors flew off their hinges. Esteban rose, peered at the door. The clatter of Moro's hooves reverberated on the wooden planks of the floor. In the middle of the cantina, Alejo held the pistol above his head for all to see. He heard sounds, perhaps of alarm, but he only saw a calm Esteban advancing toward him.

The men at Esteban's table jumped up. Kerosene lamps threw curved shadows against the wall. The men arranged themselves alongside Esteban; he motioned them to sit.

Smiling, he explained, "It's my godson." He extended an arm toward Alejo.

Alejo looked down at Esteban's confident smile, into his mouth, saw the small even white teeth.

"It all ends here."

He aimed, shut his eyes, fired.

The loud blam and the powder flash spooked Moro. He reared; Alejo nearly lost his seat. He opened his eyes, waited for the curtain of black smoke to clear. He saw his target. Esteban lay on the floor. The ball had entered through the nose. A red halo spread beneath the dead man's curly hair.

To the paralyzed audience he heard himself announce, "I am Alejo Durcal from Alamos. I have killed the man who murdered my father. I swear to give myself up to Sheriff Antonio Alcázar."

He returned the pistol to the knapsack, then spun Moro out of the bar. As he galloped away, people in sleepwear raced past him toward El Estribo, but his mind sped toward the strong arms of Felipa.

With a penetrating timbre the word "Mother" had rung in his head the moment Moro bolted out of the cantina. He had denied himself the comfort of its sound and the solace of her strength until now. Until now, when he had restored balance into his world.

HE DID NOT spare Moro on the return ride. Halfway home, the horse swerved to avoid a head-on collision with Felipa astride a panting Coqueta.

Felipa's silhouette loomed against the moonlit sky. Alejo's heart leaped.

"Mama!" His voice was not his—it seemed. Incredulous, he repeated, "Mama!" He jumped off Moro, grabbed both bridles.

She slid off the horse, her hands fiercely clasping his face against her breast. "You fooled your brothers but not me. Alejo, am I too late?"

He wrapped his arms around her waist, using her strength to keep himself upright. "It's finished. Done."

The sweetness of his message ended when a stinging slap sent him reeling on the heels of his boots. He hit the dirt—hard. Looking up, he saw the narrow outline of a riding crop bearing toward his head. He dove for his mother's feet, burying his head between them; his strong hands seized her ankles. He pulled, brought her down over him.

Alejo heard Felipa wail to the heavens. Her cries filled the night, poured over the earth where they lay. Frightened, and against his will, he found himself sobbing too. He rested his hand against her shoulder blades. Her back was drenched; it seemed as if the depth of her cries would rip her in half.

"Shhh. It had to be," he whispered. "You knew that."

She nodded. "I had other plans. Sueño is home."

"Today it was Sueño. What about tomorrow? Esteban wanted to destroy us. Nothing would have stopped him."

"I would have."

"No. The work was mine."

Felipa looked at him, heaved a sigh, reached for his hand, raised it to her lips, kissed the salty calloused palm. She smelled gunpowder, horse sweat. "You must leave Alamos. Now."

"No. I want a trial." He stood, hoisted Felipa to her feet. "Alamos will see what the Durcal name means."

"Durcal *name?*" Felipa's voice was bitter. "You did this for a *name?*"

"Our name. Father's dream—that our name would live."

"Bah! He took that name because he had none of his own."

Hurt, Alejo ignored the cut of her words. She's afraid, he thought, afraid of the Escobars. He needed distance from her.

Their mounts had strayed; he hurried after them, picked up the reins, and, placing himself between the horses, led them back to the Alamos road. "They need walking."

Felipa trailed behind. "The Escobars . . ." she called. "You don't know what you've done to yourself—to all of us. I beg you, leave! It means the paredón!"

Alejo slowed his pace to answer. "No. My jurors will be Alamos people who will remember Father's murder. Before witnesses I swore Alcázar would have me. And he will." He turned, quickened his pace.

Felipa shrieked, "You killed an Escobar! If not the paredón, then the bartolinas. Leave! Run!"

Alejo continued walking. "Run? Where could I go that the Escobars couldn't hunt me down as a coward?"

"Go where Tacho took you."

"Impossible."

Felipa stood pinned to the road, and watched her son, her love, who had killed for his father's dreams. Beneath the moon, standing between the two horses, Alejo's long narrow frame seemed fragile.

No, she would not tell Alejo the story a mezcal-filled José had told her one night. How he had taken the name Durcal from a newspaper in Sinaloa, because "it sounded strong." José had been barely older than Alejo when, after burying his mother, he had migrated to Sonora in search of a place where "no one knows la triste historia de mi madre."

That was the only phrase José ever used to describe his

mother—a woman taken, then abandoned. She had supported her son by washing, ironing; alongside Indians, he had worked other men's fields, designed another life for himself, then waited for her to die.

Years ago, thought Felipa, a stranger had planted his seed into a helpless woman. *His seed is now killing me.* How could her Alejo survive the blows rushing toward him at this very moment? How much of his sweetness must die for him to survive those blows? The ranch had failed to protect him. You're a fool, Felipa, she thought. Alejo has the proud foolishness of men. In a moment they kill, destroy all they swear to love. And their actions continue to kill long after their own death.

She had been so careful to keep Alejo close to her. He preferred the ranch over Alamos; he seemed content to be with her and the animals. Clearly, José's ambition had shaped the other two. José lived in them. Ashamed, she realized that she was thinking of Alejo's life as finished.

Her perspiration had dried. Her face felt tight. She hurried to bridge the distance between her and Alejo. As was the way with him, he had presaged her thoughts. At the crest of the hill he stood, hand extended, waiting for her.

10

ACCOMPANIED BY FELIPA AND HIS BROTHERS, ALEJO TURNED himself in the day after the shooting. Sheriff Alcázar listened in stunned silence. He did not, however, imprison Alejo.

An eye on Felipa, Alcázar advised Alejo, "Your crime has left your mother alone with two boys. Put your ranch in order. Find workers. Your trial will begin as soon as we hear from Don Escobar." To the deputies he ordered, "If he tries to run, or if you suspect an escape, shoot him in the head."

Alejo saw that Alcázar was more worried about his mother than about him. And the sheriff emphasized the word "crime" to describe his act. No mention of revenge or honor. And Alcázar had spoken as if his mother were already alone. He must ready himself to go to prison.

His guards trailing, Alejo raced on Moro to nearby rancherías to contract Mexican day workers. Too expensive. They wanted Sueño's uncut males as payment. Mature male Indian workers had disappeared. He had been careless, hadn't noticed that while he had been planning his revenge on Esteban, the government had emptied the area of its Indian labor force.

Neighbors praised how he looked on Moro, sympathized with him, invited him into their homes, asked for extra details of the shooting. Politely, Alejo refused their hospitality and their questions. He remembered: none had come forward to describe José's wounds.

Patting him on the back, everyone agreed, "The sentence will be light." "You did what you had to do." "Honor demanded it."

Before the shooting, all he could think of was killing Esteban. That obsession gone, he saw the ranch in his absence. Alcázar was right. His mother would be alone with sons who knew more about Alamos than the ranch. His brothers could read books, yet could not read the eyes of a sick calf.

Right now his brothers would give their lives if asked. Now, with neighbors' eyes upon them, with the Durcal and Escobar names on people's lips. What would his brothers do when the hellish dry months came? Or when winter winds cut their hands, cracked their lips? To them the day had finite hours; his brothers counted the hours they slept. They checked their hands for blisters and slivers.

The young ones were frightened. In his head Alejo now called them young ones. *Is it because I killed?* His conscience remained clear. He had had no option.

Alejo studied his brothers. Hector's alert, wide-eyed glance had narrowed. He monitored Alejo's every move, watching, studying how his older brother worked. His mother and Tía Mercedes had always described Andrés as the happiest of the three boys. His good-natured patience allowed him to try again if he failed. Hector however, was used to succeeding immediately. A teacher had described Hector's mind as a "lance." Piqued at the time, Alejo remembered how his father had bragged about Hector for years. Alejo wondered what his father would say about the shooting. Would he, Alejo, still be branded as merely "good"? That stupid, simple word which pleased only his mother.

Alejo was grateful that his mother kept herself in the background of his work day. He couldn't speak to her of prison, or of his fear. His mother showed up out of nowhere to feed her sons three meals. The guards she made eat in the porch.

Driven, Alejo labored from early light to night. His brothers kept up. The guards complained about the long hours; Alcázar divided their day into twelve-hour shifts.

Alejo forced himself to concentrate on what needed doing by anticipating his family's needs during his absence. He gave his brothers errands that required little skill. They went to town to buy oats and wire. At night, the guards held kerosene lamps while Alejo reinforced wheels, sharpened the plow, axes, knives.

Willingly his brothers cut and stacked wood for the kitchen and fireplace. At a loss for what else to do, Alejo focused on the outhouse. To dispel the odor, he had the young ones gather the ashes from the stove and fireplace, throw them down the hole, and toss in lime. Alejo supervised while his brothers scrubbed every board of the outhouse with a mixture of boiling water and creosote.

The boys were still working when Alejo saw Tía Mercedes's wagon rattling toward them. Even from a distance he could see that the darkly clad man next to her was not Mexican. The torso was long, narrow; he sat straight on the seat next to his aunt and balanced himself smoothly as the wagon rolled toward the well. The man's braid fell to his waist.

"Un Chino!" cried Andrés. He dropped his bristle brush and

hurried toward the wagon. The guards followed.

"Alejo," called Mercedes. She pointed to the man. "Hong—for the fields. I will pay him."

Hong stepped down and offered a helping hand to Tía Mercedes. She ignored him, steered him toward Alejo.

She spoke, out of breath with enthusiasm. "He came this morning looking for work. The American left. Took his cattle with him."

Frowning, Alejo surveyed the man, who smiled shyly in his direction. He wore loose black pants and a black top that reached his knees. His boots were thick-soled, the type worn by American miners. "You're sure Cameron won't return?"

"He took everything," she said emphatically. "Hong was there the night we took Sueño." She chuckled to herself. "He saw the whole thing." She stepped closer to Alejo. "Yaquis and Mayos are hiding—for good reason. Hector and Andrés can't work the fields. Hong can. Do you want your mother to have to sell land to buy hay?"

Alejo knew the neighbors had no field hands to spare. He didn't dare consult his mother. "He's just one man. I won't give him a horse. And where will he sleep?"

"In the barn," said Hector. "Tía's right, we need him."

"Chinos sleep anywhere," offered a guard.

Alejo saw how everyone had encircled the man and spoke of him as if he weren't there. How must he feel? "You can work the fields? Hong?" The name felt strange in his mouth.

The man nodded. Alejo tried not to stare at him. He had seen Chinese selling pastries or working as tailors. He had heard how well they sewed up people who had been badly cut. "Where are your things?"

Hong unloaded three full sacks from the wagon. Alejo took one and headed for the barn. Hong followed.

*   *   *

THE DAY BEFORE the trial, Alejo entered his mother's bedroom. Candle in hand, he stood at the foot of the bed. "Alcázar is right. I have left you alone."

"Women can work cows, chickens, and horses. It's for you that my heart bleeds."

"I would do it again, you know that, don't you?"

Felipa moved from the middle of the bed over to the edge. "Yes. Put the candle on the table. Lie next to me. We'll sleep with the candle lit."

THE TRIAL WAS held a week after the shooting. The courthouse was full. The judge who had ruled José's death an accident presided over the trial. He seemed irritated to be back in Alamos so soon. Too grief-stricken to travel, Don Escobar would not be present. Nevertheless, the hacendados were represented by a dozen European-garbed men who sat as a block directly behind the Durcals.

Rafael Castillo had returned without Ana María. Alejo listened for gossip. None about the lawyer. Alejo saw no change in the lawyer's behavior toward him. Castillo announced that he was donating his services to the Durcal family. He entered a plea of justifiable homicide.

Castillo begged the court's mercy, noting Alejo's age, claiming "extreme grief" and "disorientation" over the brutal death of his father. The lawyer closed, saying that the unfortunate shooting merely had finished an incident started by Escobar himself. The audience murmured in approval.

Overriding Castillo's protests, the judge ordered every witness at El Estribo to narrate the events of that night. Each told how young Durcal had burst into the bar on a big black horse and raised a pistol over his head. The unarmed Escobar identified Durcal as his godchild, and rose to greet him. Durcal then fired a single shot into the face of Escobar, announced that he would turn himself in to Sheriff Antonio Alcázar, and left.

Her head covered in a black rebozo, Felipa sat next to Alejo. She felt her hands and feet grow cold. She had forbidden Alejo to describe that night. There had to be more to it, no? The man they described seemed inhuman. No, Esteban had done something else to provoke her son into firing the pistol. She leaned into him; he returned the pressure, then repositioned himself to rest fully against the dip in her side. Horrified, she realized he was at peace with whatever happened.

She looked at Hector and Andrés. They too seemed undisturbed. What had Alejo told them? And when? Perhaps it was the very night of the shooting when they were in the barn, talking, working. She had gone to draw water from the well when she heard Hector's heated questions: "You closed your eyes? You didn't even see his face?" Felipa consoled herself. Surely someone who closed his eyes was not inhuman.

Felipa had prepared her sons for a guilty verdict. "No matter what that judge says, you will behave like men with honor. No crying, cursing, or threats." She expected that Alejo, being sixteen years old, would receive, at most, three years in the Alamos jail. There she could take him fresh linen and good food. His privations would be minimal.

No one was prepared for twenty years in the bartolinas.

Ranchers, farmers, businessmen, wives, screamed in protest. The hacendados said nothing; they stared at the judge.

When someone yelled, "Better the paredón!" they craned their necks to see the source.

Cries filled the courthouse. "Bartolinas, paredón, same thing!" "It's a death sentence!" "Unjust" "The code of honor has been sold!"

Furious, Felipa rose. "Juez vendido!" She felt her legs cave in.

The hacendados left, leaving ample room for her to lie down. Her sons and Tía Mercedes crowded around her.

Alejo knelt beside her. "I'll be all right." Shaking, he pressed her hand to his cheek.

His face blanched, Castillo spat bitterly at the judge. "Do you see who will suffer your cruel sentence? A woman and three boys! The bartolinas are Mexico's greatest shame. Have you no conscience?"

Scowling, the judge cleared the courtroom except for the Durcals and Castillo. Alcázar ushered people out and leaned against the door.

"Stand on the other side," said the judge. He clicked his poorly fitting dentures and waited for the sheriff to leave. With heavy steps the judge came down from the bench. He was short, grayhaired. Flesh sagged beneath his eyes.

He pushed the younger boys away, but drew Alejo to his side as he leaned over the semiconscious Felipa. "You publicly accuse me of being bought off, señora. No matter what you say, your son murdered an unarmed man." He turned to Alejo. "Isn't that correct?"

"I never denied that," answered Alejo. He stepped out of the judge's reach.

"So you understand my sentence?"

"No sir," said Alejo firmly. "Nor did I understand your decision about my father's murder. He too was unarmed when Esteban shot him."

"Where was the proof that it was intentional? Where?" The judge moved his head in a searching motion. He raised an index finger. "Where was *one* witness?"

Felipa struggled to sit up. Mercedes moved behind her and helped her to a sitting position.

"You sentenced Alejo to death," murmured Felipa, "because old Escobar ordered you to." She pointed to the empty seats behind her. "That's why those buzzards were here. Well, they're gone. We're alone. How much do you want to change the sentence?" She tightened her rebozo around her, and scrutinized the judge's face. "Look at yourself," she demanded. "Look at him." She pointed to Alejo. "Tell me, what can old Escobar do to *you*, another old man?"

Her question resounded through the empty, silent courtroom.

Alejo stretched himself to full height. The judge seemed to wait for someone to answer for him. He clicked his teeth, drew up a chair, collapsed into it. With a clumsy gesture he invited the group to sit. No one moved.

He looked at Felipa. "I'm old. But I too have children and grandchildren to think of." He regained his official composure and solemnly announced, "The sentence as stated must be recorded in the state capital." He pursed his lips. "Let's be truthful. The boy killed an Escobar. If, however, after two years, he's still alive, well ..." He paused. "He could serve out his sentence in the army."

"Judge," cut in Castillo, "not after two years in the bartolinas. Those pits kill fast. We both know that. Judge, Alejo obeyed the code of honor Sonora men live by. He obeyed the same code you and I would teach our sons and expect them to follow. Am I wrong?"

The judge shrugged and turned away from Castillo. "Well, the army may need him earlier, who knows?"

"Where in the army?" asked Castillo eagerly.

The judge raised both hands to signify, who knows? "Wherever his country needs him." He rolled his eyes to Alejo. "You look strong. Make a good showing, who knows what can happen, no? What do you think? Will you live?"

Alejo felt his family's eyes on him, felt a hot, familiar certainty. They have such large eyes, he thought gratefully. His limbs responded to the ardor. *I can ride myself through this.*

With all the dignity he could summon, he asserted, "I won't die in prison, Judge. I won't die for my father's murderer. But grant me one request."

The judge angled his head as if to hear better.

Alejo cleared his throat. "When I was six, my father and I saw soldiers walking two white men toward the bartolinas. The men were naked and barefoot. Their arms were chained to a mesquite branch. Father asked where they were taking them, and the soldiers said las bartolinas. I don't want to go like those men. I want my mother to go with me as far as possible."

The judge nodded. "If you want her to see that, I can write out the order."

"Effective?" asked Castillo.

The judge lowered his head, stared at the floor, and answered in a dead voice, "Now. I can't return to the capital until he's in."

The judge stood, opened his mouth as if to add something. He sighed instead. Stoop-shouldered, he hobbled toward the exit. "The sheriff already gave him a week. Alcázar will have to answer to the governor for that leniency."

ALEJO TOOK CONTROL. Since he had ridden Moro to the courthouse, he would ride through Alamos to the bartolinas. He was adamant. "People will last see me on Moro."

His mother was to return to the ranch with Moro tethered to the wagon. The horse would live in the back corral and there stud for his keep. No one was to ride him.

Alcázar and a guard escorted the family and Castillo to Mercedes's house. Neighbors brought the family meat and pumpkin empanadas. They ate little. Mercedes packed the rest for Alejo. He was allowed a blanket, a change of clothes, a spoon, cup, and dish. No boots, hat, belt.

Alejo went to a back bedroom to wrap a blanket around his belongings. Castillo followed. Alejo saw that the lawyer was clearly crestfallen. "You did your best," Alejo said.

Castillo's voice shook. "Had I been here for the inquest, perhaps it wouldn't have come to this."

"I told the judge the truth. Esteban's death won't kill me."

"If I petition Governor Corral, can I say you're willing to serve in the army?"

"Twenty years?" Alejo smiled bitterly. "No. Demand a total pardon. I'll live until old Escobar dies."

"Those holes are ugly!" Castillo blurted. He collected himself. "When you're there, don't think, especially of home."

Woodenly, Alejo tucked the small bundle under his arm and extended a hand to Castillo. "Mother's waiting in the wagon. Please check her bills of sale. Her addition is fine, but she doesn't read too well. Hector reads, but he's impatient."

Alejo walked into the parlor and saw Tía Mercedes and Andrés with their arms around each other. They wept openly. Hector stood in a corner, his face a mask of outraged grief. Alejo opened his arms to his brother. Hector shook his head.

Alejo went out the door, nodded to the neighbors that lined both sides of the street, then swung onto Moro.

Hector raced out of the house. "Alejo!" He pulled at his brother's leg. "Don't die!"

Alejo leaned down to kiss his brother. Castillo and another man tried to pry Hector loose. They were struck by Hector's wild flails. The men recoiled. "Don't leave me!" Hector hollered

Felipa leaped off the wagon; her strong arms embraced Hector into submission. "Stop!" He heaved himself against her; her grip held.

Alejo dismounted, grabbed Hector's jaw, wrenched his face toward him. "I'm not going to die. Damn you if you doubt me."

NICHED IN A pocket of sky, the sun prepared to descend. Alcázar and the guard kept their distance ahead of Felipa and Alejo. She had let her son set the pace as they moved through town and toward the city limits.

He rode alongside, looking down frequently as if to assure her that he was all right. But she could feel his fear. Hector's outburst had nearly shattered his control. She knew the ride through town had soothed him. So many familiar faces—some from as far back as her mill days. Their encouraging words had helped Alejo regain the poise he had sustained throughout the trial. She saw no sign of the hacendados, but they would receive reports of her son's behavior.

Had a mother ever been so proud of how her son rode to prison?

she mused. This past week she had hidden her despair from him as he fought against time, trying to foresee their needs. She thought of that man—Hong. Who could replace her Alejo? Why did people doubt a woman's strength? Fools. If they could only see the current boiling through her veins. She felt strong enough to rip open the bellies of the rolling hills that surrounded Alamos.

What ached was that secret self, the part she called *Lipa*—her father's pet name for her. She barely remembered his face, but the word had remained in her head. That part of her was wounded, marked by a red pain buried beneath her left breast. The pain had started with José's late nights. No, she corrected herself. The pain had started when she was pregnant with Hector. José and the Yaqui girl. Everything from then to now had struck that same spot. She looked at the seldom-traveled back streets of Alamos. And at the end of this ride waited the greatest blow.

She heard Alejo say, "I love Alamos." He was looking back at the tower of the Purisima Concepción, the church where his birth was registered, where Tía Mercedes and Esteban had baptized him.

They advanced; the tower disappeared. Soon the flat adobe structure that garrisoned the soldiers came into view. In front was a wagon hitched to two mules; a low-bellied mount was tied to a post. Felipa noticed that the place was unlit, though it was dark enough for lamps.

Alejo stopped. "I'd feel better if I drive myself in."

He dismounted, tied Moro to the back, boarded the wagon, removed his boots. His narrow pale feet looked blue in the dusk. His long toes were bony, seemed fragile. Where were the soft, padded child's feet she had kissed so often? She handed him the reins to the wagon. Seeing the seriousness with which he took them drove another shaft through her heart.

Alcázar galloped ahead, calling, "Captain!"

Two khaki-clad soldiers emerged, stood at attention beside the door. One carried a rifle. A short pear-shaped man in a khaki uniform and knee-high boots appeared in the doorway. While Alcázar talked, the man carefully put on his captain's cap, adjusted the visor low over his eyes. Nodding, and at the same time stroking both sides of his mustache, the captain listened to Alcázar, then walked at a furious pace toward the Durcal wagon.

Felipa took in the officer's girth, short legs, heavy arms. He's from the south, she decided. She saw no fear in Alejo.

"Señora Durcal," boomed a baritone voice. He saluted her, ignored Alejo. "I am Captain Carrasco. The sheriff says you have permission to accompany the prisoner. That's not possible."

Teeth clenched, Felipa said, "I saw the judge write—"

"My orders are from Governor Ramón Corral himself, who only answers to President Porfirio Díaz," said Carrasco.

"What can it hurt?" asked Alcázar. "Look at the sentence."

"I am. Prisoners with sentences like this go right into the bartolinas. No civilians can go near those pits."

Alcázar leaned closer to Carrasco. "The boy is sixteen. Don't put him in the pits. Put him in the caves. At least a man can look out of a cave."

Caves? Pits? Felipa took hold of herself. Her arms encircled Alejo's waist. He seemed at ease.

Alejo pointed to a low hill half a league behind the garrison. "Is that the bartolinas?"

"No. That's where the caves are," said Carrasco, still not acknowledging Alejo with his eyes. "You're supposed to go into the bartolinas, the pits that are dug into the ground. They're around the bend."

A long silence followed. In a strong voice Alejo asked, "May my mother come as far as the base of that hill?"

Alcázar prodded, "It can't hurt."

Out of the side of his mouth, Carrasco bellowed, "Ombligo! Trae luz!" He turned; at a furious pace he scurried back to the garrison and disappeared into the dark doorway.

Felipa, Alejo, Alcázar, and the guard looked at each other. They lowered their heads to prevent laughing until Carrasco was out of hearing range.

"Let's see what Ombligo says," sputtered Alcázar.

Felipa's pain eased knowing that the last moments with her son would be supervised by a guard nicknamed Belly Button. Carrasco had frightened her. Everyone knew that federal soldiers were often assigned to Sonora as a form of punishment.

A man much shorter, much heavier than Carrasco waddled out of the garrison. In one hand he held a giant lantern that illuminated the wagon, in the other a knot of chains, which he heaved onto the wagon bed.

Hearing the clang, Alejo snapped the reins, trotted the mule toward Ombligo. "Sheriff, tell him. No chains."

Alcázar galloped ahead. "No chains. I guarantee the boy's behavior."

Arms folded across his chest, Carrasco reappeared in the doorway. "Chains. Ten days. Everyone."

Felipa stood up in the wagon. "The judge said no chains!" She spoke in vain. Carrasco had retreated into the darkness.

Ombligo smiled up at her. The lantern made his round face glow. It was obvious that his shirt had not fit him for some time; intricate string webbing held the front together. Only one side of his mouth had teeth, but they were long, thick. He aimed the toothed side toward Felipa and smiled again. He hung the lantern on the driver's side and waved Alejo over to him.

Alejo's belongings in hand, Felipa jumped down. "I'm coming."

Ombligo said, "Of course, señora. Sit next to me." He patted the passenger side. "Your boy can ride behind."

Before boarding, Alejo stroked Moro's neck and loosened the cinch. Watching, Felipa pressed her son's belongings to her chest. Alejo picked his way over the chains and rested his head against her back as the wagon lurched toward the hill that was now a dark swelling rising from the earth.

"Watch the Durcal wagon," Alcázar said to the guard and followed.

"I'll put him next to Charco tonight," said Ombligo, kindness in his voice. "The captain doesn't ride out here."

"Charco?" asked Felipa. "What kind of a name is that?"

Ombligo's shrill giggles floated into the warm night air. "Charco is a horse thief—young like your boy."

"Is he white?" asked Alcázar.

"We don't know. They found him with Yaquis. The captain brought him to the caves because we got down to two prisoners. You know how it is, Sheriff—they die but we got to keep working. Charco has blue eyes." Ombligo giggled. "That's why Carrasco won't shoot him or send him to Yucatán."

The smell of human waste filled the air. Alejo found his mother's hand.

Ombligo braked, climbed down. "Charco! You awake?"

An angry voice rasped, "Careful with my stone, Ombligo."

Ombligo reached for the chains. "Señora, this is where you say goodbye." Playfully he ran the chains across the bars where the voice had come from.

"The orders say no chains," said Alcázar. "Read them."

Ombligo waddled along the base of the hill and yanked back a heavy metal grid that blocked a narrow hole that had been dug into the hill. "I don't read. The chains aren't heavy, and they go in front." He held out the shackles as if to prove his point.

Alejo embraced his mother, pressed his lips to her forehead, whispered, "I won't die." He eased himself down. He shook Alcázar's hand and, fists extended, stood before Ombligo. Alejo figured the guard to be at least two hands shorter than he.

Ombligo snapped the manacles around his wrists. With labored breathing, he bent over to manacle the ankles. He joined the top and bottom cuffs by threading the end rings with a short thick chain. This held Alejo's hands below the waist and prevented him from standing to full height. Ombligo secured the end links with a heavy padlock. His hands retraced the procedure. Satisfied, Ombligo grunted and stepped aside.

Alejo drank in Felipa's silhouette, tall, straight against the night sky. He had to crouch down on his haunches to enter the hole.

Huffing, Ombligo slid the metal grid across the opening, then hammered a long stake through a ring into the ground. He shook the bars. They held. He wiped his hands on his trousers.

"His things!" cried Felipa. "I have his things!" She tried to get down.

"I'll bring them in the morning," said Ombligo.

"But the empanadas!"

Alcázar dismounted, took the small pies from Felipa, and handed them to Alejo through the bars.

Alejo stashed the pies in his shirt, away from the stench.

On hands and knees, he watched the wagon pull away, saw the lantern sway, grow smaller and smaller.

11

FACE AGAINST THE METAL BARS, ALEJO SCANNED THE DARK sky, until his neck gave out. He remembered the santuario where those same stars were an arm's reach away. Tacho.

Don't think!

He sat back, wiped the rust off his cheeks by hunching his shoulders. He tried to grope for the dimensions of the cell. He couldn't raise his arms above his waist. What had they said about caves and pits? Were the pits worse than the caves, or was it the other way around?

He managed to lie on his back and with a slight leg stretch his toes touched the top. Dirt. The sides too. He guessed he was in a low rectangular cave. Too much like a coffin. He turned, pressed his shoulders against the bars, and stretched out. His toes touched something slimy in back of the cave. He gasped, drew his knees to his chest.

A mocking voice asked, "What scared you, Yori?"

Alejo remembered. The horse thief. The voice seemed to enter his cave from outside. "Where are you?"

"In the cave next to yours. Talk through the bars."

Alejo pressed his face against the opening. "How big are these holes?"

"I can sleep."

"Are you chained?"

The answer was a loud rattle followed by a threatening, "Yori, you stepped on my night. When they brought you in, did you kick my stone?"

"I didn't see one," said Alejo, irritated. He lowered his head, looking for some rise along the flat earth. "And I still don't see one."

"Her name is Dolores. She's got my mark," he boasted. "You'll see her in the morning." Now he spoke with a playful lilt that reminded Alejo of Andrés.

Tired of the stone and the voice but afraid to feel alone, he offered, "I'm Alejo Durcal. Who are you?"

"I heard Ombligo tell you." He used his raspy voice.

"He called you Charco. What's your real name?"

"Yoemem call me El Charco." He enunciated his name with grave respect. "Nice women call me Charquito," he said with gentle affection. His voice became a snarl of contempt. "Yoris call me Charco cabrón!"

Alejo laughed quietly.

Charco asked, "Are you a thief?"

"I shot someone." He heard the pride in his voice. Embarrassed, he explained about his father, Esteban, and his own twenty-year sentence.

Charco ended the dialogue, scoffing, "No twenty years for you. Yoris can kill anyone. Tell me a good story before they come for you."

I hope you're right, thought Alejo. He decided to tell Charco his best story. Moro and the river.

"Bah! I've done that," Charco cut in. "Say something better."

"I don't know more. You talk. Who called you Charco?"

Silence. Fine, thought Alejo. He fumbled around, trying to fit himself into the narrow oblong space. Nothing worked until he lay flat on his back and angled his long legs up against the sides of his cell. Finally, he felt comfortable. And the stench seemed lighter if he kept his head down, close to his chest.

Would they come for him? Breath steadying, he let his shoulders drop, relaxed his eyes, watched the black night change shades.

SHARP STINGS WOKE him. The biting pain came from his stomach, shot to his chest, then down to his groin. Fighting panic, he spread his hands as far as the chains allowed and ripped open the front of his shirt. He slapped blindly at his middle.

"What are you doing?" asked Charco.

Alejo churned wildly in his cell, slammed against the sides. Thin dust flew into his eyes. Sharp stings pierced his fingers. "I'm covered!" He shook the bars. "Mochomos!"

The predawn purple offered little light.

"The ants like your mother's empanadas," said Charco.

Alejo butted his head against the grid. "I need out!"

"Your clothes! Throw out them out!" ordered Charco.

Howling in pain, Alejo sat cross-kneed, and curled up into the smallest possible ball, crossed his wrists, and holding the front of the shirt, inched the back up and over his head. Now the shirt hung from the chains. Growling, he gnashed his teeth into the cotton, ripped it off piece by piece, and threw it out.

"Everything!" urged Charco.

Alejo undid the front of his pants, slid out of them, and pulled down first one side then the other. When they reached his knees, he ripped the seams and forced the pants out through the bars.

A sticky substance—what remained of the empanadas—clung to his middle. Panting, he reached between his legs, broke the surface dirt with his fingers, dug up handfuls of damp earth to cover himself as far as his chains allowed.

The shackles cut into his wrists and ankles. He didn't care. Frantic, he tossed dirt out of his cell as fast as he could, shoved out more with his heels until his body was covered with sweat.

"For sure you moved my stone now!" yelled Charco.

"Shut up! Charco cabrón!"

Alejo threw dirt out until a new layer of soil carpeted his cave. Round hot bumps covered his stomach and the tops of his thighs. When the itching started, he scratched with unchecked frenzy.

The morning sun broke over the hills to his left. He leaned against the bars to catch some light. A maimed red ant faltered across his knuckles. He crushed it.

He rechecked what he could of his naked body. No ants. He knew the pain would last all day. No matter. He knew its source. Outside his cell his clothes lay buried in a heap of dirt. Somewhere in that mess lay a well-meaning neighbor's pies.

He was very thirsty. "Charco, when do we get water?"

"Go to hell, pendejo."

Alejo remembered his cruel words. "Sorry if I moved your rock."

"It's a stone." After a while, Charco added in a friendlier voice, "Small places are hard to protect."

To ignore the bites and his thirst, he coaxed Charco to talk.

The boy claimed to have lived everywhere. Under a table, in a stable, in Mayo and Yaqui villages, with Mexicans and gringos. He didn't know if he was Mexican or Indian and he was glad. ". . . because in Sonora everyone shoots someone, sooner or later. Like you. Best if people don't know what you are."

Clapping in cadence, Charco sang out town names he said he knew. "Osobampo, Torocobampo, Jubarebampo, Memelobampo, Barebampo, Bellubampo, Mochibampo . . ."

Listening to Charco recite Sonora's countless "bampos," Alejo realized how little he knew outside the ranch.

The rising sun let in more light, enough for him to check the back of the cell. The slime his toes had touched was moss. Strange how the earth changed, even in a small cave dug to keep a man from standing or stretching out.

The creaking of wagon wheels alerted him. Eventually he could see Ombligo heading toward them.

"He's alone!" said Charco. "We can shit outside!"

"Muchachitos!" Ombligo called merrily. He threw down some sandals. The wagon tilted precariously as the guard got down and slid his wide feet into worn huaraches. From the back of the wagon he unloaded a shovel, a blue metal pot, tin plates, cups, and a rifle.

Standing in front of Alejo's cell, he let out a high-pitched, belly-shaking guffaw. "I warned your mother, told her I'd bring your things today." His foot rummaged through Alejo's half-buried clothes. "Lástima empanadas!"

Alejo felt foolish.

"Make it a good day, Ombligo," purred Charco.

The guard pulled out the stake, jerked back the grid. A chained, naked Charco emerged. Ombligo unlocked the lower padlock. Charco unraveled the rest of the shackles. He rubbed his wrists, his ankles, then stretched, raised his palms to the sky. His sinewed back and leg muscles told Alejo the boy had worked long and hard.

Charco scratched his scalp, ran his fingers through his short, thick black hair, picked up the shovel, and strolled out of sight. When he returned, he searched the area in front of his and Alejo's cells. "Dolores is gone."

Ombligo got on all fours and picked up a pea-size pebble. He gave it to Charco. "Here she is. Sorry."

Charco checked it carefully, then, pebble clutched between index and middle fingers, he crouched angrily before Alejo. "Chingado!" he yelled. "I told you, you moved Dolores. You made me lose!"

Alejo didn't care about the stone. He was eyeing Charco's face, the narrow blue eyes, the square determined chin. From the young boy's fury, Alejo caught a strange, intensely personal heat. He knew this face.

Charco turned. Intuitively, Alejo directed his gaze to the base of the spine. There it was. The same scythe-shaped birthmark that he and his brothers bore.

Ombligo was ladling out food. He tossed a large metal pin high into the air. "Charquito, let Durcal out."

Charco caught the pin in midair, yanked out the stake, and effortlessly lifted back the heavy grill. Shielding his eyes against the sun, Alejo crawled out. When Charco bent down to unlock the padlock, Alejo scrutinized the birthmark. Identical. He barely caught the shovel an incensed Charco tossed at him.

While defecating into a hole, Alejo calculated Charco was about Hector's age. But he *felt* much older. And was he Yaqui? He was dark, but looked Mexican. His frame was narrow, his arms long like a Yaqui's, but unlike Yaquis, he liked to talk and make noises. Strange.

Doubts about his father flooded his mind. Were there other Charcos? Had that been a forged IOU Billy Cameron brought to the ranch? Rafael Castillo had verified the signature. Is it possible his father had bet Sueño?

Ugly doubts. Did his father love his mother?

Dangerous doubts. Esteban had murdered his father, no?

He found Ombligo and Charco sitting on the ground, eating oatmeal, still talking about the Dolores, the stone.

Ombligo pointed to a full plate. "Come. Fill up good, Durcal. I put honey in it. You won't see me for two days."

Charco grunted, gulped down more food. "You'll learn what that means."

Alejo drank water, then ate. "Tell me about the stone." He avoided looking at Charco for fear of staring.

Ombligo laughed. "It's an old game. The prisoners bet anything they have, anywhere in the world. Money, a burro, a knife, a saddle. They bet for water, food, a bath, sometimes a woman."

"You push the stone with your piss," explained Charco, his mouth full of food. "You push it to the finish line. Today I lost a bridle because of you."

"No, I'll give you another chance, Charquito," said Ombligo. "Durcal moved it. We'll start over." The guard asked, "Alejo, want to bet?"

Unsure if he understood, he asked, "What against what?"

"Whatever you got against whatever you want."

Hesitant, Alejo ventured, "A sack of feed for a day outside?"

Ombligo's round friendly face became sour; only the tips of his teeth showed. "You're supposed to be in the pits, Durcal. Back there." He waved his hand. "I was nice and put you in the caves near Charco because you're young. In the pits, you wouldn't be offering me no stupid sack of feed. You'd be *giving* me your black horse for a bucket of water."

Ombligo ran an index finger across his gums—top and bottom—and rinsed out his mouth. "You can't even piss out of the pits. Those are the real bartolinas."

Alejo finished his food in silence. Where was he? he wondered. The caves aren't the bartolinas? He looked at his cave. It was one of four holes dug into the base of a low hill. The pits were worse? If it weren't for the black grids, passersby wouldn't see the caves.

He checked the sky. It wasn't yet noon of the first day. Twenty years. His head, his entire body hurt. The pull in his throat told him he was close to tears.

Out of the corner of his eye he saw Charco shovel his cell clean in swift efficient moves. He shook out a frayed straw mat and a long colorless rag that must have been a blanket. When finished, he asked, "Ombligo, can I wash?"

The guard rolled from side to side on his buttocks, pitched himself forward, then stood. He climbed back on the wagon and dipped a gourd into a barrel strapped to the driver's seat. While he poured, Charco, an apparition of his father, scrubbed his face and body.

Hand raised invitingly, Ombligo called, "Durcal!" His face had softened.

"Thank you," said Alejo, rising. He placed his feet over Charco's footprints, noted his own were longer.

"Make mud. Put it on those bites. I brought you a mat and your blanket. Careful with the guards tomorrow. They're federales."

Alejo rinsed the dirt out of his hair and guided the cool water down to the ant bites. He saw where he had torn his skin. "What about the soldiers?" He bent down to knead the water and gravelly dirt into a mud pack.

"Don't bet with them," advised Ombligo. "They've seen you and your mother. Saben que vienes de mata buena."

Furious, Alejo said nothing at hearing his mother likened to a fine plant. He slapped off the water, grateful for the full hard movement of his arms. He put mud packs over his stomach, legs, and groin, and placed an extra muddy mound just outside his cell.

"Bet with me," challenged Charco, hitting his hand against his chest. "You must have a saddle. I'll need one when I leave."

Alejo unearthed his clothes from the heap in front of his cell, knotted them into a ball, and tossed it onto the wagon. "You have a horse?" asked Alejo. Who was this boy?

"I had six when they arrested me. The Yaquis took them and left me behind." Charco and Ombligo laughed.

"So you have no horse?"

"Bet a saddle—that's if you got one," Charco goaded.

"I have a saddle," said Alejo evenly. He paused. *"And* a mother to weep for me." He added, "But *you* have nothing I want." He turned his head away.

"Right now!" Fist cocked back, blue eyes narrowed to slits, Charco thrust out his chest. "Let's see who has more."

Now he looks like Hector, thought Alejo. "All right. A saddle—but against what?"

"A Mauser," said Charco.

The arsenal in the santuario. "Done."

"Find you a stone, Durcal," giggled Ombligo. He rubbed his hands together in excitement. "Hurry."

Alejo scoured the base of the hill for a round pebble similar to Charco's. Every one had a sharp edge. They laughed watching him search. He glimpsed a rose-hued pebble with only a slight tip on the end which he broke off with his thumbnail. He ran it between his palms; it moved at an angle. Tired of their gaping, he nodded in readiness.

They tossed their straw mats and blankets into the holes. Alejo chose to remain naked. Impassively, Ombligo rechained and recaged them—Alejo first.

The guard handed them tin cups filled to the brim. "Drink slowly," he cautioned. Then he hand-swept the ground in front of their caves. He positioned the pebbles a hand's length from the grids. "Where's the finish line?"

"Mark out five paces!" called Charco.

Ombligo laughed. "That's too far, Charquito."

"I'll go for five," said Alejo.

"Muchachitos!" Shaking his head, the excitement gone, Ombligo measured out five paces. "We won't have a winner."

"Mark it," ordered Charco.

"Mark it," Alejo echoed.

With a shovel, Ombligo etched a vague line across the hard earth. Again, he shook his head at the distance. Obviously disappointed, he repacked the wagon and waved halfheartedly. "See you in two days."

Charco hollered, "Ombliguito, I promise, you'll have a winner!" Once the wagon was out of sight, Charco let out a low moan. "There goes a saint."

Alejo laughed. He had only heard older women like Tía Mercedes use that expression.

"Laugh at me, pendejo. You'll pray to see him again."

"Maybe," conceded Alejo. "Are the soldiers bad?"

"Carrasco is a snake. He makes everyone bad."

"Charco, how long have you been here?"

No answer. Alejo wasn't sure if the boy had fallen asleep or if he hadn't heard. He asked again, louder.

"Shut up! I'm trying to count," Charco snarled. "I can't tell. Carrasco kept me tied to a post—day and night." Moments later he murmured, "Ombliguito persuaded Carrasco to untie the reins they had around my neck. That's how I got here. Ombliguito brought me."

The broken ends of the straw mat rubbed against Alejo's back. He pressed down the small of his back and scratched himself. The itching returned. He reached out to replace the now-dried mud with a fresh pack and discovered his reserve pack had baked solid.

The sun's noon rays threatened to enter his cell; they stopped just outside the grid, at the mouth of the opening. Alejo was amused that the same cave that held him prisoner now protected him from the heat.

"This is better," said Charco in a tired voice that Alejo visualized as coming from a young boy.

"*Luula katec,*" Alejo said in Yaqui, referring to the time. He wanted peace between him and this boy. No one deserved to be tied to a post.

"*Ehue.* Time to sleep," answered Charco in a tone that seemed to accept Alejo's offer. "Hold your piss."

BEADS OF SWEAT gathered at Alejo's temples. He blocked out images of Ana María and Tacho. In the silence of the hot afternoon, he disobeyed Castillo's warning and thought of home. By now his mother had everything ready for supper. Covered by a damp cloth, the large mass of white dough for the flour tortillas would be resting on the kitchen table.

Charco. Of course his father had had other women. All men needed other women—not him. He had sought no one after Ana María. He forced Ana María's face away.

What part of his mother's love had failed his father? He let tears flow. Did she know? Had she grieved? He felt embarrassed for her. Pitied her.

He fought the doubts that had surfaced the moment he saw Charco's back. How many seeds had his father scattered? Had he seen them? Did he love them?

How could two of José Durcal's sons end up side by side in these bartolinas? Surely that meant something. He needed to know more about this boy.

Alejo studied his torn, chained hands; saw his maleness, recumbent, safe from the scorching midafternoon beams. His arms ached to work. Only work could stop the swirl of demon doubts dancing in his head.

"TUA KUCTEO!" CHARCO's cry announced late afternoon.

Alejo smiled; his bladder felt full. He had no doubts about winning the race. He had always won such contests with his brothers. They had not pushed objects but had tried to see who could piss farther or arch higher along the side of the barn. More than once his mother had caught them, and slapped them with her apron. But his father had remained undisputed champion, beating them by such distances that they avoided playing with him.

He heard Charco's chains rattle. "You ready?"

"Ehue," answered Alejo. He sat as close to the bars as possible; his knees got in the way. He changed positions, lay on his side, knees bent, back arched. Although the angle was tight, even painful, he figured he could rest his penis on the lowest bar of the grid. The metal burned him.

Charco started with a strong jet that hit Dolores and got her going. He whooped, hollered, *"Lola!"*

Alejo aimed, hit his pebble, but his spray bounced off. The pebble held. Afraid to lose power, he held back, changed strategies. This time he aimed to the left, counting on the smoother side to give way. It moved!

Meanwhile Charco was moving Dolores with hard, quick bursts. His pebble was halfway to the mark when suddenly he stopped.

Alejo stuck to the same tactic, moving his target by aiming at the left and letting it slide along the smoother right edge. He felt himself lose pressure, and he too stopped. He compared distances. He was clearly losing.

"You have a better rock," he said, angry at himself for choosing so carelessly.

"Let's bet money," said Charco.

"Are you changing the stakes?"

"I need money more than the saddle. Aren't you rich?"

"No. We have a ranch. I have nothing to bet."

"What about the gun you killed with?"

"It's a black powder "

"Bah. No Colt .45?"

"Rurales took everything," said Alejo. "You have nothing I want and I have nothing to bet."

"When they come for you, take me out. Pay Carrasco."

Alejo reached for the cup of water and sipped. The sun had warmed it. Would Castillo bail out this boy? Perhaps if the lawyer came alone and saw Charco's birthmark.

"Charco, what does Carrasco want from you?"

"To know where Yaquis are hiding."

"Do you know?"

Charco laughed. "Get me out, Durcal. I'd pay you back. I know horses, cows, fields."

The thought of his mother seeing Charco wearied Alejo. "Drink more water. Let's race. If I win, will you tell me anything I want?"

"No. Can you bet a mule?"

Alejo thought of what he had. "I have new silver spurs." He liked the thought of Charco having their father's spurs.

"If I tried to sell them, they'd say I stole them."

"You're always with Yaquis?"

"Of course. Yoemem are good to me. But Yoris are taking them away. I must work. Mexicans are mean. With gringos I could learn to make cement!"

"Cement?"

"A powder. With water it becomes a smooth stone that never breaks and never moves. I saw it at a gringo's house."

The boy was lying, but Alejo didn't want to argue. He knew Charco would win the race. "I have the silver spurs."

"Keep them. Buy me out of here. I'll work for you." The boy spoke with pained urgency. "Carrasco—"

"Ah. You do know where Yaquis are hiding." Alejo felt victorious. At last. A straight answer out of Charco.

Silence. Then Alejo heard chains rattle. Next he saw a narrow stream shoot across his cell and hit his pebble! The well-aimed spout hit right behind the target and moved it by alternating between the left and right sides. Soon it was aligned with Dolores.

"There. The pebbles are even. We can start again," said Charco.

"No," said Alejo. Moved, he surrendered to tears for the second time that day. *"If* they come for me, I'll ask Carrasco how much he wants for you."

12

On the second night, while Charco spoke of the wonders of cement, Alejo curled into a dreamless sleep. At dawn he thought he heard chains rattle. Peering out, he saw two pairs of legs in front of Charco's cell.

A voice ordered, "Out."

Charco did not answer. Moments later, the two silhouettes tossed the boy into a wagon and drove off.

Alejo tried to call out, to ask where they were taking him. Speech and sight eluded him. Again he slept.

By noon, he was very awake. His water had run out and hunger pangs made him wish he had eaten more of Ombligo's honeyed oatmeal. And he needed to defecate—not in the cell. He forced himself to wait. He emptied his bladder, aiming at his pebble. He hit it but failed to move it.

Charco. Charquito. Strange boy.

The wagon returned. The guards pulled a bundle wrapped in a crude blanket off the wagon. They held the ends and, swinging, heaved the bundle into the cell. A guard reached in and jerked the blanket out before replacing the grill.

Alejo asked, "What are you doing?"

Next, they removed his door. The shorter guard motioned him to come out. Wary, Alejo crawled on all fours. He peeked into Charco's cell; he was unconscious. Bloody welts dotted the boy's back, legs, and buttocks.

Horrified, Alejo asked, "What have you done?"

Face blank, the same guard pointed him toward the wagon.

To avoid the guards' hands, Alejo hopped onto the wheel and hurled himself over the side. He was trying to stand when the driver struck the mule, jerking the wagon forward, dropping him to his knees. He wished he had thought to grab his blanket.

Fear intensifying, he asked, "Where are we going?"

The guards ignored him, continued what seemed an important personal conversation—something about new boots and blisters. Striving for control over his bowels and his fear, Alejo scanned the horizon; his eyes absorbed the nearby chestnut hills that rose gracefully from the flat Sonora land.

Hot sun warmed his shoulders. Good, he thought. He stretched his legs so they could share the heat. His bites and scratches, he noticed, were changing from red to brown.

The ride ended outside the barracks, where Carrasco sat on an empty powder keg tilted against the wall. Alejo noted the similarity between the keg and the captain's body. The man wore his cap low over his eyes. His front teeth clasped a short unlit cigar; he held a long dried reed in his hand. His knee-high boots glistened in the sun.

The guards jumped off, grabbed Alejo's ankles, dragged him off the wagon, and stood him up, at arm's length from Carrasco. The captain waved the reed and the soldiers left Alejo.

Again, Alejo wished he had grabbed his blanket. He kept his cuffed hands together, hoping the chains might hide his genitals from Carrasco's line of vision.

"Yaquis broke the Ortiz Peace Treaty—killed four soldiers last night. Took everything. Left only the naked bodies." Carrasco spoke without removing his cigar. "Charco knows where they're hiding in the Sierra Bacatete. He knows their forests."

Alejo felt the weight of his full colon. He tightened his buttocks.

With the tip of the reed, Carrasco pointed to the bites on Alejo's stomach. "Hurt?"

"Not much," Alejo muttered, head down. "Captain, a shovel please."

"Charco knows a lot he won't tell me. He might tell you. Has he talked of Tetabiate?"

Alejo's rectum trembled. A thin liquid burned down the back of his leg. "If not a shovel, then let me go there." He nodded toward the stables.

With the reed, Carrasco slowly moved the chains aside and as he spoke, stared at Alejo's groin. "I suspect Yaquis stole Charco. He's Mexican. I've written a bulletin describing him. Someone in this godforsaken state will claim him. There may be a reward."

"What do you want?" begged Alejo. Despite the heat, cold sweat bathed his forehead.

"Make friends," said Carrasco. "Find the Yaqui route up the Bacatete. Find out if Tetabiate is responsible for the killings."

Carrasco would keep him standing until he agreed, Alejo realized. "All right," he muttered. Without waiting for an answer, Alejo turned toward the stables.

He had hobbled a few paces when Carrasco leaned forward and

pierced the back of Alejo's knee with the reed. He stumbled to both knees. The handcuffs prevented him from breaking his fall. He tottered, crashed facedown on the hard earth.

"Chingado!" he yelled. He rolled over on his back.

Carrasco leaned over him. "I'm not finished, Durcal. Hear my conditions—"

Alejo heard his colon release itself.

Eyes wide, Carrasco pulled himself upright—too slowly. Hands between his legs, Alejo was already shoveling his waste at Carrasco.

FELIPA CONCEDED HONG's worth to herself and to Tía Mercedes. The man learned quickly, moved ably with tools, and stayed out of her way. He understood his place at the ranch. She trusted him with her sons, especially Andrés, who was fascinated by him. Ignoring her reprimands, the boy constantly touched the man's skin and hair and asked him questions about a city up north, San Francisco.

Hong seemed to enjoy the attention. When Andrés offered Alejo's sketching charcoal to Hong, the man drew pictures of that faraway locale which Felipa knew was in California where her father had searched in vain for gold.

With Hong, animals were fed on time. Water troughs were kept full; fruit and vegetables were picked with perfect timing. He cut hay and stacked and moved it as fast as Tacho and his men.

Hector rode Coqueta and supervised the range with help from neighbors or Mexican day help. But unlike Alejo, who worked at a steady pace and then stopped to admire his own work, Hector worked fast and drew no pleasure from his efficiency. Felipa read discontent in his sullenness, defiance in his demand to ride Moro "while I'm the oldest." Afraid she might strike him, she sent him on errands to Tía Mercedes, trusting her to calm him. The boy returned with fat books—biographies and histories—which he read every evening. Only then did he seem happy.

Now that the weather was warming, the cattle would be moved

less, fed more, as they were prepared for sale. After the sale, she would allow Hong to help with the range. Yaquis had vanished. Word was they had returned to their pueblos.

Maybe they could rent a horse for Hong from one of the neighbors. She had to be careful about gossip, and about having a man living at the ranch, even if he did sleep in the barn.

Uneventful days opened and closed. The ranch ran smoothly, a circumstance that, in truth, meant nothing to her without Alejo. The place had been José's dream; he had decreed the same dream for his sons. Alejo, the only son who shared his father's vision, was gone from the ranch and her. The void he left had forced her to look inward.

She saw how men's dreams had shaped her life—her father's search for gold, her husband's desire for land. Then Sueño, then Moro, and now her son's rash belief that blood could redeem José's death. Would she always be trapped?

And what were these changes she felt within herself? Her red pain had disappeared, eclipsed by a silver-gray fog. Its inviting softness promised respite from the heaviness that clung to her thighs, loins, arms. Afraid to surrender, lest she be unable to reclaim herself, she hurried through each day, barely staying beyond the fog's fingers.

That first sleepless night without Alejo in the house, she had moved her statue of the Virgin of Guadalupe into his room. *Just to remind you to bring back my son.* A votive candle burned day and night before the Virgin.

Her nights were bouts with anger and guilt. Why hadn't Alejo let her kill Esteban? Why did she detest every smile, every laugh that came from Hector and Andrés? Who cared if they worked long hours? How dare they take their freedom for granted?

Holy Mother, will you punish me for these thoughts? You've taken my soul. What is your will for Alejo?

In the mornings, too ashamed to look at her sons, she fed them double portions. She baked coyotas, sweet pastries that took too long to make. Her sons thought she was rewarding them and kissed her gratefully. When she turned away her head, they lifted her hands to their lips. Infuriated, fearful of her wrath, she gnawed the inside of her mouth.

ALEJO HAD BEEN gone almost a month when Hong asked to drive the wagon to the nearby reed beds. He pointed to the fruit trees, the vegetable garden, and the well, pantomiming water flowing through to all the plants. Curious, she allowed the half-day trip—making sure Hector and Andrés went along.

They returned with the wagon loaded with carrizo. Hector and Andrés helped Hong strip the leaves off the long reeds. The reeds were yellowing, hardening, their pliant green softness gone now that the rainy season had ended.

Hong motioned to Felipa and her sons to watch him. First he sorted out the widest reeds—about two fingers in diameter. Then, wielding a short knife in his thin, strong fingers, he halved the reeds lengthwise and carved out the joints, leaving a slender smooth channel. Using the stripped-off leaves, he tied together six reed halves and laid them flat among the garden rows. Next he fitted single reeds perpendicular to the main channel. He whittled equally spaced holes into the single reeds.

Restless, the boys tried to help. Hong shook his head in a polite but firm no. The family stared in silence as Hong decorated the garden's rows with long yellow reeds. He rechecked every angle, leveled various areas, then clapped his hands. The message was clear: watch.

He walked to the well and filled the buckets of the shoulder yoke. Then he slowly poured the water into the wide channels at the head of every row. The liquid flowed, wending its way down one row and edging sideways along the perpendicular channels. Felipa and her sons followed its trail.

"I see how it works!" shouted Hector.

Andrés pointed to the fruit trees. "Can we do those?"

Hong looked to Felipa.

"If you cut yourselves, don't tell me," she said. She went into the house and emerged with two small knives.

Hector stepped back. "Mama, those belong to Alejo."

She gave each a knife. "That's why you'll be careful."

From the porch she watched the boys follow Hong's direction. She suspected that his strangeness inspired their zeal. Although he used basic words when speaking to her, he spoke freely with them. She could not describe to herself the sound of his voice. It came from the nose and the back of the throat. She could get used to it, she decided.

PUTTING ASIDE HER personal suffering, Felipa decided that the main problem with Alejo's absence was Moro. She could not look at the horse without reliving the strife he had caused. The ugly pride José and Alejo assumed when riding him. Though to herself she admitted the magnificence of the animal, she could never understand why men had to straddle everything they valued.

Without Alejo to exercise him, Moro had become obstinate, mean. When a rancher brought a mare to him, Moro had chased the man out of the corral. The man barely cleared the fence.

Denied visiting rights to Alejo, she needed to see that he was all right. Sheriff Alcázar had tried to convince her: "Give him time to learn the routine. Habit is everything."

But Alcázar had failed to look at her when he spoke. He knew something she didn't, she decided.

Rafael Castillo too had promised to check on Alejo. She trusted Rafael, but when he failed to report, she designed countless tragic possibilities, each more feasible than the last.

Indignant at these men, she took control. The next day she rose before dawn, intending to drive the wagon to Alamos, then to the prison. Hong helped her hitch the mules.

As she boarded, an idea came to her. "Of course!" she said, laughing aloud. She tapped her forehead. "You fool," she murmured to herself.

She returned to the barn and threw a saddle blanket on Moro. The horse snorted. When she lifted the bridle, he flattened his ears. She slapped his neck with the reins.

She reentered the house for a saddle. Shrouded by blankets, José's and Alejo's saddles lay side by side next to the fireplace. Her hand trembled as she reached for José's heavier saddle. It would be an ill omen to use Alejo's.

Once she was outside, Hong hurried to help her; she stopped him and hefted it on by herself. Remembering her height, she lowered the stirrups before leading Moro out.

She lifted her skirt and mounted. The horse spun. Reins taut, she dared him to move without permission. "The food," she whispered to Hong.

He handed her the sack, and she tied it to the pommel. She lowered her black skirt over her knees. When she felt ready, she let Moro walk. Out on the road, where Hector could not hear, she let him trot.

"Muchachitos!" Ombligo's high yell reverberated inside Alejo's pit.

Alejo pulled down the blanket that he had threaded between the bars to shield him from the sky. Daylight. The bright sun cut his eyes. Why is Ombligo here? Alejo thought, alarmed. He covered his eyes to listen better. More than the wagon. Horses, not mules.

Next, he heard Ombligo insist, "Please, señora, go back. We'll get him. The señor can help me."

Mother? wondered Alejo. "Charco," he called. "Wake up. I think they've come for me." He paused. "Maybe."

"Ya," Charco answered, his speech unclear, "A'ios, Yori."

The weakness in Charco's voice worrried Alejo. "I haven't forgotten our bet. I won't leave without you. I won't."

Several nights ago, soldiers had again come for Charco. Though he was gone only a few hours, the boy had barely spoken since his return. Last night Ombligo had paid them a quick visit. Riding a burro, the guard had come alone; as a treat he had given them pinole and peeled oranges. Alejo was certain Ombligo was there without permission.

Ombligo had been unable to let them out, and though Alejo had not seen Charco, the guard's consoling phrases told him the boy was seriously hurt. Alejo admitted he was relieved that it was Charco and not him Carrasco had sent for. Filled with remorse, Alejo vowed he would not leave the bartolinas without Charco.

Alejo heard the wagon approach his pit, heard the springs creak as Ombligo got down. Footsteps. Then Ombligo's girth blocked the sun. Squinting, Alejo also saw the thin frame of Rafael Castillo.

"You've come for me!" exclaimed Alejo.

Puffing, Ombligo bent over the iron grid. "Grab the other side. Slide it just enough so the boy can climb up."

Alejo saw two sets of hands grip the bars, heard metal grind against the gravelly soil as they slid back the iron cover. The men moved out of his line of vision.

To prevent cramping, Alejo kneaded his calves and thighs. He rose slowly. At full height, he stood chest-high in the pit.

Cupping his eyes, Alejo saw that the lawyer had retreated, holding a handkerchief to his nose. Ombligo carried a shovel and a bucket of water toward the pit.

"Sorry, Rafael," yelled Alejo. His throat felt tight, unused. "I don't smell it anymore."

He put one palm on the grid, the other on the hard earth, and hoisted himself out of the pit. When he sat on the edge of the pit, pebbles pressed themselves into his bare buttocks. Moaning softly, he lifted his long legs out of the narrow hole and straightened them over the flat earth.

"You look terrible." Castillo stuffed the handkerchief into the pocket of his black serge coat and approached. "I'm the one who's sorry," he said gravely. "I haven't come for you. The governor hasn't even acknowledged receiving my letters."

"It's not all bad news," cut in Ombligo, putting the bucket down. "Wash up. Your mother brought food and clean clothes. She's waiting for you." He pointed to the bend in the next hill.

Damn you, Castillo, Alejo thought. He splashed water over his hair, face, and shoulders. He scrubbed hard. His mother must not see this filth.

He tried to stand, then remembered: standing had to be done in stages. Hands around a knee, he drew back one leg, then the other; next he squatted on his haunches; from there, he unfolded himself upright. He waited for his head to clear before walking.

"Ombligo, can I wash myself more?" he asked.

The guard nodded. "Save your clean clothes. Put on those blue trousers."

Alejo ladled water out of the barrel and wet down his groin, legs, feet. He slipped into the old, soft pants. Nice. He folded back the waistband to keep them on.

"These bartolinas are worse than ever," said Castillo. He stepped away from the six holes whose severe thick bars stained the patternless flatland. "How many have prisoners?"

"We're only three," said Alejo. "We got a new one two weeks ago." He tried to press down his hair. Impossible. He looked at his shadow; unmanageable bristles crowned his head.

"They're sending all prisoners—not just Yaquis—to work in Yucatán or the Valle Nacional in Oaxaca. The boys like to sleep during the day," Ombligo explained to Castillo. "In the pits, prisoners always prefer the night."

"They can't clean their cells at night," scoffed Castillo.

Ombligo shook his head. "We see good by moonlight. We got lamps too. The boys come up most nights. They wash, walk around, stretch, talk, laugh. I always make sure they get something, don't I, Durcal?"

Pointing to Ombligo, Alejo said, "He's a saint."

Ombligo frowned at Castillo. "If only one of us comes, it's too hard to slide back the top. We have to drop their food down through the bars. There's no other way."

Before walking to meet his mother, Alejo said, "Ombligo, let Charco out. Please? Give him the food Mother brought. Rafael, will you help?"

"Carrasco better not find out," said Ombligo, already moving toward Charco's pit.

"Rafael," said Alejo, "check my friend's face and back. Not the scars. *Here.*" He pointed to his own birthmark.

ROOTED, FELIPA WAITED while the barefoot, shirtless Alejo walked toward her.

They collapsed into each other's arms. Stepping back, Felipa pressed his head to her chest, heard him gasp for air. No matter. Already feeling the ache of parting, she clasped him tighter, her gut and chest unwilling to let go. Hugging, seeing, weren't enough. She wanted to breathe him.

She felt his hands move behind her. Turning, she saw he was trying to include Moro in the same embrace. She stepped aside. Moro recognized Alejo's voice; he let the boy stroke him. His nostrils, however, did not accept Alejo. The animal snorted his passages clear.

Alejo laughed. "I stink." He scratched Moro's chest.

She wet her thumb and rubbed his cheeks and forehead. "You're yellow," she said. "Why, with all this sun?"

"It's better to hide from it." He pulled his head back and stood between Moro and his mother—standing as close to each as possible. "Ombligo says the sun made the gachupín crazy."

"You can't mean the same old gachupín loco? He's not dead?"

"He's in the farthest pit. I always thought he was one of the

crazy stories about the old days." His hand caressed his father's saddle. "Mama, you rode Moro?"

"You've *seen* the gachupín?" Felipa realized Alejo did not understand the horror he spoke.

"Once. When he arrived a few days ago, the soldiers made me
and Charco dig a new pit for him. He's too old to dig. His white
beard is out like this." He made a wide circle from ear to ear. "No
hair on top. The sun cooked his head. Mama, *you* rode Moro?"

Hand to hip, she stated proudly, "Who else?"

He laughed and kissed her. "Hong, he's working?"

His breath shocked her. "Yes. Tell me what you eat."

"Watery beans, bread, water. Ombligo makes us oatmeal.
Enough to live, Mama."

As he walked the horse, she studied her son's stride, his carriage.
It mattered not that he averted his eyes, nor that he bore himself as
naturally as possible. Thinner, paler, he showed no signs of illness.
But he was different.

He hurts, she thought. There's more—that almost cruel curl to
his upper lip. In a month, the boy in him had *turned*.

He cut into her thoughts. "Castillo already told me about Governor Corral. The pardon will come. Be patient."

Felipa knew different, had seen it written on Castillo's face that
dawn when she had awakened him and forced him to come with
her to the barracks so she could see her son. Too embarrassed to say
no, the lawyer had dressed hastily. He personally had bribed Carrasco to allow her to see Alejo.

Not until the barracks were in sight did Castillo tell her that
Alejo had been moved from the caves to the pits. "It's all within the
letter of the law," he had explained. "Maybe now we can persuade
Alejo to go into the army. I have a proposition he may accept."

With Castillo's plan in mind, Felipa worded her question carefully. "Alejo, how long do you expect your family to see you suffer?"

Eyes burning, he challenged her. "I know you want me to

choose the army." He stopped, his mouth groping for words. "If I get out that way, I'm admitting I'm a murderer. Mama, that old ga-chupín has lived in bartolinas all over the state for more than ten years. I'm stronger, younger!"

She wanted to rip out his tongue. "You compare yourself to that monster who cut the bellies of pregnant Yaquis? Has the sun cooked your head too?"

Alejo lengthened his stride, slapping the dirt with his heels. "Yes, I wish I was home. But I won't admit to murder. The Durcals are not murderers. I'm not sorry for what I did. That pardon will come. It has to."

Felipa changed tactics. She squeezed his hand. "No fighting," she pleaded and stroked his cheek with the back of her hand. "Before I go, ride Moro. Don't raise dust. Carrasco."

He mounted. His thighs, legs, and groin felt the stretch of his father's wide saddle. Good pain, he thought. His legs dangled freely. Moro moved at will while Alejo breathed in the day's warm air deep into his lungs.

For a month he had striven to make himself smaller to sleep comfortably in the pit. He had trained his mind and body to associate star-sprayed nights with freedom. Days were for sleeping. Nights marked the beginning of a new day.

Now, awed by the power of daylight, he surrendered sight, stopped thought, and allowed the vast countryside, the countless subtle browns with their sparse green tufts, to enter him. Tears stung his eyes. *Mi tierra.*

And if he were to ride away? Ombligo had told them of the few who had escaped the bartolinas. The sun killed them. He would not be one of those. More often, escapees returned after the govern-ment had taken family members hostage.

He shook his head violently, resentful that his mother's love had weakened his resolve to hold out until the pardon came. Not the army, not with men like Carrasco. Never.

Taking his time, he steered Moro past one hill and around the next until he found the caves where he had spent his first three nights. Leg wrapped around the pommel, he stared at them. Strange how they evoked emotions he expected to feel only the next time he saw home. How comfortable the caves look, he thought. He smiled. Ah, but the pits are well worth what I did to Carrasco.

Still smiling, he recalled the soldiers idly watching the waste-bathed Carrasco vent his rage by stomping him. The pear-shaped officer would have ground him into the earth itself had his boots not become mired in shit.

When the fatigued captain had finished, the soldiers had returned Alejo to the cave. Sometime during the night, he and Charco were bound, gagged, blindfolded, and tossed into the pits. Holes a meter and a half deep and two armlengths wide.

That first day he slept until the midafternoon heat woke him. Seeing the dimensions of the pit with slits of sky overhead, he panicked, yelled, "Charco! Charco!"

Finally came a raspy weak "Durcal." Later, the only response he received was an ongoing "Mmmmmm."

That was enough for Alejo. He got busy, took in fresh air by pressing his face against the bars. While scraping the dry feces off his legs with dirt, he noticed the chains were gone.

Somehow, the freedom to move his hands made the pits bearable. Yes, the pits were small, but the chains were gone. He grabbed the bars overhead; pulling, he stretched his back. He curled his legs, gripped the bars, and lifted himself up and down until his body was bathed in sweat. With pleasure, he licked the salt off his arms and shoulders.

For two days, silent soldiers came to pour water and gruel down to them. Alejo ate, drank. He clawed out a narrow hole, defecated into it, then covered it. Other than "Mmmmmm," he heard no more sounds from Charco.

Then Ombligo came alone at sunset. Through a long tedious procedure the guard chained Alejo's grille to the back of the wagon and moved it enough for him to squeeze out. He helped slide back Charco's grille.

A shocked Alejo climbed in for the inert boy. The gruel the soldiers had poured down lay baked over his head. He also understood why Charco had not spoken. The sides of his mouth were slit open. "Carrasco," whispered Ombligo. "He does this with rope."

Together, he and Ombligo bathed Charco head to toe. Alejo cradled Charco while the guard cleaned out the punctures with alcohol. Once, Charco feebly tried to wriggle out of Alejo's clutches; he couldn't. After that, he held himself so still, Alejo was sure he had fainted. Checking, he saw that Charco was very much awake.

In the vanishing twilight, while Ombligo drained the last of the alcohol into the wounds, Alejo witnessed the boy's blue eyes become dull stones that stared at nothing. He had seen that same unflinching look in Tacho. *Sangre Yaqui.* In the boy's expressionless face José lived.

After that, to Alejo, Charco became his "wild brother." He could not describe this love to anyone. *Is this what my mother feels for me?*

What if Carrasco punished him as he had Charco? *He won't,* Alejo decided, *not while that snake can drain money or fresh food from the Durcals. But Charquito has no one.* Two days ago the silent soldiers had come for him again. And done what?

Standing in front of the caves, Alejo looked up at the sun. By now Ombligo and Castillo should have tended to Charco; Castillo would have seen that two sons of José Durcal were in the bartolinas.

He led Moro toward his mother. She stood as he had left her, tall, straight, her love palpable in those large black eyes that had remained fixed to the direction he had taken.

To please her, Alejo gave the horse full leg. The animal lurched; Alejo reined him in. Checked, Moro pranced in place. Felipa clapped. Alejo hugged Moro.

Dismounting, Alejo folded her fingers around the reins and embraced her. "If this was to weaken me, it almost worked. I'll speak to Castillo."

*   *   *

HE FOUND OMBLIGO and Castillo by the wagon crouched over a prostrate Charco. The boy had been cleaned. Ombligo was pouring sugared water down his throat by wringing a cloth over the cut lips. Despite the swollen face, the likeness to José Durcal was unmistakable.

Welts covered the boy's legs, back, shoulders. Alejo lowered his pants, showed Castillo his birthmark, then turned Charco on his side and traced the scythe.

"I *understand*," said the lawyer. He motioned Alejo away from the guard. "In truth, the governor will reprieve this boy before he does you."

Alejo eyed the lawyer closely, noticed the trimmed hairline around the neck, the combed mustache, the clean, evenly pared nails. *This man may have a choice of how to look and how to smell, but Ana María never loved him.* Relieved, Alejo asked, "Did you know Charco's mother?"

"Of course not," said Castillo. "But the boy is Durcal. Who knows where or how these things happen? Your father adored Felipa. He kept no other woman. I would have heard."

"But would you tell me?"

Castillo met Alejo's eyes. "Why lie? José traveled. Things happen to us men. He was human." Castillo glanced back at Charco. "Una copa. Un jalón de trenza." He smiled almost coyly. "I doubt if it was more than that. He is half Indian."

"Yaqui," corrected Alejo, embarrassed to hear Charco's life starting with a voyage, a drink, and the yank of a braid. "Charco was caught with Yaquis. They escaped with stolen horses and left him behind, probably because he looks Mexican. Get him out, Rafael. Carrasco's going to kill him."

"I'll describe him as a Mexican in the petition to the governor. He looks old enough to go into the army."

"There's no other way?"

"I doubt it. He has no family, no one to claim him. With bands of Yaquis hitting everywhere, better to say he's Mexican."

Ombligo was helping Charco sit up. To shield his eyes from the sun, the boy leaned into the shade of a wagon wheel.

"*I'll* claim him," said Alejo angrily. "Call him Charco Durcal! He'll live with us."

"Does the boy know about José?"

Alejo shook his head. "He claims no last name."

"Sit down." The lawyer sat on the bare earth and waited for Alejo to join him. "That's not as noble as it sounds. How will Felipa feel? Your brothers? Can't you imagine the jokes?"

Alejo understood. Always the wrong people suffer. "You're saying Charco must go into the army?"

The lawyer scratched a circle in front of Alejo. "Listen. Pay attention. Every year thousands of men are forced into the army." He made several X's in the circle. "Every year hundreds desert." Castillo drew wild lines going in all directions out of the circle. "The ones who aren't caught and shot escape to mountains, hills, jungles, valleys—never heard from again. Some get to the United States."

"Charco likes gringos," mused Alejo.

"Does he know any that would help him escape?"

"I don't know."

"Alejo, the Peace Treaty of Ortiz is over. War with Yaquis is inevitable. Soldiers and whites still occupy Yaqui pueblos. Let me work this to your advantage. If you and that boy go into the army, in a few months I could plan your escape to Arizona. You would never be listed as a deserter. Meanwhile, you could stay with friends."

Castillo lowered his voice, spoke carefully. "From there we could negotiate a pardon. You'll be safe. We'll take our time—pay the men close to the top. That's how it's done."

Alejo listened for any mention of Ana María living in Arizona. He felt trapped. "I have no desire to leave my country. We were talking about Charco, not me."

"The governor will sooner accept two soldiers than one. Sonora doesn't contribute many men into the army."

"You're telling me to forget the pardon?"

"I'm reminding you the hacendados are powerful. You killed one. You're lucky to be alive. But you won't last long out here. Who would notice if you took sick or died?"

Exhausted, Alejo realized it was best not to fight Castillo's words. Too many people were involved.

Alejo watched Charco walking with Ombligo at his side. How did Charquito do it? He recalled what Tacho said about horses and Yaquis getting their strength from the land. *Even in the pits, Charco's on Yaqui soil.*

Nodding toward Charco, Castillo said, "That boy won't last. Does he even know the answer Carrasco wants?"

"Whatever he knows of Tetabiate's men, he'd never tell."

"If anyone can save him, you can," Castillo said.

"Would Carrasco let him go?"

The lawyer smiled. "I would phrase the letter so that Carrasco is credited for adding two soldiers to the Republic." Castillo laid a supporting hand on Alejo's shoulder. "Of course, we will have to pay Carrasco to leave the Durcal name out of all documents. We'll use your mother's last name. Robles."

Alejo shook off the hand. He stood up. "Change my name? Rafael, I killed Esteban to protect that name. I won't give it up!" He erased the lawyer's circle with the ball of his foot. "I don't want to be a soldier. I wouldn't know how, and don't want to know. A soldier!" He spat in disgust.

Castillo scowled. "You know very little, Alejo. Not all soldiers are like Carrasco. Some are innocent victims. Forced conscription is one of our country's greatest cruelties. When the government press gangs raid a town, they haul away sons and husbands. Tie them like beasts to wagons. No goodbyes to mothers or wives. Nothing. The men simply disappear."

The lawyer's words whirled in Alejo's head. *I'm losing something.*

"You can get out of these hellholes. The army, Arizona, and

from there, a pardon. You'll get home faster. Of that, I'm sure."
Castillo leaned closer. "If not for you, then for that boy you claim
and for your mother." He pointed to the pits. "She's in there with
you."

In silence, Alejo assented.

IN THE MONTH that followed, Charco was no longer tortured. Carrasco received permission to move two prisoners to the army barracks near the Yaqui Valley.

As the oldest Durcal male, Hector was allowed to deliver Alejo's
boots. Afterward, Hector did not return to the ranch. Instead, he
shadowed his brother's movements for the rest of the day.

From a distance he witnessed Alejo and another young man
joined to a chain gang of twenty naked men whose arms were
strapped to wooden mesquite stakes. The procession stayed clear of
Yaqui forests, making it impossible for Hector to follow without
being seen.

Escorted by government troops, Carrasco moved the men on
foot. Those too weak to walk were shot.

Twelve survived the seven-day journey.

PART

TWO

13

Two months later—
the port of Guaymas

I AM ALEJO ROBLES.
Alejo Durcal stayed in the bartolinas outside Alamos.

WE ARE SOUTHBOUND for the port of San Blas in Nayarit. The water around this rusty boat is bluer than the sky. Color gives me no pleasure. In an airless hole below, Yaqui families and other prisoners are packed tighter than I was in the bartolinas. A sodden stench invades the air, flows through me, unrolls itself across the deck.

I shut my eyes and still see the faces of those we shoved into the lower decks. Shame clings to my palms.

I listen. Nothing. I would welcome their curses. It matters not that Charco and I were forced to do this. It matters that we did.

Charco sits huddled against the hull, his knees bent, head buried in his arms. He's taken his boots off again. He avoids my eyes and I am grateful. If our eyes met, my shame would double.

*   *   *

IN THE BARTOLINAS Charco and I learned to see into each other.

I recall an evening Ombligo stayed with us until dawn. He brought an extra barrel of water so we could take complete baths, what Charco calls baños de ricos. Neither Charco nor I questioned this extra kindness. Ombligo waited while we shoveled out our cells and aired our mats. He urged us to eat, to stretch. He made us walk until we complained.

Finally Ombligo told us that he was going away and didn't know when he would be back. "We're picking up prisoners," he said. "I'm driving the wagon."

"Yaquis?" asked Charco.

"And Mexicans."

"Good!" said Charco.

Ombligo scolded him. "No, Charquito, it's bad business. Bad for them, bad for you two. Only four soldiers will stay behind. They don't like coming way out here."

I heard the warning. I saw Charco hadn't.

Before we climbed back into the pits, Ombligo gave each of us a handful of crushed cloves wrapped in sackcloth. "Smell this when you need to. Chew it when you hurt."

I climbed in first, and Charco helped Ombligo slide the grid over me. He closed Charco's pit with the help of the mule.

I saw only the outline of Ombligo's belly as he announced in a high voice, "Muchachitos, I'm leaving a pail of water out here. While I'm gone, use the prayer my Huichol grandmother taught me. Pray to God and the Holy Virgin to help you throw all sadness into this pail. Say, *I am a divine, powerful being and all that lies inside my God lives in me.*"

Ombligo sounded like a woman. Charco and I laughed.

"Stop!" cried Ombligo. "Listen to me. If you sleep with sadness, it will soil you. Every night, before you fall asleep, wash your thoughts or you will become ugly men."

Charco laughed. "I could never be ugly."

Ombligo left. I could not see him, yet I knew he was unhappy with us.

Ombligo was right. We saw only the soldiers.

After weeks of their tossing gruel down the hole to us and refusing to let us out, the sadness Ombligo spoke of came, wrapped itself around us, turned us into howling beasts. We beat against the grid, tore the skin off our fists. We hurled our shit out at the guards, hailed them with insults.

"Hijos de mula!"

"Cobardes sin madre!"

Laughing, they answered, "Lenguas zurradas!" and sprayed us with their urine. They told us Ombligo was dead and would never return. Father—Tacho—Ombligo.

We cried, grieved day and night without shame. Our eyes swelled shut. Charco's wail became my companion, mine his. We lost our voices. Time sealed itself around us. We recognized night and day only by changes in temperature.

It was in that void that the knot again appeared inside my chest. I remembered it from the day I killed Esteban. The knot bore the same ugliness as before. But it was familiar and so I bowed to it, made room for it, treated it like a guest.

I sat still, careful not to frighten the knot away. Then with my eyes, I circled it several times to hold it tight. When I was certain it could not move, I willed it to my throat, then rolled it into my mouth, where it almost ripped my jaws apart. I gagged, breathed through my nose, filled lungs and stomach with air. I held my breath till I nearly burst, then I exploded the knot out into Ombligo's pail.

The emptiness freed me to sleep. Once I had rested, pain took hold of me. I chewed cloves and received the gift of numbness.

I called to Charco, "Do what I tell you. Find your sadness."

"I don't have any," he claimed.

"Yes you do," I insisted. "Think of Ombligo,"

"All right," he murmured.

"Wrap it and throw it out," I said.

Nothing happened. He wouldn't leave his pit.

"Stop fighting me," I argued. He stopped talking to me. I begged, threatened, bribed. Nothing would make Charco talk.

Then one day while praying the words Ombligo gave us, I found myself inside Charco's pit. I saw his blue eyes. They were half open as if trying to decide whether to roll back into sleep or stare at the deep lines he had scratched onto the walls. Beneath his folded body, I saw he had torn his straw mat to shreds.

He must have felt me, because he screamed, "Sierpas!"

That broke my concentration. I found myself back in my hole, assuring him that I had been in there with him. He refused to listen until I promised that Ombligo's Huichol prayer would keep away the demons. I didn't tell him about Mother and me.

We prayed until we met in the empty wooden bucket outside the pits. At first we only saw each other's eyes. Next our faces. But our meetings seemed uncertain. Were they imagination? We devised messages. His first word was "Dolores"—the firm-breasted woman who visited him nightly. My picture was Moro. Eventually Charquito grew skilled at the game.

The praying ended the morning the soldiers pulled us out, fed us, and let us wash. They ordered us to the pit of the gachipín loco. We could smell the old crazy Spaniard was long dead. The guards had to help us open the pit, because we could barely stand up.

I didn't want to go down after him. He was rotten—flesh had peeled off his skull except for a curious black strip of tongue which lay trapped between his long front teeth. His face looked like a mask trimmed with white horse hair.

Charco argued with the soldiers to let us shovel the pit closed. "It's already a grave."

The soldiers aimed their pistols at our heads and fired next to our ears. Our heads buzzing from the blast, we jumped into the pit. I couldn't hear myself or Charco scream, yet I know we were hollering all the while we tossed out the dead man's parts and fitted them into the square ammo box the soldiers brought for a coffin. After that, burying the old man was nothing.

The soldiers stuck a marker over the grave which read:

GENARO BALTAZAR DE CULEBRA FRIA—ESPAÑA 18—
FALLECIÓ—ALAMOS, SONORA 1899

Captain Carrasco marched us north, then west out of Alamos territory, past the Río Mayo and near the Río Yaqui. Carrasco shot the weak prisoners, but Charco and I sent each other ánimo and because of that, we did not die.

Ten armed federales came to relieve Carrasco. As the only officer present, Carrasco remained on his mount. I could tell he was displeased to be met ahead of schedule. He spoke about us as if we weren't there. "They're dirty, but capable." He did not list those he had shot. If the federales saw us as pitiful, they did not show it. I was learning about soldiers.

To an older soldier, Carrasco called out each prisoner's name, his place of origin, and anything the prisoner was entitled to keep. All possessions were spread out before us. An accordion, smithing tools, and several pairs of boots.

After the prisoner's name was written down, two soldiers removed the shoulder yoke and chains from the prisoner and walked him into a circle guarded by federales. Once freed, the prisoner either cupped his balls or covered the deep shoulder cuts. The change from criminal to soldier went smoothly, except for me.

Carrasco called out the name Alejo Robles. I felt the yoke and chains come off. All I had to do to become a soldier was take a few paces. But while I was walking from one group to the other, a dizziness came over me. I staggered, fell. I was more than naked, I was stripped of flesh and memory. Two angry hands grabbed my wrists and yanked me into the circle. Men and earth spun around me. I imagined the sound of Tacho's voice, and using it, I ordered myself up.

Back then I blamed the dizziness on my new name. Now I'm

convinced it was the unchaining. Much as we cursed the yokes and chains, we felt halved without them.

Since Charco gave no last name, the soldiers laughed and placed "Un" in front of "Charco." They placed "El" in front of a man called "Lagarto," and "La" in front of a skeletal man dubbed "Lombriz." They toyed with our names, amusing themselves, until Carrasco announced his immediate return to Alamos. His soldiers tossed yokes and chains onto the supply wagon and got into formation.

Carrasco ignored the nearby shade and kept his men at attention in the sun. He adjusted his visor and hand-pressed the front of his uniform as if preparing for a formality. He waited. We waited with him. My tongue started to swell. Ants fed on our bloody feet.

"El sargento."

A wagon and a rider moved toward us. The driver of the wagon turned out to be the sergeant. He was not much older than me— maybe twenty-two. The rider was also young, dressed like a rancher, though the sergeant called him Cabo. Their speech told me they were criollos from Sonora.

The sergeant reread the list of names and studied us. He gave Carrasco a wordless salute and ordered a ladle of water for each of us. Then, single-file, we followed his wagon to makeshift barracks, several hundred meters from the main garrison. Denied the pleasure of watching Carrasco and his white horse disappear, I swallowed unaired curses.

Our new quarters consisted of four high adobe walls, a dirt floor, and a thick wooden door. No roof. There we joined eight other criminals-turned-soldiers. We were now a group of twenty. Under guard, we scrubbed ourselves with cold water and lye soap. When they shaved our heads and forced us into itchy blue government uniforms, Charco and I laughed, and no one heard.

Dinner that night was all the beans, tortillas, and water we wanted. We dug a latrine behind the garrison, and most of us hurried to it before we were ordered into the barracks to sleep behind a padlocked door. No one tested the door. On the other side were six armed soldiers.

The danger was not outside. Charco and I stayed together, waiting for each man to claim his place. In silence, each demanded enough space to sleep stretched out. Each knew when to step aside. In the end, el gallo más gallo—the toughest of all—was a short, powerful man called Saltillo. He took the back wall facing the door.

Charco and I took what was left. Beneath the open sky, I felt unprotected. In the moonlight, I saw everyone slept as we had in the bartolinas—with our knees to our chests.

At dawn the sergeant mustered us out. "You have been given another chance at freedom by serving your country. But first I must turn criminals like you into soldiers. You will become a working unit. You will march."

He called out the names of us who had our own boots. The others were given hard army boots. Charco refused them. He told the soldier to let him wear the topless Yaqui sandal, "or else let me walk barefoot."

The sergeant heard this. He ordered Charco to stand at attention and warned, "That sandal will land you in chains." He seemed unable to decide if Charco was Mexican and if so, by how much. Charco widened his eyes and stared straight ahead. Afraid for my brother, I looked away. In the end, Charco's blue eyes saved him.

The walk to the Río Yaqui had torn my feet. Marching hardened the wounds into rocklike calluses. I ripped one off and was left with a bleeding gash. I could no longer fit into the boots Hector had brought, but because they were listed among my belongings, I was refused another pair. I marched with my toes curled.

We marched with unloaded rifles. Soldiers forced into service are not given ammunition unless they go into battle. We marched before and after every meal, marched in the cruel midafternoon sun, marched in sudden thunderstorms, marched when the moon rose and sometimes after it set. Our chests grew, our legs hardened. We regained lost strength. Some men spent their gains on cruelty.

The accordion belonged to Lombriz. Every night after lockup he played polkas, only polkas. Every night Saltillo threatened, "Don't play polkas to men who can't dance."

The skinny long-faced Lombriz played anyway. I think he felt safe because armed guards were on the other side of the door. One morning Lombriz missed roll call. The soldiers found him dead, facedown in the latrine.

An investigation of the death kept the sergeant busy. This freed Charco and me to fix our real problem: our feet. We cut the tips off our boots. With rags we strapped our feet to the hard army soles. This gave Charco more freedom to walk and allowed me to straighten my toes. If the sergeant noticed, he said nothing.

After Lombriz's death the sergeant moved cautiously around us. He made sure the group stayed in front of him. He and his assistant carried their loaded Remingtons everywhere. The group's marching improved, probably because the sergeant and his cabo matched us step for step. Some thought they were brothers. I, who boasted I could tell if calves were related, saw no similarity between them. Yet somehow they were connected. I could feel it. Their closeness made me miss my brothers. I wondered if they knew how much I loved them.

I looked to Charco. No. Although we had the same birthmark, we only shared the blood of one parent. One thing was sure. He had never seen his own birthmark. Just as well, I thought. What good would it do if I told him?

One hot afternoon the sergeant pulled me aside. He asked that I follow him over to a jito, a giant tree beloved for its shade. He said my mother had been denied permission to see me. I sensed his embarrassment.

"She said you're the young Durcal sung about in the corrido. I've heard about the Durcals." He paused briefly. "She brought your carving tools. I explained bartolina soldiers aren't allowed to have knives. She asked that I tell you she was here."

I was glad he had seen my mother. Maybe in another place he

and I could have been friends. We both used silence. What you say, you give to others. He seemed to know that too.

In secret Charco and I wondered if our new life was any better than the old. We greeted the return of night and day, though at first the days were too bright and the nights not dark enough. When our barracks was issued a few cots we let the others argue over them.

Both of us feared the prisoners from the bartolinas of northern and central Sonora. I followed Charco's lead. He knew how to move among bad Yoris. We never spoke, always avoided their glances, and stayed beyond their reach. Charco had told me of men using men as women. We watched out for each other.

These were no longer men. They raced rats, but to make sure they controlled them, they cut the tendons. When they spoke of women, they talked of parts. Nipples. Breasts. Crotches. Thighs. Buttocks. To them, women were for chewing, riding, piercing, swallowing, wearing. The men's night noises told me something had cut loose their souls. And though my eyes never absorbed their faces, their laughs told me these men belonged to no one.

We had been there a month when two wagonloads of women came by our barracks. We were washing clothes. The soldiers told their drivers we had no money, and they should continue to the main garrison. We grew restless. I remembered Tía Mercedes describing soldiers who came to town as "fleas in search of a dog."

That afternoon the soldiers rechained our ankles—three men to a chain—and locked us in. Throughout the long evening and night, we grabbed our groins while the federales whooped with pleasure.

During the night Saltillo yelled, "I can smell the women!" He stood, yanking the other two men up with him. Saltillo tore off his uniform. No one said anything while the naked Saltillo slammed himself back and forth against the door. He moaned into the raw wood until he finished.

On easier days I dared hope Rafael Castillo had been right. The lawyer's promise of an escape to Arizona seemed possible. If I grew careless, my family's faces slid into my head. I saw Hector's impatience with the ranch, and Andrés making fun. As always, Mother's face threatened to destroy me. From clouds up high I saw the Durcal ranch. Moro and Sueño. I kissed the sweetness of my past and vowed to reclaim it.

WITHOUT NOTICE, THE sergeant entered the barracks at dawn and told us we were going to Guaymas. Criminals from all over Sonora were being shipped out of the state. We bartolina soldiers were to escort them and stop anyone from escaping—even though our rifles were still unloaded.

On horseback, the sergeant and his assistant ordered us to "double-step." Balancing the Remington on his knee, he warned, "The one who runs, dies."

Our legs burning, our shoulders cut raw, we arrived at the seashore in the afternoon. We weren't allowed food or water until we had set up camp. A group of federales set up security against desertions. The town was off limits to bartolina soldiers.

The news left the men evil-tempered. To avoid them, I volunteered Charco and myself to care for the horses, a pair of godforsaken saddle-bruised geldings.

Using strips of coarse blanket, Charco and I brushed the horses' coats to a bright sheen. We untangled their manes, cleaned their bit-torn mouths, greased their fly-bitten ears, and stood them in ocean water to ease their swollen splints.

In Guaymas I saw the ocean for the first time. Charco laughed when I tasted the water to find out how salty it was. All my life I had heard of the port of Guaymas. Everything new to Sonora had sailed through this endless flatness that moved even as it stood still. My brother Hector spoke of *crossing* the seas?

With federales watching over us, bartolina soldiers were to sleep in the open until the prisoners arrived. I gave the sea my complete attention, clocking its every change. The sky, an endless sheet of blue, commanded the water beneath. In the morning the water was green, later turquoise, then black with stars bouncing over the top.

One afternoon while eating fresh mojarra cooked over coals, we heard a voice announce, "Here they come!"

In the distance, beneath a cloud of dust, I saw a horde marching toward us. Soldiers with rifles kept the lines moving. Charco elbowed me and pointed to a wagon that inched alongside the group. Some immense weight pitched the wagon way over to one side.

"Ombligo!" We dropped the steaming fish and ran toward the wagon.

Bullets pinged around us. We hit the ground, keeping our arms high in the air. Looking back, I saw the sergeant had unsheathed his pistol and was yelling for his horse.

A piercing whistle came from the wagon. Ombligo waved at the sergeant to stop. "Son míos!" he called.

Ombligo reined in the mules and hurried down. Huaraches dragging, he waddled toward us, all the while waving his arms at the officers behind us. He scooped us up by the collar, pressed our heads into his warm chest and pinned us to him until the sergeant lowered his gun.

The smell of Ombligo brought tears to my eyes. "They said you were dead," I mumbled into his shirt front.

"You left me!" cried Charco, angrily. His narrow blue eyes softened when Ombligo removed our caps and ran his hands over our shaved heads.

"That's where I've been." Ombligo motioned to the human mass beside us. "They've rounded them up by rail, cart, or foot."

Charco looked. "Those aren't criminals," he said.

Turning, I saw Yaqui women walking with their bodies straight, their belongings balanced in bundles on top of their heads. Their children walked alongside them. Herded separately in the back, hands bound, were Yaqui males, some not older than twelve. Charco got set to run toward them.

Ombligo grabbed hold of Charco's neck. "No, Charquito. If the soldiers take you, you can't help them."

I looked closer at the worn faces, and saw not only Yaquis, but Mayos, Chinese, even Mexicans. "Help them? How?" I asked.

"Sometimes a few drops of water is enough," whispered Ombligo. "Be good soldiers and you'll find what to do. These soldiers haven't been too bad. The children have been able to keep up."

The mounted sergeant trotted over to us. Ombligo pushed us behind him. "Forgive me, Sergeant. These boys are from the Alamos bartolinas. They—"

The butt of a rifle knocked me to the ground. Chest out, arms by his side, Charco stood still and waited for horse and rider to turn so the sergeant could kick him in the chest as well.

"Back to your wagon," he ordered Ombligo.

On all fours, we scrambled back to our troop.

OUR FIRST TASK as soldiers was to count and separate Mexicans, Chinese, and Indians. The Chinese totaled a dozen. The sergeant ordered them shackled and assigned Charco and another soldier to guard them over by the loading dock from where all prisoners were to be shipped the next day.

The rest of us were ordered to wait. Finally an older man in a fancy military uniform arrived and loudly proclaimed before the soldiers and prisoners, "Enemies of the state, present yourselves."

Everyone was silent while the federales marshaled the twenty or so Mexicans over to a small cell. I saw their bruised faces and torn lips.

"They've been tortured," I said to Saltillo.

Saltillo said, "In a month they'll beg for the firing squad."

"Why?"

"They're going to the sugarcane plantations in the Valle Nacional." Saltillo spat. "No one returns from there."

"What did they do?" I asked.

Saltillo shrugged. "Díaz has spies everywhere. The fools probably wrote something and were turned in."

We moved toward the Indians. Adult males were separated from the women and children, who were then ushered into a temporary corral. There we fed them a sour pozole, watery beans, and rice. We had no milk for the children. Some had been sick, all had been thirsty.

MY CHANGE OF name from Durcal to Robles has been a blessing—it frees my eyes, loosens my hands. The silence of examined women, the unflinching faces of children being searched, the cracked lips filled with dried blood, the dust-covered eyelashes, the dragging legs would have haunted Alejo Durcal.

Durcal could not have searched the women's bundles for weapons the way I can. He would have been ashamed of the pleasure he felt as his hands checked beneath skirts. He would not have suspected children, nor would he have guessed that spoons, tin cups, strips of rope could become weapons. No, Durcal could not have tightened slip knots, could not have cursed at or pushed those who fell behind.

And that first night as the bartolina soldiers hungrily prowled among the women, Alejo Durcal would have tried to stop them. Instead, Alejo Robles shut his eyes and joined them.

ALEJO DURCAL WOULD have remained loyal to the Yaqui. He would have remembered the Yaqui legend Tacho taught him. According to this legend the little girl, the prophet Yomumuli, translated the words from the talking tree. Those words warned of the coming of the white man and the railroad. Sadly, Durcal would have seen the dark part he played in that legend, a legend that saw the Yaquis expelled from their own land.

14

The state of Nayarit

OUR ORDERS ARE TO MARCH SOME TWO HUNDRED PRISONERS from the port of San Blas to Tepic. One hundred sixty kilometers. Every day we move, sleep, eat in the slime of hot heavy rain. The sun that has blistered my face and cracked my hands hangs powerless over this wet jungle, turning the rain into steam that rises from our bodies and from the earth.

When I touch myself, my hands touch a strange body—a body that allowed its ugly hunger to feed itself on unprotected women. The beard on my face—no time for shaving—is thick with blood. Here in Nayarit mosquitos have teeth. A raw rash has claimed my groin, neck, and waist. My uniform falls loose around my hips, the pants legs drag through the mud.

Bartolina soldiers must move the prisoners through a narrow ravine the rains have cut through the jungle. We've placed the prisoners in the center with old people, women, and children in front. Male prisoners are more docile when they can see their families.

Charco and I guard women and children. I force myself to avoid their faces, blur them into a silent mass that we must roll across the mud. I march to the sound of sandal and boot sliding in and out of the muddy trail.

Behind us Saltillo's group drives men—Yaqui, Mexican, Chinese. Sometimes we can hear beatings, and I ask myself, would I prefer a bullet? Then I remember when I was a prisoner. And I can't recall ever preferring a bullet to prison. Even now, I think if I were those men, I would do what they're doing—choose the marching with the beatings over death. I prefer being a soldier to being a prisoner. So does Charco, and that's why he is angry.

Saltillo says there's always a worse place than the one you're in.

And if we imagine such a place, then our place isn't so bad. That is of little comfort. Why must we choose between bad and worse? Who sets up the choices?

My instinct tells me that if we can imagine a worse place, we'll make sure someone ends up there. That must be how evil places get started. That's how Yaquis got chained—someone thought of a worse situation than his own, then he created it.

Above us, the federales ride along the banks of the ravine. They demand we give them the prisoners who are too weak to keep the pace. I busy myself with my boot as a soldier hands over an old man to the federales. No one looks as they drag him into the jungle. Rain mutes the reports of rifles. The line of prisoners quickens its pace. Federales know how to make us move. Each time that happens, I say, *Alejo, you have a mother.* I call her face into my head, connect her to the ranch, to my brothers, to Sonora, and I return by land over the mountains and through the jungle—back to me.

As always, after a shooting Charco locks his eyes to mine. *Run.* I shake my head. Not now. Every morning his blue eyes sweep the surrounding jungle. His look is easy to read. Yes, I answer, if we could climb out of the ravine, past the cordon of federales, we could disappear into that thickness. They'll never find us if we stay on our bellies. The bartolinas taught us how to lie still.

We carry old Mausers to shoot whoever tries to escape. We'll never fire them. The women will never leave their children, and the males are hobbled, hands tied behind their backs. The federales with their Remingtons are watching us.

Saltillo says we're the only ones they worry about escaping. He calls us the suicide squad. If the Yaquis hit anyone, it will be us. If we run, the Remingtons will pick us off.

The allotted eight-day march to Tepic is in its tenth and final day. We're late because of the rain and because we stopped for funerals. Funerals for children.

When the federales complained about stopping, the sergeant was angry. "If we don't let them bury their young, we'll be fighting women too." The federales blame him for the delay. They're not from Sonora. They don't understand Yaquis and burials. Yaquis and religion. Yaquis and God.

The women carry their few belongings in knapsacks. Yet every child they've buried has had several Yaqui rosaries resting on its chest. Those little wooden beads that mean so much appear out of nowhere. Even here, Yaquis keep their faith. How? The padrinos and madrinas of the dead babies are untied long enough to dress the child and dig the grave.

Charco and I volunteered to stay behind while the Yaquis finished their burials. The federales let us help with the first few. But the babies kept dying. After that, the federales decided it was taking too long. They slid down the ravine and snatched the dead babies. The sound of rain slapping leaves drowned out the women's cries. God, why do you let this continue?

Control yourself, Charco. I argue with Charco that he is not a *torocoyori,* a Yaqui traitor who has gone over to the enemy. I remind him of Ombligo's words that we can help them best by being good soldiers. Charco says there are no good soldiers.

We cook in the morning. The federales have the better food. They give us their leftovers, and we give ours to the prisoners. The beef jerky got wet, and now it's full of maggots. It takes too long to cook garbanzo or beans, so we eat atole, bananas, and coconuts.

The midday sun disappears behind dark clouds that gather one over the other until the entire sky turns black. Whips of lightning rip open the darkness and release fat drops that cuff down branches and flood the trail.

Panicked voices scream, "Tromba!" The entire line stops. All order disappears.

We stand paralyzed, blinded by an endless sheet of water. In minutes a muddy paste rises to our knees. The federales run for cover. Guards and prisoners stumble into each other looking for higher ground. Charco and I see our chance. We ditch our heavy rifles. Barefoot, he climbs swiftly up the muddy bank.

I follow, but the soaked earth collapses under my feet. On his belly, Charco reaches down to pull me up. His eyes scan something over my shoulder. He points to a woman behind me. I turn, see her drop her belongings as she lifts a child above her head. Next to her stands a second child pulling on her waist. Her possessions sink into the mud.

I reach for Charco's wrist. "Pull!" I holler at him.

His eyes stay with the woman as she searches for her knapsack and topples with both children into the mud. Charco frees himself from my grasp, then leaps over me into the mud. I'm halfway up the bank. Turning, I see him lift her body out of the paste. She finds the children and presses them into the muddy folds of her skirt.

Charco recovers our rifles and with his head, motions for me to keep going. He turns his back, and with long furious strides establishes distance between us. The bank is clean of federales. Prisoners and guards hug the walls of the ravine.

A woman stands lost in the rain. Charco encircles her with his arm around her shoulder and gently steers her toward the group. The sadness of his gesture overwhelms me. I start crying, blubbering over myself. Ashamed, I see my part in this terrible cruelty. I'm grateful for the rain and chaos that drown out my sobs. The moment vanishes. I let myself slide down the bank to join Charco.

The storm ends. The sun returns, and with it, human steam. Federales regroup and count heads. Children whimper. We make holes in coconuts so they can drink the milk.

I couldn't leave Charco, couldn't leave knowing that to my brother these prisoners are family. He did more than help the woman when he raised his arm to guide her back. He tore away the curtain I had used to separate me from the eyes of prisoners, from those I'd been trying not to notice.

I have kept myself alive with a secret belief that once I'd suffered enough, my life would be like before. Except without Father. I was to continue his dream. I had answers to my questions.

But now, one by one, the prisoners—each with independently

accusing eyes—crowd into my head. I cannot forget what my eyes tell me. I ask God, what blood runs through my veins? How can I still stand? Why wasn't I struck down in Guaymas when I joined the men who abused the women? If I did not make this situation, I made it worse when I took a faceless woman against her will.

After the tromba, everything is heavier and dirtier. Nothing is stronger than human stench. I want to smell horse and saddle, and I will yearn for that smell for the rest of the journey—all the way to a corral near the army post in Tepic where we deliver the prisoners.

WE EAT SUGARED bean tamales, our first unhurried meal in ten days. The sergeant calls us over to him. He stands on a wobbly platform and reads from a dirty piece of paper. The look on his face tells me he too can't believe the next directive. Men and women will remain separated, he announces. Chinese and Yaquis will stay together and build their own sleeping quarters under the eye of the federales. Enemies of the state must stay in the brig until they're taken to the Valle Nacional in Oaxaca to work the sugarcane plantations.

Soldiers mumble that they want no part of that. Saltillo repeats what he had said earlier, "No one ever returns from there."

The sergeant's gaze shifts nervously when he adds that bartolina men must guard the female prisoners. I want to scream. *We musn't be allowed near them.* I know why they're doing this. They know how we will exact payment. We will pay ourselves with the women. That's how they control us.

Charco elbows his way to the front, cups his hands, and calls down the sergeant. They move out of hearing range. Charco's beard is beginning to sprout. He is almost as tall as the sergeant. While Charco argues—chest out, eyes burning—I see a true son of José Durcal, known as a defender of Yaquis. But am I the son of José Durcal? Not when I fear death more than how I manage to live through this. What will we do to these people? Why don't I know? Why haven't I asked?

Charco returns, frowning. "He won't give me his Remington."

I laugh. "Are you innocent or just stupid?"

Charco paces before me. "He said I could stand guard. Are you with me?"

My chance arrives. "Of course, but you know these rifles are worthless."

Charco smiles, lifts his shirt. I see a knife handle.

"Who will that stop?" I ask.

"One will be enough."

I will guard women I abused barely ten days ago.

15

THE BARTOLINA SOLDIERS HAVE PITCHED CAMP. THEY COME to tease the women.

Armed with switches Charco cut for them, the women quickly form a circle, placing their young and old in the center. The stronger ones use the switches to keep the soldiers at bay.

Laughing, the men take turns trying to break the circle by pulling or lassoing their feet.

A balding bartolina soldier is determined to have one of the Yaqui women. He tosses a lasso at his selection, a pretty girl— maybe fifteen years old. She grabs the rope around her ankles, yanks it out of the soldier's hands, then chases after him. Before he can outdistance her, she loops the lasso under his feet, pulls, and brings him facedown into the dirt. Charco and I cheer and whistle. But the Yaqui girl stays mad. Before the soldier gets up, she's on top of him, keeps him down by driving both knees into his chest. She pummels his bearded face with her fists until two soldiers pull her off.

The soldier staggers to his feet and strikes her across the face.

Charco calls out, "Leave her alone!" He moves toward the soldier.

I grab Charco by the seat of his pants and reach down for the knife he's got tucked in his belt. "They'll kill you," I whisper. "Please, Charquito." I hold him tight until he agrees, then I toss the knife to the sergeant.

Someone yells, "Let her fight!"

They let the woman go and she lunges at the soldier.

They bite fingers, scratch faces, kick and swing with full force. Somehow the girl manages to stick her middle and index fingers inside his mouth and grabs hold of his cheek. He howls in pain as she spins him around, forces him to the ground, and gouges at his eyes. He kicks her off and manages to stand up. The two circle each other, panting loudly. Their clothes are nearly ripped off. Blood from her nose and lips colors her breasts. His eyes are swollen nearly shut. Bloody scratches X his chest.

They don't stop. We won't let them. We want more of what they're giving us. The day's exhaustion falls away. It falls off all of us. Yaquis, Mexicans, prisoners, soldiers. Yaquis and soldiers root for their own. The women are counting on her and the bartolina soldiers are betting on him. The federales hear our laughter and come to add their clapping and whistling.

The girl and the soldier crash again and roll on the ground. Every time the soldier pins her down, up she snaps and down he goes. He may be stronger, but he can't hold her long enough to end the fight.

Our noise catches the attention of the rurales that are stationed in Tepic. Wearing their coned hats, they stroll over with that casual laziness of power I've learned to recognize. They frown at us bartolina men and federales—filthy and ragged from days of marching over the mountains. The rurales' glare silences us. But the Yaquis continue their wild cheering.

The girl wins. She bests her opponent with a pair of short punches to his eyes. The soldier holds up his hands to signal enough.

A rural steps forward and strikes the back of her head with a rifle butt. Everyone is silent as she drops to her knees. A second blow breaks her front teeth. He drags her back to the circle. Two other rurales clap chains on the weary soldier's wrists and ankles and haul him away.

The girl howls angrily. Her yell fills the air that moments before held cries cheering her to victory or defeat.

THE CAMP SEEMS peaceful now. The women's circle is quiet. Ours—mine and Charco's—contains the only fire. The sergeant sleeps near us. Charco is angry at me for not letting him defend the girl. Her name is Luz María. Charco tried to help her after the fight, but the Yaqui women sent him away. He took fresh water to her anyway.

After the fight the captain of the rurales called for the sergeant. When the sergeant returned he asked if he could join Charco and me to watch the women. He told us his name was Gustavo Saldaña and asked that we call him that when talking to him. "I need to re-member it," he said.

The Saldañas are wealthy hacendados from northern Sonora. Gustavo told us that he studied in Europe and when he returned to Mexico, "my father bought me a commission with the state militia. You were my first troops." We laughed.

"What happened to your friend, the cabo?" asked Charco.

"He went home," Gustavo said. "I had to stay."

I remembered how my father had cursed hacendados for raising their children in Europe: "And then they bring them back to run the country with European ideas."

Gustavo told us, "I saw what lay ahead for me—the boring rou-tine of running the hacienda. I knew I had done nothing, just study and travel. I said I wanted to work." He spat into his hands. "I'm no good at this."

*   *   *

LAST NIGHT I thought the rurales had reprimanded Gustavo for letting one of his men fight the girl. But it was more than that. This morning while the women were trying to start cookfires, a handful of rurales moved through the women's circle grabbing boys who looked ten to twelve years old away from their mothers.

They ordered the youngsters to form a column and prepare to march. Any woman who held on to her child was immediately beaten by two, three rurales. The plan worked. To spare his mother a beating, a boy obeyed. I saw that people who love someone can always be controlled.

Stunned, unable to do anything, Charco, Gustavo, and I watched them break up families. "Why hurt them more?" I asked.

"The rurales want to break the Yaqui women," said Gustavo. "They say that if they control the women, they can control the Yaqui men." He seemed unconvinced.

"Cowards! Gustavo, get us guns," Charco begged. He slapped his thighs and circled the sergeant with wide steps.

"We can't stop rurales, Charco. They report only to President Díaz."

"We can't be part of this," I said. "Help us escape. You can do that."

"Yes!" Charco agreed, clapping his hands.

Gustavo spoke as if to a child. "Charco, the rurales would torture, then hang us. I'll find the right time. Right now, you two stay here. Don't move, no matter what."

He walked toward Saltillo and other bartolina soldiers. "You men watch the Yaqui boys. Stay with them."

The Yaqui boys were brave. They kept their silence all morning. Charco stood at attention and faced them, and, in a voice I never knew he had, sang,

> *Alcuna te vichaca sehuahui vichaca*
> *tabuico sea taliqua*
> *tabuico sea taliqua*

cenu cutataca machiliata tuyule
cenu cutataca yoyuquemta tuyule

Not one boy turned to look as Charco told,

We found that flower while looking for a different one.
It is a tree that loves the light of day.
It is a tree that likes enchanted rain.

The song forced me to remember how free I had thought I would be once I had killed my father's murderer. I had found *this* bitter flower while looking for a different one.

At noon, federales took the enemies of the state out of the brig and lined them up behind the boys. Some enemies were so weak they couldn't lift the chains around their ankles, so the soldiers had to drag them. These men were bound for the dreaded sugarcane plantations in Oaxaca. What could these enemies have written?

Rurales oversaw federales, who in turn oversaw bartolina soldiers as they marched the Yaqui boys and the enemies of the state to a waiting train. If the boys were afraid, I couldn't tell. It was the bartolina soldiers who seemed terrified of leaving. They craned their necks, and hollered at Gustavo to keep them in Tepic.

"They should be frightened," said their former sergeant, sadly shaking his head at them. "They know they will replace those who die before they reach Oaxaca. I tried, but there's nothing I can do," he said, unashamed of his tears. "Nothing."

The rurales let Gustavo keep two dozen bartolina soldiers to supervise the remaining Yaquis. He asked that Charco and I be counted as his assistants. "They allowed me two assistants," he said. "I chose you."

He also told us that the Yaqui boys were going to Mexico City to be sold to labor contractors from Yucatán or Tabasco. "Twelve-year-old boys can be sold as male adults," he said.

My friend the strong Saltillo was ordered to go with the boys. I waved goodbye, but he never looked back. I know I let him down when I went to join Charco in guarding the women. Saltillo had warned, "Be careful, Alejo, you live in a dangerous country."

To me, Saltillo was the bravest of us bartolina soldiers. When he marked his space, no one crossed it. Seeing Saltillo march with his head down behind the Yaqui boys sickened me. If they did this to him, what could I hope for?

I realized the importance of being Gustavo's assistant. Gustavo was spared having to go to the Valle Nacional because his father was an hacendado. Charco and I were spared because of Gustavo.

I NEVER LIKED to fatten cattle before selling them. I remembered this as we were ordered to increase the prisoners' rations.

The Yaquis are being fattened before we bring them to the capital, where buyers will look them over.

The prisoners receive other privileges. Soap and water. Some days the women are allowed to cook for their men. Still, nothing breaks the women's silence. Luz María still refuses to talk to Charco. He still takes water to her.

The rurales' plan is working. Sending the boys away hurt all of us. At night, a sadness creeps through the camp and covers me. My mother's face returns and I see my life with fresh eyes. I see no future for myself and my past is blurred. I live in one long narrow day, putting one foot in front of the other and working constantly not to see.

Charco, Gustavo, and I continue to guard the women. That's good. The men stay away.

Gustavo has finally found out how far we're going. Yucatán.

"Where is that?" asks Charco.

"On the other side of Mexico," answers Gustavo. He keeps reassuring us that he's planning our escape. We have no choice but to trust him.

We wake to calls announcing, "The trains are coming!" We're

ordered to prepare the prisoners. Federales hurry the women along with a cruel promise: "You're going to find your sons."

Mexico City

I haven't seen much of the nation's capital. My orders are to stay with the prisoners.

We arrived with the Yaquis packed into cattle cars. Tired federales and bartolina soldiers stood in admiration as fresh, precision soldiers formed a human corral to escort the Yaquis to an army post. The soldiers' uniforms were spotless. Boots too. The men moved as if commanded by a single mind. I remembered the inside of Father's watch.

I said to Gustavo that Mexico must have more soldiers than any other country in the world, and he said that President Díaz needed every one of them to watch his back.

When I first arrived I had trouble breathing. I couldn't fill my lungs. The soldiers had talked of the city's thin air, so I kept reminding myself to breathe. Even when I did, I felt I hadn't. The cold night air cut through our uniforms.

It's clear we bartolina soldiers aren't considered much better than the Yaquis, whose clothes are even thinner than ours. Only federales get blankets.

We feed the prisoners twice a day—morning and noon. We eat three meals of beans, rice, and corn tortillas. Yaquis get no rice. Corn tortillas make them and me sick. In Sonora we eat flour tortillas and feed corn to hogs.

Charco and I were on guard duty one afternoon when Gustavo showed up with a man dressed in a full suit and homburg hat. With them was a group of women also dressed up. The dandy's name was Javier Alonso. He was Gustavo's age, and like Gustavo had studied in Europe. Gustavo and Javier spoke in French of cities they knew.

"The ladies came to see your famous wild Yaquis," said Javier. "Tell that boy to bring them closer."

Charco stood between the visitors and the Yaquis, and he refused to move.

The group moved around Charco. All they saw was hungry, tired men and women huddling to keep warm. The more curious visitors put their faces against the bars.

"Please step back," I said, annoyed at their staring.

They ignored me.

Suddenly the women started screaming and running toward the door. I thought they had been attacked. Charco. He had dropped his pants and was pissing at them.

The women tried to dodge out of reach, but Charco's wide arc gave their skirts a solid soaking.

The angry Javier demanded, "Beat this man!"

Gustavo said, "You have my word. This soldier will be punished. But please, let's not offend the ladies with violence."

Turning to me, Gustavo said, "Put him in chains."

I moved toward Charco. He pulled up his shirt, giving everyone a full view of his nakedness. The women renewed their screaming.

Gustavo begged Javier, "My friend, help me protect the ladies. Escort them out, please!" Speechless with rage, the man had no option but to leave.

After they left, Gustavo came back and laughed until he cried. I liked that he had protected Charco instead of siding with people of his class.

That night Gustavo invited us to a brothel. He told us not to worry about money, he would pay for our night out. It wasn't far, he said. In fact, it was a small room in back of a residence near the barracks. And there was only one woman. Her name was La Francesa.

Charco and I bathed out of a bucket and put on shirts Gustavo had found for us.

After Charco was dressed, he announced, "I'm not going, Alejo." His face seemed terribly calm.

"Of course you're going," I said. "Women at last, Charco! You've been talking about them for months."

He pointed to where the Yaquis were kept. "I can't leave them." I laughed. "They'll be here when we return."

Charco sat back on his haunches and stopped talking. It didn't matter that I tried to pull him up or that I told him he was afraid of women. He remained as he was—eyes and ears closed.

Gustavo arrived, and he couldn't budge Charco either. As we were leaving, Charco rose and returned to the Yaquis.

That night was the first of two I went to the brothel. The first time I was too nervous and stayed outside with other soldiers and waited for Gustavo. The soldiers let him go first because he was a sergeant.

The second night I entered La Francesa's cold room—bare walls and a narrow bed. The room smelled of lamp oil mixed with rose water. A dusty kerosene lamp on the floor gave off more smoke than light.

La Francesa's large breasts were hidden by a man's sweater. Over that, she wore a long robe. She was naked from the waist down, except for socks. Money in hand, I unbuckled my belt, sat on the bed, and let her pull off my pants. "You're not ready," she said. She rubbed her hands together, then bent down and cupped my parts with a warm soft hand.

"Are you sick?" she asked, looking at me.

"I'm worried about my brother," I said. That's all I could think of to say. *Ana María.*

She kissed me on the mouth and took the money Gustavo gave me.

I returned to Charco and his Yaquis. I told him I hated him and his prisoners, and he nodded as if he knew what I meant.

He's been nursing a skinny, white-haired man with a severe cough. Whenever he can, Charco brings him hot yerba buena tea. The man looks sixty. Charco calls him Abuelo, and says the man has no family. Charco stays busy helping Luz María and Abuelo.

At night, I sleep on the cold dirt floor next to Charco and think of La Francesa's large breasts and full mouth. I won't think of Ana María again. She makes me weak.

Each day that we remain in Mexico City I see less. If I go for a walk outside the army post, images of the Yaquis go with me. I can't escape the faces of the prisoners. I see their silence. Their waiting. I hear Abuelo's cough. I see the pretty Luz María and her broken teeth. The mothers who lost their sons. All go with me. I hate them when I'm with them, then hate myself when I leave them.

We're with the Yaquis constantly, except when labor contractors come to look them over. Gustavo makes sure we never see this and sends us to the laundry to scrub clothes.

I want the Yaquis to fight. Tacho said they were Sonora's fiercest warriors. He told me how they charged bare-chested up a hill and threw themselves against the mouth of a cannon until they clogged it with their flesh. But then, Tacho also said their land is their strength. That must be why here, in the army post, hungry, cold, away from land and family, they seem to wait for death.

That must be what Charco saw the night Gustavo invited us to the brothel. I envy Charco for knowing what to do.

Gustavo took us out of the barracks for a walk this morning. "I want to be where no one can hear us," he said. "Saltillo and the nine others escaped."

Charco and I clapped.

"Wait," he said, his face working for control. "They had two days of freedom before rurales and agents caught and shot them. They caught three in a brothel and tortured them until they gave the whereabouts of the rest."

"Saltillo can't be dead," I said.

"They were foolish," said Gustavo. "They lost their heads. Do you still want to desert? It means a firing squad if we're caught."

Charco and I nodded.

"Then listen closely. A friend of my father's said Yucatán is the safest place for us to disappear. It's far enough away from the capital to get lost. Our big problem will be getting on board the steamer from Yucatán back to Veracruz. Security is tight. We'll be able to buy false papers. He warned me not to get caught buying them. It means jail. But if I can get myself back here to Mexico City, he guarantees me safe passage to Sonora. Do you want to try?"

"Would you go if we didn't go with you?" asked Charco.

"I have to," said Gustavo, eyes lowered. "I've written to my father and told him I'm coming home."

"Take me with you," I said, thinking of Castillo's plan to send me to Arizona.

"Take me too," said Charco.

The port of Progreso, Yucatán

I'm with Charco and Gustavo in the back of a hot empty cantina. The cantina sits on a pier that reaches deep into the ocean. We're drinking horchata. The cool sweet rice water tames the heat that begins before the sun rises and stays after it has disappeared.

We left the capital on the transoceanic railroad bound for Veracruz. There we loaded the Yaqui prisoners on a cargo steamer for an ugly five-day journey to Yucatán.

We are deserters waiting for Anginas, an old Maya who has promised to smuggle us to Veracruz. From there we will find our way back to Sonora. Our plan is to disappear before the army misses us. If caught, we'll be shot—like Saltillo. No trial, no hearing, no questions.

Through a glassless window I watch the white-hot sand of a beach that seems to go on forever. Crowds of coconut palms face the bay. At the far end of the pier, hundreds upon hundreds of bales of henequen wait to be loaded onto a steamboat whose flag I don't recognize. I ask Gustavo about the flag and he tells me it's English. He knows a lot and is surprised we know so little.

Gustavo is nervous. He lowers his head every time someone looks in. This amuses Charco and me. We're comfortable being criminals.

We wear huaraches and white cotton shirts and pants to look like Yucatán workers. A barber gave us Maya haircuts, but our hair wants to stand up. We're using the straw hats to flatten our hair. Also, Gustavo's bone-white feet look strange. The sun has never touched them. The Yucatán sun has darkened Charco's skin, making his eyes bluer.

Anginas sent us to a photographer, who took our pictures. No questions asked, not even our names. He said he would give them to Anginas, who promised us papers that prove we're free men. We left our belongings with the photographer.

Anginas warned that if the police caught us without identification, we could be sold as slave labor to the henequen plantations. In fact, he said, the police could make the government bid against the planters for us.

Short and stocky, Anginas barely reaches my chest. His beaked nose juts out from busy dark eyes. He moves quickly, barely lifting his sandals off the ground. When he walks, he leads with a shoulder pushing against an unseen obstacle. When standing, he sways in all directions until he decides where he's going and then he darts off.

But what is most remarkable about this strange man is his voice. When it comes out, it doesn't sound human. His sound starts deep inside him, and a growl is somehow formed into words.

I first saw him at the San Ignacio train station. We were delivering a chain of Yaquis bound for the Molina plantation. Anginas was dashing up and down an old brick ramp looking into the soldiers' faces. I thought he was some old crazy until he put his face up to me and in his raspy voice asked, "Mejicano, where are you from?"

Without thinking I answered, "Sonora."

"Don't worry, I can get you home."

Next he fixed on Charco and trotted after him. "Uxmal!" said Anginas. "Save your people!" Charco ignored him, but Anginas kept calling him, "Uxmal! Come with me."

Gustavo tried to shoo him off. This was the day we had chosen to desert, and the little man was attracting the attention of other soldiers.

Again, in his most military manner, Gustavo pushed the old man. But Anginas grabbed the front of his shirt and pulled. "Mejicano, I can help you escape," he whispered in his torn voice.

"Get away," ordered Gustavo. Charco and I prepared to move the pest.

"I'll be waiting," he said to us.

He scurried away, but not too far. I felt his eyes on us as we signed the Yaquis over to labor contractors. That's what Gustavo and I did, hand them over. Charco accompanied Abuelo and Luz María as far as he could. Then he joined us, and from a distance we watched the contractors and their helpers count the prisoners as they pushed them onto open-air cattle cars pulled by a smoking engine that belched, then slithered off into Yucatán's interior.

It's possible to feel death.

I felt mine when I delivered Yaquis to men who speak the language I speak.

I turned over Sonora men and women I have known all my life to men who paid sixty-five pesos a head for them.

Sixty-five.

My father had tried to make me curious about my country and failed. Now I'd crossed my homeland, ocean to ocean, and my country poisons me. My ears listened for a word of hate from our prisoners. They voiced none. They emitted it.

Once we had delivered the Yaquis, our orders were to report to Mérida. Two weeks' leave with pay awaited us. The soldiers broke into clusters. Anginas lurched toward us, and we followed him behind a stone wall. Out of a sack, he pulled out the soft white pants and shirts we now wear.

"Before you put on these clothes, buy huaraches." His voice rumbled. I wondered if talking was painful to him. "Don't wear boots. The police will arrest you."

We accepted the clothes. I asked, "What do you want from us?"

"I'm always here when the train comes," he said. His eyes danced at some private joke. "I come to look for men like you, soldiers with shame, Mejicanos with shame who want to run away." He smiled, victorious with his answer.

We said nothing. Gustavo tried to pay him for the clothes, but Anginas waved the money away.

He lowered his voice. "Go to Mérida for your huaraches. You have big feet. They won't remember you there." He was enjoying his secret. "Go here for your pictures." He pressed a piece of paper into Gustavo's hand. "When your pictures are ready, you'll have your papers."

Impatient, Gustavo asked, "If it's not money, then what do you want?"

Anginas seemed to be waiting for that question. He stepped back as if to see better. His black eyes settled on our faces.

"I will show you my Yucatán and you will tell the world what you saw."

16

IT'S NOON OF THE SAME SAME DAY. OUTSIDE THE WATER HAS turned from blue to silver. Anginas is late.

Gustavo calls us fools for trusting Anginas. We quarrel. We don't understand his suspicion of the old man, and remind him that we have no way to get aboard the steamer without papers.

Angrily, Gustavo says, "Why should he help us? We forget we're Mexicans, which, from an Indian point of view, makes us enemies."

"No!" we shout. I am surprised by the feeling behind the word. Have we forgotten the Yaquis we delivered to the labor contractors?

Gustavo wants to leave. He plays with his hat. "As a Maya, Anginas has no reason to trust us, and every reason to turn us in to the secret police." Gustavo says fifty years ago the Mayas fought a bloody caste war against criollos, the landed whites of Yucatán. "I've heard my father say that the Mayas nearly won."

I ask, "Why did they lose?"

"I don't know what happened," admits Gustavo.

Charco asks, "Was it the fault of Mexicans?"

"And the Díaz government. And the fault of criollos and Americanos and everyone else," Gustavo says.

We share a silence.

"No," says Charco. "He won't turn us in. He said he wants to show us his Yucatán. And I want to see it."

"True," I say. "He said he wants us to tell the world what we saw."

Another silence.

I'm thinking that Yucatán doesn't feel like Mexico. Mérida, the white city, truly is all white. The men's clothing, the women's huipiles, the houses and their lime rooftops. White.

I imagine that from up high, Mérida's long narrow streets would look like animal ribs after buzzards and sun were finished with them. Strange that the land that surrounds Mérida is almost solid rock. Flat, barren. No trees. We are told that only henequen can grow here.

ANGINAS ARRIVES. HE walks by the cantina a few times before he peeks inside and motions us to follow him. Outside, the sun's rays burn firm, merciless. Gustavo and I hurry to keep up with the old man, who has a tight hold of Charco's arm. Charco seems pleased by this and looks back at Gustavo with pride.

Anginas walks us toward the countless bales on the pier and points. "Do you know what these cost?"

"Who cares?" Gustavo asks impatiently. "Have you brought our papers?"

"First," says Anginas, "answer that question."

"It has to do with the Yaquis," says Charco, more to Gustavo than to anyone.

Anginas's laugh is a loud wheeze. He gives Charco a playful tap on the cheek. "Uxmal, you understand!" He grows serious. "When the sun weakens, accountants will come to count the bales before they're loaded on board."

That makes sense. In the short time we have been standing, my head and eyes feel the effects of the sun. Its rays are crueler than any I've known.

Anginas walks to the bales and peels back some of the protective sacks. We see bright yellow fibers. "Henequen!" he bellows.

Gustavo scoffs at Anginas. "You mean *hennequin*. The word is French. It means ingrate."

Anginas says, "To us the word means suffering."

"To the rest of the world, it means the finest rope ever made," says Gustavo.

I remember the ropes Father brought home years ago.

"But to the henequen kings it means one cent per pound in gold," announces Anginas. He waits for our response.

I look at the number of bales and see tons.

The old man inches closer to Charco. "Criollos murder Mayas for this. Now you're bringing Yaquis." His short fingers fumble to pull out some henequen, but the fibers won't give. He holds his hands out to us anyway.

Gustavo moves away. "If you won't give us the papers, we'll find another way to get on the steamer."

Anginas finds this funny. His laugh is a rumbling growl. "I want to see you prove you're free men."

"But we are free men," says Gustavo. He has become a sergeant again and is dealing with an insubordinate underling. To Charco and me he says, "We can prove we have two weeks' leave."

"Go if you want, Gustavo," says Charco softly. He lowers his eyes. "We're staying with him."

I realize my brother has spoken for me and that I will do what he wants. Frowning, Gustavo stays.

Charco blurts out, "Anginas, did you fight in the war?"

"I'm still at war," he answers. He peers at us, turning his head waiting for more questions.

"He means the caste war," says Gustavo curtly.

Anginas becomes very serious. "I continue to fight the caste war. Years ago, I was one of the Talking Crosses," he says proudly. He laughs at us. "I don't speak in riddles to you." From inside his shirt he pulls out a small wooden cross tied to a string around his neck. "You've seen these?"

We haven't.

"Years ago, Mayas listened to Chan Santa Cruz. The Holy Cross. From the Cross came the courage to push the evil *dzules* into the sea. When I was a young man in Quintana Roo, a mestizo priest chose me to be one of the voices that called for war. I joined the Crusoob. One cross became many and soon we were everywhere."

"You do speak in riddles," says Gustavo.

Anginas starts to laugh, but a heavy cough overtakes him. He spits. "Our temples housed these crosses, which spoke to people when they came to worship."

"You tricked them?" I ask.

He's offended. "No. The crosses talked. They awakened our warriors' courage, not their rage. Courage builds. Rage destroys. Our voices cleared the vision of our warriors to look beyond the dead enemy to a time when Mayas once again lived on their own land."

"The criollos are still here. The Mayas fought and died for nothing," says Gustavo.

"We all fought," says Anginas, apparently not bothered by the sun nor by Gustavo. "The henequen kings took me prisoner. They let me live, but they put burning coals down my throat. As a lesson to the rebels I was dragged from village to village wearing a sign that said, 'Talking Cross.' " He rests his throat a moment. "Others had their hands cut off. I was fortunate. I learned to speak again." He sways back and forth, then asks, "Do you know of our fight?"

We look to Gustavo to answer. "I know it was long ago. My father said Mayas had most of the state. What happened?"

"All Yucatán was ours except Mérida and Campeche. It will be ours again. What happened? We Mayas must obey the seasons, and so we stopped the fighting to plant corn. Our families must be fed. Tell your father that we wait to replace the men we lost. Soon we will take up arms again."

"Are Mexicans your enemies?" asks Charco.

Anginas touches Charco's face with a gnarled hand. "No. Díaz sided with the henequen kings. But Mexicans aren't our enemies. They too have lost their country." He points to the English flag on the steamboat. "Díaz is giving it away to the señores distinguidos."

Gustavo stiffens. "Careful. This is dangerous talk. Mexico is a sovereign state. All its citizens are free."

Anginas laughs, shakes his head. "You have not seen the kingdoms of Yucatán. You have much to see, and much to tell the world."

MÉRIDA SWELLS OUT from the large plaza at its center. Around the plaza are colonial homes, government offices, and a large stone cathedral with two large towers. Despite the dozens of shade trees and benches, few men linger about. As we cross the square, I look for signs of the secret police Anginas says are everywhere.

"It's too hot for the women," says Anginas, explaining the plaza's emptiness. We follow his quick-trot step. "I'm looking for Pacal, a driver for the plantation. He will take us inside."

We exchange looks. "We're not going inside," says Gustavo. To us he says, "This has gone far enough." We ignore him and follow Anginas.

Pacal is nowhere to be found. Anginas walks toward the church and continues walking along its outside wall. His busy eyes search for something in particular.

Excited, he calls to us, "Mejicanos!" He points to a stone high above his head. We follow his lead and see that one of the stones has a design carved on it.

"Templo Maya," he says proudly.

We study the design on the stone, a half-circle with a dot in the center.

"What does this mean?" I ask him.

He stares at us as if he can't believe my question. "Everything," he says finally, and smiling, he disappears into the church.

Gustavo says, "Indians were forced to make churches out of their temple stones. It's the same everywhere."

"Not in Sonora," says Charco proudly.

The church is dark and cool. I feel the skin tighten on my face. We wait in the entrance until our eyes grow accustomed to the dark. I am surprised by the poverty of the church. The main altar is almost bare.

Anginas is not here to pray. He darts in and out of the side alcoves until he emerges with a thin, young male. Pacal. He looks to be about fourteen years old or younger when compared to Charco and me.

They speak in Maya. Pacal looks us over. His narrow, slanted eyes rest on Charco. He approves. About me, Pacal shows no response. He frowns at Gustavo. Anginas scolds, and Pacal shrugs. It's obvious Pacal will do as he's told.

We follow them out of the church and down one narrow street, then another, and another. We're lost, which is what they want.

We stop in front of a food stand. Anginas says, *"Itz, Put."* The vendor gives us sweet potatoes and papaya. He sprinkles chile over the fruit. The combination of hot and sweet makes me hungry. We eat until we can eat no more. Anginas motions to Gustavo to pay. He reaches into the pouch tied around his waist and tosses out some coins.

In back of the food stand is a tavern. Its front has no wall, allowing what air there is to run through. Half a dozen men are drinking and playing cards on wooden tables.

Anginas pulls us aside, reaches into his shirt, and pulls out a small bundle. He hands me three sets of papers.

The names mean nothing. Our pictures are glued to the top left

of each document. I sort mine out. I look strange in the Maya hair-
cut. Charco has never seen himself in a picture. He's happy with
what he sees.

Gustavo asks, "You're giving these to us now?"

Anginas says, "Pacal was ordered to find free men who know
about cattle. Look here." He points to a square that says: "Deudas:
Ninguna." He looks at Gustavo and dares him, "Those papers say
you're free. Go, if you want."

Charco and I watch a nervous Gustavo decide. He puts away the
papers and stays.

I think something is wrong. Cattle in Yucatán? In this heat?
What cattle could live here?

Anginas says, "Show the majocols the papers. They usually
don't even ask for them. They're celebrating the big henequen ship-
ment. Pacal will take us in with him tonight, when he drives the
majocols back to the hacienda. Each plantation has its private mule
car." Anginas turns to Gustavo. "Don't worry, Pacal drives in and
out all day. I work in the hospital."

"What's majocols?" I ask.

"Whippers," says Anginas, nodding toward the men at the tables. "Every plantation has them."

"To prevent uprisings," adds Pacal. He gestures to us to remove
our hats. We follow.

Pacal approaches a swarthy, broad-backed man who's squeezing
lemon over jicama. "I have the men you wanted."

The man ignores Pacal. He continues to squeeze the lemon half
even though the jicama is overflowing with juice.

"Señor majocol," repeats Pacal, "I found these men in the plaza.
They said they know about cattle."

Slowly, the majocol turns his head to Pacal and stares at the
young man's thin face. Pacal keeps his eyes down. I also lower my
eyes and lament my height.

The majocol squeezes the spent lemon over Pacal's head. The
men in the tavern stop their card game and watch. The majocol

drops the lemon over the boy's head, then covers the boy's face with his wide hand and squeezes.

Pacal moans, then buckles in pain.

"Martino, stop," says another man. He's also broad-backed, and tall. He stands and pries Pacal loose. "Go wait," he says to us, pointing to the back wall.

His arm around Pacal, Anginas leads us toward the farthest wall of the tavern, and we sit on the floor. Gustavo and I have trouble folding our legs beneath us, and we sit, knees to chest.

I cover Gustavo's white feet with my hat. He nods in gratitude. Our former sergeant's frightened. He probably wishes he had left. I side-glance at the old and young Mayas. Their faces are fearless. Anginas turns to me. "No tenga pena," he whispers. Again, his face draws me in.

How different we Sonora men look. Our hair, noses, eyes resemble the majocols'. The similarities shame me.

The tall man talks to the others. "Martino doesn't know when to stop. That's why the mayordomo fined him."

The man called Martino is sulking. He stares at the floor in front of him.

"Maybe the Indian died because he was sick," says a voice.

"We shouldn't have to pay if they're sick." This comment meets wide approval.

The tall man says, "My administrador counts to six between lashes." The man pulls out an imaginary watch and places it in front of him. "He signals to me with his finger, like this." He teases Martino by wiggling a little finger. "Then, *pas!*" He slams an open hand against the tabletop. "Fifteen lashes later, the man's back is full of praying lips."

"Do you soak the lash?"

"All night," says the tall man. "But you should use the six-second trick. It's scientific. The man's mind tortures him while he waits for the next lash. Sometimes they faint. The mind does it. I tell you, if you wait six seconds, you'll never have to give more than fifteen lashes." He nudges Martino. "And the peons won't die on you." He laughs till his stomach shakes.

Martino frowns and tosses some jicama into his mouth. "The mayordomo fined me five hundred pesos for a slave that was worth sixty-five. He pocketed the difference."

"If the peons rise again, the mayordomo will wish they'd let us majocols do our work," says a voice.

"That's right," says Martino, grabbing the muscle of his right arm. "We're all that stands between them and the Indian machete."

This meets wide approval.

Martino walks over to us and motions to Pacal, who jumps up immediately.

Martino points to Anginas. "Who is he?"

"Anginas, the hospital worker. You know him."

"Patrón," says Anginas to Martino. He pulls out his papers, but Martino focuses on us.

"You know about cattle?" We nod. "Let's see your papers." We give them to him. "Stand. Hold out your hands, palms up."

We obey. His thumbs test our calluses. I see him take in our height. He asks Gustavo, "Where did you learn about cattle?"

Gustavo answers, "I learned from my father when I was a boy."

"Where did you learn about cattle?"

Charco answers, "Born on a ranch."

"And you?"

"Born on a ranch too," I say.

He looks the papers over. I remember that we didn't bother to read them. I want to run. The entrance is far away. Now all the men look us over. I remember Anginas's words, "I want to see you prove you're free men."

Martino walks to the tall man and whispers to him. They agree about something. The tall man goes over to the tavern keeper and whispers in his ear. The tavern man is not pleased by what he hears. Frowning, he disappears into the kitchen.

Martino looks us over. He waves a thick index finger at us.

"Lies. You are not Yucatecos. I suspect you are deserters. From where, I'm not sure." To me and Charco he says, "Your accent is norteño." To Gustavo he says, "You," he pokes Gustavo's chest, "you with the white princess feet. Criollo?"

"We've done nothing," says Gustavo. "We are free men."

Martino yells, "Quick! Give me the name of your village." He snaps his fingers.

"Santa Cruz!" Charco calls out, his voice strong, sure.

"Santa María!" I say, following Charco's lead.

Gustavo stammers, then manages an unconvincing "San José."

Martino finds this very funny. He turns to the men. "No one from Santo Niño? What a shame we don't have La Sagrada Familia." They all laugh.

Martino folds and refolds the identity papers down to a small square, which he tosses back at Gustavo, hitting him in the face. Slowly Gustavo stuffs them into his pouch.

The tavern man comes out from the kitchen carrying several lengths of rope. My stomach and legs shake uncontrollably.

Martino takes the rope. "Turn around, free men."

"Stop!" says Gustavo. "This is a mistake. My name is Gustavo Saldaña . . ."

I see his head crash into the wall, then his body slowly slides down.

Martino flips Gustavo onto his stomach, straddles him, and while tying his wrists, warns us, "Make up your minds that you're going to be with me until I'm finished with you."

Charco and I surrender our hands. I hope my brother remembers to flex his wrists while they bind him. That way, the rope will be looser.

17

Hacienda San Jacinto, Yucatán

A BELL WAKES US. WE HAVE SPENT THE NIGHT LOCKED UP IN A small shed. They untied our hands, but ran a rope connecting Charco's, Gustavo's, and my neck. We can't lie down. The ends of the rope go out an opening in the shed and are tied to something solid outside.

Charco and I slept sitting straight up. Not Gustavo. All night he cursed Anginas. "The old Maya sold us."

Pacal unlocks the door. "Follow me." It is pitch-black outside. He carries a torch and waits while we relieve ourselves. Dawn must be hours away.

"Where?" asks Gustavo. He walks too fast, causing the rope to scrape our neck.

Pacal says, "To eat before I take you to Martino."

"You're breaking the law. I am a free man," says Gustavo.

I'm sorry for Gustavo. Last night his head bled after Martino pushed him against the wall.

"Don't escape," whispers Pacal. "You will only run to another hacienda and there you have no friends."

"You're not friends," says Gustavo. His voice is unpleasant, making everything worse.

"We're not bad." Pacal stops to hand us several hot corn tortillas. We eat in silence. A strange taste, but good. Gustavo takes a few bites and, frowning, gives us the rest. Pacal waits until we finish.

Gustavo must stop talking. He's making people notice us, forcing us to make our circle smaller. If we're to escape, we need the Mayas. We don't even know where we are.

We know last night when Martino brought us here, tied to the platform of a mule-drawn trolley, we crossed under a big archway and entered a place with an immense feel to it. It's not a ranch, it's more, but I couldn't see what the place looked like. I saw only a walk made of flat white stones.

Necks tied, we follow Pacal down a narrow alley. We stumble toward what looks like a main square lit by torches. The square is large and feels full of people. Silent people.

Pacal's torch joins other torches in the square. I was right. There are many people, and they're separated into groups and lined up several rows deep, facing the square. The square is outlined by a long arcade with tall arches. Against the night sky I see the roofline of a wide building. A government building? There's the dome of a chapel. Is this another town?

The torches give enough light for me to see a foreman of sorts walking up and down the rows calling out names. To each name, a voice answers. The caller of the roll carries a stick that looks like a walking cane. With it he swats those who take too long to answer.

Torches throw light and dark shadows across the faces of men and women. I see enough for me to identify eyes and cheekbones. Yaquis. Body numb, I pray God forgives me.

I move back to give Charco my vantage point. He sees, then, lips tight, asks, "Who is he?"

Pacal whispers, "The capataz. He assigns the workers."

Charco and I exchange glances. I know his next question. "Yaquis?"

"Yes. Also Mayas, Mayos, Chinos, Coreanos."

Charco's eyes tell me, *We did this.*

Dawn begins as the long roll call ends. Two guards lead out four men to the middle of the square. The prisoners' feet are hobbled. I study the men. Yaquis. The square is empty except for a large rain barrel and the majocol from last night. Martino.

One of the foremen comes to the center. "Running away is forbidden. Failure to meet your daily quota of two thousand leaves is forbidden. Abuse of a henequen plant is forbidden. All fighting is forbidden."

Martino reaches into the barrel, takes out several thick, meter-long ropes, and tosses them onto the ground. He prods them with the tip of his shoe before choosing one, swinging it over his head until it whistles. When he's ready, he signals the guards to remove the first man's shirt. The Yaqui holds his arms out, keeping the guards at bay, and rips off his own shirt, then gives his back to Martino. I close my eyes and count the blows. Fifteen.

Martino takes his time, making his movements large and visible to everyone. Eventually, all four prisoners lie before him. The square is silent. From nowhere, Anginas comes out and bends over them, checking their backs. He raises an arm and young boys swarm forth to drag the men away. Martino tosses the ropes back in the barrel.

One by one the torches are extinguished. Issuing more warnings about work and escape, the foremen march their groups toward the arcade, where wooden tables are piled high with what looks like small rounds of bread. Each laborer takes one.

We stand with Pacal at the end of the line. Charco is restless. He pulls at the rope so he can watch where the workers are going. He asks Pacal where they're going. Pacal says to the fields, but we're to wait for Martino at the stables. For now, says the boy, we eat the same as the workers.

Gustavo reaches for the food first, tastes it. What he doesn't spit out he throws on the ground. "Masa!"

Immediately, Pacal swoops it up and cleans it. He's angry. "Corn is sacred."

Looking closer, I see that what I thought were loaves of bread are soggy balls of uncooked corn dough. I've never seen such masa. It has the pungent smell of fermented corn.

"Sorry," says Charco to Pacal. "It's that we don't know the food here."

"It smells like liquor," I say.

Pacal remains angry. "Then don't eat it. We don't. My family is free to cook their own meals. But we never lose respect for masa." The boy's young face transforms before my eyes. He is a scowling old man. "We give our portions to the workers because they're only allowed this to eat—only *this!*" He holds out the balls of fermented dough. "At sundown they get beans, tortillas, and sometimes boiled fish."

"They don't die?" asks Charco.

"Yes, they die," says Pacal, wrinkling his high forehead. "They die from the work and the beatings. But men like you bring more men. You bring Yaquis and others." The boy is tired of us.

Again Charco pulls at our rope as he strains to learn the layout of the place. His eyes are busy looking for an opening somewhere. "Is the work that hard?"

"Standing all day in our sun? Cutting two thousand leaves?" Pacal grunts and takes away our dough balls.

"Women and children too?" I ask.

"Everyone works in the fields. Unmarried women work alone. Married women help their husbands. Small children clean plants. When they're twelve they get their own row."

Charco moves closer to the boy's ear. "Pacal, why don't the workers escape? There are many of you. Why not fight?"

"Mayas fight."

"All men should fight. It's many against few. Take me to where they work. I want to see."

"No one escapes from the haciendas," Pacal says. "If they run, the sun kills them or they merely end up at the next hacienda. Some get as far as Mérida, but they have no papers, so the police bring them back."

"I'd find a way," insists Charco. "Show me the fields."

Pacal is tempted, but something stops him. Gustavo. Pacal shakes his head, picks up the rope, and pulls.

The square is empty now, and except for the rain barrel, there's no sign that anything ever happened there. Pacal leads us to an open-ended cart hitched to a mule. We sit so that our feet drag on the ground. Pacal wraps his end of the rope to the seat. Daylight and heat have begun.

Charco asks, "What's that?" He points to a large building the size of the Palacio Municipal in Alamos.

"La casa principal," calls out Pacal proudly. "And in back is La Capilla de San Jacinto, and that's the priest's new house."

I turn and see the boy is boasting. I point to buildings across the way. "And that? I ask, hoping he has forgiven us.

"The store and the factory. They make our clothes there. The big house belongs to the mayordomo primero. He runs this whole hacienda. The overseers have the smaller houses. The capataces and the two majocols live in back."

"The owners don't live here?" asks Gustavo.

"Administradores and owners live in Mérida. But the owners also have the casa grande here. I'll show you," says Pacal. Clearly he's happy to do this.

He turns sharply away from the square and down a smooth road paved with fitted stones. From here I can see that the hacienda is really a town whose center, though smaller, is designed like Mérida.

"You said Martino is waiting for us," says Charco.

"We have time. After he works, he returns to his house for a bath and breakfast. Then he goes to the casa principal to meet with the administrador."

"Do you know why he wants us?" asks Gustavo.

I worry that he will again anger Pacal.

"No. He just said you're his gift from heaven." Pacal knows what he wants to talk about. "The owners live here in the casa grande or else in Mérida. The ladies sleep during the day and come out only at night. See those rails? Their trolley brings them to evening mass. I have brought them."

"There's more rail in one hacienda than in the whole state of Sonora," says Gustavo.

Charco says, "How strange to pray only at night."

We bump along in silence toward clusters of large shade trees. The road runs beneath them, and in the distance I see the casa grande. It's as big as the casa principal. White columns line the front. In its center, beneath the wide arch, is a huge door. The house spreads out, big, powerful, like a resting queen. A wide porch surrounds the house. The porch stairs lead to the road.

I look at the hard land around the house. How did this union of stone to stone come to this lifeless flatness? What kind of people are in there? Who can live here knowing what happens in the square in the morning? Do they know? I see no sign of life.

"It's closed," I say.

"Because they're asleep. But at night the house is full of lights. Wait," says Pacal. We circle to the back and see gardens, stables, a six-seater trolley. Servants sweep a grass patio. Pacal whistles, and they wave.

"They all know me. I was born here," he says. "I was the driver until I turned sixteen. They say I'm too old to drive the ladies. Now I work for Martino."

Pacal is no longer happy. He returns to the road we came by. I see heat waves. "Where do you draw water?" I ask, thinking if we were to escape we would die out here.

"Cenotes. Our rivers and lakes are under the earth. The water is so pure that the Empress Carlota bathed in the cenote of the hacienda Mucuyche. A true legend."

Gustavo laughs. "Pacal, help us leave this hacienda. We have family waiting."

"I can only drive you when I'm told to. I know all the roads. After Martino, I'm to take you to the hospital to Grandfather."

"Anginas is your grandfather?" I ask. Pacal nods.

"I have money for you now," says Gustavo.

"Money? For what?" asks Pacal. He finds this funny.

"Pacal," says Charco softly. He whispers the boy's name like a prayer. "Before we see Martino, show us the workers."

This time Pacal nods. "You still think you can escape. Here, all eyes belong to the henequen king." He says this with great pride, as if he were connected to the king. "I'll show you the hacienda because Grandfather wanted you to see it. That was his plan before Martino caught you."

"He wants *me* to see it?" asks Charco.

The boy looks at Charco. "He wants you to tell the world what you see in Yucatán. He says you were sent to him. That's how Grandfather talks. But now Martino has you, so I don't know how you're going to get out."

"Martino doesn't have us," says Gustavo angrily. "We are free men. We are here with federal troops."

Pacal tugs playfully at the rope. "You're not free. And you're not in Mexico. You belong to the king."

"Show us everything," says Charco, yanking the rope out of Pacal's hands.

Pacal shrugs. He takes up the reins and gives the mule a light slap. He drives down the streets behind the main houses. They have small gardens in back. I admire the wide streets paved white by large flat stones.

We pass corrals. Quickly I take in the sweet smell of livestock. The boy moves by too fast.

Pacal points to a bright yellow field. I have never seen so much of a single color in my life. Up close, I see the vast field is really long yellow strands hung over ropes in rows. The rows extend over hundreds of meters. Pacal waves an arm and announces, "The drying yard."

Weak, lifeless men and boys move slowly through the rows turning henequen fibers to the sun. "What's the matter with them?" asks Charco. "They look bad."

"They say they're sick," says Pacal, displeased. "This is where the sick work. They get half pay."

"Wait! *This* is the plant?" asks Charco, very upset. "This is what Yaquis work? This, this yellow hair?"

"They call it gold," says Pacal, ignoring Charco's anger. "They send *our* henequen all over the world."

The boy enters an empty stable area and circles it several times. We exchange nervous glances. Is he delivering us to Martino? I see no sign of the majocol. All we see in the courtyard is two workers arguing about how to start a fire. In Spanish Pacal asks them for Martino. They shrug, shake their heads. Pacal seems relieved, and we leave.

I see a large one-room building surrounded by a tall wall with cut glass on top. "The jail?" I ask.

"The dormitory," Pacal says.

"I want to see. Stop, please," says Charco.

"We don't have time," says Pacal. He stops anyway.

Two guards doze in chairs tipped against the wall. They wear holsters with guns and keep their rifles and machetes at arm's reach. Pacal points to us. "Son de Martino," he says.

They nod. I feel their eyes on us as Pacal leads us inside. Hammocks, hundreds of them, swing from the ceiling. "Unmarried workers sleep here. Armed guards, inside and out," he says to Charco as if to prove there's no escape.

Charco says, "So any escape must start in the fields."

Pacal shakes his head. "No. You'll see."

A rotten smell surrounds us. "Something's dead. What is that?" I ask. The stench is hard, solid as a wall.

He takes us behind the dormitory. Bare-breasted Indian women are grinding corn to make masa. Big steaming pots rest on open-air stoves. "You smell the fish in the beans," Pacal says. "They're making the workers' meal."

"They eat one meal all day?" I ask.

"And the corn dough in the field," he says. "And we give them ours, remember?"

"Pacal, show us the fields," says Charco urgently. "Take us."

Impatient, Pacal looks at Charco. "There's no escape from there or here. Why can't you believe me?"

18

CRUEL ROCK COVERS THE EARTH'S CRUST, FORMING AN IM-
pregnable barrier between man and the soil beneath. Blood
is inevitable should a worker's foot scrape itself over the rock's
craggy surface, which clings tenaciously to huaraches. Workers
must pull their feet away. Only the henequen plant lives on this
rock.

In its struggle to find sun, the henequen must burst through
rock. To do this, it assumes the shape of a hand or the claw of a
powerful creature. Surely a plant that can shatter the earth's rocky
mantle belongs to a terrible demon seeking freedom from the bowels of the earth. The thorns of the plant are too sharp to be only
thorns. They must be talons.

Neat straight rows of henequen extend for miles in all four directions. The plant itself is two, three meters wide and at least two
meters tall. A leaf measures one, two meters long. Triangular briers
border both sides of the leaf, ending in a sharp spearlike tip that
measures three centimeters. Workers call the leaves swords. Indeed, from a distance, the leaves in a henequen field resemble an
army with its swords drawn, pointing, challenging the sky.

Henequen is harvested year-round; year in, year out. The earli-
est light will find gangs of men with machetes working their rows.
Every worker must cut two thousand leaves a day. From each plant
his machete cuts twelve of the largest leaves. The worker must
leave thirty leaves which will mature in three months. He will be
beaten if he miscounts and leaves one leaf more or one leaf less on
the plant.

The worker gives each leaf several carefully placed cuts. The
first cut separates the leaf from the mother plant. Further cuts trim

the sharp briers off the leaf's edges. If the worker cuts the briers crookedly, he will be beaten. The final cut severs the crowning spike.

The trimmed leaves are piled into bundles, which the workers haul to the end of the row and toss onto a movable-track mule-car line. The car takes the leaves to a steam-powered stripping machine. Its metal teeth grind down the leaves into a green, hairlike fiber. Henequen. In the drying yard, the sun bleaches the fibers from green to gold.

Work rules are clear and the same for men, women, and children. No rest periods during the twelve-hour work day. No time to eat. The worker's only food is the ball of fermented corn dough. No way to cleanse punctures or cuts.

The rules of the field must be obeyed. Men on horseback are ready to whip the slow worker, the idler, the talker. Men are whipped standing. Women must kneel.

Workers are either full-timers or half-timers. Both receive twelve and one-half cents a day. Full-timers are allowed to keep their families on the plantation. Families live in a one-room hut set on a small patch of ground. Half-timers must sleep with the unmarried men locked up in a dormitory. When not working, half-timers are not allowed to seek other work. Every half-timer wants to work full-time. Full-timers live longer.

THE SUN BURNS directly above. Pacal untied us so we could crawl through the fields unseen by the capataces. The workers walked around us, their eyes fixed only on the next step, the next leaf, the next cut. So many hands with machetes controlled by one horseman with a gun and whip.

We squat to let Pacal retie the rope around our necks. "They'll leave you alone if they see you're tied up," he says, and he laughs.

Charco is strangely silent as we march back to the cart. Pacal searches to make contact with him, but Charco is angry. He lowers the brim of his hat. Head down, blue eyes narrowed, he walks avoiding all of us. My brother's brooding pleases Pacal. Their squabble has ended. Pacal has won. There's no escape from the plantation.

Gustavo and I need water. He's bleeding. His foot brushed a rock. My eyes and throat burn from the dust of the fields. I tasted the sap of the henequen plant. Bitter. The skin of my forearm is red and swollen where sap fell on it. I've tried to lick it clean. No use.

Pacal goes for water.

Once we're alone, our fear surfaces. Gustavo argues we could get out if he got word to the comandante of the federales. He insists we were taken illegally. "The federales wouldn't know we were deserting."

"Federales aren't worth shit here. Did you forget what Pacal said?" asks Charco, chest rising in anger. "This isn't Mexico. The only law here belongs to the henequen king."

"Do you believe that boy?" Gustavo asks. "We could pay someone to—"

"Stop!" screams Charco. "Where are your eyes, Gustavo? There is no escape. If Pacal knows all the roads, then let's force the cabrón to take us out of here."

Fear is making us mean. "We can't hurt him," I say as strongly as possible. "Let's find Anginas."

"I'll kill that old son of a bitch next time I see him," vows Gustavo. "And why should we trust Pacal? He has no mind of his own. One minute he's proud of this place. The next minute he's telling us how terrible it is."

"Gustavo, Anginas is a good man," says Charco tiredly.

Pacal returns with a gourd. We drink the cool, sweet water. Gustavo cleans his cut. I rinse off the sap.

"Martino's waiting." Pacal's voice is tight, nervous.

"Is he angry?" asks Gustavo.

Pacal says, "He's working with fugitives. Every time a slave escapes, the neighboring hacienda can claim him. He's still a slave, but we can't prove he's ours."

Forgetting the rope around his neck, Charco lifts a fist at Pacal. "Hey you, why do you say *ours?* You don't own Yaquis. You're trapped here too."

Pacal is unafraid. "No, I'm not trapped. I live here. This land was ours before it was an hacienda. The father of the father of my father, all of us are from here."

"Say you don't *own* Yaquis," insists Charco.

"All right. I don't own them. But they're now on our land. Hacendados don't care if Mayas die so long as they have Yaquis. Don't you understand?" asks Pacal. He's hurt by Charco's anger.

Pacal's boy-face changes. He's finished talking. Something has ended between us. A sour taste fills the air. He boards the wagon and waits for us take our seat. He slaps the mule into a trot. He wants to be rid of us.

We return to the stable. Two Mexican workmen are waiting for the cart. Pacal jumps down, grabs the rope around our necks, and leads us to Martino.

The majocol's in the courtyard, stoking coals banked by large stones. He wears a white straw hat, and his face is soaking wet from the heat of the fire. Under the noon sun his hands are larger, his back broader. Loose folds of flesh hang from his neck. His mustache is thick, but not as thick as it seemed last night. Martino is an ordinary man, I realize, and am terrified by what I've seen this ordinary man do.

Near a goat pen six fugitives—feet bound, hands tied behind— sit on the ground. They're naked. Their clothes hang over the pen's fence. Three of them are Yaquis in their twenties. The others, about the same age, could be Opatas or Mayos. How did they end up here? Who brought them? Each man has a rope around his neck and the rope is wrapped around a post. What will Martino do?

My mind races, remembering: a goat is slaughtered with one hoof tethered to a post. By trying to escape, the animal positions itself to be killed, neck stretched, jugular exposed.

Martino takes one of the irons out of the coals and inserts the hot tip into a bucket of water. Steam shoots up, hiding his face for a moment. "Well, señores del norte, Pacal says you've seen the hacienda. Forty square miles. What do you think?"

He returns the iron to the coals, then pulls out another. He holds it out an arm's distance and nods approvingly at the heat waves. He walks to the post and presses the hot end into the wood, leaving a dark *X*.

"We have bigger haciendas in Sonora," says Gustavo.

"With slaves?" asks Pacal.

"No," we murmur.

Pacal grunts. "You have slaves. Grandfather saw you deliver them."

"Where is that Judas?" asks Gustavo.

"I told you, Grandfather works in the hospital."

Martino returns the iron to the fire. He's not listening. His fingers pull at his mustache as his eyes shift from the coals, to us, and back to the naked men.

Suddenly I see the majocol's plan. I turn to Charco. My brother also sees and shakes his head. We agree. Death first. Death, the cleanest, simplest measure.

Martino unties Charco and points to the Yaqui closest to us. "Brand him," he says.

Charco nods several times before voicing, "No."

"Here, in the hip," says Martino, slapping his own hip.

"Never," says Charco.

Martino calls out, "Látigo, Pepe." The workman brings Martino a coiled leather whip. Martino snaps it loose and cracks the air with it. Eyes hard, he stares at Charco. My brother gently tosses his hat away, removes his shirt, and looks calmly at the majocol.

The first lash catches Charco by the ankles and brings him down. He quickly turns onto his stomach and buries his head in his arms. In silence, my brother takes six blows before his body becomes soft, inert. With his foot, Martino cautiously turns Charco over. My brother's eyes are closed into narrow slits. His lower lip is bleeding.

The courtyard is silent except for Pacal's muffled whimpering. The boy is huddled against Pepe the workman.

"Go get Anginas," Martino says to Pacal.

They pull Charco to the side and Pacal runs off wiping tears away.

Martino looks at me. I steel myself, shake my head. "Never."

He unties me and I lie flat on the ground before him. The first lash catches me unprepared. I hear myself gasp. I bite my lip and prepare for the second blow.

Pain echoes, moving in waves from the outside flesh to the body's center. The next blow yanks the pain back to the top. I lose the first wave somewhere inside me. My mind scrambles, crazily trying to keep track of each burning wave of hurt. And then another lick comes, and another, and I'm spinning in a swirl of singeing pain. I lift my head and my eyes lock with those of the Yaqui closest to me. I hang on, reaching to hide inside him, seeking to enter him through his eyes. I try to gather the surges that course through my body by driving my groin into the earth.

The next blow falls to the sound of voices. Gustavo is yelling. His hands turn me over, sit me up. He rips off my hat and fans me with it. I see Martino's boot and crawl on my knees toward the Yaqui.

Gustavo follows me. "I told him I'd do it." He lowers his voice. "He wants to see how it's done so they can keep working afterward. He crippled the last group."

I hear Charco's voice. "Never." He's sitting up, vomiting liquid.

"He said he'd let us go," says Gustavo.

"The coward's lying," says Charco.

Martino's whip flies at him. Charco lifts his feet, the whip misses.

Martino rolls the whip back up and moves toward Charco.

I hear myself. "A la chingada!" I dive for the iron, grab it, and still on my knees, drive it into Martino's lower back, and hold. He stands paralyzed and yells, "Pepe!"

Machete in hand, Pepe comes at us. Gustavo trips him, grabs the machete, and ends Pepe.

Martino, legs rigid, stumbles forward. He drops the whip. Turning, he reaches for me. Charco lunges and hugs Martino's ankles, bringing him down. Again the iron. I bring it full force down on his head. Martino is silent. A bloody stain swells around his head.

"El Yori," says the Yaqui, jutting his chin out. "He'll sound the alarm."

The other worker is running away. Quickly Charco cuts the Yaqui loose and tosses him the machete. The Yaqui darts after the man.

Charco, Gustavo, and I stand over the bodies. We're shaking. "Now what?" asks Gustavo, lips trembling.

"First, they go." I use the heat of the iron to free another prisoner. Gustavo and Charco untie the rest.

The first Yaqui returns, out of breath. He shakes his head. "He ran toward the fields."

"Chingado! They'll be here soon," says Charco, limping as he picks up his shirt and hat.

"I know what to do." I empty the bucket, fill it with straw from the stable, and toss coals over it. I tell the men, "Move. Burn the drying yard."

In seconds the men pull on their pants and shirts. They take the coals and grab the whip and machete. I look for Pacal's cart.

A low growl rumbles behind us. "Que pasó?"

Behind me stand Anginas and Pacal. Slowly, the old man circles the dead Martino. "Ah Chhuy Kak came for Martino?"

"No, your meddling did this," shouts Gustavo to Anginas.

Pacal says, "No, Grandfather means Ah Chhuy Kak, the god of violent death."

To me and Charco, Anginas says, "*Sábila* will heal your backs."

"We don't have time for your gods," says Gustavo.

"No, he means *sábila,* the plant," says Pacal.

Charco throws his hands up in the air. "We can't understand each other!"

We hear three shots followed by another three. We turn to Anginas.

"Follow," says Anginas.

19

ANGINAS HAS SENT PACAL TO THE CAPATACES WITH DETAILS OF our escape. The boy is to give our whereabouts as being in another part of the hacienda. We walk slowly, single-file behind Anginas, hiding the difference in height between us and him by staying low and hugging the walls. This helps Charco's walking. His legs keep buckling. The back of his clothes is bloodstained. I suspect I too have bled through.

The sound of gunshots continues. It comes from all directions, yet no one looks up. No one turns his head. Outside the hacienda's general store, men continue loading a trolley with supplies. Sweepers continue cleaning the wide streets. *Don't notice me, please,* they say by working through the sound of shots.

Anginas is taking us to the hospital, where we'll be safe. "Nobody goes there because nobody likes to see what happens to the workers."

Gustavo still does not trust Anginas and tells him so. He argues, "Your grandson was proud to work for Martino."

Anginas offers no defense. "Pacal is impressed by strength. Ask to see his back."

We walk beneath the arcade around the square. I see the casa principal where the mayordomo works. Yes, there are the trolley rails we saw this morning. For a moment I wonder if Anginas is turning us in to the overseers. But then he enters a narrow alley that leads to the rear of a low square building next to the casa principal.

The trolley rails follow the same alley and end in a dirt yard behind the low building. Anginas goes down some stone steps that lead beneath the building. He uses his shoulder to push at a pair of thick wooden doors. The doors open to a large room, a dark, damp, windowless basement. It's almost cool down here. The floor is part earth and stone. The room smells of damp earth, sweat, and urine.

Charco enters and falls on his stomach. I too let myself drop. Anginas removes Charco's shirt and checks his lacerations. Gustavo helps me take off my mine. Blood holds the shirt to my back.

The basement has several rooms, small narrow cubicles without doors. Anginas lights a candle, rubs something over Charco's back. He finishes and passes some leaves to Gustavo. *"Sábila?"* Gustavo asks.

Anginas nods. *"Sábila."* He rises and shows Gustavo how to squeeze the liquid out of the leaves. Anginas's gnarled hands feel strong yet light on my back. I close my eyes as his fingers trace where Martino's whip fell. Good.

Anginas brings us a cántaro of water. We all drink. "Now we wait," he says.

"What plan do you have?" asks Gustavo.

Before Anginas can answer, a bell rings outside the basement. "All hands to the drying field," calls a voice.

Anginas opens the door enough for me to see a guard on a mule-drawn trolley. "I have no helpers, only sick women."

"Everyone can carry water," says the guard.

Anginas shuts the door. He trots through the narrow rooms, his gravelly voice urging, "Come on, you don't want him to come for you."

The old man makes several trips, loading nine women onto the trolley. They wear fragments of dresses. Their hair is matted and their legs are brown summer reeds. I'm touched that he takes the women pallet blankets to cover themselves.

"You too," says the guard.

"I know what to do," answers Anginas, closing the door. To us he says, "The drying yard is on fire."

"I told the Yaquis to burn it," I say, feeling proud.

"Bad plan," says the old man. He opens the door and points to black clouds. "That's your *kinán*. All anger, no focus. Destruction, not change."

I'm bitten by his words. "No, it's a good plan, because we had to move unseen. Here, henequen is god, more important than human life. Even the mighty henequen kings bow to it. While the hacienda tends to its burning god, we could have escaped from this hell you brought us to."

"Many will die," blares the old man before going out.

He leaves us in a glum silence. "It was a good plan," I say out loud to myself. Charco and Gustavo nod, yes.

In silence, we lie on the floor while outside the basement angry voices shout, "Shovels! More water!" Footsteps race. Acrid smoke seeps in under the door, and we cover our eyes. Outside, the fire howls and the air grows pungent, thick. Gunshots ring. More shouts. More gunshots. I close my eyes, aware of a strange pride. *I did this to this evil place.* I search within for shame but find none.

ANGINAS HAS BEEN gone long enough for the sun to lose its force. No heat and little light enter the room when he opens the doors. He's covered with soot. He drinks water and cleans out his eyes. "You started more than a fire," he says to me, wiping his neck with a big handkerchief. "They chant, *Mataron a Martino, Mataron a Martino,* and bring pain to the fields. They cut a capataz to pieces. He looked at the sky for an instant."

From a corner, Charco applauds. "Their machetes should cut down this whole place."

"I see that even in death Martino will kill," growls Anginas. "Yes, Uxmal, sometimes we must touch violence to end violence, but not here. Yaquis should not fight here. There's nowhere for them to go. Their blood should feed their own soil. If they spill their blood here, this land will demand more, perhaps even your blood."

I can't answer the old man's words.

Charco stammers, "You promised to get us out of Yucatán."

"Did you kill Martino?" Anginas asks me.

I nod. "With the branding iron."

"Did his last breath fall on you? Think back. Did a drop of his blood touch you? Were you the last person he saw? If Martino knew he was dying, maybe he gave you his *et p'iz*. Each man is born and dies with a load to carry. You don't want his debts. Careful you don't lose your way."

"Viejito cabrón! Your stories can't scare us," says Gustavo. "We're Sonorenses."

Charco struggles to sit up. "It's not his stories. Read his scars. They tell the wisdom of this land. What's not true elsewhere may be true here in his land."

Listening to Charco, I begin to believe Anginas. I worry about Esteban's *et p'iz*.

We hear the trolley outside and hide behind the door. "Anginas!" calls a guttural voice. "Get rid of these!"

Anginas yells, "Leave them! I'll move them."

The old man goes outside, and drags in the first body to the farthest side of the room. After the trolley leaves, and Anginas signals that no one is around, Gustavo and I help him stack ten bodies against the wall.

The thick smell of the dead forces Gustavo and Charco outside. They sit on the stone steps trying to breathe. The fire is out but the smoke remains. I stay with Anginas.

"What killed them?" I ask.

"Bullets, fire," says Anginas.

"And my *kinán?*"

"And your *kinán* and the Yaquis' *kinán*."

The old man is wrong. "I didn't kill these men."

"Perhaps. But the power that did this," he says, pointing to the bodies, "is the same power you used to lift the iron that killed Martino. Maybe Martino brought the iron down on his own head when he became majocol." He stares directly ahead, eyes wide. "Or maybe I killed everyone when I brought you here. It's the same circle."

Charco and Gustavo come running inside. "The trolley," says Charco. "More bodies."

Anginas goes out. We listen for the ping of trolley wheels on rails. Instead, we hear the guards. They're coming inside.

We haul the bodies from the top and make a space for Charco to burrow in. Next, Gustavo and I climb in. We jerk and pull on the remaining bodies until we've covered ourselves with them.

The doors crash open. "Crazy old man! How can you breathe!"

Footsteps move toward us. "Uno, dos, tres!"

A body lands on us.

Somewhere Anginas's voice pleads, "Leave them to me."

They go for another. "Uno, dos, tres!" More weight.

I can't breathe. They're burying us in bodies. Some already cold, others still soft. I must breathe. If I could just turn . . .

"Uno, dos—"

"Not that way," says Anginas. "Let me . . ."

"Eusebio!" A thunderous voice calls down the steps and silences the basement.

I must breathe . . . lift my chin . . .

"Sí, mi capataz," says the counting voice.

The capataz's voice comes down the steps. "How many?"

"Eighteen."

"Anginas!" yells the capataz. "Nothing happened here, understand? Nothing! Tomorrow, during roll call, these bodies disappear. Don't burn them. Drop them in the cenote. Take the guards."

"Usted manda, mi capataz," says Anginas. "Pacal and I know where to take them. Let the guards watch the wounded."

The capataz says, "There are no more wounded. Those were the last ones."

Desperate for a shred of space, I press my head back and slowly raise my chin. My nose hits a mouth. The mouth is breathing. The man above me is alive. I breathe in him.

Anginas says, "Mi capataz, I know what you want. I swear to you, we'll be finished before the sun rises."

"Eusebio, tomorrow, you're majocol."

"I'll soak the ropes tonight."

The doors slam. Air! I push and the bodies roll off.

20

WE GASP IN THE DARKNESS.

Gustavo breaks into loud sobs.

"Sargento." I too start sobbing. "Sargento," I say, reaching in the darkness for him.

My hands find his shoulder. Emitting cries of terror, Gustavo cowers and slaps wildly at his face. I force down his hands and hug him. Charco finds us. We touch each other's faces and weep again. I weep because I'm no longer alone. We embrace, pull each other's hair, pinch arms, squeeze hands, grateful for a response, grateful for the smell and sound of each other's breath that assures us we are alive.

We jump when the doors swing open. Anginas enters with a small candle. Pacal is behind him.

I remember the mouth above me. "Anginas, one of them is alive. Get a torch."

Gustavo rises and grabs Anginas's shirt. "You caused this! You brought us to this nightmare. There's no way out of here!" He shakes the old man with a violence that lifts him off the ground.

Charco and I pull Gustavo off Anginas.

"Gustavo's right," says Charco to Anginas. "We believed you and got whipped for it. We did nothing to deserve this day."

Anginas lights a torch and glares at us. "This day? Is it only happening to you?" He points to the stacked bodies. "Tell *them* about this day! Is your horror the only wonder of this day?" The power of his voice paralyzes us. "Foolish boys."

I hear a moan and search for the man above me. "I knew it!" I say and sit him up. "Anginas, bring the torch!"

He holds the light up to the man. He's sooty, and cut, but I recognize the Yaqui from the goat pen, the man who gave me the strength to endure the whip.

I ask, "Remember me?" He nods. "Say your name."

"Juan."

Charco moves the Yaqui's head closer to the light. "How did you get this?"

"Grazed by a bullet when I was setting fire to the drying yard." Juan takes the torch from Anginas and, still sitting, searches through the bodies. "There. See him? He pulled me out of the fire. He took the next bullet."

Anginas gives Juan a ladle of water. "Stand up."

Juan has trouble standing. We grab him under the arms and pull. He weaves, then gestures us to stand back. He's weak, but stands.

"See him?" asks Anginas. "This is his day too. You come from the same land. Different cribs, same land, but here, you're the same. Ask yourselves why this day is fighting to keep you alive. Now hurry before the capataz sends guards to help me move the bodies."

"Hurry where?" asks Gustavo. His alarm resurfaces.

"To the farthest end of the hacienda, where I'm to throw the bodies into a bottomless cenote," says Anginas, in his lowest voice. "From there, Pacal will take you by cart to Progreso. By six tonight you can be on your way to Veracruz."

Gustavo lowers his head. "Let them shoot me. I won't go near those bodies again," he says, his voice quavering.

"It's the only way. I won't let you give up," says Anginas. His tone is low, threatening. "To live you must obey me." His dark eyes bounce off and on each of us. "Guards are searching everywhere for you. The neighboring haciendas have sent men to help."

"We'll put you near the top," says Pacal gently.

"Eat this," says Anginas. In his gnarled hands he holds out several fermented balls of corn dough. "It's all I have. This and *balché* to drink."

"Why do you give them *balché*, Grandfather?" asks Pacal.

The old man doesn't answer. Again he offers us the corn dough. Charco takes some and pops it into his mouth. I take a generous pinch and swallow it right away. The taste burns into my nose the way strong mezcal might. Gustavo waits to sees us swallow before taking his. Juan also eats. Next Pacal and Anginas. We eat it all.

"Now we load the trolley," says Anginas. He opens the heavy doors and returns for the first body. The old man drags a corpse that leaves behind a wet trail.

Gustavo's eyes fall on the trail. "I had that on me." His voice breaks. "I can't."

Charco takes him by the shoulders. "We'll wrap your head in something. You're taking us home, remember?"

Anginas has carried out three bodies. I rise, grab a wrist and ankle. The weight startles me. Is Anginas that much stronger? Gustavo refuses to move, and I motion to Charco to help. With Juan, we haul the rest to the door.

Suddenly, I'm light-headed. My tiredness has vanished. I can do this horrid task and feel nothing. The hacendados have thought of everything, I realize. I understand why they feed the workers fermented dough. I don't even smell the dead anymore.

Outside, Pacal helps Anginas finish fitting the bodies into the trolley on their sides. They alternate, feet to head, head to feet.

Anginas returns. He holds a gourd out to Gustavo. "You first. The *balché* will calm you."

Frowning, Gustavo accepts. "Why do I listen to you, old fool?"

I'm next. The liquid tastes honey-sweet and something else I can't place. I'm allowed a few sips before Anginas passes it to the others. Pacal seems especially pleased to drink.

"That's good," says Gustavo. "What is it?"

Anginas's voice is very low. *"Balché* is my gift to you and to myself. Strength will return to me as I give you this gift. I have caused you suffering and have brought you and myself harm."

"Balché is for important ceremonies," says Pacal.

"Tonight we separate," says Anginas, his voice heavy with sadness. He puts an arm around Charco. "Uxmal, Juan, tell your Yaquis it's better to fight in their own land than to die here in exile. Every year it's worse. More henequen. More slaves. More death. Tell them about Yucatán."

"We fight, same as Mayas," says Juan. "We fight Díaz, we fight the state." He drinks. "There's many against us. They take peaceful Yaquis and force us here." He looks at us, eyes burning. "The life of the Yaqui is very hard."

"Yaquis and Mayas are trapped between the hacendados and the government," says Anginas.

He turns to Gustavo. "The trolley will pass the guards on the way to the cenote. Pacal has his cart in place. While it's still dark, he will take you to my friend the photographer. Daylight should find you safe with him. Trust him. He and I have moved many out of Yucatán. He knows how to get you on board a steamer bound for Veracruz. He'll make whatever papers you need."

"Him too," says Charco, pointing to Juan.

"Of course," says Gustavo. He reaches for the gourd.

The drink makes me lie flat. "Why must I lie down?"

Pacal laughs. He also falls back and sighs. "Ah, *zacil!* The Maya's holy drunkenness."

"It's time," says Anginas. He opens the doors and we follow him into the quiet darkness. I feel loose, giddy, and I want to yell out, "We go to lie with the dead!" We drink more *balché* and climb in. Charco gets in between two dead, then Juan, also between two bodies. I stretch out on my side. My flesh is numb to the coldness of the dead. Gustavo is last. Anginas drops a cover over us.

The trolley moves slowly and Pacal must snap a whip to coax the mules. We gain speed, gliding through turns that toss us into each other. Eventually the guards force the trolley to a stop.

"What have we here, old man?"

"U uay yab," Anginas says in Maya.

"We have plenty of ghosts," laughs Pacal.

The cover is pulled off us. "Drunk bastards!"

I hear Anginas and Pacal laugh and laugh.

A guard says, "Move! I swear I'll shoot you!"

Again the cover falls over us. We're moving. Anginas and Pacal are still laughing. The top of my head feels wide open. I feel us gain speed.

Above me Anginas hums a strange melody. Pacal joins.

I listen. I know how the melody is going to break, pause, and rise. I'm certain where it's going. In my head, my voice joins Pacal and Anginas and I see that I was right. I do know that song—even though I've never heard it. It's inside me, inside us all. The melody shatters my thoughts. I'm frightened.

A voice vibrates through me. "Return to your country. Be priests of this vision, and you will be men of action, be men who move without doubt to turn Sonora into a land of generosity. Tell them what you saw here. When they enslave men there, they enslave us here. Tell them. That is why you have been saved. Be drops of water that penetrate and soften the land. Leave prints for others to follow."

We move in silence for a long while before we stop again. Anginas removes the cover. "Finish the *balché.*"

We sit up and take the gourd. The stars are a kiss away. No one talks. The melody Anginas hummed for us still flows through my head. We are at the edge of the henequen field. On one side the cruel plants tower above us. On the other side, an endless flatness quivers beneath the cold moonlight.

The trolley moves on, its wheels singing over the rails, leaving behind the henequen fields.

After the trolley swerves sharply around a grand flowering tree, Pacal stops. Clusters of orange-and-red blossoms cover the tree's long arms. Incandescent blooms light the darkness.

I climb out and stand beneath the blossoms. Charco and Juan and Gustavo stand with me. Anginas is beside us. My arms reach for the flowers, but they're too high. *No matter,* says the tree, *climb.* I obey. The rest follow and soon our heads are surrounded by flowers that form a net of joy that cradles me. My laughter becomes tears—both unstoppable—wondrous to own and release. Anginas, Charco, Juan, Gustavo rest in the same net. I cry and laugh until I'm empty and weak with a sweet tiredness I've yearned for all my life. I rest my head against the trunk, close my eyes, and hear the voice of the tree speaking with all the voices I have known— Mother, Ana María, Father, Tacho, Hector, Andrés, Tía Mercedes—all are together and separate. All and none. My eyes open and my gaze falls on Charco. His face is mine. Gustavo, Juan, Anginas are me. *In lak'ech.*

A voice. "Take the word of the ceiba, the *yaxché,* the tree of life through which all creatures live. The harmony of its smallest leaf contains the harmony of the heavens. Submit to the *yaxché* and your *kinán* will heal the cruelty of your land."

It's still dark. The trolley is gone. I see only Pacal's cart. Charco, Gustavo, and Juan are fast asleep.

"Anginas!"

"He threw the bodies into the cenote and took the trolley back," says Pacal. He nods toward those sleeping. "Wake them up. Dawn is near and I have orders."

"Pacal, first tell me the name of this tree."

"That's our sacred *flamboyan.*"

THREE

21

One month later, January 1900—
the Durcal ranch, Alamos, Sonora

FELIPA IS ALONE WHEN SHE SPOTS TWO MEN DRESSED IN SUITS and hats driving Tía Mercedes's wagon toward the house. Alarmed, she throws on a shawl and walks out into the bracing cold to wait.

It is early afternoon. Hector and Andrés are out on the range and Hong is delivering firewood to Tía Mercedes.

The taller man drives, and the way he leans forward to allow the mules more rein reminds her . . . but it can't be. She tightens the shawl.

There—the way he compensates for his long legs . . .

She bolts toward the wagon.

Alejo!

ALEJO FINISHES HIS prayer thanking the Virgin for his safe return as his mother had demanded, then turns to Felipa. "Charco has our

255

birthmark," he says. His mother has stared hard at Charco.

"I'm not a child. I know he's not to blame," she says, wondering how many more Charcos are wandering around Sonora. "But why bring him to this house?"

"I couldn't leave him in town. You can see he's got Hector's face—has the same temper. Someone is sure to notice, ask questions. If they arrest him, they'll trace him back to me. Anyway, I haven't told him yet."

"What's his real name?"

"Charco is the only name he uses. He says Mexicans named him that because they found him in a puddle. He's also lived with Americans, says he speaks English. But he'll tell you his heart is Yaqui. He returned to live with them as soon as he could. His blue eyes saved him from the firing squad in the bartolinas. I'm not ashamed to tell you, Mother, I'm here because Charco kept me going. I owe him my life."

Felipa remembers the fat guard at the bartolinas saying he would put Alejo next to Charco. "Let him stay," she says, "but don't ask me to like him. Get your things."

"We just have a portmanteau."

Surprised, Felipa raises her eyebrows. "A what?"

Laughing, Alejo draws her nearer. "Remember my sergeant? Gustavo Saldaña? He's the son of an hacendado. He's been good to us—bought the suits, hats, and travel bag. Charco and I promised to wear them until we were safe. We're all Gustavo has left of his first command. The clothes brought us to Alamos undetected."

"Undetected? Alejo, you've deserted! Why? Rafael Castillo has land for you in Arizona. You agreed to wait for his instructions. Are you mad? Desertion carries a death sentence. Did anyone—?"

Alejo presses her hand to his cheek. "Don't be frightened. No one saw us. Castillo knows everything. Gustavo is with him in Alamos. He must leave too."

They return to the living room to find Charco playing with the parrots. He's cajoled a male onto his shoulder.

"Did your father shoot that deer?"

"No, he bought it."

"Huh," says Charco, unimpressed.

"But he made the whole house," says Alejo. "Table, chairs, doors, beams. Everything."

Charco surveys the beams and fireplace. "It's good."

Alejo goes for the luggage, then calmly describes to a wide-eyed Felipa their smooth trip from Mexico City to Alamos.

Charco interrupts, "We can do anything in these clothes." He balances the parrot on his index finger and kisses the bird's beak. "People are happy to wait on us. If we asked for chocolate they brought it, and we never had to carry anything."

"They treat you as they see you," says Felipa.

She sees that Alejo's pride in Charco is almost fatherly. Every joke and gesture amuses him, and with good reason, thinks Felipa. Charco has a playful quality Hector doesn't have. José had it. In Charco's quick movements and watchful eyes, she sees evidence of the temper Alejo mentioned.

Alejo feels his mother is tranquil enough for them to tell her about Yucatán. The sale of Yaquis, the henequen plantations, the majocols, Anginas, and the false papers that returned them safely to Mexico City.

He monitors Charco's storytelling. Martino beats Yaquis, but Alejo doesn't kill him. Anginas saves them, but they don't hide among dead bodies to escape.

"Gustavo returned from Mexico City with Juan as his servant. We traveled as brothers," says Alejo, wishing he could take back the word "brothers."

Reluctantly, Felipa agrees they had no choice but to desert and adds, "You were in terrible danger there. But things are dangerous here too. The Yaquis get worse every day. They stole my Cocinera." Her eyes fill with tears.

Alejo leans over, tries to console her. She waves him away, and continues. "They raided Francisco Flores's Rancho de Aguacaliente. After that, and Cocinera's disappearance, Hector bought two rifles. Thank God for the soldiers."

Her words embarrass Alejo. He should have prepared Charco for her views about Yaquis.

Charco is flushed with anger. "Señora, you've been afraid of starving Yaquis?" The parrot squawks nervously. "What can they take? Skinny winter cattle? Didn't you hear what we saw in Yucatán? Maybe you didn't understand. The Yaquis weren't dangerous. Yoris were. We saw them—"

Alejo cuts in, keeping his voice flat. "Enough, Charco. Mother, in Mexico City Gustavo heard of a big push to end the Yaqui wars once and for all. The popular saying about Sonora is 'New century, new land. Forget coexistence.' Secretary of War Bernardo Reyes will give Sonora everything it needs to subdue the Yaquis."

Carefully but emphatically, Alejo adds, "We witnessed the government's cruelty against Yaquis. If necessary, we will fight to stop their deportation to Yucatán."

"Alejo," sighs Felipa. How she would like to slap these ideas out of his head. She longs to hold him, to trace his hairline with her hand as she did when he was her little shadow and looked to her for everything. She forces herself to concentrate on how handsome he looks in his elegant wool suit and black polished boots. The last time she saw him, he was gaunt and dirty.

She recalls the darkest day of her life, the day she escorted him to the bartolinas. And what is today, the day he returns safely to her? No. Happiness never erases suffering. She upbraids herself. Felipa, be grateful. He's here, he's alive.

And he's foolish. On the brink of shouting, she asks, "So, soldaditos, you've returned to fight against your own? You're not only deserters, you're traitors too. You'll find the firing squad you're looking for." She stops, takes several deep breaths. "Alejo, go to Arizona," she pleads.

"First we tell the Yaqui chiefs about Yucatán," says Alejo curtly. "Yaquis must know what awaits them if they don't negotiate a peace here." He tries to soften his tone. "After that, I promise to go to Arizona. Believe me, I never want to go back to prison." He waits, then, "I need to see Moro."

"I'm the only one who's ridden him," Felipa says. Alejo has hurt her. She irons the folds of her skirt with her hands.

"I also want to see the famous Moro," says Charco, returning the parrot to its cage.

Felipa's eyes follow Charco's surefooted strut across the living room. He can only be José's son, she thinks.

Playfully, Alejo slaps the side of Charco's head and races out of the house toward the barn.

"Señora," says Charco, excusing himself, his boots pointed toward the door.

"Yes, please go," says Felipa.

Alejo stands at the entrance to the barn and inhales every possible scent. He waits for Moro to turn his head. Moro is fatter than when Alejo last saw him.

"Moro." Alejo chuckles. Moro's ears and nostrils move toward him, but the horse does not turn around. "Bastard, you know I'm here."

Alejo notices the tools—oiled and stacked according to size. The floor is swept, and the entrance area, always a muddy mess during the rainy season, is covered with neatly fitted bricks. The sacks of feed are closed tight. He sees a small bed in the farthest corner. Shirts hang from nails. Hong. He must warn him about the federales.

"Alejo, I should have bet you more than a saddle," says Charco. He stands next to Alejo and surveys the barn. "You're rich."

"No. Gustavo's rich. We have land, cattle—and Moro."

The horse turns and lowers his head, allowing Alejo to stroke the long neck. He savors the strength of Moro's head nuzzling against his shoulder. *This is the best feeling in the world.*

Charco walks to the other side of the horse. Moro shies toward Alejo.

"He's skittish," says Alejo. "I told you about breaking him in."

"Too many times," says Charco. "Alejo, why didn't you tell your mother about us leaving for the Bacatete tomorrow?"

"Later. Not everything at once. Charco, I must tell you something about José Durcal."

Bored, Charco says, "I know about El Centauro Durcal, and how he won Moro with three queens and he—"

Alejo points to the base of his spine. "Charco, you have a mark on your back, *here*. Same as me, same as José Durcal, same as your half brothers Hector and Andrés."

Eyes narrowed, Charco removes his jacket.

Alejo stops him. "You can't see it without a mirror. You've seen mine. Believe me, it's exactly alike. We're half brothers, Charco. And when Hector and Andrés come home, you'll meet two more brothers."

Charco scowls at Alejo. "How long have you known? Why tell me here? Why tell me at all?"

"You deserve to know," says Alejo, surprised at Charco's reaction. "I've known since we were in the caves, and since then I've thought of you as my brother. Truly. Every day I thought of telling you. Something bigger always happened. First we were prisoners, then soldiers, then deserters." He laughs dryly. "Now we're Anginas's messengers. Besides, what would have changed had I told you before we got back to Sonora? At least here I have things to show you about your father."

Charco's anger seems to dissolve, exposing a forlorn look Alejo has never seen. "All I'm wondering about is if El Centauro Durcal did to my mother what we saw those Yoris do to the women." He looks directly at Alejo. "Did you think of *that* every day?"

"Charco, you're asking the wrong questions. Ask why we survived. Ask what you can do with your life. Start here, with your

brothers. As the oldest son, I offer you our father's name. Durcal."
Alejo rests a hand on Charco's shoulder. "You look like Hector."

Charco slaps Alejo's hand off. "Your mother knows about me,
doesn't she?"

"I had to tell her."

"She doesn't like me."

"She's jealous. Forgive her. Think how she feels."

Charco explodes, paces back and forth, pummeling his thighs
with his fists. "Chingado! Chingado! Mil chingados!" Moro snorts,
stomps his hooves as the sound of Charco's footsteps grows louder.

"You shouldn't have brought me here, Alejo! Better yet, you
shouldn't have told me, or told me, and left me in town with Gustavo, then gone with Juan to the sierra. Yoris have no honor."

Impatient, Alejo orders, "Stop!" He presses Charco's head between his hands and jerks it right up to his own. "You're being a
fool. I'm sorry about your mother. I'm ashamed of my father, all
right? Like it or not, we have the same blood. We're connected. Remember what Anginas taught us? Each man is born with his *et p'iz*.
His own load to carry. Don't lift our father's weight. You don't
want to be a Durcal? Fine, don't be." He pushes Charco away.

Charco wipes off the sides of his head where Alejo touched him.
"I hate talk. We promised Anginas that we would tell the Yoemem
about Yucatán. We will do that, right?"

"That's our trust. Nothing has changed. Help me bring in Tía
Mercedes's mules for the night."

FELIPA FRIES UP carne seca with onions, potatoes, and green chiles.
She makes flour tortillas, pinole, and pumpkin empanadas sugared
with piloncillo.

She sets the table, placing herself and Alejo at the ends. Hector
and Charco will sit opposite each other, Andrés next to Hector.
Outside, she hears loud whooping and laughing. Hector and Andrés must have seen Alejo.

The boys' noise ends abruptly. Hector must be meeting Charco. No matter, men always forgive each other. Is the boy's mother still alive? Is Charco his only child by her?

Felipa recalls how she threatened to move back to town if José didn't throw out the Yaqui family. How reluctantly José helped them pack. Where did they go?

Tía Mercedes said the family had gone to work at La Colorada Mine, but José hated mines. He wouldn't have gone after her. No, she thinks bitterly, Charco was sired here.

DINNER IS QUIET. Alejo can think of nothing to say. Before him sits his favorite food in the world, but clashing thoughts and ugly pictures won't let him enjoy it. Charco and Hector exchange glances with every bite. The two share Father's face, the thick wavy hair, but only Charco has his eyes.

Hector eats in silence, stabbing the food with his fork. But Charco, out of what can only be stubbornness, is ignoring his fork, choosing to eat Yaqui style—meat pushed onto the tortilla, which is then folded over and held with both hands. Charco's chewing and lip-smacking is the loudest noise in the house.

A huge grin on his face, Andrés eats only empanadas. His eyes dart back and forth between Charco and Hector. Felipa taps the back of Andrés's head several times to no avail. The boy nods at her, then quickly smiles back at Charco and Hector as if expecting them to disappear the moment he looks away.

Alejo compares the intense, volatile Hector and Charco to the even-tempered Andrés. Only Andrés could laugh here. If it weren't for him, this dinner would be unbearable. I suppose together, we're a balance, he thinks.

He looks at the deer over the fireplace. Father, what did you do to Charco's mother?

He forces his thoughts back to the table. Warily, Alejo discloses to Felipa that they actually arrived in Alamos two days before. "We stayed at the Fonda Elizondo. Nobody recognized me."

"So," asks Felipa, a sharp edge in her voice, "Tía Mercedes knew you were here?"

"We sent a note asking her to lend us the wagon. People know she rents it out. Don't be angry at her. We had business with Castillo. I begged her not to tell you," says Alejo.

Felipa is pleased that her aunt respects Alejo's wishes, then wonders if her aunt doesn't pity her because her sons want to leave the ranch as Tía Mercedes's sons left the mill.

Hong enters and goes to the kitchen to serve himself. Before he's out the door, Felipa asks, "Hong, did Tía Mercedes tell you they were here?"

"No, señora," says Hong.

Alejo turns to him. "Hello, Hong." He has forgotten how tall the man is. "The barn is in good order. Thank you. I must warn you, the federales are taking Chinese, for no reason."

Hong nods. "I have heard. Many new soldiers are in town. They speak of a Yaqui war. I stay away from the plaza. I avoid men if they're drinking."

"They take them to Yucatán. There's no escape. The haciendas are guarded day and night. They work and beat people to death." Alejo's voice rises. "I saw Chinese and also men they call Coreanos who look like you."

Hong nods. "I know of those men. Thank you. I will be careful," he says and leaves.

Andrés says, "Hong and I are going to San Francisco."

Felipa sighs, and starts stacking the dishes.

Alejo pushes his chair back and tosses his napkin over his plate. He orders his brothers, "Come to the barn."

Charco rises along with Alejo. In silence, Hector and Andrés wait a few minutes before slowly following them out.

Alone, Felipa thinks about the look in Alejo's and Charco's eyes, and remembers how years ago José set up traps to catch jackrabbits. Pleased with his success, José brought them in for her to kill and cook. Instead, she burst into tears, turned the rabbits loose, then locked herself in the bedroom.

"Their eyes," she cried after José coaxed her to open the door, "they're too human." She claimed she could *hear* the rabbits' fear through their eyes.

Alejo and Charco have that haunted look—that of a creature hunted and caught. The look is there when they don't know anyone is observing them. Yet, there's a new strength in Alejo. He's always been strong, she quickly corrects herself. But now, the tranquillity, that special softness of his, has been replaced with . . .

Precise words elude her. No matter. For now she's content to have remembered where she saw that look. And now she's convinced that they have not told her all they saw, nor have they told her everything that happened.

She feels the bond between Alejo and Charco, and hurts for her other two sons. How left out they must feel. She will speak to Alejo about it. He must praise Hector and Andrés for working the ranch so well in his absence.

ALEJO PLACES TWO lanterns on the newly laid bricks. The barn's best, he thinks. The house is full of Father's loud presence and Mother's hurt feelings. Parents are like shoes—they either pinch or rub. But here, with Moro, my *kinán* is free.

Not too long ago, this ranch was all I wanted in life. Now I have no desire for it, he thinks sadly. He can still see his father's face squeezing, hurting his hands as he placed them over his heart. He can still hear those words: *Make the Durcal ranch a wheel that turns by itself. If I fall, swear to me that you will complete my dream.*

Unfair.

Hong is not around, Alejo notices. How homesick this man must be. Where is his family? How did he end up here? Alejo understands Andrés's affection for this quiet man.

Outside the day is ending, spreading an evening chill. Charco,

Hector, and Andrés wait in the doorway for Alejo to direct them. He throws down saddle blankets and motions for them to sit.

Alejo turns to Andrés. "What was so funny back there?"

Andrés points to Charco. "Nothing was funny—except now we know one of Father's secrets. When I look at Charco I see Father. Hong said people aren't dead forever. Sometimes the dead come back. I wondered if what Hong said was true, in a way."

"That's stupid," says Hector. "Mother's warned you not to talk about religion with Hong."

"Death isn't religion. It helps my sadness to talk about Father's death with someone."

"Then talk to me," says Hector.

"Hector, you won't talk about it. I know Charco isn't Father. It's nice to look at him and imagine. What's wrong with that?"

Charco says, "I don't want to be a dead man, especially one I never knew. Alejo says we're brothers—so what? He brought me because he said he needed my help to tell you about some things." To Alejo, "Tell them."

Hector asks, "You needed him to tell us about what?"

Alejo has no trouble beginning. "After Carrasco took us to the Río Yaqui . . ."

With Charco's help, he tells his brothers about Mexico's writers who were branded as enemies of the state, then sent into the Valle Nacional. They describe the Yaqui exile, include every detail: the breaking up of families, the raping of women, the beatings, the shooting of the sick and old, the thirst and hunger.

Alejo feels his body shake as his voice rises. Words come fast to him. "Have you ever seen starvation? People's skin turns gray. Their eyes sink into their head. Their skin opens. Liquids come out of every hole God gave us. And through all this, the Yaquis are silent."

Next they detail the henequen plantations. The slavery, the whipping, the brandings, the countless deaths. Their harrowing escape and their vow that Anginas demanded of them: to tell all what awaits those the government sentences to Yucatán.

Alejo sees he is shocking his brothers. They're barely breathing, they're so frightened. Good, he thinks. He swells with passion. "We must tell Alamos, tell everyone."

"But *you* can't tell anyone," says Hector. "You're a deserter. You'll be shot if they catch you."

"After Castillo wins our pardon, Charco and I will return to spread the word—not just in Sonora, but throughout Mexico. Meanwhile, tell others what we've told you. Before we go north, we will tell the Yaqui chiefs."

Andrés says, "Hector's right. What if the secret police or the army or Sheriff Alcázar captures you?"

Alejo thinks about this question, then what was merely a vague idea crystallizes. "Neither of you has asked why we did nothing to stop what we saw. Neither of you has asked why we went along. I'll tell you why. Because when you see torture and death, all you fear is your own death. Honor becomes a useless word. Both of you could have done anything we saw the soldiers do. Done it, or let it happen, just so you wouldn't die. So to answer your question, what if I'm caught, the answer is I will kill myself. Better dead than see myself become . . ." He searches for words. ". . . the worst kind of man," he says simply. "And if they chain me, one of you must find a way to kill me."

No one answers.

Alejo adds, "I won't go through prison again. Put a bullet in me. One of you, promise me you'll do it."

Charco looks at Alejo. "I'll put a bullet in you if you're taken. Swear you'll do the same for me."

"That part is sworn and settled—at least with one brother."

The group is quiet. Hector and Andrés exchange glances. Andrés bites his lower lip.

Hector speaks deliberately, his voice low, resonant. "I too swear. I saw how Carrasco marched you from the bartolinas to the Río Yaqui. I should have killed him."

"Don't go to prison for Carrasco, Hector," says Alejo. "But this I do swear, and it doesn't matter if you protest." He stops, looks at each one separately. "If any of you here is taken prisoner, I will shoot you.

Upset, Andrés draws his legs into himself. "You can't do that if we don't want it."

Charco leans over and whispers, "You'll want it."

Hector cuts in, "All of this is talk. What is more important is what you said about Yucatán and the Valle Nacional. Slavery is against our Constitution. To sell a human being is treason. If Díaz permits this, then he's a traitor. That is what we must speak of. I agree that we should tell everyone."

"Exactly," says Alejo. "But be careful where and how you speak of this. Spies are everywhere. Enough about us. What are your plans?"

22

On a road outside of Alamos, Rafael Castillo checks his watch. Three hours to daylight. Wrapped in layers of blankets, he sits in his wagon waiting for his new client. Gustavo Saldaña has been overdue since midnight.

Castillo is nervous. Gustavo and Alejo must get out of Alamos territory. Already townspeople are speculating about the young men who arrived dressed in three-piece French-cut suits. One of the travelers has been described as a "young José Durcal."

Those rumors brought Sheriff Alcázar to Castillo's office. "Nonsense," said the lawyer. "I'm in contact with Felipa. The woman is still inconsolable."

When Alcázar arrived in Castillo's office, Gustavo was sitting, tilting back comfortably, his chair balanced on two legs.

Smiling, Gustavo introduced himself to the sheriff and said, "I know who you're talking about. I traveled with those two from Guaymas. They came to find out about the Alamos garbanzo bean. Is it really the best in the world?"

Flattered that an hacendado knew of his city's famous product, Alcázar said, "Undoubtedly, and it improves with every crop. Our own Alvaro Obregón developed it. Though I doubt our garbanzo would grow as well anywhere else."

For the moment, Gustavo's charm satisfied Alcázar. Yet, had Alcázar realized the truth, Castillo knows the sheriff would not hesitate to put the deserter in chains.

CASTILLO HAS FOLLOWED orders, strange as they seemed. Every rider must have his own supplies. Four horses, four Remingtons with bullets, four gourd canteens, tin cups, separate portions of jerky, separate quantities of pinole and flour tortillas.

Why? Were they taking separate routes to Arizona? Thinking of the border, Castillo moves his gloved hand inside his coat to double-check that the heavy envelope filled with documents is there.

He praised Gustavo for the explicitness of his directions, only to learn that Alejo gave the orders. Who would have thought that the tall gangly Durcal boy would become such a methodical planner? He always seemed a dreamy ranch boy. Castillo's godson, Hector, is the one to reckon with.

Can't complain, Castillo thinks, watching his breath in the white moonlight. In two days I've earned more with Gustavo than I have in two years. Winning him a pardon for desertion won't be easy. Maybe impossible. But the Saldañas have deep pockets. Whether or not Gustavo gets his pardon, I will have an hacendado client. Finally.

The lawyer hears the rattle of wagon wheels. He lights a lantern, which he waves toward the sound.

"I was just thinking of you," he says lightly to Hector Durcal, who's driving the wagon.

A sullen Hector barely nods. He lifts a bundle of blankets and Alejo, Gustavo, and two more men jump out.

Something is wrong, thinks Castillo. They all look grim, purposeful. He also notices that they are dressed in the faded denim trousers and cotton shirts worn by Yaquis. Alejo and Gustavo wear boots, the other two huaraches.

"You're late," says the lawyer testily. "I was about to leave. It's all here. With all the troops in Sonora, good horses were hard to find. You might find better ones at Ures. If you're careful, these will get you to Tucson."

Alejo checks the mounts. He's clearly dissatisfied. "These are old range horses. Before Arizona, we're going to the Sierra Bacatete."

"The Bacatete? That may be north, but it's also west." Irritated, Castillo asks Gustavo, "Does he speak for you?"

"He speaks for all of us," says Gustavo, standing next to Alejo.

"You've been away. There's much you don't know," argues Castillo. "The Bacatete is full of soldiers. General Torres is leading an army against the Yaquis. You could be stopped, and dressed like that, shot on the spot."

Juan mutters bitterly, "Francisco Torres, the Yaquis' executioner."

Alejo grunts in accord. He offers Charco a boost to mount, and does the same for Juan.

Juan says, "The name of the mountains is Bacatebe, not Bacatete."

The lawyer argues, "If you go now, you may be caught in the middle of the battle."

Charco's clear voice fills the night sky. "So what? Then we'll know that was where we were meant to be, and that was where we were meant to fight."

Castillo recognizes Charco as the Durcal bastard and ignores him. "This is insane," says the lawyer, thinking, will I lose my new client so soon? "Alejo, Gustavo, now is the perfect time for you to slip straight up to Arizona. People's minds are on this battle. Every man and gun is committed. Soldiers have been brought down from Baja California."

Alejo grabs the mane of his horse and hoists himself up. "So you say. But we have an obligation to fulfill. First that, then Tucson, not before."

Charco and Juan trot away in the darkness. Alejo turns his horse in the same direction.

Castillo works to remain calm. "Alejo, it's not for me, or for yourself. It's for Felipa. She's suffered enough. In the months you've been gone, she's given me no rest. Every week she came to town—always on Moro—urging, begging me to find land for you around Tucson."

Alejo seems hurt to hear of his mother's suffering.

The lawyer sees an opening. "And I found exactly what she wanted. You are all that's missing. It's a good stretch of land and it's ready."

"And paid for," says Hector. "Don't forget that."

"That's also true," Castillo adds quickly. "Your mother used this year's cattle sales to pay for it."

"And my university money," says Hector.

Castillo reaches inside his coat and pulls out the envelope. "Here's the papers you need. My wife's family will help you until you're settled. It's arranged. The place is called Crittenden. It's near Tucson, close to Nogales." He shakes the envelope in front of Alejo. "Take it. It's good land."

"Don't, Alejo," says Gustavo. "Don't take anything that could identify you. If you're caught, your family will lose everything."

"True. Take them to my mother," says Alejo. "I'll come back for them, or Hector will bring them." He raises a hand of farewell to Hector, and follows Charco and Juan.

Castillo turns to Gustavo. "As your lawyer and counselor, I warn you not to go. Save yourself. Think of your family. Everything the Díaz government wants dead is in that sierra." He lowers his voice. "Look, I didn't tell the others, but rumors are that the attack may be today or tomorrow. It's useless for you to go."

Mounting, Gustavo says, "I appreciate your advice. But we can't take our freedom until we've delivered our message to the Yaquis."

"You're not heroes. You're deserters!" cries Castillo, spittle around his mouth. "If you're caught with the Indians you'll be traitors too. What could you say to the Yaquis that others haven't already said?"

"That I don't know," says Gustavo. "But if the Yaquis don't negotiate a peace here, in their own land, the government will deport them to Yucatán. They must know what awaits them there. Goodbye."

Castillo stands up in his wagon and calls after Gustavo, "Listen! Have a second plan of escape ready. If you survive, get to Magdalena, board the train to Tucson. I'll wire my in-laws . . ."

"What they're doing is important. Let them go," says Hector. "And anyway, you're more worried about Saldaña than about my brother."

CASTILLO HURRIES TO the Durcal ranch. He is stung by the Durcal brothers' insolence. He will be frank with her. How dare Alejo dismiss a year of his work? Work undertaken without payment? Does she expect him to defend Alejo if he's arrested?

When he arrives, Felipa is rolling a water barrel up a long board onto the wagon. Andrés and Hong try to help, but she moves too fast for them.

It is daybreak, cold, and Felipa is working without a wrap. She stops, long enough for him to see the deadly fury in her eyes. Castillo rethinks how he will protest Alejo's going to the Bacatete.

"Why are you so mad?" she asks.

"Alejo refused the papers, told me to bring them to you. Let me help," offers Castillo.

"Hitch up the mule," she says and swings a full sack of feed on the wagon.

I couldn't do that even as a young man, he thinks. He notices the wagon is fully packed. A saddle, a portmanteau, blankets, food, even a pick and shovel.

He backs the mule into the harness. "Felipa, Alejo and his friends are talking treason with their crazy ideas about Yaquis and peace. If the government catches him, he'll be shot. No trial. Nothing. Alcázar's already asked about him, so he can't come back here."

She goes to the barn for Moro and tethers him behind the wagon. "That's why I must go after him."

"You're crazy too! They're going to the Bacatete. How will you find him? You don't know your way around there."

"I know I'll go crazy here. Give me the papers."

"Please, don't tell me you're taking him to the border. That's four hundred miles—at least thirty days away. You've never—"

She holds out her hand. "The papers."

23

THE FOUR MEN RIDE EAST, STAYING FAR ENOUGH FROM EACH other not to raise dust. Alejo leads them quickly out of Alamos territory, bypassing Navojoa, where he shot Esteban, then he turns north, near Esperanza, keeping all of them a safe distance from the Yaqui pueblos.

It is midday when they camp against a low butte with a clear view in all directions. Tonight they will move again, pushing the horses to their limit. Meanwhile, there's enough green here for the horses to graze.

What they've crossed thus far—flat ranchlands, broken by mesquite, low shrubs, willowy paloverde, pitaya, creosote bushes, and rows of cottonwoods near green riverbeds—is familiar to Alejo. But tomorrow they will be in lands unknown to him.

The Bacatete—fifty miles of sacred mountains that shoot up from the plains. Allowing for detours around government troops, they estimate a three-day ride to the sierra.

Any doubts about going to the sierra were dispelled just before they met with the lawyer. They found Juan hiding in a hovel. He told them that his wife and two children had disappeared.

Immediately Charco swore, "Yoeme, count on me. We'll find them."

"Me too. To the end," said Gustavo.

Alejo shook the images of the boat, the long walk, and the cattle trains out of his head. Bowing his head to avoid the low thatch, he saw his friend's despair.

Juan's former employer, a Mexican rancher, had told him that for months government troops had been sweeping the Yaqui River area, methodically forcing rebels into the Sierra Bacatete. Wandering Yaquis were shot, or imprisoned to await deportation.

"If my sister Pilar heard of the raids, she would have come for my family," said Juan, his voice level, free of hope. "If they're not with her, I'll return to Yucatán."

It was dark and the wind had whipped up a wavering column of dust, but Alejo could see the implacable anger in Juan's face.

Juan's older sister, Pilar, was a renowned warrior who had escaped from jail twice, once from a fort outside Hermosillo and another time from Guaymas. She had fought hand-to-hand, disarmed her jailers, killed four. Then, dressed as a soldier, she had returned at night, causing chaos by freeing all the prisoners.

"She's been with the mountain bands most of her life. Yoris will pay five thousand pesos for her head," said Juan proudly. "Somebody would have heard if she was captured."

Juan's information was correct, according to Gustavo. He had chatted with merchants, listened to gossip, and because he knew that the Díaz government controlled all the press, he read *La Constitución,* Sonora's most important newspaper.

Editorials full of praise confirmed that for twenty days straight,

General Torres's brave forces had combed the Guaymas Valley, that dense, thorny, desert jungle of maguey, barrel cactus, mesquite, nopal, and deadly cholla.

In the end, the general's plan to herd the Yaquis out of the river valley and into the mountains had succeeded. His next tactic had been to force the Yaquis out of their mountain hideouts toward a single spot: Mazocoba. Torres had his stationary target.

WITH A STICK, Charco holds four tin cups of water over a tiny fire, while Alejo and Juan tear saddle blankets to wrap cold compresses around the horses' splints.

"Now the paper only talks of the Campaign of Mazocoba," says Gustavo. He offers a newspaper, which no one takes.

"What does that change?" asks Charco. The water is hot, and he drops a generous pinch of pinole into each cup.

"It makes the public hungry for a big battle," says Gustavo. "People like war." Frowning, he adds, "Here's something else. This article claims the Yaquis are holding a priest and four nuns as hostages. It says that there's little hope that they are still alive."

"What does that mean?" asks Charco, handing each a cup.

"A slaughter," says Juan.

"Is that true?" asks Charco.

"Probably," says Gustavo. He points to the newspaper. "They have four battalions, plus a regional company, and the National Guard to fight two thousand Yaquis."

"They're counting the old and the children," says Juan. "Hungry families that must eat *sawum* roots or magueys."

The word "maguey" hangs in the air between them.

Alejo wonders about the maguey, which is food in Sonora, and compares it with the hennequen, which brings only suffering in Yucatán.

He feels his chest swell with reverence as he gazes at the landscape around him. Sonora is most beautiful in the winter when colors dress the soft brown of the land. The mesquite turns pale green, and the tall cottonwoods sway under veils of new, tender leaves.

Rows of purplish-red and bright yellow flowers push up overnight. Flowers. Yaquis say flowers were a gift from heaven, a miracle that came to pass as drops of Jesus' blood fell from the cross.

How certain he had been that he would die without this when he first went to the bartolinas. And now? Sadness fills him as he remembers his brothers' future plans. No one wants the ranch.

Andrés's sole desire is to travel, and he would begin by going to San Francisco. "I want to go see." The urgent hunger in the request did not allow Alejo to disregard it.

Hector's stand was as firm. "I'll work until you return. That's fair. You defended the family's honor. But after your pardon, give me money to go to the university as Father promised I could. I won't forget about Yucatán. But Alejo, telling people about it won't change anything. People must be pushed to change. I'm ready to do that."

The strength of Hector's words did not surprise Alejo. It was no secret that Alamos considered Hector to be José Durcal's greatest promise.

Alejo did not tell his brothers that Castillo had offered him little hope of a pardon. "People can understand your killing your father's murderer," the lawyer had said. "But under the Díaz government, desertion is unpardonable. You agreed to wait to hear from me. I was ready to pay someone to take your place. But now you're on every wanted list."

Alejo doubts if even a pardon could lure him back. He has changed, and for now, that is enough for him to accept.

To his question "Doesn't Father's dream mean anything?" Hector and Andrés had offered no answer.

What was Father's dream? That the name Durcal live after him through his sons and the ranch?

Small dream.

Well, thinks Alejo, I will change El Centauro Durcal's dream.

Father said, "A man must make good dreams—if not, he is capable of the worst." I say a dream should be bigger than one man's ranch, or one man's land. I killed more than Esteban when I fired that gun. I killed Father's old dream too. No, made it bigger—to include everyone. And I need not step through his ghost to live my dream. I will stand on his shoulders to carve my own dreams.

Through me, Father's dream will be realized. His name will live.

Alejo feels liberated by that thought.

Now? José Durcal's sons have land and don't want it. Yaquis want their land but it's stolen from them.

Fondly, he looks at Charco, Gustavo, and Juan and remembers the *flamboyan* tree in Yucatán. They too abandoned their personal dreams.

Anginas changed us, he thinks, united our *kinán*. From Anginas his mind drifts to Tacho. He stops. That sore is too raw to touch.

BY MOONLIGHT, THEY follow Juan. Separately, they move slowly yet steadily over the flat, broad stretch of land. "If I can hear your horse, you're too close," Juan said.

The night is quiet. In the distance, a solitary Alejo sees where the series of mesas that make up the sierra form jagged shadows like gaping mouths reaching to taste the sky. Lonely spires crown the Bacatete.

At closer range on the land, Alejo admires the rare outline of a cactus or pitahaya whose tenacious fingers have broken through the flat plain. Beautiful. He hopes that from a distance he and the others resemble these strong, single desert guards.

Juan has said that dawn will find them at El Cerro de Tres Hermanos. From there they will cut across the Valley of Aguacaliente. "We enter through the Pass of Bacatete and climb the long slope to Mazocoba. Three hundred meters."

Whatever other questions Alejo has about what they're going to do he keeps to himself. As they near their goal, Juan and Charco seem withdrawn into a unit of two. They sit separately, talk in Yaqui, spit into the dirt the way Tacho used to, and they exclude Gustavo and himself.

They reach Tres Hermanos before dawn. After they eat and rest their mounts, Gustavo chooses the strongest horse and leaves, his field glasses dangling from a string around his neck, to "assess the government's strategy." Irked by Gustavo's military talk, Alejo asks himself, what happened to the unity we shared a few days ago?

Gustavo returns and gravely motions them to gather around him. He's a lieutenant again.

In the dirt Gustavo draws a row of several circles. Above and below these he draws more circles of varying sizes. When he completes a convoluted maze of circles, he says, "That's the Bacatete, and this big one here, at the north end, must be Mazocoba."

Juan and Charco aren't looking at his circles, but he doesn't notice.

"Say what you saw," says Juan dryly.

"The government has posts of food, water, armaments, and medical supplies all around the mountain. Plus at least a thousand soldiers." Then solemnly he adds, "Before we left, Castillo told me the attack was due any day."

Everyone is quiet. Juan and Charco show no emotion. Alejo wonders if he is the only one who is afraid.

Charco says, "We must get past the sentries."

"I already know how," says Gustavo. "All their posts face the mountain. They don't want anybody leaving the sierra. We're going into it. That's our advantage. Guards change every three hours. The last change is at three in the morning. After that, things quiet down. Soldiers aren't afraid of dozing on duty, because no one will catch them. We have from then until dawn."

THEY RIDE SEPARATELY for several miles before reaching the area which Gustavo says has the greatest distance between posts. There they abandon the horses. Strapped to their backs are the saddlebags packed with food and bullets. They tie the gourd canteens to their rifles, which hang at an angle down their backs.

Juan says, "We meet at the bottom of the long slope." And he leaves, crawling on his belly. They hear nothing as he disappears into the darkness.

Charco is next.

"Your turn," says Gustavo.

Alejo gets down and crawls. At first the ground beneath is hard, so he moves swiftly, silently. Then he hits a thorny jungle of thick desert shrub. He sees that the wall of shrub is what lies between the government posts. He lowers his head to push through.

A thorn breaks with a loud, snapping sound.

Heart pounding, he takes off his pack and claws at the base of the plant. Hard crystals burrow into his nails, but yes, under that, the ground is softer. He smells moisture and digs, hand over hand, until he has a groove, deep and wide enough for his head and shoulders. He squeezes himself into the hollow above the roots and beneath the shrub where the growth is newer, more pliant.

Thorns tear, scrape his back, but they bend, don't snap. He squeezes past one bush and pulls his belongings through after him. He begins on the next, then the next. It's slow. But finally the wall of brush is behind him.

Ahead is a narrow stretch of open space that leads into an opening in the sierra. The Pass of Bacatete, he thinks. Terrified of creating a silhouette against the open space, he drags himself across on his belly before darting around the lip of the pass. He walks a few meters more, and finds himself standing before Mazocoba, the highest peak of the sacred Bacatete mountain range. For generations this has been the Yaquis' traditional stronghold.

Alejo studies the mountain, sees the long slope leading to the top, which is enveloped in a misty fog. Doesn't look difficult, he thinks. He jumps when Juan and Charco appear behind him. In silence, they wait until Gustavo arrives, then start as dawn begins.

Again Juan leads. He walks around the base of the mountain

until he finds a wash with shrubs growing between the loose pebbles. "We'll go up this, until we have to climb," he says, scrambling on all fours up the wash.

The others follow, grabbing the hardy sacatón to pull themselves up. They move, scrambling and pulling themselves at an angle, around the mountain. Curled cacti and barbed shrubs cling to the mountainside and to their pants legs.

Alejo hears a muffled groan, then makes one of his own when his open hand lands on some cat's claw, a cactus that punctures the palm of his hand.

They reach a narrow ridge of hard rock. It rises at an incline. A light dew has descended over the dense volcanic mountainside, causing Alejo's hands and boots to slip off the wet rock.

Pendejo! How did I plan to get up there? he wonders. Since they left for the Bacatete, he has always seen himself on top of the mountain talking to the Yaqui chiefs Opodope and Tetabiate. He saw himself describing the voyage to Yucatán and detailing the treatment of Yaquis. The chiefs would listen intently, and devise a plan to keep their people here in their homeland. Never had he envisioned himself climbing a mountain with heavy equipment choking him.

It seems to Alejo that they are spiraling their way up Mazocoba. Finally Juan leads them to a ledge wide enough for them to stop. They strain for breath. Alejo and Gustavo sit down. Charco squats. Juan remains standing.

Alejo looks down. We're more than halfway up, he thinks. High enough to get hurt if we fall.

"The way we're going is taking too long," complains Gustavo.

"We left no trail," says Juan. "Now we climb. Watch."

Juan climbs as if he were embracing the mountain. Huaraches swing from the rope around his trousers as his arms reach out, fingers probing for the next break in the basalt wall. His bare feet seem to enter into the mountain.

Alejo climbs, digging his fingertips and the toes of his boots into any narrow crack. His thighs shake violently. "Is this possible?" he whispers to Charco.

"They say children have done it," grunts Charco, hugging the mountain. "Watch Juan."

"I can't do that," says Alejo, face bathed in sweat.

Gustavo says, "Don't go straight up. Move at an angle."

Charco follows Gustavo. Soon they're out of Alejo's sight.

Alone, Alejo stays pinned to the side of the mountain. The morning sun has burned off enough fog for him to track Juan's ascent. He's encouraged when, minutes later, he sees Juan standing on what looks like another fair-sized ledge.

Holding his breath, he forces himself to follow Juan's trail, positioning his hands where Juan's have been. The feel of rock cutting into his hands comforts him. He forces the toe of his boot onto a stingy ledge and gains another step. One tiny bit, then another.

Above him, Juan waits, lying flat, and prepared to pull him up. Calves burning, Alejo extends a shaking arm to Juan. The strength of Juan's pull lands Alejo facedown on the porous ledge, where he remains until his sweat dries.

"Good," says Charco.

Alejo sees Gustavo and Charco standing next to Juan.

"How did you get up here?" asks Alejo.

"There's a path around the back," says Gustavo. "It must be a false trail, because it leads right back to here."

Suddenly blasts of gunfire surround them. The four lie flat as shots come from behind and from both sides. The shots continue, forcing them to hug the mountain to protect themselves from a hailstorm of shattered rock.

Over endless deafening volleys of gunfire, Charco screams, "What is this?"

Dust covers Gustavo's face. Rock fragments bounce off his head and shoulders. "They're attacking Mazocoba!" he says, cupping his ears. "We're too late!"

"Move," screams Juan, pointing to the top. They shake their

heads, refusing to move. Juan drops his gear. "Wait here," he yells. He climbs out of sight.

Unable to see who's shooting, they stand flush to the side of the mountain and wait for a break from the deafening shots. None comes. Instead, the volleys seem to thicken as if joined by fresh, eager recruits.

Gustavo shields his eyes from the falling debris and looks up. "They're firing at the top of Mazocoba, but I can't see from where." With his field glasses, he scours the side of the mountain for Juan. "Too much smoke."

"Give me those," says Alejo. He grabs the glasses. Staying flat, he surveys the area. "Look down there." He points to a nearby mountain peak on the other side of a steep canyon. "They're firing at us from that mesa. I bet they have the whole mountain surrounded."

"We must do something!" screams Charco, body tight, poised to leap anywhere.

"Juan said to wait," says Alejo. His stomach feels as if it's turned over. A bitter taste fills his mouth.

"This is the battle we were trying to stop," says Gustavo, a wild look in his eyes. "I say we go down."

"No!" shouts Alejo. "If we move, the soldiers will see us and shoot. So will the Yaquis. We wait for Juan." He yanks Charco and Gustavo down next to him, keeping his arms around them until they nod that they will stay.

For hours, they sit, backs pressed against the mountain, heads buried in their arms. Rock fragments and clods of dirt pile up around them.

Smoke and dust darken, thicken the air. Alejo drinks from his canteen. Charco tears off a piece of his shirttail, wets it, and drapes it across his nose. Alejo and Gustavo do the same.

"What time is it?" asks Charco, yelling into Gustavo's ear. Gustavo pulls out his watch. Three o'clock. It's dark. The sun's rays cannot break through the sheet of smoke. Through the glasses

Alejo sees a canopy of smoke connecting Mazocoba to the next mountain.

A powerful voice calls to them from somewhere up the mountain. Squinting, Alejo sees Juan drop a rope to them.

Pushing away the rope, Gustavo shouts, "It's suicide! The minute we start climbing, we become a target."

Alejo shouts, "They can't see us through the smoke."

"I'd rather die up there than here," yells Charco. He straps his and Juan's saddlebags to his back, tests the rope with several hard pulls, hoists his feet up so that they are perpendicular to the face of the mountain, and climbs. From below, he seems to be walking up the side of the mountain.

Alejo sees raw fear in Gustavo's eyes. "The battle of Mazocoba has started, Alejo. What do we know about fighting?" His voice falters. "Why should Yaquis accept you and me? Because we're dressed like them? Juan and Charco belong up there, we don't."

"We belong on the right side. That's up there," answers Alejo. "Besides, with them we stand a chance of escaping. Yaquis must know an escape route. We don't."

Alejo points to the mountain across from them. "See those soldiers? They're carrying full packs. They have to go down that steep canyon and then come up again before they begin climbing Mazocoba. They might not even get here."

"They will, Alejo," says Gustavo sadly. He reaches for the rope. "And once the soldiers get this far, they will be inaccessible to Yaqui guns." He tightens his gear and climbs the way Charco did.

Alejo looks down at the canyon. Gustavo is right, he realizes. Once the soldiers start climbing, they'll be beneath the Yaqui's line of fire. They'll make it, and I'll fight in the battle I tried to prevent. He notices his stomach no longer aches.

He grabs the rope, pulls himself up, past ricocheting bullets, past flying rock fragments, until he reaches the top. Once there, Alejo uses his feet to push away from the mountain. He swings out and returns with enough momentum to swivel his legs over the edge.

Alejo sees that the rope that held him is tied around Juan's waist. Also around Juan's waist are the strong arms of a stocky, powerful woman. Pilar, Juan's sister. She wears a long faded calico skirt, a man's shirt—crossed cartridge belts around the chest—and hat with two hawk feathers in it.

Tacho's voice awakens Alejo's memory. Only defenders of Yaqui territory may wear hawk feathers. The thick braids that trail down her back represent the power and wisdom of the woman to control the destinies of the tribe. Pilar is barefoot.

Juan nods at Alejo, then turns his back to him. He leaves, moves cautiously, body close to the ground. It's clear Alejo is not to follow. Pilar remains. She stands straight, heedless of the soldiers on the opposite mesa firing in her direction.

Transfixed, Alejo watches her coil the rope as she strides to the very edge of the peak. She lays down the rope and takes up an old Winchester with a tubular magazine beneath the barrel. Standing erect, face calm, she grips the rough rim of the mountain with her toes as she fires fifteen rounds at the soldiers across from her. Finished, she spits. With an open hand, she presses the hat down on her head. Turning, she catches Alejo's eyes upon her.

Embarrassed, Alejo wants to say something—anything—to her. Here, in the midst of the tumult, beneath a blanket of smoke, heat, and the endless thunder of rifle fire, he wants to praise her. He opens his mouth, but words are useless before Pilar's stony expression.

He fumbles with his backpack, but he can't untie the leather straps around his chest. Pilar moves toward him. Out of nowhere she produces a knife and with a single thrust cuts through the straps. She hands him his backpack, wraps a hand around his neck, and leads him like a child to a narrow opening between the rocks.

She leaves, and Alejo sees Charco join her. Alejo hollers, "Charco!" Neither Charco nor Pilar looks back.

Alejo is hurt and angry with Charco and Juan. Why are they ignoring him? Alejo sees Gustavo firing at the soldiers across the canyon. He shows no sign he ever hesitated to climb to Mazocoba.

From his limited vantage, Alejo sees why the Yaquis consider this peak impregnable. Mazocoba is a flat table of volcanic rock. The vertical rocks around the top form natural barriers, allowing the Yaquis to fire safely through narrow openings. Their enemies will know to get directly beneath them, so the Yaqui bullets won't reach them. How much ammunition do the Yaquis have? he wonders.

Alejo estimates the time. Four o'clock. He lifts his rifle. Charco has abandoned him. The first bullet he fires releases bitter tears. The sharp pain that wends its way through his chest connects him to the shattered Mazocoba.

SMOKE AND DUST burn his eyes, close his throat, fill his chest. He opens his canteen and drinks.

Through the smoke he can barely see the sun in the west. He guesses it's around five o'clock. The soldiers have been shooting nonstop for almost eight hours.

His thoughts turn to the fearless Pilar. He wants to see her, to prove himself to her. Why did she leave him here? He knows the answer. He's a Yori.

Then a piercing toque de asalto cuts through the rifle fire. Countless bugles echo this official call to arms. The shrill bugle cries rise to Mazocoba, surrounding the peak with terrible threats.

Alejo and Gustavo exchange glances. They know that call to arms means an all-out order to attack. Government troops will make the final climb to the top.

They must find their escape route now, Alejo thinks. They don't know their way around Mazocoba, and their clothing doesn't make them Yaquis. They could be shot.

Alejo low-crawls toward Gustavo. "Where's Juan or Charco?" he yells.

Gustavo shrugs. Together they hurry toward the center of the

mesa. Pilar is ordering the people swarming around her to the farthest side of the mesa.

"That must be the way out," says Alejo.

They hasten in that direction. "Good God," says Alejo. "There
are *thousands* up here." The top of Mazocoba is a pueblo, he thinks.
He looks closer. A torn, hungry, thirsty pueblo.

But not everyone is leaving. Some families head toward the middle of the mesa. They're seeking shelter in a large rock fortress con-
structed of stacked stones. He wonders if that's where the Yaquis
will make their last stand. But that fortress can't hold all this multitude.

Others hide behind parapets of tightly fitted stone four feet high.
Hiding space is precious. People, their faces turned away from the
dense hot smoke that laps every crevice in the mesa, scurry past the
fort and walls. Alejo offers his canteen. A hand takes it. His food
goes as quickly. He realizes he has lost Gustavo.

The pace around him is hurried, but not hysterical or panicked.
It's solemn, as if the participants have prepared for this all their
lives. He listens, but hears no wails of panic, no cries of desperation,
no complaints about the fumes that have turned breathing into
agony. Children do not weep when silent women hurry them
along. He trips over pieces of ancient muskets, empty carbines,
empty shells. They have no weapons, he realizes.

A voice announces, *"Yoris!"* He turns. The Mexicans are at the
top.

Frantic yelling tells Alejo that the enemy has arrived from a
place no one expected. He sees government soldiers lying flat on
their stomachs firing at the crowd, turning it into a wave rolling
across the mesa.

More soldiers arrive. They stand at the very spot he and Gustavo
have just left. The soldiers fire, catching the Yaquis in a cruel cross-
fire.

Quickly, Yaqui warriors surround the stone fortress and fire
black-powder firearms. Soldiers fall. More replace them.

Alejo now sees hundreds of people racing toward the farthest side of the mesa. Staying close to the edge of the mountain, he too runs. He passes the rock fortress searching for Charco, Gustavo, Juan.

Turning, he sees the soldiers are still shooting, but they have stopped advancing. More and more soldiers reach the top. It's as if the mountain itself were giving birth—first head, then shoulders, chest, finally legs.

When that part of the mesa can hold no more soldiers, the order comes, "Al ataque!" and the soldiers' battle cry merges with blasts of gunfire into a resounding call for blood. The Yaquis answer with their own proud readiness.

Alejo watches.

The soldiers—some with guns, others with rifles and fixed bayonets—advance inexorably toward the stone fortress. Yaqui warriors—men and women—form a line of defense between the soldiers and the fort.

As if in released longing, the enemies clash in full abandon— two, three, four embrace, meld, fall, and even on their knees, arms keep rising and falling, hacking and mutilating long after the opponent is still.

A bugle orders the soldiers' retreat. They haul away some of their wounded, regroup, reload, then fire a thick lead rain at the stone fortress.

Alejo sees where the bullets that pass the first line of defense will find their mark—it's among those protecting the children. He races toward them.

Bone fragments spray the air. A woman loses the top of her head, yet she turns and reaches her hand out to a child just beyond her. Another woman is shot through the neck. Her head drops, but her arms remain around a half-dozen children.

Pilar appears. She shoves the dead woman aside and leads the children away from the fort.

Hands outstretched, Alejo yells, "Give them to me!"

He takes the hand of a stunned five-year-old boy, the head of a chain of six worn-out children, and steers them through the melee toward the far side of the mesa.

Gone is the solemnity of moments before. The Yoris are on Mazocoba. People push, shove each other out of the way and over dead bodies. A world is ending.

Alejo sees Pilar's eyes on him. He will not disappoint her. Proudly, he holds up one of the children. He gestures, *Can I go to you?*

She shakes her head. With her rifle, she vehemently points him to the most extreme part of the mesa. It's an order.

Anguished, Alejo watches her take her place among the warriors in front of the fort. Body low to the ground, she places one leg in front of the other. She's ready. Except that her hat with the feathers is gone. No. The person next to her wears the hat. Charco.

Though filled with jealousy, Alejo sends an impulse of love to his brother, then follows Pilar's order.

Before him, a river of people descends from the mountain. The river disappears into a thick bank of smoke. Ahead of him he sees Gustavo, an old woman clinging to his back.

The woman's hands are locked beneath his chin. Her eyes are closed. Alejo elbows his way toward him. He does not tell Gustavo about Charco.

Gustavo screams, "It all ends with the next charge."

Alejo lifts a boy and girl whose legs can no longer carry them. The other children grab hold of his legs. Their small heads press against him as desperate adults race to evacuate what they thought was an impenetrable fortress.

The descent proves more treacherous than the climb up. Every foothold is occupied. The side of the mountain is alive with people scaling, slipping, sliding.

Fumes smelling of human fear, feces, urine, blood, and gunpowder fill his nostrils.

Alejo tries to lower the children first, but they're barefoot and the shrub covering the mountain is full of spikes. He sees that Gustavo has moved the woman to his front so that her hands now hang around his neck. This protects her.

Alejo does the same with his two children. The other four he will move one at a time, descending first, then reaching for them. He arches his body around them. The children work well, moving rapidly, helping each other. The blanket of smoke prevents him from gauging how far he has to go. No matter, nightfall is near.

To his left a man helps a wounded woman whose arm hangs limp and useless by her side. Her shoulder is a bloody mass. Suddenly the man falls backward and disappears into the smoke. Before Alejo can reach her, she also falls. The people on the other side of him also fall back. It's as if the mountain itself had shoved them off. No sign of Gustavo.

A bullet strikes the spot from where his foot just moved and spews rock shards over him and the children. In disbelief, Alejo screams, "No!" as he realizes that they are being fired upon from *behind.*

That means the soldiers know about this exit. He turns, searching for the source of the bullets, but he sees only smoke.

"Who's behind us?" he hollers, but his voice is lost. He's talking to the mountain.

Alejo makes his legs reach farther, and the children respond by moving faster. "Good, good," he says, patting their sharp shoulder blades. He assumes he has made progress, because he can no longer see the mountaintop.

A rapid line of bullets pelts the area above him. Fear grips him. Teeth rattling, he leans against the children. No doubt. "They're behind us!"

Now others understand this new offensive. They hurry, slip, crush his hands. Looking up, Alejo sees that the river of people has become a frenzied torrent, heedlessly seeking its doom.

But from below, under the smoke, he hears desperate warnings. Torn voices fill the inferno. *"Torocoyoris, torocoyoris!"* Traitors, traitors!

The body of a man falls from the sky and crashes into him, almost pulling him off the mountainside. Another body hits the cliff wall, then bounces off. More bodies.

From the number of people falling, Alejo concludes that the final charge has occurred and the soldiers have gained possession of Mazocoba. Charco, he thinks. Charquito.

"Almost, almost," he whispers to the children.

A bullet crashes into the mountain, ricochets, and penetrates the lower part of his leg.

A wetness fills his boot. *I can't be shot.* Heat fills his leg, then a dull pain enters his knee. He can't reach the children because his body is broken somewhere and he's tipping over. *Pilar trusted me.*

Falling through the smoke, he realizes he had longer to go than he thought.

24

FELIPA ARRIVED AT THE BACATETE THE MORNING OF THE GOVernment's attack on Mazocoba. She passed easily through the government posts. They seemed almost empty.

Not until she crossed the Pass of Bacatete did a corporal from the National Guard detain her. "My orders are to shoot anyone approaching Mazocoba."

Seeing his fear, she spoke cautiously, veiling her rage with helplessness. "As well you should. And that's my fear. My son is here somewhere. He's young and foolish. He and his friends heard rumors of a big battle and came to see. They left without permission. I've been traveling three days looking for them."

He kept his Remington trained on her. "He's not with a regiment?" He eyed Moro.

"Absolutely not! As I said, he's young and . . ."

At that moment, the government forces opened fire on the mountain. The power of the coordinated blast made them both jump. Moro shrieked, tried to break loose.

"Señora, I'm going to shoot!"

Felipa lifted the reins. Without looking back, she raced half a league before stopping. She remained in the wagon the entire day, getting down only to give water to the mule and Moro.

She faced the mountain and witnessed.

NIGHTFALL.

The battle is decided.

Lantern in hand, she plows through brambles and brush toward the base of Mazocoba. A half-dozen exhausted, dehydrated soldiers call out to her. Two of them approach her. Each takes an arm and tries to turn her around.

She towers over them and with little effort shakes herself free. She holds the lamp up to her face so that they may see her clearly. "A ésta madre no la paran, cabrones!"

They laugh. Victory is theirs. The woman is unarmed. They wave her through.

Her search begins. The smoke of the battle has settled over the ground like a giant cobweb. She watches her footing over the broken surface dotted with sharp, unyielding rocks.

The first body she finds is a woman, lying facedown, arms outstretched. Felipa asks herself why she only anticipated finding males when at day's end she saw every kind of human form fall from the peak. Maybe because these acts belong to men.

She sees other lanterns, hears male voices barking in Spanish, for efficiency and speed. Ah, the cleanup, she realizes. She hurries, hears the incoherent calls of the wounded, goes toward them, but doesn't go too near. She will know her son.

*   *   *

"I MUST GO to the Bacatete," he said to her the night before he left.

After the meeting in the barn, while Charco entertained the younger boys in the living room, Alejo came to be alone with her in her room, his arms loaded with supplies.

She watched him oil and test his wood-carving tools. His face changed, grew softer, handsomer, more beautiful. Yes, my son is beautiful, she thought, aware that she could not say these words to him.

With charcoal, he drew what looked like a giant maguey on the longest board he could find. "I'm going to carve this," he said. "Someday." He claimed the plant was much bigger than the magueys of Sonora. "Over two meters," he said, his eyes wide with wonder. "They kidnap people for this. Take them from their families, and work them to death to make rope with this plant. So you see, I must go."

"And if your mother forbids you?"

He kneeled before her, hands around her waist, and whispered, "Listen to me. Remember how things are with us—between you and me. Remember how we *know*. If there's a battle, I know I will not die there. If there's a battle, you come look for me. Find me."

He rested his head on her lap, allowing her to caress him. She understood this was his gift to her. He stayed until midnight, when Charco knocked on the door reminding Alejo of their appointment to meet Castillo.

"Remember, come look for me," he said before leaving.

His intensity had convinced her. Until morning.

SHE SEES SILHOUETTES separate the wounded from the dead. Piles of each surround the base of the mountain. Some soldiers tie crude bandages, while others offer water. The wounded mumble names. "Isikio." "Dominga." "Antonio." She listens for Alejo's voice.

Tracing her way farther around the base, she enters an area with much heavier casualties. The bodies are in heaps, draped randomly

one on top of the other in such numbers that the soldiers are loading them onto two-wheel carts they have hand-pulled through the
thick ravines. Some men carry lanterns; others use kerosene-soaked
brush as torches.

She moves closer, lowers the lantern over several individuals.
Her pulse quickens. Her legs tremble. These aren't soldiers. She
sees old people. Infants. Children. Entire families. Other than
death, they share something else: they have been shot several times
in the back.

"Qué buscas?" demands a faceless voice in the night.

"Mi niño," she stammers, not recognizing her own voice.

She lowers the lantern, frees her arms, and begins moving bodies, tossing the dead and lifting the wounded with care. They seem
weightless, slight, thin. Horrified, she realizes they are children.

First she sees the toe of his boot. He's lying faceup, with two
children over him. One is unconscious, but breathing. To the shadows moving in the darkness she calls, "Come for this child. She's
alive." Felipa lifts the girl off Alejo and rests her on a bed of shattered rock.

She locks her arms around Alejo's chest to lift him off the bodies
beneath him. She goes back for the lantern, and checks those below
him. They're soft, warm, but dead. Felipa sees the soldiers are moving in her direction. In the semidarkness, she carries, drags, her son
until she finds a flat space. There she cradles him on her lap and
lowers her cheek to his nose. He's breathing.

She shakes his head, calls into his ear. "Alejo! I'm here! Alejo!"
She taps his cheek until he moans.

"Look at me, Alejo! Answer!"

Eyelids barely open, he gazes at her and squeezes her hand.
"Le . . ." He points, drops his hand on his thigh.

She opens his pants leg up to the thigh, then she probes downward. Her fingers find the shredded leather boot. She tears apart
what is left of the boot and slowly slides it off. The niche between
shin and ankle is wet, hollow. She rends the hem of her skirt and
ties a constricting band around his midcalf.

"Alejo, help me get you to the wagon. The soldiers mustn't find you. You'll be taken prisoner. Do you understand?"

He doesn't. He needs air, she thinks. She stacks two bodies on top of each other and props Alejo against them. She fans furiously with her skirt until he lifts his head.

Firmly she says, "Alejo, I'll hold you up by the waist. Keep this arm around my neck. Carry the lantern with the other."

They take a few steps, and Alejo screams in pain. She lifts him higher, transferring most of his weight onto her hip. "Better?"

"Yes." His first complete word.

THE ARMY'S CLEANUP lasted all night.

By dawn, she has ripped off the Yaqui clothing, put him into one of José's shirts, washed him, and tied a strip of rawhide around his calf. She waits for daylight, afraid to move, lest guards stop her.

Wrapped in a wool blanket, his back to the mountain, a dazed Alejo rests against the water barrel and sips pinole as the sun rises. The hot sweet liquid opens a throat sealed by gunsmoke.

First light shows Felipa the battle's tally. Walking toward her must be a thousand people. In torn bloody rags, faces sooty, burned, lips blistered, cut, they move in slow, heavy silence.

Outraged, Felipa demands, "Dónde estás, Virgen Santa?" She shakes a fist at the sky. See this maimed, broken multitude—these old men and women, these maidens, these boys, these mothers whose children emit not a single complaint, tearless children whose stonelike expressions ask for nothing. Holy Mother, doesn't this silence wring your soul?

She takes a ladle of water to the child closest to her. He drinks, the mother nods and moves on. Felipa refills the ladle several times until a soldier on horseback forces her back to the wagon.

"These people need help," she argues.

"There's help four leagues from here in Tetacombiate," he says. "Who's he?" He's looking at Alejo.

"My son. A volunteer."

Before leaving, the soldier circles the wagon, making sure it's only a Mexican woman, a wounded boy, and a horse.

Felipa moves slowly, careful not to call attention to herself. Eventually she sees wagons like hers in the area. Most drivers are women. Is this all that we're for? A familiar anger rises.

She corrects herself. No, most drivers aren't women. Some wagons have couples in them. A soldier maneuvers a buckboard packed with Yaqui children through the parked wagons. The children are young—five at most. Good, she thinks, at least some people have come for the orphans.

A man stands up, points to a child, and pays the soldier for his selection. Numb, Felipa can't believe what she sees. The soldier puts the money into a sack and goes to the next wagon for the next sale.

Choking with rage, she says, "Alejo, we're moving. Hold your leg." She doesn't wait for him to respond. She slaps the mule and it jerks forward.

Alejo hollers, "Stop!" He's trying to lift the ankle by holding up the calf. His face is colorless.

"Keep it high," she says, thinking she'll wash the wound after she crosses the wall of dust raised by wagons, horses, soldiers, and prisoners.

Bumps are unavoidable. Alejo groans but stays flat. Good, she thinks, he won't see this misery. God only knows what part he had in creating it.

He's hurt, but this brooding, the way he keeps his head turned away from the mountain, is from something else.

Her plan was to find Alejo, give him the papers, and send him on Moro to the border. Now she realizes she must take him. She has no idea where Arizona is, but she will ask until she gets there.

Already the obstacles begin. Frustrated, she sees that her route will be much shorter if she cuts directly through the mass of prisoners. She steels herself, vowing to look only straight ahead. As the wagon moves, the horde parts and closes behind her. She imagines she feels their eyes following her. She is too ashamed to look back.

For the most part, few soldiers escort the prisoners, except for a cadre of National Guardsmen that surround the remnants of what must have been the core Yaqui fighters—most of them men, most of them wounded.

Ahead of her, marching barefoot abreast the line of warriors, she sees a small figure, in torn bloody clothes. He wears a crushed hat with broken feathers sticking out of it. She recognizes the wide swing of the arms, the raised chin, the familar arrogant strut of Hector and José.

Charco.

Her mind races. I need a plan. What? What? Los pesos fuertes. She reaches into the narrow inconspicuous box nailed beneath the seat, pulls out a five-peso coin, and slips it into the waistband of her skirt.

She steers the wagon alongside Charco. "Get on," she orders. "Quick!"

Before the boy can move, a soldier spurs his horse between them, knocking Charco to the ground.

Felipa brakes the wagon and stands up. "He's mine!"

The soldier draws his gun and points it at her. "That's a prisoner of war. Who are you?"

She jumps down. "Felipa Robles de Durcal from Alamos. And I say that's my son. Look at his eyes. Blue. Look at his back. He has a mark like this." She outlines a scythe with her index finger.

The soldier accepts her challenge. He dismounts, slaps Charco's hat off, and peers into the boy's bruised face. With his boot he turns Charco over and yanks down his pants.

"That boy in the wagon is his brother. He fought as a volunteer on your side and he has the same mark."

The soldier is thorough. He checks Alejo, who stifles a scream during the stranger's harsh inspection. Next the soldier drives his sword through her supplies. No firearms. No Yaquis hiding.

Felipa approaches the soldier, whose head barely reaches her shoulder. She leans down and in a low voice coos, "Give him to me. Not everything is easy to understand. Just believe we're Mexicans. This *one* is no danger to you."

She presses the gold coin deep into his palm. She holds her breath until she feels his fingers tighten around the blessed amulet. Nodding toward the horde of prisoners, she whispers, "You fought bravely and won. You still have much to do."

Brusquely, she yanks Charco to his feet. "Get on the wagon, disobedient boy!"

Charco tries to pick up the hat, but the soldier covers it with his boot. Charco pauses, looks at Felipa, then walks to the side of the wagon. He curls his toes around a wheel spoke and leaps up.

25

THE FIFTY-MILE PROFILE OF THE BACATETE BEHIND THEM, Felipa stops to study Alejo's wound. She traces where the bullet ripped the boot, entered the leg, then tore its way through the shin and inner ankle. Both lower leg bones are shattered. The thinner outer bone is a pointed shaft. The thicker inside bone is splintered.

Charco looks over Felipa's shoulder. "Did he fall?"

"Shot."

"I know how to take out a bullet."

Alejo mumbles, "You know nothing." He turns away.

"Ha!" says Charco. "You're mad because Pilar ordered you off the mountain."

Alejo looks away. "You and Juan left us. We were supposed to stay together."

"You're a Yori, 'Lejo. Pilar couldn't let you fight. We brought Juan home, so she helped us. Without her, we'd be dead."

Alejo lifts his head as if to argue, but falls back.

Felipa puts her hand on Charco's chest. "Move."

Charco climbs out of the wagon and watches while she ladles water over the mangled flesh and covers it loosely with a sleeve of a shirt of José's. While Felipa works, Alejo grits his teeth, emits a low growling sound.

Felipa removes the thick leather belt around her waist, tosses it to Charco. "Take the machete. Make more holes," she says, her hands wrapped around Alejo's calf. "Make it small enough to tighten around the leg."

Charco admires the elaborately tooled leather. *"Sewam,"* he says. "Señora, not the machete. It will make ugly slices in this."

"Look through Alejo's tools, under the seat. Hurry."

Charco chooses a swivel knife to poke holes through the leather and hands the belt back to her. "Alejo's father chose Sonora flowers for his belt."

She decides not to tell Charco that she chose the flowers. She tightens the belt around the calf. The foot seems to darken by the minute. What if I hadn't come? she wonders. She picks up the reins and prods the mule into a faster pace.

MIDAFTERNOON.

Felipa asks herself, where does Sonora end?

She's never left the Alamos region. The stars tell her she's driving north, past the leanest country she has ever seen. A few magueys and creosote bushes, an occasional mesquite or a furry cholla dot the land ahead and around her. Out of reach, distant hills look fuzzy with wild winter growth. The rest is solid rock or sandy gravel.

Her son needs a doctor and she needs directions. She's abandoned hope of finding a town, and looks for a cow, a dog—any sign of people.

"Charco, do you know Sonora?"

"I've been everywhere," he boasts. "Everywhere—though not for too long." He's sitting in the middle of the wagon holding up Alejo's foot. "There's nothing around here. San Lorenzo is two days away. Lend me the horse. I'll go find a ranch."

Alejo opens his eyes. He struggles, but manages to throw the enamel cup lying by his side and hits Charco across the nose. "Horse thief!" He screams in pain.

Charco laughs, then grows serious. "I would never steal Moro." He tosses the cup back. "Alejo, you were still helping when you carried the children."

Felipa remembers the young bodies she found around her son and feels Alejo's humiliation. "We'll camp here," she says, unable to stop the sorrow swelling in her for her son and Charco, the wanderer whose feral eyes have seen too much cruelty.

She watches Charco with Moro and the mule. He waters, feeds, and brushes them with the care Alejo would have used. He leaves with a hand ax, and returns with enough wood to start a fire, small, but strong enough to boil water.

She rubs her arms and hands, numb from hours of driving. She doesn't dare move Alejo, merely tucks the blankets around him and turns him so that his leg rests on the wagon seat. Over the coals she heats flour tortillas and makes carne seca tacos. She passes around piñon nuts and slices of dried quince.

Alejo raises himself on an elbow while he chews a handful of nuts and drinks water. Charco washes down several tacos with cups of pinole and packs his mouth full of nuts and fruit. For herself, Felipa pours hot water through a gauze bag filled with ground coffee, cinnamon, and sugar. When they finish there is a little bit of day left.

Not waiting to be asked, Charco unloads the saddle so that Felipa and Alejo can sleep in the wagon. Out of the saddle and saddle blankets, he fixes himself a pallet directly beneath them.

"I'm here, señora," he says. "Alejo, how's your leg?"

"Hot. Are Juan and Pilar dead?"

"Not Juan. He found his family and left before the Yoris got to the top. I heard Pilar tell him to leave."

"How? Mazocoba was surrounded."

"She told him to hide with his family in the caves beneath the ridges until the battle ended. Juan took his saddlebags and mine. Pilar told him how to walk to Arizona. 'Walk north, past La Colorada and Minas Prietas. After you cross the Valley of Concepción, walk the chain of mountains to Arizona.'"

Angry that her son wasn't helped, Felipa asks, "Why didn't she tell the rest of you how to get out?"

"Señora, Yoris aren't Yoemem," answers Charco.

"So many fell from the mountain," says Alejo. His voice is weak.

"I know," says Charco. "The Yoris got there, and we ran out of ammunition. We fought with our hands, rocks, anything. The Yoris clubbed the wounded or shot them in the back of the head. *Tiro de gracia.* Then when the soldiers started taking prisoners, the Yoemem threw themselves off the mountain." Charco pauses. His voice is barely audible. "More than a hundred jumped. Women with children. I couldn't—didn't have the courage."

After a while, Alejo asks, "It took us so long to climb—how did the Yoris get there so fast?"

Loud, clear, Charco begins, "I'll tell you what the Yoemem told me this morning. One of our own betrayed us."

"Who?" asks Alejo.

"Pluma Blanca, Tetabiate's second in command, joined the Yoris. He took them to Mazocoba and showed them one of the secret entrances. He betrayed us—that *torocoyori!* He who calls himself Loreto Villa. He showed the soldiers how to get into the meseta. The fourth and eleventh battalions climbed up the way we did."

"If Juan had shown us the entrance," says Alejo, "maybe we could have left with him."

"I doubt if Juan knew. He isn't a mountain Yaqui. They say the mountain life is the hardest life a Yaqui can live. Juan had a family. Anyway, let me finish. Now all the Yaqui chiefs are gone. Opodope fought to the end—died in knee-firing position. I don't know what happened to Tetabiate. I think he got out. The soldiers found the Yori priest and nuns. The Yoemem had put them away safely in one of the fortresses. What the newspaper said about the Yaquis killing them was a lie. And Gustavo?"

With effort, Alejo stammers, "Our friend vanished. He was ahead of me, carrying an old woman. If he's alive, he must be with the wounded. I lost him when they started attacking us from behind."

"That was the twentieth battalion!" says Charco, angrily. "Cabrones never even fought. They hid in the ravines and brush behind Mazocoba waiting for the Yoemem to come down the mountain. When the mountain was full of people, they opened fire. They had unlimited ammunition, I heard. They hunted Yaquis instead of fighting them."

Felipa thinks of what she herself saw—that area filled with old and young corpses. She hates hearing about killing, but at least Alejo and Charco are talking to each other again.

Charco recites every detail to Alejo. *Etehoi,* the Yaquis call it. Tellings. *Etehoi* is how Yaquis record events, according to José. He'd keep after Tacho, saying *"Etehoi, etehoi,"* until he'd prodded the old man to tell him again of the Cajeme days.

Charco continues in his storytelling voice. "Finally the fighting ended. They pulled the survivors to their feet, and separated the men and women. Then a soldier found a boy hiding with the women and dragged him to the men's side. The boy was about my age. His girlfriend ran to him, and, holding hands, they jumped off the mountain. It happened fast, and left everyone—Yoris and Yoemem—shaking, maybe because the heat of killing was over."

"Pilar?" asks Alejo, fighting sleep.

"Hay, Pilar," sighs Charco. "She was the best. Everyone is staring at the empty space where the boy and girl jumped, and sud-

denly Pilar runs full speed at the soldiers. She grabs three around
the neck and takes them down with her."

Charco's voice is shaking. Felipa can't tell if it is pride or grief.

"She was the best," echoes Alejo.

THE FOLLOWING MORNING, Alejo wakes, face wet with fever. Felipa
checks the wound. The center tissues have swollen to twice their
size, and the edges of the outer skin have shrunk away from each
other like the collar of an open shirt. The foot is black.

She remembers her father's death—his blistered lips, flushed
skin, and the blood inside that had boiled until he burst. She hurries
the mule northward, searching for anyone who can point them to a
town. Only the wheel ruts in the dirt tell her she is on a road.

By noon, Alejo is delirious, babbling "Moro," and "Tacho." She
rechecks the wound. The smell is foul.

"Charco, saddle the horse," she says.

The boy moves quickly. "I'll go find a ranch."

"No. Drive the wagon. Stay on this road."

She rides east and west, up knolls, searching. Nothing. Why so
much war if Sonora is empty? She hears Tía Mercedes: "Because
men's huevos need a lot of room."

She remembers Charco's talk last night. La Colorada Mine is
north. Miners have doctors or medicine. She races ahead. Moro is
generous, and soon the wagon is out of sight.

NESTLED BETWEEN TWO hills, she spots a three-room adobe ranchito,
with a low thatched roof. "Gracias, Virgen."

A clean-shaven mestizo, maybe thirty, stands in the doorway.
His thick eyebrows hide small, deepset eyes. Arms folded across his
chest, he looks wary of the lone woman on horseback who has scattered his dogs and chickens all over the yard. Grudgingly he says,
"San Lorenzo is two days away, La Colorada four—even on that
horse."

Felipa hears young children playing in the house. A tiny, pretty woman joins him. His wife? Felipa wonders. The young woman is Indian, possibly an Euleve.

Felipa explains that her son's been shot in an accident. "What medicine do you have?" she asks.

"Enough for ourselves," he says.

"Alcohol? I'll pay."

"Bacanora and a little mezcal."

"What's the matter with him?" asks the woman.

"I need a place to clean his leg. If not, it must come off." That's the truth, she realizes, losing her breath.

He steps back. "You don't know what you're asking. We can't help you with that!"

"He will die out there," shouts Felipa, hands choking the pommel. "I will do everything. Lend me your cutting tools." They're silent. "Please!" she yells.

"Bring your son here," says the woman.

THE CHANGE IN the foot horrifies Felipa. Yes, she must cut it off. Every instinct to shield her son from pain riots within her. Hardly breathing, she wrestles with this truth.

Alejo opens his eyes. They look glazed, but as he continues to gaze at her, they clear and, for an instant, they fix on her. "Cut it."

To Charco, standing behind Felipa, Alejo says, "Help her."

"Are you sure?" asks Charco.

Alejo closes his eyes.

She wraps a blanket around the leg and rests it on the seat. She orders Charco, "Stay on this road. Keep the mule at a trot."

Night nears. She races to the ranchito. When she stops to let the horse rest, her mind continues to race, searching for everything she has seen or heard about treating wounds. José cured his own animals. He cut, cauterized, sewed. To each step she allots its separate clarity.

The kitchen has a tamped dirt floor. One kerosene lamp burns. She sees a square table with stools. The woman has a good fire going in a brazier. When Felipa enters, the woman ushers two small children to the back room and lowers the blanket that serves as a door.

On the table are a bottle of bacanora, a jar of mezcal, an ax, a machete, a saw, and three knives. Felipa drops the blades of the machete and knives into the fire.

"Eggs?" she asks.

The woman gives her two. "It's all we have. We had more this morning, but we ate them."

This tiny woman is apologizing to her. Wordless, Felipa cups the woman's hands with her own. "Aloe?"

The woman brings her a clay pot, in it a whole plant.

Outside the dogs bark. Felipa hurries out. The man follows. He helps Charco lift a semiconscious Alejo onto the kitchen table that only accommodates his torso. Charco takes a stool and holds Alejo's injured leg in his lap. The rest of Alejo—head and other leg— droop onto the other stools.

Outside, Felipa unpacks her skirts, blouses, and shirts and rips them into long strips. She ties the strips together and makes several long strands, which she braids into a single thick cord. She stops when she realizes the braided cord is longer than the wagon. Pay attention, Felipa, she chides herself.

She fills her lantern with kerosene and returns to the house. "I need something to sew with."

The woman brings a needle and thread. "I doubled the thread. Here's more. What else?"

Felipa checks, counts, itemizes. "A bowl, your molcajete, another lamp, and . . ." She has trouble saying it. "Something for the blood. A bucket perhaps."

Charco says, "I've seen an arm cut off before. You're supposed to wrap the stump in maguey peel."

"That's true," says the woman. She pulls the machete out of the fire and hands it to Charco. "Out back. There's plenty behind the goat pen." She takes Charco's place holding Alejo's leg.

The smell of rotting flesh fills the room. The man brings in another lamp, making the room much brighter.

With a hot knife, Felipa chops the aloe leaves into the molcajete and uses the pestle to grind them into the egg whites, making a thick paste. As she works, she says, "My name is Felipa Durcal. My sons are Alejo and José." She nods. "That's Alejo."

Hand covering his nose, he stands next to his wife. "We are Manuel and Carmen Peña."

"Thank you, Manuel and Carmen Peña," Felipa says.

Charco enters, his arms full of maguey leaves.

"Will we need that many?" asks Felipa.

"We might, we might." He drops them on the floor. "I'll clean them."

Felipa hands him the braid she made from the clothing. Vigorously, Charco wipes the maguey leaves to a shine, then cuts long, narrow rectangles inside the thorny oval leaves. "I'll peel when you're ready."

The room is silent, except for Alejo's labored breathing and his incoherent mumbling. The stillness seems to thicken the stench.

Felipa motions Charco to bring the lamp closer. How far up the leg does the rot go? With her fingers she separates the torn flesh around the shin. Alejo screams, almost twists off the table. Manuel runs out and returns with rope and leather thongs. Everyone helps strap Alejo to the table.

She ignores Alejo's low wail and continues her study. On one side, the outer flesh is bright red, like a burn. She raises the leg. The tissue beneath is black shreds, twisted into coils. The skin has shrunk back, allowing her to see the splintered bone protruding through the flesh. Was this there before? She tests the bone with the tip of her index finger. Already, the bone is dry.

The smell overwhelms her. She lifts her head, closes her eyes until her head stills. "Felipa," she whispers harshly to herself, "cut the foot. You've butchered animals. You know how to cut a leg."

She checks the tools, aware that she knows how she will stitch up the leg long before she has decided how to cut it off. Her eye falls on a carving knife with a six-inch blade. She tests its weight. The size and shape are familiar. Then she remembers. She takes Alejo's leg from Charco. "Go for Alejo's tools," she tells him.

"I'll need the entire leg on the table," she says. "Don Manuel, please bring the saddle."

Felipa fits the saddle over one of the stools, then raises Alejo. He screams as she and Don Manuel lift him high enough to recline his head and back on the saddle.

Charco stands with Alejo's tool kit in his hands. She takes the carving knife and rubs her thumb across the blade. "Una chaira."

The man places a rectangular whetstone on the edge of the table. He also hands her a long staff of ironwood. "I prefer this," he says.

She runs the blade and point down the staff of ironwood, then drops the knife into the fire.

Quietly, Manuel leads his wife into the back room.

Felipa plans to disjoint at the knee where the tissues are certainly clean. Ligaments and muscles are tough, but once they're cut, she knows she can carve around the kneecap. The joint should snap loose.

"The bacanora," she says.

Charco puts the bottle to Alejo's mouth. Alejo sips, coughs, spits it out, falls back.

Felipa holds Alejo's head. Hot sweat covers his body. "Help us," she hollers sternly into his ear. She pours in the liquid, holding his chin up until he gulps.

She holds the bottle up to the lamp. He has four fingers of bacanora in him. His head sways loosely on his shoulders. She forces more down him. He gags, but she clamps his jaw shut until he swallows. She waits until his head hangs, dead weight from the neck.

She runs the lantern up and down the leg.

"Where?" asks Charco.

"I'm thinking of the knee, or *here.*" She points to the upper calf.

Alarmed, Charco says, "Señora, cut below the knee. Alejo must still ride."

She rechecks the leg. The calf would be faster, she thinks. The blockage is in the shin area. She sees that the saw is a crosscut saw—cuts only on a forward thrust.

"Charco, bring the rasp," she says.

She stares at the foot, and isolates it. For the first time, she sees it for what it is. The smell identifies the enemy that would rob her of her child. A serenity enters her. Her son will live if she removes the source of this foul stench. She's suddenly eager to move against the would-be killer of Alejo that has blatantly announced itself. She is grateful that her son's enemy is so tangible.

Her mind clears. She holds out her hands. Steady.

She hugs Alejo, whispering, "Hijo, we will win."

Charco returns with the rasp. She stirs it vigorously into the jar of mezcal, then holds it over the fire. A blue flame dances through the fine teeth.

She reties José's belt firmly below the knee and pulls back the outer skin. A drunk Alejo tries to sit up. Charco pins down Alejo's head and shoulders. She ties a second cord below the belt, leaving a space of a finger between the two. She'll cut there.

She pulls the carving knife out of the fire, then lowers the machete's blade into the flames. Charco inhales loudly.

After the carving knife has cooled, she raises the leg and carefully, evenly, cuts her way around the flesh and through the red muscle. Alejo arches, shrieks loud and long. She waits until he falls back unconscious.

When she loosens the belt to locate the artery, she's unprepared for the wild spurts that douse her chest and face. She pinches the artery shut, and looks despairingly at the thread the woman left her.

"Charco, quick! Horsehair. Moro."

Calmly, Felipa waits, her fingers clamping the artery. Her son's eyes are half-closed, his mouth open. "You won't die, Alejo."

Charco returns with several strands. She takes the longest one and knots the artery tight. It holds.

She retightens the belt. Despite the tourniquet, blood flows, lands into the clay pot below.

"Turn him on his side," she says.

They release the straps. Alejo is limp as they roll him so that the wound faces up.

"Come. Hold the leg steady."

Charco stands in front of her, both hands on the knee. She feels him staring right at her.

With the rasp, she makes several runs across both bones. When she can see the grooves, she takes the saw.

"Now, come hold the foot steady," she says.

The outer, thinner bone takes three thrusts. The inner, thicker bone takes seven.

Charco falls back, holding the foot to his chest. Eyes wet, he whimpers. He holds it in front of him. "Alejo."

"Take it outside." Her voice is hoarse. "That's *not* Alejo."

Everything—flesh, tendons, muscles—is red. The tissue around the artery is white. Charco returns and holds the lantern while she carefully picks off bone fragments left by the saw.

With the hot machete blade she cauterizes the soft inner tissues. She hears a loud, sizzling sound, and smoke fills her face. The smell of scorched meat fills her nostrils.

The bleeding stops.

With the carving knife, she trims the edges of the skin, then she tugs the flaps until they meet evenly over the wound. She bites off the knot of the thread, inserting the needle at right angles to the edges of the flesh—first one side, then the other.

Tiny stitches, not too deep, not too tight. We don't want a ridge, she tells herself. Once she has the wound closed, she sews back over the stitches to fasten the thread. She holds the stump while Charco daubs it with the egg and aloe paste.

She straightens up. Her back feels as if it's been hunched over for years. She tries to walk. Her feet shuffle at first. She circles the stump, checking her work. The end is sewn tight. "The maguey," she says.

Charco warms the leaves over the fire, just enough to loosen the ends. Slowly, carefully, he strips off the clear, sticky peel. Felipa recalls how skin can shrink and tighten, so she pushes the thigh muscles downward toward the cut while Charco crossbands strips of maguey peel around the newly stitched surface.

When he's made several layers, she cuts off a strip of the braided material to use as a bandage and coils it up Alejo's thigh and trunk as far as the waist. She rolls Alejo onto his back and, raising both his legs, turns him around so that the stump rests high in the saddle. His head hangs over the end of the table.

She hears the dogs fighting outside. The leg. Charco is still stripping peels off magueys. "Stop!" she says. "Go bury the leg. Leave the door open."

"I'll bury the leg and leave the door open," he answers evenly. "But I'll stay in the wagon." The boy's face is wet. Tears? Sweat?

She remembers they have not eaten all day. "Are you all right? Eat, Charco."

As he leaves, the cool night air races in. Felipa raises her head, savors its touch. She puts out all but one lantern, grateful for the stillness in these kind strangers' home. Where are the Peñas? It doesn't matter right now. The only sound comes from the fire settling in the brazier.

She must sit down. She takes a stool and nestles Alejo's head on her lap. Her hands thick with dried blood, she strokes Alejo's face and combs his hair back with her fingers. "Now what?" she asks him.

More air rushes in. Good, she thinks. Night winds, clean this room. A dark, shadowlike form threatens to envelop her and Alejo. Nothing will separate them. Quickly, she takes what is left of the braided material, wraps it around her son's chest, then around her own waist.

She turns his head to one side so he can breathe easier, then rests her head on his chest. His heartbeat is strong. The black form looms nearer. Focusing on the cadence of Alejo's heart, she closes her eyes. Surrenders.

26

SOMEONE, SOMETHING, VIOLENTLY JOSTLES FELIPA, TRIES TO wake her. She listens for a familiar sound. None. The frantic urgency continues. Unwillingly her eyes open, and are stabbed by a bright light. Daylight fills the front door—still ajar from last night. Her head, she realizes, is on Alejo's chest. But his torso is twisting, trying to buck itself free from her.

Fully alert, she sits up. The stump is making wild circles in the air. The force of the spasms wakes Alejo.

He releases a loud, low "Aaaahhhhhhhhh!"

I've done something terrible, she thinks.

Frightened, she unties herself from her son. From outside, Charco and the Peñas, followed by two little girls, rush into the kitchen. They stand around the wooden table staring at Alejo's stump.

Alejo continues his donkeylike braying. Felipa tries to hold down the leg. It twirls away from her. She fears applying her strength.

Charco steps in, clasps his hands together, and lowers them over Alejo's upper thigh. Crazed, Alejo strikes Charco's head, shoulders, attacking him with closed fists.

Tiny Carmen Peña puts an arm around Felipa's waist. "Manuel, move the boy to the bedroom."

Her husband stands across from Charco. Together they lift Alejo. Carmen slides out the kitchen table. In a clumsy two-step dance, the men carry a screaming Alejo into the back room and lower him onto a straw-filled mattress.

Felipa follows with the saddle. The windowless room is small and crowded by an ornate chest of drawers, out of keeping with the humble home. The children's pallets cover the floor. Carmen drags them out. Felipa places the saddle at the foot of the bed. Her son's stump thrashes uncontrollably. His face, hair, body are a lustrous shine from fever.

Carmen returns. "Perhaps the bandages are too tight," she mutters, staring wide-eyed at the spasmodic leg.

"That's possible," answers Felipa, grateful to receive direction. "Hold him," she asks of everyone. "I must get closer."

Barefoot, Charco squeezes into the space between Alejo's head and the wall. He grabs the flailing arms, crosses them, and sits on them. Alejo's torso arches. His shrieks become guttural growls, his eyes white orbs.

Manuel Peña drops, full weight, on both of Alejo's thighs; Felipa removes the cord from around his waist and thigh. The bands of maguey peel remain tightly in place, she notes. But the stump flares out like the ends on a spool of thread.

"Look," she says to Carmen. "It wasn't like this last night."

Carmen tests the swelling with her fingers. Alejo screams. "Feels like water. Maybe it's blood," she says. "Manuel, what do you think?"

He shakes his head. How sorry he must be that he ever saw us, thinks Felipa.

She goes for Alejo's carving knife. Manuel and Charco pin down Alejo as she slowly wiggles the tip through the maguey bandage and into the side of the swollen stump.

A gurgling, dark-brown liquid spurts, covering the Peñas' blankets. All stare at the foamy discharge until it slows to an oozing trickle.

Alejo calms as the stump's wild motion slows. His dark eyes, made blacker by the deep circles beneath, take in the people in the room. All strangers.

Felipa dips her fingers in the liquid and smells. "It's not rotten." Head turned, Manuel says, "Must be the bone draining."

"Of course, that must be it," says Felipa. She sees the soiled covers. "I'll change these." With a single pull, she yanks the covers out beneath Alejo.

She goes to the wagon for her blankets. Returning, she sees several strips of maguey peel lying on the kitchen floor. Overnight, they have dried, curled into long, thin tubes. She picks them up.

In the bedroom, she sees the stump is almost motionless except for sporadic jerks. Alejo moans as she widens the hole she made in the bandage. She trims the edges of one of the curled peels until it fits neatly into the hole. She leaves the tubelike peel in place, then steps back to wait. Eventually, brown liquid seeps into the curled peel.

She looks at her son's drawn, exhausted face. He's nodding asleep, his breath thick with the alcohol she forced down him— when was it?

"What time is it?" she asks.

"Past noon," says Charco.

Manuel holds down Alejo's hands as Charco eases himself off the mattress.

"Past noon?" asks Felipa. "I slept a long time," she murmurs, more with wonder than embarrassment.

She looks at the Peñas—the surly, square-shouldered man who was ready to deny help to her yesterday, who today gives his bed to Alejo. The seemingly timid Indian woman with thick, waist-length braids, who gives up her home.

"I will find a way to repay you," says Felipa.

"A mother trying to save a son has no debts," says Carmen. "You will need water to wash him."

"And I have cheese to make," says Manuel.

The Peñas leave. Charco stays with Felipa. His narrow blue eyes seem to be assessing her. He would do anything for Alejo, she thinks. She extends both arms to him. "How can I repay you?" she asks.

Charco lowers his eyes, stares at the floor. "I'll bathe him," he says, eyes still down.

Tacho cleaned José's body when it lay on the table. My God, she thinks, that was barely a year ago.

"Carry the water for Carmen," she says. "I'll call if I need help."

Carmen and Charco bring water in pots, gourds, jugs. They help Felipa force it down Alejo by squeezing a water-soaked cloth over his mouth. Thirstily, Alejo drinks.

The stump rests on the saddle. But stubbornly, it continues to twitch. With each jerk Alejo releases loud, terrible screams. If only the leg could keep still, thinks Felipa.

As if reading her mind, Carmen enters, dragging two mud-filled sacks. From the chest of drawers, she pulls out a rebozo, which she drapes across the stump. She sets the weighted sacks on either side of her shawl, creating a ballast for the restless limb.

Felipa says, "Carmen, not your rebozo. I'll find something else. A woman's rebozo lasts a lifetime. You must have carried your children in that."

"Yes, I carried my daughters in it." She laughs coyly. She rests her small hands on Felipa's shoulders. "That's why I know nothing can hurt it." She leaves before Felipa can say more.

The sweetness of the young woman's touch nearly brings Felipa to tears. She's tired. She yearns to scream her tiredness to the world. Instead, she looks down, amazed at how easily Carmen stopped the leg spasms. At last, she thinks, she can wash Alejo. He is heavy but malleable.

She sits him up to wash his back, and stops when she sees the long, red scars across his shoulder blades. Angrily, she calls Charco, demanding an explanation.

Without hesitation Charco stands at the foot of the bed and begins. "The story of Martino," he says. *Etehoi* again, she thinks impatiently.

He recites the complete story—beginning with Martino's kidnapping of them, ending with the bloody death of the majocol at

Alejo's hands. Proudly, Charco points to the feverish Alejo. "He saved me, Juan, and Gustavo."

Felipa's skin aches as Charco ends his telling by showing her his scars. "The newer ones are from Martino. The old ones are from Carrasco at the bartolinas," he explains. He closes with precise details of their escape, turns on his heel, and goes out of the dark, close space.

Her faith shaken by his words, Felipa remains inside the room, afraid to leave, afraid to find out more about her Alejo, the one son she thought she knew.

She has no trouble accepting his killing a man who was clearly evil. But now she must see her son as a man who will kill obstacles that stand before him. Esteban, Martino, who else?

Lying alongside him, Felipa strives to reconcile the frightened rabbit look she saw in Alejo when he first returned with the Alejo Charco described. Alejo perplexes her. Fury and anger she associated with Hector, never Alejo. Tía Mercedes was right: women never know their sons. Yet if she must lose this most beloved son to an unknown place called Arizona, at least she can trust him to defeat his enemies.

In the end, that's what mothers fear, she thinks, a cruel force robbing their child from them, thus reversing the order of life and death. She can't help but feel proud of Alejo.

Gently her index finger traces the intricate curve of his hairline—so similar to her own. His head thrashes, ending her caress. She sponges his face and torso with cool compresses, blots his forehead, resumes her caresses.

"Remember the baby bear your father brought home?" she asks the unconscious Alejo. "You said bad things happen to those with no mother. Alejo, your mother is here."

She talks to Alejo until evening, when Carmen brings a lantern and food. Felipa is surprised to see Charco sleeping on the floor next to the dresser. She never saw him come in. She wonders if he spent the day there.

Felipa knows Alejo will need her strength. She eats, though she can't taste, a stew of onions, potatoes, and a few strands of what might be chicken. The tortillas and goat cheese are better.

The food makes her sleepy. Before ending the day, she raises the flame on the lantern and checks the tube of maguey. Dark fluid continues to drain out—more slowly, but visibly. She lies down next to her sleeping son and closes her eyes.

SHE WAKES TO find herself and Alejo in the same position. He's sleeping, but still feverish. She must do something else. The lantern has gone out. The Peñas have lowered the blanket over the doorway. She needs air. First she removes the soiled maguey tube and inserts another.

In the kitchen she finds her own food, cooking utensils, the sack of feed, Moro's tack, and the rest of her supplies neatly stacked in a corner. She opens the front door, and is shocked to see that the bed of the Durcal wagon is now a makeshift tent.

A length of barbed wire is wrapped around the seat and extended to the end of the wagon, where it's tied around a long, crooked mesquite limb that serves as a support pole. Draped over the wire, Felipa recognizes her blankets, the Peñas' covers— washed clean—and a heavy material that once was a portmanteau.

In the faint light, she sees Charco's blue eyes and smile as he builds a roaring fire. The two Peña children sit beside him, feeding twigs into the blaze.

"I tried to wake you. Carmen said to leave you and Alejo alone." Charco points to the tent. "I did that, took a pole from the goat pen."

Speechless, Felipa manages, "Where is everybody?"

Moro whinnies, stomps impatiently at the sound of her voice. He's tied to the branch of a bush, away from the house. She goes to him. He has not been exercised in two days, she realizes.

"They took their cart to fill your water barrel. I lent them the mule. They're due back."

Felipa says, "Can you ride Moro without a saddle?"

Charco takes his time before answering, "After breakfast."

BREAKFAST IS COFFEE, fried chorizo, and day-old tortillas. Felipa vows to help Carmen by making a big batch of fresh ones. She will use her own mix, not the Peñas'. They have already given so much.

Felipa feels the little girls' dark round eyes on her. They've never seen a woman her size before. She supposes she should ask them their names, but knows she can't make herself sound remotely interested.

The older girl, a five-year-old, whimpers, "No eggs?"

"No," mutters Manuel. "The horse scared the chickens."

"Moro?" asks the younger girl, maybe four or younger.

"Moro," answers Manuel. He points to the horse.

"Moro malo," blurts the girl and hides behind Carmen.

"I'm ready," says Charco, still chewing. He tosses his scraps to the dogs, who are keeping a safe distance from the horse. He goes for the tack.

Felipa and the Peñas watch Charco slowly slip the bridle on Moro. He leads the horse away from the ranchito, all the while whispering to him, stroking his chest, legs, barrel.

A stone's throw from the door, the barefoot Charco hoists himself up. Moro rears, bucks, spins. Charco stays on. The Peña girls clap. Shaking his head, Manuel takes the pail he is sitting on and heads toward the goat pen.

Felipa and Carmen check on Alejo, who is breathing through his mouth. The fever continues as before—not worse, not better. The tube is clean. No brown liquid.

Felipa asks, "Could he die from fever or pain?"

Carmen nods. "Or fright."

Felipa washes her son, then goes to the kitchen. She mixes lard, water, salt, a dash of baking powder, and handfuls of flour. She kneads the dough furiously into a large sphere, then reshapes it into two dozen egg-size balls, which she covers with a cloth.

A hesitant Carmen says, "My people use yerba mansa to cure fevers and cuts like this. I don't know if you believe in our ways, but I have seen cures with yerba."

It sounds familiar. Perhaps José used it with the animals. "Does the herb grow near here?" Felipa asks.

Carmen says, "There's some growing along the edges of the creek where we went for water this morning. It's marshy. The yerba likes swamps."

Outside Felipa hears a strong gallop racing toward the house. Moro. She rushes out. Moro is alone. Felipa takes the reins and climbs on the wagon to look for Charco. She scans the horizon in all directions. No Charco. She'll find him later.

From the wagon she mounts Moro. She tucks the folds of her skirt beneath her thighs and knees. "Carmen, let's find the yerba mansa."

"What about your other son?" asks Carmen.

Effortlessly, Felipa swings the slight Carmen onto Moro's hindquarters. "Hold on to my waist."

ON THE OTHER side of the creek Felipa sees the swamp. They take off their shoes and climb the flat overlapping rocks that lock in the stagnant water.

Carmen points to tall stalks with thick brick-red leaves.

Not familiar, thinks Felipa, studying the rounded succulents with basil leaves. She strips off a few leaves.

"The strongest part is the root," says Carmen.

Felipa puts her shoes back on and goes around to the riverbed side, where she undresses down to her underwear and wades into the swamp. The cold surprises her. Her feet sink deep into the softness. She squats and lets her hands trace a thin stalk to its root in the oozy alluvial bottom.

She grabs an entire root. Pulls. The plant comes easily. She tosses it to Carmen. "How many?"

"More than this," says Carmen, who looks as if she were standing on her head—her small frame prone on a flat rock. Her hands barely reach the water. She rinses off the mud and studies the dark gnarled root. "This is yerba."

Felipa uproots more plants until Carmen says, "Enough."

FELIPA WATCHES CARMEN peel the scaly outer covering off the root ball. The inside is thin, fibrous, similar to parsnip, and smells like a mixture of pine, mint, and camphor. Carmen boils water and makes a tea of the herb. Some she leaves fresh.

Taking no chances, Felipa calls Manuel to hold down Alejo's arms while she and Carmen undress the wound. Sweat has weakened the peel's adhesive; it comes off without causing Alejo pain.

Carmen gasps

"Looks bad," says Felipa. Her legs cave. She staggers to the back wall, lets herself slide to the floor. To have come so close to saving him, she thinks.

The wound is an ugly, bloody mouth, mutilated into an unrecognizable aperture. Felipa remembers the women after the battle of Mazocoba.

Manuel looks. "No. The skin is mending. It needs a good cleaning—you should've washed it sooner. I've seen worse on older men. Give me the yerba."

He wrings a cloth dipped in the solution directly over the wound. The stump reacts—lifts in jerks—without Alejo waking. Next, Manuel wraps the wound in yerba-soaked compresses.

A tired-looking Charco leans in the doorway, sees Felipa on the floor. "Moro is too much horse," he whispers.

She raises an arm to him. "Moro malo," she says, in a little girl's voice. He flops down next to her and lets her hug him.

From the floor, they watch Carmen hold Alejo's head while Manuel pours a full cup of yerba mansa down the throat. "Give him more later," he says to Felipa and Charco. "When the swelling goes down, move the end around so it won't stick to the bone. It's going to hurt him."

"Manuel is from Cananea," Carmen explains to Felipa. "He's seen accidents like this."

Irritated, Felipa asks, "You know how to cure?"

"No," answers Manuel firmly. "I've heard miners talk about lost arms or legs. I've never cut one."

That night the fever breaks. Alejo sleeps, waking only when Felipa forces more yerba tea down him.

ALEJO FIGHTS HUNGER and pain.

Ravenous, he stuffs himself with tortillas and cheese the first day. Moments later, he's hollering in pain from severe cramps. Manuel and Charco rush, carrying him far from the house so he can defecate. They hold him over a hole Felipa has dug for this eventuality.

"Phew! Chingado!" Charco screams. "We could have killed all the federales with this!"

Other than watered-down bacanora, there is nothing to give Alejo for pain. They keep him half-drunk. When the bacanora runs out, Manuel offers to buy more from a ranch nearby. Felipa gives him money and the mule to fetch it. "Buy all you can," she urges.

TIME TO PUT a thorn through my heart, thinks Felipa, describing the several times a day when she applies the yerba solution to Alejo's wound. She ignores his tearful protests, his insults as she massages the wound. No matter how gently she works, any movement seems to drive him out of his mind.

He refuses to listen to explanations of why she must massage the scar. Sullen, he drinks the yerba tea, and barely nods when she asks if he likes it. He won't speak to her, won't meet her eyes. It's the liquor, she hopes.

She can't shake the guilt she feels toward him. This enrages her. Bonito cuento, she thinks.

He defies her, goes off to be a hero, gets shot, and when he sees death, he begs her to cut off his leg. Now he's angry with her.

His rapid healing eases her guilt. The skin is mending. The swelling is down. Well, she can be as stubborn as he is. She will wait for him to speak first.

Not Charco. "I did what you said. Helped the señora."

"I'm sorry I said it," says Alejo. He's pale and needs a shave.

"You'd be dead now."

"I wish I could see the whole thing." Alejo points to his leg. Lying flat, he only sees the back of the stump resting on the saddle. Reaching hurts too much. "Find a mirror."

The Peñas' only mirror is attached to the dresser. Alejo would have to stand on the bed and lift his stump to see it.

"It looks exactly like this," clowns Charco, squeezing his lips into a grotesque shape.

Alejo bursts out laughing. Felipa can't believe what she sees. She was ready to cuff Charco across the neck.

Alejo is drinking tea with bacanora. "Come here. I want to tell you something."

Charco bends down. Alejo spits tea into his ear.

Felipa watches them roar, shake with uncontrollable laughter. The shaking seems to hurt Alejo, but he does not mind. For hours, their laughter rings in her ears.

27

ALEJO STARES AT THE CEILING, WAITING FOR HELP TO SIT UP. His back and buttocks ache. He counts the lines he's scratched on the adobe wall with his fingernail. Fourteen. Fourteen nights he remembers falling asleep without his mother lying next to him.

Once when she came to massage the scar he heard himself snarl, "Now you can say you were right."

He wishes he hadn't said it, yet feels no gratitude when she comes to clean the wound and give him that tea. He could throw something at her when she starts to move his scar around. His head picks up her anger for his going to Bacatete.

He can't sort out his thoughts. The bacanora muddies his thinking, stops his comparing the pain from day to day. Every morning he's determined not to drink it anymore. He hates it, hates the smell, hates the burning it leaves in his throat. The hot compresses help for a while. But when the shooting pains start, he hears himself cry for bacanora.

Every morning he rediscovers his leg is gone. Though even in a drunken stupor, he feels his toes hurt all night.

He runs his hand over his face. The pretty lady, Carmen, shaved him a few days ago, left his face smooth. Nice hands. Charco nicked him to death around the jaw.

Alejo chuckles, glad that Moro threw Charco. How could his mother let Charco ride Moro?

Daily Charco assures him he will ride again. "You have your knee," he says. "You even have Moro in your knee. The señora tied something in your leg with Moro's hair. You say we're brothers because we have the same father. Now you and Moro are brothers."

TODAY CHARCO BRINGS breakfast. "Buenos dias, Mocho."

"Where's my mother?" asks Alejo.

"Washing. They're boiling cloths for you. Everything is for you, 'Lejo. Food, sheets, staying here forever—all for Alejo." Charco is not joking.

Alejo signals that he wants to sit up. Charco lowers the food to the floor. Slowly, Alejo pulls himself up while Charco holds the stump and moves the saddle toward Alejo.

"Leg, don't wake up," Alejo pleads. "Too late." He leans back against the wall and groans.

Charco hands Alejo a large clay cup steaming with pinole. He rests a wooden plate on Alejo's lap.

Alejo looks at the marmalade-covered flour tortillas toasted over coals. His mother made this for him. She knows that's what he likes in the morning.

He admires the wooden plate decorated with alternating long and short curves like a flower in bloom. First time he's noticed it. I'm better, he thinks, and wonders if the man, Manuel, carved this. The plate is thin, but solid. Ironwood. Not perfectly round, but the carver buffed it to a sweet rich brown.

Lying across the foot of the bed so that his head rests on the pommel, Charco stares intently at Alejo.

Right now he could be Father, thinks Alejo, still amazed at their likeness.

Charco says, "Stop being a cabrón with her, Tejo. I already told you, you were the one who said, 'Cut it,' and you told me to help her. Maybe you're sorry you said it. And maybe you spoke from *the other side*."

The tortillas are especially good, thinks Alejo. "Maybe I was on the other side and scared. The last thing I recall was hearing about Pilar's jump. I have strange pictures in my head. Shadows. Mostly I have tristeza."

His throat catches. He swallows. Tears pass. He could say this only to Charco. Only Yaquis understand how tristeza can kill a person.

Charco warns, "Best you stop. Don't let tristeza grab you. Think of the new ranch. You have so much."

Charco runs a hand through his hair, then continues. "You have a mother that won't let anything happen to you." He laughs. "You think you're angry. You should have seen her. You're lucky you weren't that foot of yours."

Charco stands. He growls, crosses his eyes as he imitates a crazed Felipa sawing wildly. Charco picks up an imaginary foot and hurls it at Alejo. *"Cuas!"*

Charco is finished clowning. Again he sits on the bed. "You

lived because of your mother's rage," he says. "I saw the rage in her eyes as she fought off death. Her passion saved you. And this is right, for that's what we are." He slaps his chest with the palms of his hands. "The flesh of our mothers. I'm unlucky. I never saw my mother's eyes or her passion. All I know is that the man you say is my father took her."

Alejo sees Charco's hands tremble.

THE FOLLOWING MORNING the Peñas help Felipa remove the stitches. Manuel cuts the outer thread with his straight-edge razor. Felipa and Carmen take turns carefully pulling the decaying thread through the stitches.

Alejo is silent. The wound bleeds slightly.

"Will we leave now?" Alejo asks his mother, addressing her directly for the first time.

"If it were my leg, I'd wait until I could stand," says Manuel. He makes a fist and rubs it into the palm of his other hand. "Tomorrow *you* move the end around with *your* hand. *You* toughen the skin so *you* can stand and walk."

Embarrassed by Manuel's emphasis, Alejo remembers what Charco said about his rudeness to his mother. "I will, and I'll carve my own leg too," he says.

He directs his gaze toward his mother, studies her. Tired. The large brown eyes he's seen spark with fury or joy look sad, her powerful shoulders thin. I did this to her, he thinks. But tired or thin, she's beautiful. "Mother, I said things I'm sorry for." He's glad everyone can hear.

She meets his gaze. "I have your tools."

To Manuel, Alejo says, "I've seen your nice plates. Would ironwood make a good leg?"

"They were a wedding present from Carmen's brother. He's a real carver. Ironwood might be too heavy. Then again, with ironwood, you wouldn't need as much wood as with pine or fir."

Manuel pulls up a stool and leans closer to Alejo. "I'm from Cananea, mining country. There, when the earth collapses, beams crush arms and legs. Men learn to work anyway. They have to. Work your leg, Alejo. You'll walk."

When Alejo wakes the next day, he finds a branch of ironwood by his bedside.

He looks at the ironwood and at the stump. He pulls himself up. The stump slides off the saddle.

He hollers. Felipa rushes in. Alejo fans her away with both hands. "Sorry," he says. "Please, my carving tools, charcoal, and some paper. A piece of cloth will do. And water to rinse the cloth in.

"No bacanora, no bacanora," he chants quietly. What did Tacho say at the sanctuary? "Give your pain a face."

Sundown. Embarrassed at the scarcity of wood shavings on his lap, Alejo continues to search for an inroad into the obstinate iron wood. Beside him hangs a half sheet, one side covered with designs of a lower leg, the other with the face of a long-haired, sawtoothed woman.

Charco and Manuel have spent the day plying him with ideas. But Alejo hasn't heard them. He knows that the proper time to learn the wood's language is when the branch is recently severed from the tree. Beneath the reddish bark, the black, brown, and red veins of the dense wood seem impenetrable.

DAY AFTER DAY, Alejo devotes every waking moment to shaping his new leg, tapering the lower part. To ride, the part that fits into the stirrup must have a heel. He'll carve that first, worry about the length later.

When he's not carving, he massages his stump.

STANDING BRINGS ALEJO renewed pain. He nearly faints at the sudden rush of blood to the scar.

Charco and Manuel stand on either side of him while he balances on his one leg, weak after a month of lying in bed. Alejo grips the thigh of his half-leg—also soft. Thin. He walks until his whole leg is too sore to move.

At first Charco and Manuel keep Alejo in the bedroom. Then comes the kitchen, where Charco loudly announces, "That's the table where everything happened."

Eventually they venture outside. The cold fresh air staggers Alejo. His mother tells him it's February. He laughs when he sees the family wagon has been turned into a lopsided tent for the Peñas.

"Charco," he says, once he's back in the room, "move the family back. I will sleep out of this room tonight."

Felipa, Charco, and the little girls sleep in the Peñas' kitchen. Despite the cold, Alejo insists on sleeping alone in the wagon. Blankets weigh down his chest. The sky is clear. He has missed the stars.

The ankle of his whole leg hurts. It bore his entire weight today. The stump also hurts. He stares directly at the pain, forcing it down until it subsides to a low moan.

I will make my leg strong, he promises himself. He thinks of the little Peña girls. How easily they switch from sitting to running, their slim ankles turning and bending without fear. They don't taste their running. Why should they? He never tasted his.

Can a one-legged man work a farm or a ranch? Shouldn't he worry more about this? It would please his mother to hear him worry out loud about his future. Crittenden. Strange name. He trusts he'll find an answer as they come closer to the place.

What haunts Alejo has nothing to do with a missing leg or with making a living. The biting question is tied to his *kinán* and *seeing* the right place for his spirit to work—knowing that he may be alone. He wishes he could think of something to wish for. In the past when he called for something, seeing it brought it. The time ahead of him is too open, too empty.

Whatever lies ahead, Alejo, you must meet alone, he thinks. José, Ana María, Tacho, Gustavo, Juan, Anginas disappeared from his life. Charco. How long will he stay? He cannot bear the thought of Charco leaving him.

AFTER BREAKFAST, FELIPA watches Manuel and Charco help Alejo measure the length of his ironwood leg. They're excited, she thinks. This is an adventure for them.

Alejo uses a crutch Manuel has made for him. From a crude charcoal drawing, he instructs Manuel exactly how to saw the wood for the leg. "Leave a niche near the end. I need to fit *into* it," he explains. "And my stump needs something soft to rest on. A nest. Do you have any cork?"

"Cork? No. But we have wool from the goats."

"We can make the nest of wool and chicken feathers," Charco suggests. He collects feathers from the yard. Using Alejo's knife, he separates the thin soft ribs from the hollow shaft and compresses them. "We need more," he says.

While Charco chases chickens, Felipa saddles Moro. "I'll be back," she mumbles and gallops away.

The men mix feathers with goat's wool to make a nest, which they wrap in cheesecloth and shape into a disk that fits into the niche. Next they take the cord Felipa braided out of clothing and thread it through a hole Alejo calls the "eye" of the leg. They criss-cross the cord up the wood to the thigh.

Alejo is ready to stand. He rests the stump on the nest in the niche. Black circles whirl before him. Charco and Manuel steady him. The whole leg wobbles, aching in protest as he balances his weight between toe and heel.

By noon he has learned to balance his weight over his pelvis. Eye fixed on the hub of the wagon wheel, he stands.

Pain be damned. He will take one step. His entire body shakes as he harnesses all his strength to force the stump forward. It moves.

But the peg leg flops back, and the nest falls to the ground.

Alejo looks at Charco's and Manuel's crestfallen expressions.

"By the time I get to Arizona, I'll have a perfect leg. It won't be that difficult."

FELIPA HAD REFUSED to see Alejo being measured for his leg. Instead she went to find the road to Arizona, a road Manuel described as "very busy. Used by everyone."

She has no trouble finding it. Big rocks have been placed to indicate a vague border along the gravelly road. Yes, this is where I was a month ago. Desperate for help.

Dismounting, she loosens Moro's cinch and sits on a rock, glad to be alone, away from Alejo and his pain. The rock cuts into her buttocks, but she dares not leave. She's determined to meet the hijo de la chingada carriage driver who was nowhere when she needed him. She will make him draw her a map to Arizona.

The road looks more comfortable, and her skirt couldn't get dirtier. She shredded the last of her clothes to make bandages. Soon she is lying on her stomach, stretched out flat across the road, chin resting on her hands. Random thoughts float in and out.

Looking back at the weeks with the Peñas, she sees a shift in allegiances. The ranchito has become her and Carmen's duty. They wash, cook, make the goat cheese the family trades with local ranches. Charco and Manuel spend the day walking Alejo or watching him carve his leg.

The picture of Charco chasing chickens makes her envious of how easily men accommodate each other. Never would she abandon her duties to care for an injured stranger who came to her door. One day men kill each other, the next they're filling each other's needs.

That's true, she argues with herself. José dies, and Alejo attaches himself to Tacho. Andrés finds Hong. Alejo goes to prison, and he finds Charco. Then they both find Gustavo, and all three find a crazy Maya called Anginas.

She stops. Not Hector. He went to Tía Mercedes, though not for

long. If any son mourned José, it was Hector, José's favorite—and
the son she has least access to simply because he seems so complete.
All he ever asked of her was permission to ride Moro, and that she
denied him.

And yet, she's relieved Manuel is helping Alejo. Now that she's
certain her son will live, she wouldn't know what to do. He acts
ashamed to let her see his leg, or to let her help him dress. But he
accepts all help from Manuel. The fruit of my tree ripens over the
neighbor's fence, she thinks. And the neighbor is kind and shares
the bounty.

The Peñas. She's never known such people. What friends has
she had? Tía Mercedes and Alejo. She extends both arms across the
road and points her toes. How wonderful this feels.

Stretched out, her body almost covers the entire road. She rolls
on her side. Above is an endless, gray sky. Around her is Sonora,
vast in its flatness, meager in its rises. Like creases in a freshly
ironed sheet. She feels small. That comforts her.

She looks forward to leaving, then stopping to visit for a few
days with the Peñas on her return from Arizona. She never imagined such freedom. Alamos would think her mad for traveling
alone. She smiles.

She will go the four hundred miles to the border. Besides, she
wants to see something other than Alamos. Now she sounds like
Andrés. No, she must go to be certain the place she bought exists.

She trusts no one and laments her lack of faith.

She has not prayed since she cut off Alejo's leg. Some might say
that's when she should have prayed more, asked the Virgin's inter-
cession during Alejo's suffering. She hadn't. Even now, she can't
formulate a prayer.

When she leaves, she will give Carmen a twenty-peso gold coin.
That will leave two for Alejo. He would be first to agree that the
Durcal debt to the Peñas could never be repaid. She hopes the
Peñas will buy a mule. Their burro is old. It barely carries the chil-
dren. Carmen cried when Felipa suggested they shoot it. "He's

been part of my family since I was a child," she said.

Felipa can see the love between Carmen and Manuel. A quiet love. They exchange few words, yet remain connected. She admires Manuel, who left home and family for Carmen. "Manuel saw me at a fair where my brother went to sell his carvings and has never left my side," Carmen told her.

His family rejected his Indian wife. Only his grandmother approved, gave them her dresser as a gift. Now with Carmen, two daughters, and a herd of goats, Manuel lives content out here, away from everyone, making cheese, which they trade for what they need.

"What else could we want?" Carmen asked, her shining dark eyes challenging Felipa to answer.

Who would suspect this barren land to house such a perfect love, thinks Felipa. How fortunate to know when you have enough.

She wishes that José had felt satisfied during their early years. Some recognize happiness when they have it. They say basta. Enough. And mean it. Others say más. And keep going until someone stops them with a bullet as Esteban did José.

One sleepless night while lying on her palette in the kitchen, Felipa heard the Peñas' lovemaking. Her first impulse was to check the Peña children, who lay near her. The girls slept soundly.

Her entire body protracted across the dirt road, she drives thoughts of the Peña couple from her head. Rolling over onto her back, she clasps her hands beneath her head.

She has seen Alejo eye Carmen, and Felipa admits she's wished he would find a good Indian woman like her.

Shocked, she sits up. What a stained soul I have.

Would I wish this if my son had not lost a leg? She knows the answer. I did not wish a good woman for him. I wished a good *Indian* woman—to serve him. Ashamed of her disloyalty to her son and to Carmen, Felipa makes a rushed sign of the cross, vows to the sky to let her sons marry who they want.

Empty gesture, she thinks, unable to wed her vow to passion.

Vows can't change this ugly rejection of people like me and those whom José called Mexico's primera gente. José was a better person.

She strokes the gravelly dirt with the palm of her hand, shapes it into cones, then crushes the tops with her index finger. People like me made the Martinos who scarred Alejo. People like me allow the Mazocobas that maimed my son.

She remembers it was Carmen who spoke up and asked her to bring her son to the ranch. Manuel, the mestizo who is most like herself, was ready to turn her away.

She thinks of Hector and Andrés, who want to leave home. If the cruel Mexico Alejo described is the true Mexico, then a mother's only hope is that her son's death be quick.

She shakes her head, wishes Tía Mercedes were here. From what little vegetation she sees around her, she supposes this part of Sonora is even drier than Alamos, where sometimes a year's rain falls in a month. Yet the land parcels the rain to last an entire year. Even in drought, flowers bloom. *Sewam,* she thinks.

Can I make the passion I knew with José fill the rest of my life? That small portion is all I'm allowed? she wonders angrily. Not enough.

More than having no man to cover her, she dreads a long solitude: the absence of a companion's weight beside her at night; arms that reach out but embrace no one; hands that grab at nothing; sighs that remain unheard. Will her mouth never stop yearning for another's breath? Will her lips never press and lock with another?

Felipa looks at the sky. No, I want my body covered. And entered. I want the reventón, the puncture and explosion José gave me *when I allowed it.* Foolish woman!

To reclaim one of those afternoons when he rushed home, in midafternoon, full of desire for her, and she, also in desire, denied them both.

At the time, Tía Mercedes had called her "a ripened woman." Well, at thirty-five, she still had desire.

Her limbs feel weak; she knows the feeling is temporary. Felipa suspects she will live a long life. She forced herself to be strong to carry Alejo past danger. Now she wonders what force is tough enough to topple her. Once she spoke to the Sacred Virgin with reverence and humility. That too is gone.

Heedless of dress, hair, everything, she rolls herself over and over, pressing her full weight onto the road. She welcomes the sharp pebbles and scratchy rock against her face, arms, hands.

She stops when a spooked Moro snorts.

28

Five weeks later—Santa Cruz, Sonora, seven miles from the U.S. border

FELIPA DECIDES TO STAY IN HER BEDROLL UNTIL THE WATER IS hot.

She hears the pumping sound of Alejo flexing his stump. No need to look. She knows he's sitting on the edge of the wagon raising and lowering the pants leg she turned into a sandbag by sewing the end shut.

He exercises even when the wagon is moving. Every three or four days, he asks for more weight in the sandbag. She or Charco makes mud and drops it in. When it dries, Alejo rewets the dirt. He asks for no pity, and she's grateful.

Alejo has claimed the wagon as his own since they left the Peñas. "Up here, I can work my leg whenever I want."

She hears the huffing, pumping sound in her sleep. By day, the sound joins the ring of the wheels as they drive toward the American border.

Charco sleeps on the other side of the wagon. Good. Without this privacy I'd go mad, she thinks. Why did she expect special treatment from these two? Already they try to put a woman in her place.

Each seems involved with something other than getting to the border. They say that every madman is busy with his little knot, she thinks.

Charco, she suspects, wonders how long to stay with Alejo. Whatever the boy decides, he will feel disloyal, either to Yaquis or to Alejo.

When Alejo isn't working his leg, he's carving another wooden leg. The wagon bed is filled with dozens of miniature, infant-size, half-whittled legs. Alejo claims he needs them all if he is to make "the perfect leg."

Felipa relives the amputation whenever she goes for food and must crawl over the maze of tiny leg remnants—calves, ankles, feet.

Every night Alejo combs and caresses Moro. He refuses to even sit on the horse until the leg is finished. "He'll know I'm not complete."

Sometimes Charco lies on the dirt while Alejo traces the lower leg. Charco never complains.

Alejo's first ride could have been tragic. Without telling anyone he rode the mule into the night. Later, pained screams filled the desert blackness: "Pull me off! Pull me off!"

The cries seemed to come from everywhere. Felipa and Charco ran in all directions searching for him. Desperate, Alejo had thrown himself off. The mule's return to camp narrowed the search area. Charco backtracked and found him. Since then Alejo rides the mule in circles around the camp.

THE FIRST STOP after leaving the Peñas's ranchito was a mining town near Minas Prietas. They bought food, feed, crutches for Alejo, and clothing for all of them. The miners were generous with advice for her son, advice he has heeded.

"Rub the stump across the dirt every day. Make a thick callus."

"Stand. Ignore the pain. Stand longer each day."

Charco quickly sought out Yaqui miners to tell them of

Mazocoba. They said they already knew, but Charco insisted they hear what he himself had witnessed. Then he argued with her for a peso to buy used sandals from a Yaqui miner. The three-point, top-less sandal which tied to the foot by a thong between the toes and around the ankle could only be Yaqui. All Sonora knew that.

"A peso is too much for something that could get you shot or take you back to Yucatán," she said.

His face up to hers, eyes blue slits, Charco argued, "I'll work it off!"

The boy ignored the Mexican miner's warning that federales were combing northern Sonora for mountain Yaquis who had es-caped Mazocoba and sought refuge in Arizona. In front of his Yaqui workers the miner said, "That's because they know Yaquis are pricks and later return to raise hell."

She and Charco compromised. He would keep the sandals hid-den until they crossed the border. Later, as a peace gesture, he volunteered to trade his faded denims, the kind worn by Yaquis, for a pair of Alejo's pants, which she gladly adjusted for him.

They followed the miner's advice, stopped only at small towns, hamlets that sold basic necessities—flour, lard, sugar, pinole, carne seca, pickled fruit, feed, water. And always, more wood for Alejo to carve.

They never took Moro into town. One of them always stayed with him at the campsite which they'd pitched against a butte or behind a knoll, away from the main road.

The Yaqui miners had given Charco a route not used by Yoris. At first Felipa had been suspicious and at every day's end she would ride out to make sure that what she herself had come to call the "Yori road" was there. It always was, parallel to the route they fol-lowed, but out of sight.

This must be how Yaquis survive, she realized. They stay out of Yori's sight. Miserable life. She had stopped checking for the Yori road.

The Yaqui miners assured Charco that if there were no federales watching the border, he would have no trouble entering the United States. Americans were welcoming Yaquis.

Felipa is happier astride Moro and away from Alejo's constant toil that only exhausts her.

Besides, Moro would rather be ridden than led tethered to the wagon. On Moro she doesn't have to hear Alejo and Charco's plans to return to Mexico. The carnage of Mazocoba has taught them nothing.

Alejo shocked her with his scheme of parading his stump to demonstrate the government's injustices. "My leg will be like Angina's voice. I'll have something to show them."

And Charco agreed. "People will listen to a man with half a leg more than to a man with nothing missing."

She had never considered her son devious. If Alejo doesn't see how his stubbornness about Mazocoba cost him a leg, then no words could change him.

And yet sometimes she understands their need to return to Mexico, especially when they speak of Yucatán. Alejo frequently speaks of their promise to Anginas to tell the world of Yucatán's cruel slavery. They aren't wrong to want to end the evil in their country, she concedes.

She's enjoying this longest voyage of her life. On Moro her eyes are free to absorb the changing Sonora landscape. She likes the human-shaped saguaros, the giant cacti that live for centuries and house countless desert creatures from owls to rats. What is the legend? God made the oceans and each drop that fell from his fingertips became a saguaro.

Dogwood is her favorite tree. Saguaros have never caught her attention, except here in northern Sonora, where they become an army. Each different, yet the same. The powerful, thorny arms turn, coil, twist, but remain steadfast in their direction. Upward. She hopes Alejo sees he is like them.

On some days the clouds separate, creating a broad aisle for the sun's setting. This gives the desert plain a uniform hue, turning it into an endless mantle, a cloak spread over the earth. Where is she on this vast cloth? At the end of the material, where edges fray into nothingness? She does not feel ragged.

Maimed and scarred, Alejo and Charco are at the beginning stage—strong fibers still free to weave themselves into beautiful tapestries. She remembers the magical change in the ocotillo when a frontal storm forced them to stop. The tiny leaves glowed, transforming the simple stalks into a luminous, beatific vision. Such a change is possible for these two boys.

Daily she teases Moro, "Remember how I once wanted to shoot you? That's why you're staying with Alejo, so you'll be happy." She hugs the horses's neck until the grief passes.

For a few days she convinces herself that her tears are because Moro is her last link to José. Then she decides, no. Moro himself is worthy of tears.

FELIPA IS STILL angry. Six days ago she and Alejo had the most bitter argument of their lives, creating six days of ugly silence. He had demanded the remaining gold coins to purchase three spotted mares from an unknown group of Indians leading a herd of horses toward the American border.

They were on the same route the Yaqui miners gave Charco, except they rode at night. "The federales or Mexicans would steal those horses," Alejo said.

The leader of the group barely spoke Spanish and relied on a Navajo translator. They looked like no Indians Felipa had ever seen. Their tribe supposedly lived in the northern United States in a land of mountains, forests, and lakes, thousands of miles away.

Charco said they called themselves Nimipu. "It means 'the real people,' " he said.

"Never heard of them," she said. "And we didn't come all this way to take up with more Indians."

To herself, Felipa admitted that these Indians were handsomer than any she had ever seen. Their faces were longer, thinner, accented with high cheekbones. They wore beaded braids on the sides of their faces. The rest of their hair fell loose down their backs. Some had cropped the hair above the forehead so that a tuft stood straight up.

The Indians—five males—said they were returning to their land after spending three years in Chihuahua crossbreeding their strange-looking horses, which they called *peluse.*

These weren't like any pinto horses Felipa had ever seen. These were spotted. *Stained,* really. An ecstatic Alejo had declared them the most beautiful horses in the world.

Six days ago the Indians made their fire close to the Durcals'. The Navajo walked to their camp and invited Alejo and Charco to join them. Charco drove Alejo in the wagon. Later, they came for Moro.

Late that night, Alejo returned bewitched. Lo embrujaron, she thought, looking at the light in his eyes.

"I've seen what I will do in Arizona," he announced to her, his voice high, trembling with a quality she had not heard since he was young and about to start a new carving.

"I will cross their *peluse* with Moro. Make a new breed of horse that will be perfect for this country. It will have endurance. Their mares are beautiful. Small, but wiry—up in the belly, with big hindquarters. Lean and well muscled down the side of the tail. They carry their head high. They don't arch the neck, like Moro. The men also showed me how to check for a heavy hoof wall. I tap it with a stone. They said the sole should be arched, not too flat or convex," he recited, entranced.

Sharply, Felipa said, "Look around you. You have five hundred acres of *this* land. Breeding takes more land than you've got. It also takes time. Remember how long it took your father to start with Sueño? How will you feed yourself until you have horses to sell? You know nothing about these horses or if the crossbreeding will work."

Charco walked out of the camp, leaving them alone.

"It will work. They already told me and Charco how to do it. I'll start small, like Father. If I give them the gold coins and Moro to stud their mares, they will give me three young brood mares."

"Alejo, these strange Indians are *giving* you nothing."

The argument lasted past midnight, ending with her throwing the gold coins at him. "Take them!" she said. "Never ask me for anything again. I have two more sons."

Alejo had dragged himself over the ground, groping through the darkness to find them. Unable to withstand the sight of him crawling, she helped him find the coins and gave them to him. Afterward, he raised himself onto the wagon bed and seemed to fall asleep instantly. Fuming, she stared at the sky, watching the starlit blackness fade to gray.

The following morning she discovered she was capable of deeper rage.

The Navajo had asked to look at the title for the property in Arizona. Using charcoal, he jotted something down on the leg of his pants and said to Alejo, "I'll bring the mares to you."

Alejo gave the coins to the Navajo. That's when Felipa realized he had paid strangers for mares he would not receive until he had crossed the border.

Charco jumped between Felipa and Alejo when she took a full swing at her son. Her slap flattened Charco. Neither has spoken to her since.

BATHED IN SWEAT, Alejo finishes working his leg. Excited, he yells, "Charco, today we cross the border."

On crutches he hobbles to the fire. Charco hands him a cup of pinole, then goes to feed the animals.

He sees his mother's gauze bag lying by the supplies. He knows it's filled with ground coffee, cinnamon, and sugar. The sight of it saddens him, spoils his joy.

Enough, he thinks. He fills a cup with water and drops the bag into it. The tin cup is too hot to hold, so he uses his shirttail. Wobbling on crutches, and trying to hold the cup, he circles over to her. She's lying down. He hands her a half-empty cup.

She sits up, accepts it.

"We don't have much time together. I need you to believe in my plan," he says.

"You don't have the mares," she says, her voice flat.

Alejo holds out his hand and slowly lowers himself to sit before her. "The Nimipu must cross at another place, at night and away from border officials. American soldiers might take their horses." His mother does not believe him.

"You never let me explain. Mother, their story is like the Yaquis'. Worse. Soldiers not only killed their people and took their land, they ordered the slaughter of the spotted horses. The *peluse* are sacred to the Nimipu. The American army killed thousands of horses to break the soul of the Nimipu."

"Killed horses to break souls? That's superstition. They're lying. Or it was long ago."

"No, barely twenty years. The Nimipu painted the *peluse* to disguise them. Only a few horses survived. These men travel thousands of miles looking for good horses to rebuild their herds. I'm lucky they saw Moro."

His mother drains her cup. She braids her loose hair.

He will not let her leave. He takes her hands. "Please. See the good fortune in all this. We survived. The *peluse,* the Nimipu, the Yaquis, Charco, me. People tried to kill us and couldn't. We're all joined somehow. I don't have the words, but I see the picture clearly in my head. It matters that I work with those who struggled. It unites our *kinán* into a circle."

Her frown tells him he should not have used that word. He adds, "I know breeding takes time. Until my herd increases, I'll plant seeds, eat whatever comes up. Remember too," he emphasizes, "that your plan was for a son with two legs. My plan is for a man with one strong leg. Meanwhile, I can work. Carve. Mend. I know you made sacrifices to buy my land. Be happy for me."

"I thank the stars daily for your life, Alejo. But understand that a mother fears. That's what we do. We fear."

29

IT'S NOON WHEN THEY ARRIVE AT THE LOCHIEL BORDER. Felipa chose this smallest of borders to narrow the likelihood of Alejo's name appearing on a fugitive list. In Magdalena she learned that unlike Nogales, Lochiel has no telegraph.

She drives as they take their place behind a half-dozen wagons. Alejo sits beside her; Charco sits behind them.

She notices the difference in border stations. Americans have an adobe single-room low structure. Mexicans have a wood kiosk. Thirty meters separate the stations. She wonders what country claims that land.

A small-framed Mexican officer looks at the papers. His uniform shirt is soaked with perspiration on this unusually hot April day. "Who is Alejo Robles?"

The question starts Felipa's heart racing.

"I am," answers Alejo.

The man takes a long look at Moro and at Alejo's stump. "You have five hundred acres?"

"We have family," says Felipa. She looks ahead, refuses to look at him.

"And lots of legs," says Charco sarcastically. He waves a couple of Alejo's leg carvings at the officer.

Frowning, he waves them through.

"Now, my sandals," says Charco.

Felipa leans forward and Charco slips them out from under her buttocks. He puts them on.

Slowly they move toward the American side, which has several officers working. The line barely moves. Americans ask more questions, she notices. She sees them checking wagon beds. For what?

She sees Pimas and Opatas crossing the border in both directions. Some carry chickens, others herd goats. Neither border station seems to notice them.

No Yaquis.

Their turn comes. A husky, fortyish, red-faced officer approaches them. Around his neck hangs a soiled kerchief, which he uses to mop his brow.

Felipa knew he would check them. His eyes have not left her or Moro since they passed the Mexican kiosk.

Alejo holds out the papers. The American ignores them and strides toward Moro.

"No brand on this horse," he says. "It's yours?"

They don't understand. Again, Alejo holds out the papers.

"No marca," says the American. He makes a branding motion on Moro's hindquarter.

Charco stands, puts his hands on Felipa's and Alejo's shoulders. "Horse es mines," he says.

The American sees Charco's sandals. "You Yaqui?"

"Yaqui, yes," Charco answers.

The officer points to the sandals. "Did the Mexicans see those? Yaquis and Mexicans—" With his index finger, he makes a dramatic cutting motion across his throat. He walks to Felipa's side. His eyes engage hers, then comb her face and stop at her breasts. "You're no Yaqui," he says heavily, and leans toward her.

"No!" yells Charco. His arm shoots out past Felipa to push him away.

Alejo stretches across his mother's lap. Felipa blocks his attempt to punch the man.

She yanks both boys back. "Los papeles, Señor," she says, snatching the papers from Alejo and forcing them into the man's freckled hands.

Every eye at the border stops to take in the scene. The red-faced man regains his composure. Chuckling, he scans the documents. "Alejo Robles. Landowner. My, my. Yaquis with blue eyes and land. Who is A-lay-ho?"

Charco signals. "Mine brother."

"You speak English, A-lay-ho?"

Alejo shakes his head.

"Papers say you were born in Tucson, but no speak English?" he asks. He mops his forehead, and with his index finger he slowly reads the papers, line by line.

Felipa feels the heat of the day rise. How she would like to take a whip to him. The American checks and rechecks the various seals. Castillo did his job.

"What's holding you up?" asks another officer. He's younger, but clearly the officer in charge.

"Why would Mexicans claim to be Yaquis?" asks the red-faced man. "They're enemies. Blue-eyed Yaqui landowners with a high-bred, unbranded stallion. Don't you think that's strange?"

"We can expect a lot of them. Some battle happened. Nogalitos is full of them. If they have no weapons, let them through. Yaquis, Mexicans, what's the difference?"

Charco grabs Felipa's shoulders with both hands. "Mi mother!" he hollers to the second officer. "Mi mother!"

"It's hot, Gerry. Finish your line," says the younger man.

Felipa is surprised to hear only Spanish as they travel through Arizona. Same country, different name, she thinks.

The assessor is Roberto Suárez, a thin-legged, narrow-footed man who seems only too happy to escort them to Alejo's land. He's talkative, eager with information about where to buy the best meat and vegetables and the abundance of apples and quince in the area.

"I know Rafael Castillo and his in-laws, Hilda and Elias Sobe-ranes. Good people, generous, helpful. I'll wire them from the post office that you've arrived. They've been waiting for your boy. Hilda will help your son arrange the inside of his house. That's how we do it here. We set up the kitchen, measure out the other rooms, then build the outside. Your son will have an immediate family, you'll see." Suárez never loses his smile. He wears a worn black serge suit.

Felipa notices his nails are bitten back. Lonely. The assessor waits while she and Charco unload the wagon beneath a tall paloverde ablaze with yellow blossoms.

The wagon is much lighter when they follow Suárez's two-wheel cart as he drives between red-flagged stakes stuck into the ground.

The low hills that frame Alejo's land only emphasize its boundaries, making it seem smaller.

"Enough to start with," the assessor says to Felipa. "I helped Castillo find this parcel. He made a good buy. I've helped him buy other property. Good bargainer. If you want to range stock, burn your grass for oacatón. Make sure there's a breeze so the fire moves fast and won't turn your soil into clay."

He takes a deep breath before leaving and adds, "Water's about thirty feet down. Rain starts June twenty-four, Día de San Juan. What's important is that no one owns the neighboring land."

Felipa is embarrassed for Alejo. She knows he feels slighted. The assessor addressed her even though he knows the land belongs to her son.

She points to a row of cottonwoods. "There's where to dig your well," she says gently to Alejo. She offers to help him get down, forgetting how hard he's worked to polish that skill.

He waves her back, hops off, and, balancing himself on his one leg, reaches for his crutches. "We need to seed this ground right away," he says gruffly to Charco.

Charco leans against the paloverde. "I'll find Yoemem to help us build the house."

Felipa says, "Castillo's in-laws are coming from Tucson to help you get started. Let them help you."

"The man said Tucson takes two days to come and go," Charco says. "Yoemem are here."

"Tucson is bigger. Go there tomorrow. We need a buckboard," says Alejo. "Take the mule. Buy fence posts."

He's overwhelmed, and needs to give orders, she thinks. Wounded by the sadness in her son's eyes, she says, "Charco, could you find fresh meat for supper?" She gives him money.

"When will you leave?" Alejo asks when they're alone.

"Soon. Before the summer heat starts. No goodbyes, Alejo. It will be easier for me to leave unannounced. I'll keep the wagon ready. I don't want to feel your eyes looking at my back when I go."

"I can understand that," says Alejo quietly. "But I don't like you traveling alone. I keep thinking of men like the gringo at the border. The wagon will be lighter. Why not follow a carriage?"

Felipa sees he is worried. "If one comes along, I will," she says gently. "I plan to follow the main road and sleep in towns when I can. I'll hurry to the Peñas."

He is balanced on crutches, and, against her will, Felipa's eyes take in the cruel space beneath his knee. She wraps her arms tightly around him, and is consoled by his solid shoulders. "Don't change your dream, Alejo. You make that new breed of horse."

30

On a clear night one week later, Felipa lies in the wagon beneath the paloverde. The boys are nearby, but sleep in the open. She hears their chatter. Tonight alone they have aired enough ideas to fill ten lives.

Alejo hasn't slept in the wagon since they crossed the border, says he wants to know his land with his body. He still sleeps with the stump raised.

How is it, she wonders, that in one week her son's five hundred acres are overrun with people and animals?

First, Charco returned from Tucson with two Yaqui families atop the newly purchased buckboard.

Smiling, he said, "I promised they could live here. They'll help us make the house and the fence posts."

Felipa looked at the boy's handsome face. José and his Yaquis. Again.

The Yaquis set up camp at the base of the farthest hill. They knew the livestock came first, and in half a day wove mesquite branches into a corral. Then they mixed adobe and poured it into molds, and while the sun cured the blocks, they set fence posts.

On Charco's heels, Castillo's in laws, Hilda and Elias Soberanes, arrived. A wizened Elias stood back while Hilda, a robust, effusive woman, introduced herself to Felipa, Charco, and Alejo, landing wet kisses on each. In minutes Hilda had unpacked a world from their wagon. Kitchen, garden, and smithing tools, bolts of muslin for sheets, clothing, gourds, pickled fruits, vegetables, seeds, and cuttings.

Felipa's big surprise was that Ana María, Castillo's wife, came with her parents. Though still pretty, she looked frailer than Felipa remembered her. She and Felipa exchanged perfunctory kisses.

At the sight of Alejo on crutches, Ana María gasped, visibly shaken. Face bathed in tears, she extended both arms for the traditional kiss an older woman gives a young man she met as a child.

After the soft brush of her lips, Alejo remained standing next to Ana María. Felipa saw Ana María's hand grab Alejo's and yank it into the folds of her skirt. He was ready. Felipa witnessed frantic, fierce clasping of hands between her son and Ana María.

Her parents saw nothing, but I did, Felipa thinks now. What did José say about La Muda? Why is she here? Did she leave? Or did her husband return her?

Castillo had brought La Muda to Alamos after a trip to Arizona. Felipa remembers Castillo saying that he had finally found a Mexican partner he could trust on the American side. At the time, Felipa and others had wondered how Castillo had won over such a young, pretty woman. Tía Mercedes had said perhaps Ana María was thrown in as part of a bargain.

Lying beneath the paloverde, Felipa's head whirls imagining what those clutching hands could mean.

Since she arrived, Ana María has quietly found a way of making herself indispensable to Alejo. When he's out in the field on the mule cutting down brush, she takes him water and food. Twice she has washed his shirts. And he looks for her when she's not around. It all looks perfectly natural. But Felipa can feel the tension between them. A thunderbolt is going to flatten them. Heart, body, soul, she hopes she's right.

SHE AND ALEJO had spent a painful first two days alone. He worked in a depressed stupor, dragging himself down one row and the next as they planted the first vegetable garden. Then as Charco would say, *"Cuas!"*—her son's luck turned.

And now the place is bursting with helpful strangers, thinks Felipa. Alejo's change of luck freed her, sending her from trying to do everything to having nothing to do.

The next twist came this morning before dawn. At first no one recognized the *peluse* when the Navajo brought them. The spotted mares had been painted a solid color with a mixture of charcoal, iron shavings, oil, and vinegar.

"The government's fort is too close," was the Navajo's explanation. He added that the Nimipu's mares were hidden in the back hills and were ready to receive Moro. They wanted Moro for a week.

This time, Felipa carefully studied the mares. Long-bodied. Good. Back length helps carry foals, keeps them from getting cramped.

It was possible, Felipa thought then, that her son had chosen the right direction. She overheard the Navajo tell Alejo that two of his mares were ready to breed.

Alejo's face lit up. "Charco, let's not wait. Let's take them to Moro now."

Felipa watched her son vault on his crutches toward the corral and draw himself to the top rung. She joined him.

Charco's face glowed with excitement as he started to bring the two mares into the corral to Moro.

The mares lifted their tails, curled them to the side, then waxed. Their legs glistened with dampness.

Felipa cautioned, "Charco, don't rush. Clean the mares. Moro could get hurt."

Confused, Charco turned as if to check with Alejo.

"She's right," said Alejo. He put thumb and middle finger into his mouth and whistled, summoning two Yaquis.

Alejo said, "Get cloth from the wagon, and wipe down the mares."

The Yaquis brought several strips of muslin. Charco held the mares' halters while the men wiped them down.

They don't know what they're doing, Felipa realized. She jumped down into the corral. "Don't wipe away the dye," she said. She took the cloth from one of the Yaquis. "Watch," she said.

Wrapping the muslin around her hand, she carefully tamped and spread the mares' lubrication over the inner buttocks and tail. "You do this to soften the hair. One dry hair could slash Moro's penis."

Alejo grimaced. Charco and the Yaquis looked away.

Men are helpless, thought Felipa. She finished cleaning the mares and stepped aside to let Charco lead them into the corral.

Seeing Moro, the mares nickered, pranced sideways, their tails, like flags, lifted above their hindquarters. Charco struggled to control the two halters.

"Let me hold one," said Alejo, holding out his hand and moving his fingers anxiously.

Charco gave him a lead rope, then led the smaller, more skittish mare back to the center.

Nostrils flared, Moro raised his head, curled his upper lip back, approached. He circled the mare, met her head to head, nickered, teased her. His muzzle sought hers. He breathed deep into her nostrils. The mare answered, breathed back to him. A halo of steam connected them.

The mare's breath told Moro she was ready. Panting, she spread her legs as if to urinate. Instead she waxed again, dappling the soil with her heaviest flow.

Moro moved behind the mare. He emitted a loud chugging pant as the mare backed herself toward him. His penis dropped. He reared and mounted. His front legs straddled each side of her ribs.

His massive blackness dwarfed her. The mare squealed the instant his muscular frame fused her to him. Teeth bared, head raised to the dawn, in a low throaty sound Moro announced his completion to the heavens.

Moro's sound vibrated through Felipa, leaving her breathless. "God bless your dream, Alejo," she whispered, realizing how long it had been since she had prayed.

FELIPA'S EYES PICK out star patterns through the blossoming paloverde. On this clear night, the light of the moon and stars highlights the tree's yellow blossoms.

Alejo says, "Charco, saddle Moro tomorrow morning. I'll ride him to the Nimipu."

"Is your leg ready? I didn't see you try it," says Charco.

"I was with Ana María. She saw me."

Charco grunts in approval. "Should I follow you?"

"No, I need you here. The Nimipu want Moro now. I want to see Moro cover their mares. I'll stay the week with them."

Felipa understands. Her son is telling her, go.

Charco groans, "You mean I have to stay with that Hilda woman for a week? She looks at me out of one eye and sees Yaqui, out of the other she sees Yori. She looks at my sandals and thinks I don't belong here."

Angry, Alejo says, "Tell her you belong here because you're my brother. No, wait, I'll tell her."

Charco lashes, "I'm no one's brother! And I don't belong here. I'm only here because I'm the son of Moro and a mare." He stops; voice low, he adds, "I don't belong anywhere on earth, and I never have—that I remember."

Felipa asks, "How much do you remember, Charco?"

Charco says, "Not my mother, if that's what you're asking. The first memory I have of me on earth is me under a table. Since then, I've learned enough about Sonora to know that soldiers probably hanged my mother, then sold me to a Mexican family who sold me to Americans. I worked for them until I found the Yoemem."

Charco stops, takes a deep breath. "But *before* that, I belonged to something big—like that sky up there, only bigger. It was huge, and I knew that though it was big to me, it was part of something bigger. No matter what happens, I don't fear death, because when I die, I'll go back *there.*"

Tears roll back into Felipa's hair. "Meanwhile, Charco," she says, remembering that Charco can't be more than fifteen years old, "come to your father's ranch, because on earth, that's where you belong. That's what's right."

"Señora," Charco murmurs.

ALEJO TRIES TO remain calm. He feels Felipa's and Charco's eyes on him as he fits his perfect leg—complete with ankle and foot— snugly into his riding boot.

The inner seam of his pants leg is cut to allow his stump to slip easily into and out of the boot. Leaning against the wagon wheel, he positions the boot beneath the stump and inserts its end down into the boot's opening. His stump fits perfectly into the upper end of the carved leg.

And the scar rests almost pain-free on the soft new cushion Ana María made for him. He had not been embarrassed to show her his leg, had not been reluctant to let her touch the scar, had not resisted when she pulled him down to kiss him, stroke him, love him. *We will have time for more,* he thinks.

"I'M HERE BECAUSE of Castillo," he had told her. "My own father couldn't have done more for me."

"He gave up waiting for me to love him," she said. "I tried. My father insisted that Rafael keep the dowry and their joint property holdings. Rafael seemed satisfied. Before I loved you, my not loving him didn't matter. After I fell in love with you, I knew I couldn't stay in Alamos and disgrace him there."

Alejo felt no guilt when he said, "More than anyone, Castillo knows we all lose something."

ALEJO LACES THE horizontal straps of the boot around the leg, then attaches it to his thigh by crisscrossing leather thongs up the leg and around his waist. He is ready to walk. Standing, he tests his stump's strength by lifting and lowering the leg. Not too heavy, he thinks.

Remembering that his mother wished to leave without fanfare, he controls his impulse to see her for the last time. He's certain she and Charco haven't blinked.

Charco calls out, "Stay there. I'll bring Moro."

"No. I'll go to Moro," Alejo says.

Alejo walks with a slight limp. Don't stop, he orders himself, frustrated because he moves so slowly. You must reach Moro without stopping. Eyes fixed on Moro's head, Alejo moves forward, face bathed in sweat. He mustn't hurry, especially when the reins are three, two, one step away. There! He presses his head into Moro's muscular neck and inhales several times. Renewed, he wraps the coarse mane around his hand and hoists himself up.

Moro snorts, stays in place. Alejo leans down to fit his boot into the stirrup. His hips glide back and forth until he fits comfortably in the saddle. Now the farthest hills are an arm's reach away. He presses Moro to a trot.

Make your dream, Alejo, thinks Felipa as she watches her son ride out of her sight. Once Alejo disappears, she looks toward the Soberanes' camp.

Charco says, "Ana María is gone. She's waiting for him over there." He points to the cleft between the hills.

Felipa says, "I must return to Alamos."

SHE LETS CHARCO help her pack. When she boards, he climbs on next to her. "I'll go as far as the main road and walk back."

"Sure you want to come? I must go thank the Soberanes."

"I don't care about her," he says, eyes down.

Felipa leans over, tries to kiss his temple. He shies away. "Bye for now, Charquito. Remember I'm waiting." She draws him to her, and he lets himself be led. "Tu casa está en Alamos."

Moments later, Felipa is laughing when Hilda Soberanes argues, "Decent women don't travel alone. Let me find a family going your way."

"Alone is how a woman stays decent. Watch my sons, Hilda." As she points the wagon south, Felipa says to Charco, "Everything already happened, right, hijo?"

Historical Note

After the Battle of Mazocoba, the deportation of the Yaquis from their homeland in Sonora to Yucatán continued, reaching its high point in 1904. Estimates for the number of Yaquis sold to Yucatán are as high as fifteen thousand. The conditions in the henequen plantations remained unchanged until the Revolution of 1910 ended the Díaz regime. At that time, several exiled individuals returned to Mexico to take part in this revolution.